SEEING THE
ELEPHANT

SEEING THE
ELEPHANT

LES ROBERTS

A SAXON NOVEL

ST. MARTIN'S PRESS
NEW YORK

10-6-94

Design by DAWN NILES

Library of Congress Cataloging-in-Publication Data

Roberts, Les.
    Seeing the elephant / Les Roberts.
      p. cm.
    "A Thomas Dunne Book."
    ISBN 0-312-07081-0
    I. Title.
    PS3568.023894S44   1992
    813'.54—dc20   91-40948
                                                 CIP

First Edition: March 1992
10 9 8 7 6 5 4 3 2 1

To the denizens of the playground of my memory:

Bob and Barb, Joanne and Don, Jimmy and Art, Anitra, Slim, Molly, Lola, Dean, Jerry,

and to the memory of Patrick Scully

SEEING THE
ELEPHANT

1

Tradition dictates that a bad-news phone call, the kind that hits you just under the heart and turns whatever is flowing in your veins to ice water, is supposed to come in the uncertain dark of the middle of the night. The one about Gavin Cassidy arrived just after seven on the first Friday evening in May, when the warm air promised summer and the sun dipped into the Pacific like a vanilla wafer into milk, making pink stretch marks across the blue-gray belly of the sky.

Earlier that afternoon I had dragged the big Weber kettle out into the yard of the bungalow I rent on one of the Venice canals just west of Los Angeles, two blocks from the ocean. It was the barbecue's maiden voyage of the season, and I put two great steaks into a marinade of coarse-ground black pepper and garlic powder and just a hint of soy sauce. Marvel, my recently-adopted son, who pronounces his name with the accent on the second syllable, had whipped up a Caesar salad as I'd taught him. I cranked open a bottle of 1985 Napa Valley Pinot Noir I'd put down for just this kind of impromptu evening. I grilled the steaks rare with some ears of corn I'd buttered and rewrapped in their own husks, and the results were simple but satisfying, especially as a rite of spring ushering in the warm weather to come. After dinner we sat out on the patio and watched the breeze ripple the canal, disturbing the cranky ducks who live there. We were considering a stroll over to Small World Books on Ocean Front Walk to work off the meal and pick up some weekend reading from their Mystery Annex, and then maybe an ice cream cone. The phone ringing inside the house was an intrusion.

"Want me to get it?" Marvel said. It was a generous offer; he had his own phone and knew the call wasn't for him, and when a teenage boy bestirs himself for anything that doesn't bring him instant gratification it is a special occasion.

I waved him off; I hate to thwart any of Marvel's selfless impulses, but he's a message botcher of the first order, and I figured I'd better get it myself. I carried my wineglass inside and lifted the receiver. A voice, sounding older than I'd remembered, said, "It's Ben—Ben Nemeroff, from Chicago."

Since I hadn't seen Ben Nemeroff in fifteen years and hadn't spoken or written to him for at least ten, I was gearing up my Ben-you-old-sonofagun-how-the-hell-are-you routine when he rushed on to say, "Gavin Cassidy's dead."

And then I couldn't say anything. A foreign object was blocking my throat, and something prickled at the back of my eyeballs. There is something especially tragic about the death of a friend of your youth, forcing that initial confrontation with your own fragile mortality, and a piece of memory, of everything that was innocence and music and carefree laughter, dried up and crumbled inside me like a fall leaf.

"Are you there?"

I swallowed desperately a few times and cleared my throat. "Yes. Yeah, Ben, I'm here."

His voice sounded hollow, as if he were farther away than Chicago, on the dark side of the moon. "He was my best friend," he said, and the simplicity of the declaration crushed me; at one time Gavin had been my best friend, too.

"Tell me what happened."

He sighed into the phone, not a pretty sound. "They found

him this morning. He'd been in and out of the hospital for the last two years, but nobody realized—"

"Hospital? For what?"

"I forgot, you haven't been around here for a while. Acute alcoholism."

I listened to the funeral arrangements for Monday and the rest of it, every word like a fist, but what it all boiled down to was that my old friend had been trying for years to drink himself to death and had finally accomplished his mission. It might have been the only time in his life Gavin Cassidy ever succeeded at anything.

After I hung up I went back out and sat by the canal, alone in a silence that was all-encompassing, sipping wine I was no longer tasting. Marvel asked me what was wrong, and I simply told him, "An old friend just died."

"Sorry," he said, instantly picking up my mood—he's remarkably tuned in to my wavelengths. He went inside to watch MTV. I could hear Janet Jackson clanking away, but for a change the noise didn't annoy me, nor did the ducks as they maneuvered for position in the canal and scolded one another with irritated quacking. I was staring at a piece of paper with the time and place of a funeral scribbled on it, thinking about the Near North Side of Chicago almost twenty years before, and a rollicking, gentle giant with an Irish mug, and an Irish thirst to go with it.

Gavin Cassidy had guided me through some of my formative years. He was a role model of hell-raising, unique in the sixties, an era when most youthful rebellion took the form of long hair, tie-dyed jeans, blacklight posters, and the discovery that minds could be bent and consciousness altered by furtive puffs on foul-smelling cigarettes and dangerous downings of sugar cubes soaked with a powerful hallucinogen. Gavin had always scoffed at such symbolic anarchy. He was too flamboyant, too old, too big, and too much the individual to follow the crowd in shaking up the existing social order—he had his own methods, thank you—and in the end he was too smart to be carried

3

off by revolutionary rhetoric, Maoist chic, or politically correct sloganeering. He never demonstrated to end the Asian war or to save the whales or to gain equality for blacks; those causes had nothing to do with him, and cosmic consciousness was as far removed from Gavin as the true meaning of the Dead Sea Scrolls. Even then he was an iconoclast, a freethinker, a self-proclaimed lover, poet, and swordsman—and a drunk.

He'd been flirting with the idea of being a professional actor when I met him. My first memory of him is of a blustery giant in leather pants and a ratty fur robe, his bulk dwarfing the tiny stage of the North State Street Theatre Guild, whose company I had just joined, in a production of *Macbeth.* That he had the title role tells you the level of professionalism of the NSSTG, because Gavin was a lamentable actor, broad and bombastic, with stage balls so big they clanked, and only the blissful gall of the Compleat Ham to get him through the tricky iambic rhythms. Macbeth's opening salvo, "So foul and fair a day I have not seen," shook the walls of the tiny theater when Gavin made his entrance; his performance, prophetically, was full of sound and fury, and in the end signified nothing.

But I didn't know that then, because I was eighteen years old, an eager and nervous Caithness to his Thane, full bursting with theatrical dreams of my own, and Gavin Cassidy seemed to me larger than life, his whole greater than the sum of his parts, the quintessential leading man. I became a willing disciple, and Gavin, with an ego bigger than his barrel chest, was delighted with even a small dollop of hero worship from a neophyte from the North Side. He drew me into his circle, into the aura of the theatrical spotlight he carried with him onstage and off. He taught me little tricks of stagecraft, the subtleties of courtship, the secret of making allies of enemies and friends of strangers, and in the process helped me to grow up a bit faster. And wiser.

He was about eight years older than I, as was the rest of the crowd I ran with: Ben Nemeroff and Dolly and Diane Keeshan and Gary Storm and Tessa Niland and the exquisite and remote

Beth Shroats. My role in this exalted company was the Kid, generously tolerated, later accepted and spoiled by my more mature friends, and from my observance of the delicate quadrille of their sap-running mid twenties I learned what adulthood was all about.

They are all the denizens of my playground of memory. But Gavin was our uncrowned emperor, leader of the pack, d'Artagnan, Monte Cristo, Falstaff and Prince Hal all at once, and we each loved him dumbly, and proudly wore his colors. Now that he was dead, part of those days were dead too, and youth was irretrievably gone to dust.

When the wine had disappeared along with the day's last light, I went inside and rapped on Marvel's bedroom door. He turned down the TV before he opened the door, and I looked up at him, suddenly aware that somewhere along the line he had grown taller than I am, and broader and wider at seventeen than the skinny girl-faced kid I had been, tagging along after Gavin Cassidy. Marvel had gotten handsome, too; his coffee brown face was clear and smooth and losing its baby fat. His eyes, so bewildered and frightened when I'd taken him in from the street a few years earlier, now flashed understanding and intelligence, along with the sparkle of a deft and sometimes cutting wit.

"You hurtin', an' shit," he rumbled. He was going through one of those adolescent stages where he made sure everything he said was not to be confused with an adult's way of speaking; at the moment he believed the addendum of *an' shit* at the end of most sentences was an expression of his ethnic individuality.

I nodded. "I have to go to Chicago tomorrow. For a funeral."

"Tha's cool," he said.

"I don't know how long I'll stay. A week, maybe."

"I'll be okay."

I went in and called my agent, Bernie Silverman, at home to tell him I'd be gone next week, on the off chance that he'd have

5

lined up an audition for me. I had recently completed four weeks' work on a film, which had given me a good chunk of money, and as was his pattern, Bernie figured it would keep me quiet for a while and he could forget about me until I began pestering him again. Thank God I had a second career.

I called Jo Zeidler, who ran that career for me, Saxon Investigations, and made arrangements for Marvel to stay with her and her husband Marshall until I returned. Marvel was crazy about Jo and shared Marsh's passionate interest in professional basketball—though he was a Laker fan and Marsh, a former New Yorker, was an unregenerate Knicks rooter—so the upheaval wouldn't make him too unhappy, and now that he was old enough to drive, getting to school in Venice from their apartment in West Hollywood would pose no difficulty.

Jo expressed her sympathy; she was my dearest friend as well as my employee, and she had heard me speak of Gavin many times. She even offered to make the plane reservations, but I wanted to do it myself. For some reason, it seemed important that I do so, that I dial the travel agent and make the decisions regarding flight time and seat location, as if the simple act of booking an airline ticket could expiate ten years of guilt.

I reserved a seat on the flight to Chicago at five minutes before midnight on Saturday, leaving the return date open. I prefer flying red-eye; it seems purposeless to sit in a cramped seat for an entire day while the rest of the world, seven miles below, goes on with life. At night the plentiful waste of time doesn't seem so great. Nights, anyway, are for sleeping, making love, or tossing and turning and reflecting. Two out of three can be done on an airplane. Being violently acrophobic, I have no interest in looking out the window, so I asked for an aisle seat to avoid having to clamber over a soundly sleeping neighbor to go to the john.

The flight took off only five minutes late. As the ground fell away from us and the lit sprawl of Los Angeles spread out below in unbelievable profusion, I thought that someday there'll be a great city down there.

I had a paperback in my lap to get me through the long hours; trying to sleep on a red-eye is like sleeping in ten-second sound bites. If it's not the air turbulence that wakes you, or the fat lady who jostles your elbow heading down the aisle to the lavatory, it's the sleek-stockinged cabin attendant with her omnipresent serving cart, asking if you'd prefer juice or Diet Pepsi. They wake you up to tell you about the emergency exits and how to buckle your seat belt. They wake you again to list the cities they're going to fly over, as if anyone cared to look out the window at Grand Island, Nebraska, at four o'clock in the morning. They wake you to warn you they're going to begin beverage service any time now, then wake you again when they do, rattling ice cubes in your ear and offering up a niggardly half can of soda in a plastic cup and a bag of sweetened peanuts. They wait ten minutes and then give you a weather report and an arrival time, as if you could do anything about it. Later they disturb you once more to remind you to check your personal belongings before "deplaning the aircraft," one of the more hideous redundancies extant. I never even attempt sleeping on airplanes anymore.

After an hour my interest in the book waned, though it wasn't the fault of the author. I had too much on my mind, too many memories to take from their velvet-lined compartment and examine for the first time in years. I put my glasses and the book in the seat pocket and walked to the back of the plane to stretch my legs. It's strange to be the only one awake on a red-eye flight, lonely and spooky. Old men with their mouths open. Young kids sucking their thumbs in innocent slumber. A soldier, not much older than Marvel, with a fresh buzz cut and no stripes on his sleeve, dozing upright at attention. On a plane everyone sleeps with a different attitude, depending I suppose on their particular state of mind and the reason for their trip.

I bummed a cup of coffee from the motherly flight attendant back in the galley, but airplane coffee, especially the kind

7

you're likely to get in the middle of the night, is on a par with airplane food, and after two sips I let it get cold, finally dumping it out in the lavatory.

Depression was hitting me hard and low. I felt empty and impotent, knowing those perennially smiling blue eyes of Gavin's would twinkle no more, that the great bass viol of a voice would never again mangle a Shakespearean quatrain. I remembered how he would sit at his favorite table at the Hard Knox College bar on Oak Street and call for a refill of his own personal and perennially empty beer stein. "Give me some drink, Titinius!" he would roar, and the new cocktail waitresses—they were always new because Stretch Knox, the crusty old proprietor who clung steadfastly to Fabian socialism long after it ceased being fashionable, could never hang on to decent help—would always be offended until someone explained to them that it wasn't lewd or suggestive but a quote from *Julius Caesar*.

Not that anyone, especially any woman, ever stayed angry with Gavin for more than five minutes. He was too vivid, too oversize to be mad at. Even when he did lousy things, which was often, they were done without malice. I don't think there was a mean bone in Gavin Cassidy's body. He committed sometimes thoughtless acts simply because he was Gavin and he wanted to, and somehow all of us cut him that extra bit of slack because we loved him and admired his dash and panache. Never was heard a discouraging word about him in those days, more amazing because of what he did for a living.

Gavin Cassidy was a cop.

After a few years of knocking my head against the wall in California, when I finally realized I wasn't going to be a star and needed a second profession to keep me solvent between acting jobs, the idea of being a private investigator popped into my head, partly because of a private detective I'd met and worked for, but also due to Gavin. In a way I wanted to be like that part of him that bubbled over with life and energy and a fierce sense of justice. Everything had to be fair with Gavin, be it a romance or a fistfight. Gavin the cop longed to make the world a little better place, and I suppose I want the same thing.

So Gavin was one of my strongest influences, a role model for me that my father, stamping out license plates in prison, could never have been.

Gavin had wanted desperately to be an actor, even though three generations of Cassidy men before him had worn the blue of Chicago's finest. He went through the police academy to please his grandfather, a retired captain, and pounded foot patrols on Rush Street and North Clark and even for several months around the dreaded Cabrini Green, the most notorious public housing development in the United States. But he never quite loosened his grip on the dream of theatrical stardom.

A year after I departed Chicago to chase my own stardust dreams on the West Coast, Gavin took a leave of absence from the department and came out to Los Angeles for an extended visit, where he made camp in my apartment for several months. But he wouldn't or couldn't do the things it took to get a foothold in the movie business. He refused to have professional pictures taken, instead distributing copies of his favorite snapshot. "What photographer could ever get this Irish mug of mine right?" He disdained making the rounds of casting directors and agents—"They're flunkies and ass-wipes!" He wouldn't even take an acting class; he thought he knew all there was to know.

"They'll stifle me," he'd say. "Push me through their cookie cutters and make me come out like everyone else. Not Cassidy, my dear friend." He used the term "my dear friend" a lot, and he always meant it.

So he sat around my living room watching game shows on TV and waiting to be discovered. Occasionally he'd visit an agent or attend an open casting call, but mostly he spent sunny days strolling Rodeo Drive and Wilshire Boulevard in Beverly Hills, clucking over the preponderance of Arabs with Rolls-Royces, or strutting up and down Santa Monica Beach with his paunch sucked in over his black shorts and a white smear of zinc oxide on his nose. At night he'd drink copious amounts of beer in the local pubs. He found and patronized the few real taverns left in Los Angeles, mainly the Cock and Bull, because most of its habitués were in the movie business. He never did have much truck with fancy cocktail lounges; in all the time I'd known him, in all the nights I'd gone drinking with him, I'd never known him to take hard alcohol. He was a beer man to the core, and though he was only in his late twenties when I met him, he'd sported the belly to prove it. Nights when he didn't pass out in the pubs or fall into a drunken sleep in his car, he'd rut noisily on my pullout sofa with young women he'd met in the taverns while I, in the bedroom, pulled a pillow over my head to block out the sweaty sounds of someone else's rapture.

What allowed me to retain a shred of my sanity was the laughter, and there was more than enough of that. Gavin was a man of great good humor, a good-time fellow with an inexhaustible supply of funny anecdotes about his life in uniform, his adventures on the stages of nearly every community theater in Chicago, and the admittedly strange characters with whom he'd rubbed shoulders. And though he never contributed a cent towards his upkeep, paid no rent and bought no groceries, when we'd go out drinking together, which was fairly often, he'd never allow me to reach into my pocket. It was a selective generosity, to be sure, but it kept me steadily entertained, as well as consistently hung over. It was the only way he knew to try and recapture the good old days back on the Near North Side.

Eventually, as much as I cared for him, his particular brand of bonhomie wore thin. I wasn't making that terrific a living myself back then, fighting for big parts and an occasional class A commercial, and the care and feeding of an aging tosspot was straining my patience as well as my bank account. I had my own life to get on with, and I didn't have the nerve to tell him. But Gavin knew it, sensed it, and one day he packed his suitcase, threw it into the ridiculous little sports car that was so small it made him look like King Kong when he sat in its driver's seat, pulled on his silly racing goggles, and with a hi-ho and a careless wave drove back to Chicago before I had to ask him to. He resumed his place on the force and from all I heard of him was a good and honest cop, kept from promotion by his drinking. But for a man like Gavin Cassidy, the taste of failure lingered on the palate, no matter how hard he tried to wash it away with copious amounts of the Ballantine beer he always drank with ice cubes.

Awash in old memories, I scooted back into my place on the plane, wrapped my seat belt around me, and closed my eyes, but sleep was hard in coming, and I knew I'd be awake in the morning when we came in sight of the magnificent shoreline of Lake Michigan bordered by the tall towers of Lake Shore Drive. I kept my eyes shut anyway, because there was no one to talk to, and all I was missing in the way of scenery were the flat plains of Kansas and Nebraska in the dark, as barren of trees or hills as a lunar landscape.

I was feeling a little barren myself at the moment, and guilt gnawed at my viscera. I love my friends and have been known to go out on a limb for them more than once. And no one friend had more of a determining influence on the person I'd become than Gavin Cassidy. But yet, save for an occasional Christmas card, which he never reciprocated, I hadn't been in touch with him for almost ten years.

2

The stewardess jarred everyone awake with a loudspeaker announcement in that peculiar patois I call StewSpeak, in which all the wrong words are emphasized: "We *have* been cleared for landing. Please check *around* your seating area and *in* the overhead compartments to make sure you *haven't* left any personal belongings. Place your seat backs *in* an upright position and be sure your seat belts *are* fastened securely." I wonder if they're trained to talk like that or if it's something that just happens when you spend your life at thirty thousand feet, like jet lag.

With the look of zombies from a George Romero movie, we red-eye commandos deplaned into the bewildering maze of concourses that is O'Hare Airport. While I waited in line for a taxi to take me to the Loop, it struck me that I had not set foot on the soil of my native city for nearly half my lifetime. I'd turned away from Chicago and all it represented to me and never looked back. I had never expected to return, couldn't have imagined a reason to, though I had a pocketful of reasons not to. Now, out of necessity, I was here, to confront old ghosts and the scenes of my youthful excesses, and everywhere I turned were landmarks of my life.

I'd made reservations at a small hotel, one of the older ones, just east of Michigan Avenue and north of the river. The cab-driver was obviously trying to qualify for the Indy 500 later that month, and I arrived so early that my room wasn't yet ready, so I took myself out for breakfast and then for a walk along what has always been called the Magnificent Mile. It's more or less magnificent than it used to be, depending on your definition. The buildings are mostly chrome and glass now, except for a few like the new NBC Building, which resembles its elder art deco sister in New York. I was comforted by the sight of the old standbys like the venerable stone Water Tower poking its long finger up into the overcast. It survived the Great Chicago Fire and will probably outlast all of us. For me there was a familiarity to Michigan Avenue, and yet it was so different that for a while I became disoriented, almost as though I'd just been dropped in the middle of downtown Beijing. All the buildings I remembered seemed smaller now than when I was a kid, dwarfed by the Hancock Tower and its big brother to the west, the Sears Tower. Chicago visitors usually find their way to the observation roofs of those two buildings, but with my fear of heights the very thought of it made my palms sweat.

Chicago is a sexy city.

Some places are sexy and some aren't. I don't mean romantic, because if you're in love, Meridian, Mississippi can be magical. But sexy in the sense that the energy in the city fairly crackles; it's palpable on the sidewalks and in the cafés. San Francisco is sexy, so is New Orleans. Paris. Hong Kong. Los Angeles isn't the least bit sexy, nor are Philadelphia, Phoenix, Detroit, or Dallas. But Chicago might be the sexiest city in the world. Walking down the street is a visual feast, as smart, well-turned-out people of both genders hurry to their destinations with a purposeful stride—not the desperate haste of the New Yorker, but the strong, head-up gait of people who're happy to be there enjoying their day. There's a lot to enjoy in Chicago.

Now I felt sad that I'd left it so long ago. At the time it had seemed the only sensible thing to do.

I finally checked in to my room, unpacked, and called Ben Nemeroff, who invited me for dinner that evening. I was of two minds about that, having set my face for Pizzeria Uno, just a few blocks from my hotel. Perhaps a hundred times I had matured and weathered waiting out on the sidewalk for a table there at one of the oldest deep-dish pizza restaurants in the United States, and arguably the best. I'd give it a try, but I doubted whether I could get in touch with myself and my roots, my old haunts and old loves, in just a few days. Or with Gavin, either.

We were very different people, of course. He was a lot tougher than I am. You can't be a cop in Chicago and not get tough quick, and his burly build, Gaelic temper, and thirst for hops made it easy for him to be a hard guy. Yet he was kind, and gentle in that special way big tough men often have. He accepted everyone at face value and welcomed them into his world no matter who or what they were; many of his friends were drunks and ruffians, and some of them were really slime. Once when I was about nineteen I got into a bar beef with one of his lowlife pals. He managed to break the fight up before it started—a good thing, too, because the bastard would've torn my head off. But like Burt Lancaster stepping between Sinatra and Ernest Borgnine in *From Here to Eternity,* Gavin was able to pull it off by the sheer force of his personality. And amazingly, neither one of us was angry with him—but Gavin could do that, spread the companionable warmth of good feeling just by being there, by grinning that sly Gaelic grin and raising both hands like a symphony conductor urging pianissimo from the brass section. Talk to him for five minutes and you'd feel you'd known him all your life, because Gavin knew the art of quiet listening as well as bombast, and he drew everyone into his magnetic field.

Why, then, had I lost touch so thoroughly, not only with Gavin but with Ben and Dolly and everyone else from my formative years in Chicago? I thought about that as I walked back down Michigan Avenue toward the canyon between the white wedding cake of the Wrigley Building and the Gothic splendor of the Tribune Tower, and my own private demons rose up to thumb their noses at me for ever having tried to escape them.

Other than a worried line that bisected his forehead, Ben Nemeroff had hardly aged a bit. He'd put on a few pounds around the middle, but hadn't we all, and behind his glasses his eyes were the clear, sparkling brown I'd always remembered, although on this particular evening they were bloodshot and turned down at the corners. He was close to fifty years old, but his demeanor was pretty much the same as it had been when he was not yet thirty. Ben's innate decency and fierce loyalty to his friends had always separated him from most of the other people I knew, and he hadn't changed much. Only now he had reached that point in life where his dreams were no longer ones of hope but of reminiscence.

His wife Dolly hovered just behind him, waiting her turn for a hug. I was there the night they met; I think I introduced them, although popular mythology says that I didn't, that it had been engineered by Gavin. I hadn't noticed any particular sparks between them at that first meeting at a party at Tessa Niland's apartment, so six months later, after they'd been dating for a while, when Ben came to me in the dressing room of the NSSTG and gleefully informed me, "Dolly said yes tonight," I'd replied with all my twenty-year-old arrogance, "Yes to what?" Somehow or other they forgave me.

Their house was typically Chicago, big and solid with lots of dark wood, comfortable furniture done in earth colors, and the smells of good cooking, and it wasn't long before they had built me a drink, ensconced me on their sofa, and made me feel as though it had been two weeks since I'd seen them instead of half a lifetime.

We caught up on the years of silence, and they asked about my career, my films and TV shows, and I told them about adopting Marvel. To their credit they didn't even blink when

15

I mentioned he was black. Both of them were color-blind before it was fashionable, and they both had always accepted the crazy things I did. I wasn't surprised that fifteen years hadn't changed them much.

Ben beamed at me. "You made it, you little shit!" he said. "You went to Hollywood; you're an actor. You were pretty good as a kid. Not great—good." Ben still shot from the hip. "And you looked the part, with your theatrical clothes and your sunglasses. Damn, I'm proud of you!"

"I'm only an actor part time," I said. "I have my own business on the side." He raised his eyebrows, and I went on, "Believe it or not, I'm a private investigator."

"You're kidding!" he said. "A guy who hated getting his hair mussed, and now you're actually doing something dangerous for a living?"

"Most of the time it isn't so dangerous," I said. "Unless I have to drive on the freeway."

Dolly chuckled. "It figured. You always loved those Bogart and Alan Ladd movies. And you even did something about it. Don't you remember?" she said to Ben. "Back when he was about nineteen he got a job as a uniformed guard with the Pinkerton Agency. You lasted two days," she added, laughing.

Recollection kicked in along with embarrassment, and I said, "Jesus, I'd forgotten that! I was working in the warehouse at Monkey Ward, unpacking blue jeans and putting them on shelves, and I was sick of it. I saw the Pinkerton ad and applied. My first job, I worked some sort of costume jewelry show at the Merchandise Mart. I was supposed to make sure everyone who got off the elevator showed me a pass. One guy didn't have one, and when I tried to stop him he told me to go fuck myself, and I decided it wasn't important enough to get into a fistfight with him, so I just let him in without a fuss. I quit the next day."

"We asked you to wear your uniform one night so we could see it, but you wouldn't," Ben reminded me. "How'd you manage to get into that kind of thing in L.A.?"

I sipped at my Scotch. "I had a small part in a TV detective

16

show. There was a private investigator who was the technical advisor on the picture, and we got to talking. He said if I wanted to make some extra money he could use me to do some legwork. I enjoyed it, kept working for him for about five years." I smiled, thinking about crusty old Vincent Mecca, his bad toupee and his five-o'clock shadow, and the malodorous cigars he always smoked. He was no stereotype private eye, hardly Bogart, unless perhaps the Bogie of *The African Queen,* but he was one of the smartest men I've ever known—street smart, that is; he never saw the inside of a college classroom. "When he retired I took over his shop. Saxon Investigations, I call it."

"We still see you on TV," Dolly said.

"I do a picture or a commercial once in a while, but I'm an investigator first and an actor second. You get to meet a better class of people—hoodlums and grifters are a lot nicer than producers and directors."

Dolly went into the kitchen to check the dinner. "How about you, Ben?" I said, "What've you been up to?"

"Not so exciting as your life. I have my own company too: *Chotchkes.* Wholesale gifts. Sometimes it's good, some-times . . ." He threw up his hands. "It's a living, what can I tell you?" With a quick look in the direction of the kitchen, he lowered his voice, leaning forward to whisper, "Lately not such a terrific living. There are good years and there are punk years, but we get by."

Dolly returned, seemingly satisfied at the meal's progress. Finally we ran out of small talk.

"Tell me about Gavin," I said. "What happened?"

Ben and Dolly studied their shoes as if there would be a pop quiz about them later. Finally Ben said, "He just got tired. That's all. Tired of life."

"You know how he was," Dolly said. "How he drank. It got worse over the years. We tried to get him to quit," she added helplessly.

"They threatened him," Ben said, "the police department.

17

They were always after him to stop, or at least to cut down. They have programs for that, the police. But when somebody wants to drink and doesn't want help . . ." His voice quivered, and he fought to keep it from breaking. "His liver was gone at the end. He died on Lincoln Park West in that same crappy hotel room he lived in all these years."

I was shocked. "I didn't know."

"Alcohol and amphetamines, they said. In lethal amounts." Ben stuck his fingers under his glasses and wiped his eyes. "There was some talk that he'd done it on purpose."

"No way!" I said with more vehemence than I'd intended. "The Gavin I knew wouldn't even have thought about it, no matter how bad things got."

Ben sighed. "That's what they finally figured too. So officially it's an accidental overdose. His police insurance is paying for the funeral. But we did all the arrangements." I could see the hurt cutting through him. "There wasn't anybody else to do it."

"Everyone kind of dropped Gavin in the last five years or so," Dolly explained. "He was . . . difficult to be around. When he came over, you just knew he'd get so drunk he couldn't drive home and would have to crash on the sofa. Finally people got tired of it." She sighed. "Everyone but Ben."

"I was the one that stuck with him," Ben said. "Nursed him through his DTs and cleaned up the puke. All those people he used to buy drinks, who used to hang around just to be near him so they could say he was their pal—they all turned their backs."

"When we were all young and hanging out on Rush Street, doing theater and drinking and being crazy, Gavin was the king," Dolly said quietly. "He was bigger, taller, better-looking than anyone else, always good for a laugh or a drink, and we all adored him. But he went to Hollywood to visit you, and out there he wasn't a king anymore. When he came back, somehow things had changed. Knox College had turned into a hippie hangout; you were gone, Tessa and Diane married. Gary de-

18

cided money was more important than old friends and went off to do his thing. When Gavin put on his blue uniform again, it was a defeat. He made lots of noise about how great it was to be back, but inside it ate him up. It was an admission to himself and to the world that he'd failed."

"He never stopped talking about the old days," Ben put in. "He didn't want to let go of that. That's when he'd been happiest. He couldn't understand why it went away. In his head he was still Macbeth, still the king, but all of a sudden he had no subjects. The rest of us . . ." He trailed off, looking within.

I said as gently as I could, "The rest of us grew up, Ben."

"That was Gavin's problem. He never saw the point in growing up—being a kid was too much fun." He wiped at his eyes under his glasses again. "He was a bitter man when he came back from Los Angeles. That's when the drinking began to get out of hand. The older he got, the worse it was."

"Ben, ten million people try to make it in the movies. All but a small handful fall flat on their faces. They don't all turn into drunks."

Ben's eyes flashed angrily at me for a moment, but then his mouth drooped at the sides and he nodded. Knowing he agreed with me didn't make it any easier.

Dolly saved the moment. "Come and help me with the roast," she said, and hauled me to my feet. I followed her through the dining room to the kitchen, and when we were alone she turned and faced me, her attitude a bit confrontational.

"Ben is completely shattered."

"I know," I said, "so am I."

"Not like Ben. How could you be? You've been away so long. I don't know if he'll ever get over it." She crossed her arms across her chest. "Along with grief he's dealing with anger—at all our friends who used to be Gavin's too, people who haven't bothered to see him for all these years because it wasn't convenient anymore. Including you."

"Me?"

19

She nodded. "You more than the others, I think, because Gavin always considered you his protégé. He was so damn proud of you. I know you did what you could for him in L.A. And Ben knows it too, really. But he's hurting now. So no matter what he might say . . . be kind."

I leaned against the sink. "Of all the people in the world, Gavin was the last one you'd figure to die alone."

"There was someone—for a long time there was someone. Marian Meyers is her name. I hope you meet her while you're here; I think you'll like her. Gavin was happier with her than he'd been since the old days, and I thought this would be the one that did it for him." She sighed sadly. "They broke up finally, near the end. She couldn't take it anymore, the drinking. And that was Gavin's choice, to go it alone with a bottle of beer and a quote from some dumb play. But while it lasted, Marian was the best thing in Gavin's life." She took some dinner rolls out of the warmer and put them in a basket, covering them with a linen napkin. "Put these on the table, would you?" she said, handing them to me.

In the dining room, as I placed the rolls in a relatively empty space, I counted four place settings. Dolly came up beside me and I looked a question at her, and she said, "We've invited Kendra. She should be here any moment now."

I was too startled to answer her. Not that she was going to give me a chance to say anything; she bustled past me into the living room to stave off any discussion.

It would have been pointless, anyway. What was done was done.

They'd invited Kendra.

Sometimes you get too much crap thrown at you all at the same time and you find yourself standing on tiptoes just to keep your chin above the surface. That's how I felt. Bad enough that I'd come here to bury Gavin Cassidy; now I was to eat dinner with the woman who had left me for him, and clearly I was expected to be mature and slick, to make inconsequential small talk.

It occurs to me that the creatures in nature that most approximate human behavior are scorpions when they engage in courtship. They do a wily, seductive dance, first approaching and then retreating. It takes a certain amount of time for them to decide whether they're going to mate or fatally sting. My romance with Kendra had been a lot like that.

I went in and freshened my drink and sat mute on the sofa, not joining in much of the conversation and only speaking when I was spoken to. I was waiting for the doorbell to ring, but when it did I wasn't ready for it. I don't know if I ever would have been ready.

Kendra Dane still had the round doll's face I had fallen in love with when I was eighteen years old and she was sixteen, and the few pounds she'd put on over the years became her. My first real girlfriend, the first woman I'd ever made love to more than twice, the first with whom seeing each other on Saturday night or New Year's Eve was taken for granted, the first to have been paired with me as a couple in the minds of others. Her gray eyes still danced mischief, and the short shag cut of her brown hair wasn't that different from the gamin style she'd worn in her youth.

She stood in the archway and examined me as if I were a rare specimen of gemstone; obviously my presence was not the surprise to her that hers had been to me. "The gray hair works," she said. It was a typical Kendra opening salvo. "Do you do anything to it?"

"Wash it once or twice a year. You look terrific."

She smiled ruefully. "You can't hit a moving target."

We moved across the carpet and met in the middle of the room. She was nearly as tall as I. Our embrace was tentative, as if we were afraid we'd bruise each other. The Nemeroffs pretended they weren't there, that they were in Pittsburgh, but it wasn't like that anymore with us—at least, it wasn't for me. More water had flowed under the bridge than could be retrieved with one chaste hug and a kiss on the cheek. Clocks only run forward.

Still, it was good to see Kendra, even though there didn't seem to be much to say.

Dolly relieved the awkwardness by announcing dinner, and when we were all at the table and the food had been passed and the wine poured, Ben beamed. "God, I never thought the four of us would be sitting down to a meal again." Then he looked down at his plate. "I wish it didn't take this to bring us all together."

Kendra put her hand over his and squeezed. She had evidently grown compassionate over the years; in her youth she affected intellectualism and brittle sophistication. But then we all had, with the exception of Ben. And Gavin, who had not a jot of intellectual pretension, even though he tolerated it in the rest of us.

"We're all devastated, Ben," she said. "But it must be much harder for you."

He ducked his head in acquiescence and then shook it to indicate he didn't want to discuss it anymore.

Dolly said, "How have you been, Kenni?"

"Hanging in there," she said. "The world of physical therapy hasn't gotten any easier."

I looked up. "You didn't stay with art?"

"Sure, for a while. I took classes at the Art Institute, but I realized a long time ago I was no Georgia O'Keeffe. I'd learned a lot about physical therapy from taking care of my father, so I decided to make a few bucks out of it along the way. I do okay with it."

Kendra's father, Alonzo Dane, had been a well-known graphic artist and the winner of several design awards despite being crippled from the hips down, the result of polio, unfortunately contracted before Dr. Salk became a household word and a hero. Lon Dane was a lovely man, pink-cheeked and happy, with a gently dazzling sense of humor, and my affection for him often racked me with guilt because of my sexual relationship with his daughter. We got hung up about things like that when I was a kid, back when sex was adversarial and

goal-oriented. Come to think of it, it hasn't changed that much.

"I somehow knew you wouldn't end up selling insurance," I said.

"Why?"

"You were always dramatic, even though you never messed with acting like the rest of us. Name me another sixteen-year-old who smoked cigarettes in a long black holder, only went to French and Japanese movies, and used words like 'obsequious.' "

"Who did I say was obsequious?"

"I don't remember. Probably Gary Storm. And you'd have been right, too."

"I was a dolt back then, wasn't I?"

"And name me another thirty-seven-year old who says 'dolt.' "

"Thirty-six, pal," she said severely, "until August, and don't you forget it."

"You don't look a day over twenty-five," I said, which was a white lie; she really didn't look a day over thirty.

Of course I had forgotten her birthday. I'm lousy at remembering things like that, birthdays and anniversaries and opening nights. Were it not that we had arbitrarily assigned Marvel my birth date, his own being unknown, I probably wouldn't remember mine.

Dinner was far from a jolly affair, given the circumstances that had brought us all together, but the excitement of renewing old acquaintances after so many years enlivened the conversation. But Cassidy's ghost hung over the table like a Tiffany lampshade. Ben was finding it hard to laugh or even to smile, and Dolly's concern for him marred any pleasure she might take from all of us being together again.

Gavin was a subject Kendra and I had avoided for many years, when we spoke at all. But his memory was not to be denied here. There was no ignoring the reason for my return to Chicago, and we talked around it for as long as we could. Finally I said, "Did you see much of Gavin before . . ."

23

I couldn't bring myself to say *before he died*. Even for someone on as close terms with sudden death as I've become in the last few years, Gavin Cassidy's demise was as difficult to deal with as it was for Ben Nemeroff.

She shook her head. "No. He and I ended badly—that we would end some day was a foregone conclusion, but there are endings and endings. I didn't see much of him after that. In fact there were times when it was years between meetings. We traveled in different circles. Our fling all those years ago was just that, a fling. What else could it be? I was seventeen years old, for God's sake." She smiled at a memory. "I'll never forget Gavin, receding hairline, beer belly and all, with a gardenia corsage in his hand and wearing a white dinner jacket at the Lake View High School prom."

Ben laughed and Dolly gave an embarrassed titter. Kendra's prom night, with a mature Gavin conspicuous among the awkwardness of first tuxedos and faces dabbed with acne medicine, was one of those terrible memories I relive on occasion when I'm coming down off a particularly bad drunk. Kendra kept looking at me, her gaze probing. "You're not still pissed off about Gavin and me, are you?"

"I wasn't pissed off then," I said. "I was hurt, not mad. No, that's a lie, I was mad as hell. Naturally. It would have been easier if you'd dumped me for a stranger. But I got over it. No one ever stayed mad at Gavin for very long."

Her eyes locked on mine, the usually mischievous little mouth frozen into a thin line. This was the first discussion of the subject in years; at the time no one had said anything, not to me or Kendra or to Gavin, either; it was like a shameful family secret everyone knew about but no one dared to mention in polite company. "Did you stay mad at me?"

"No. Well, longer than I did at Gavin, but eventually . . ." I shifted uneasily. I would have been happier if it had stayed unmentioned. The presence of two other people didn't make it any more comfortable. "It was twenty years ago, Kenni. How can anyone stay mad for twenty years?"

"Gavin dated everyone back then," Dolly broke in, and I've never been so grateful for an interruption. "Not me, but just about everyone else—Beth, Tessa, and legions of women whose names have been forgotten."

Kendra's pretty face grew ugly for just a moment. She looked up at me and then away. "Gavin was eclectic, all right. He slept with whoever he wanted, regardless of race, creed, or national origin. I think he looked on it as a favor he was granting us." She laughed, but there was a catch in the back of her throat. "You think that's where the term 'sexual favors' originated? With Cassidy?"

"But somehow it didn't matter," I said sadly, looking across the table at the first woman I ever spent the whole night with, the first with whom I'd ever had a real relationship, the one I'd remember when the others faded, simply because she'd meant the discovery of romance and adulthood and responsibility to another human being, with all the angst and intensity of first love. 'Because nobody ever stayed mad at Gavin."

3

North Side Catholics simply call it "Our Lady," although its official moniker is Our Lady of the Sacred Rosary. It's a Gothic cathedral on Sheridan Road, an ornate but lumpish survivor of the neighborhood's disintegration over the last thirty years, and Ben and Dolly chose it for Gavin Cassidy's funeral because it was the closest Catholic church to their house. Though he was Irish to the bone, I could never remember Gavin talking about religion in all the time I'd known him, so it was a safe assumption that he had no home parish, and since it didn't matter, I suppose there was something to be said for convenience.

Our Lady had held its ground bravely while a Puerto Rican barrio sprang up around it to force out the middle-class Jewish and Irish families that had once lived in the neighborhood, and as I walked from the bus stop, wearing the only dark suit I owned, the smell of spicy cooking wafted through the crisp air and rapid-fire Spanish rattled from front stoop to sidewalk and back.

A crowd of stiffly-dressed people milled around outside the church, but no one looked familiar. Most of them were big, hard-looking Irishmen wearing their little-used Sunday suits, and I had to assume they were Gavin's police comrades. They stood smoking cigarettes, and the hushed tones in which they spoke melded together in the spring morning like the muttering of bees. They looked down at the sidewalk or up into space in the way of mourners, not wanting to make eye contact with anyone, uncomfortable with this evidence of their own mortality. There is no fraternity as tight-knit as the brotherhood of badge wearers, and when one passes the bell tolls for each, whether they die in the line of duty or on the floor of a cheap hotel room on Lincoln Park West.

A hand clapped me too hard on the shoulder, and the hair on my wrists prickled, the way it does when I'm angry. I don't like being touched unless it's by someone I want to have touch me, and I turned quickly to confront the broad, smiling face of Gary Storm. He removed his hand from my shoulder to squeeze my own hand in a wolf-trap grip.

"Stranger!" he boomed. "I thought you were in California."

"Ben called me," I said.

"Sonofabitch, it's good to see you!" he said, still pumping my arm, "but I'm sorry it had to be under these circumstances."

Gary is one of those bluff, too-loud people who is always ready with a laugh, usually at someone else's expense. The muscular build of his youth had thickened to solid middle age, and his hair had turned snow white, much whiter than mine, and was teased into an Elvis cockscomb in the front. His sideburns were unfashionably long, and he affected a slim mustache and goatee, also white, which gave him the look of a satyr past his prime. He was nine years my senior and looked at least twenty years older. We had never been close but had tolerated one another because of our mutual friends. His eyes still didn't smile along with the rest of his face, even as when we hung out together at the bar at Hard Knox College.

"Have you run into any of the old crowd?" he said. "Everyone's going to be dying to see you. Uh-oh, that was a lousy choice of words." Lousy it may have been, but deliberate, and he fairly beamed at the perceived witticism. "We catch you on TV now and again, all of us—but how come ten years or so, not a word?"

I shrugged. "Things happen, Gary; you grow away."

"I know. I never see the gang much anymore."

"Did you see Gavin?"

He moved around to the other side of me so the sun was no longer in his eyes. Of course now it was in mine, but a little thing like that wouldn't bother Gary. It haloed his white hair, in contrast to the Mephistophelian mustache and beard, and his beetle brows were knit. "I didn't have much to say to Gavin. We had a falling out."

"What about?"

"It's not important," he said, dismissing it.

"Then why are you here?"

"You know somebody thirty years, you want to say goodbye, whether you were on the outs or not." He looked over his shoulder toward the door of the church. "Are you staying with the Nemeroffs?"

"No, I have a hotel."

"Give me a ring," he said. "We'll tie one on for old time's sake."

In a pig's ass. Of all the things I might do while in Chicago for the first time in years, going out drinking with Gary Storm was pretty low on the list—right below a midnight stroll through Cabrini Green wearing a Rolex and a gold neck chain and flashing a roll of fifties.

"You coming in?" he said.

"Not yet." I watched his broad back as he trotted up the steps. He was wearing a double-breasted blue blazer with gold buttons. He also had on white pants, a white shirt, and a light blue ascot, as if he were doing lunch at Cannes. Just the ticket for a funeral.

I stepped out onto the sidewalk and fired up a cigarette. A parochial school education stays with you, whether you remain Catholic or not, and I somehow felt funny about lighting up on Church grounds. It was a stupid hang-up, I admit— nowhere in the catechism does it say "Thou shalt not smoke." But that didn't stop the nuns from smashing your knuckles with a flexible steel ruler if they caught you at it, so now, pushing forty and long backslid from the tenets of Catholicism, I preferred doing my smoking just off the Church's property line. Just another case of what we used to call RCPD—Roman Catholic personality disorder.

By the time I'd tossed the butt into the street Tessa Niland was bearing down the sidewalk toward me. Now in her mid forties, she was married to a successful businessman and lived in the suburbs with a twelve-year-old daughter, and since her husband Stan had little interest in the group of crazies from whose midst he had plucked her so many years before, she had left the Near North Side and the wild days of her youth behind her and gone on to other things more befitting a middle-aged matron.

She enveloped me against her ample bosom and squeezed tight, and when she backed away to look at me there were tears in her eyes. "Welcome home," she said.

"God, I've missed you, Tessa. You look fabulous."

"Well, I'm no movie star like you, but I do my Jane Fonda aerobics and stay out of the midday sun." She looked at the door of the church, at the people going inside. "This is terrible," she said. "I still can't believe it. He was so—life-affirming. He's the first one of us to go. When your former lovers start dying on you, the ticking of the clock just gets louder."

"Did you see him much toward the end?"

"I hadn't seen him in about five years. But then I don't see anybody." She waved her hand in the general direction of Gary and of the Nemeroffs, who had appeared on the steps of the church. "What we all had twenty years ago, it's old news. We were kids, we were crazy, and my God, we had fun! But now I hardly ever get into Chicago anymore. I'm busy doing my quiet suburban life. Stan prefers it that way, and so do I. It's just easier." Her smile echoed a million memories, and she brushed at a tear that was rolling quietly down her cheek. I didn't know whether or not it was for Gavin.

The organ music from inside the church grew louder and more insistent, and we walked up the flagstone pathway to the ornate door. Kendra Dane met us there and touched cheeks with both of us, and then we all went inside to say good-bye to our friend.

Neither Kendra nor Tessa had been raised Catholic, and I had been so long away that I no longer considered myself one of the faithful, so we all ignored the font of holy water and moved down the aisle of the church to the mournful peal of the organ, the morning sun outside bringing to life the stations of the cross on the stained glass windows. We sat in the fourth pew from the front, beneath the benevolent gaze of a statue of the Blessed Mother in a niche to the right of the altar. I looked around and saw several people I'd known slightly from the Hard Knox days, and a few who had been members of the North State Street Theatre Guild. A couple of small-change politicians were there, too, guys from the Fifty-fourth Ward

Democratic Organization, sitting all in a row up near the front where they could be seen. Huddling together for warmth.

I caught the eye of Al Patinkin, my mail carrier–philosopher friend; he was sitting off to one side, and he raised his eyebrows in surprise at seeing me, then smiled and nodded. The Nemeroffs were in the first row, chief mourners, along with a stunning dark-haired woman I didn't know. Ben's eyes were red from crying and Dolly's lips were thin and almost bloodless. Her grief, I knew, was more for Ben's loss than for Gavin himself, and that was all right, too. Each of us deals with the death of someone we care about in a different way.

The casket was pearl gray, decked with flowers and a large, ostentatious wreath that I was later to find out came from the guys at Gavin's old police precinct. It was closed at the moment, but I knew that after the mass they'd open it for a final viewing. I wasn't sure I wanted to look. I've seen more than my share of dead people, and it's never pleasant. I thought I'd rather remember Gavin as he was in life, quoting Shakespeare as he waved a tankard of beer, but I supposed that I'd have to file past the coffin with everyone else when the time came.

The priest came forward in his vestments and stood beneath the enormous crucifix. He looked to be about twenty-nine, and that disturbed me. When priests and baseball players are younger than you are, you know that time has sucked away your youth, that spring for you is just another season when the grass turns green and the cold wind grows warm. This stripling who was about to send Gavin Cassidy over was too young to have known him. It was just part of his job.

The High Requiem Mass got under way, and it was all too familiar to me. The last one I'd attended had been at my own home parish, Saint Aloysius, farther north, and the honored guest in the flower-covered bier had been Kathleen Ryan Saxon, my mother. I'd managed to steer clear of churches and funerals since then.

My mind wandered, back to Hard Knox College, to a small table in the corner at which Gavin Cassidy always held court.

He'd sit there against the wall, which was a huge blackboard on which anyone could scrawl anything he found amusing, things like "My mother made me a homosexual—send her the wool and she'll make you one, too." His friends and admirers would come by to say hello and share a moment, then move on. People always came to Cassidy, he never went to them; that's the way it worked.

"Sit down, my friend," Gavin had thundered at me, waving a hand in which a cigarette always smoldered between the second and third fingers. "Such a long face! You look as if the X rays came back positive."

I sat down with my drink, glancing up at the mirror behind the bar, feeling as young as I looked. I had only a splash of gray at one temple then, when I was twenty-two, but it didn't make me appear older; I just looked like a young actor half made up for the role of an elderly man.

"I need your advice, Gavin."

He'd loved giving counsel, reveled in being all-wise and all-knowing; it was the basis of our friendship.

"I'm thinking about leaving."

"Leaving where?"

"Chicago."

His brows knit together. "Where would you go?"

"California."

His blue eyes twinkled. They always twinkled unless he was three sips from losing consciousness. "Are you going *to* someplace, or are you running *from* someplace?"

I shook my head. "I can't stay here anymore. Too much crap."

"You can't run away," he'd said. "You'll only meet yourself in California. You'll be tanner, but you'll still be you. No one thinks less of you because your old man is in the joint. No one much thinks about it at all."

"It's not only that. If I'm going to be an actor I have to go where the work is, Gav. I've got my degree now, and I have to start my life."

31

He shrugged his massive shoulders and drank down half the beer in his pewter mug. It was Gavin's own personal mug that Stretch Knox kept behind the bar for him, and the ice cubes in it rattled as he gestured.

"It's the only life you have," he said. He wasn't slurring his words just yet, it was too early in the evening for that, but his voice was beer-loud and full of flourishes. In another half hour he'd be in full bloom, roaring in iambic pentameter, so that any stranger who happened in for a drink and a look at the bohemian crowd couldn't possibly ignore him. "And if you feel that way, press on. Go for broke. But don't waste away unfulfilled. Open the throttle wide, follow your heart, and do it!"

He reached out and clapped me on the shoulder. "We shall miss you, sir. It won't be the same here without you." Leaning close to me, his face serious, he'd struggled for the right quote. " 'This above all,' " he'd finally said, " 'to thine own self be true; and it must follow as the night the day thou canst not then be false to any man.' " Then he'd grinned at me with those Erin-go-blue eyes. "Did I get it right?"

As I listened to the priest drone on in Latin—at least he wasn't so young that he conducted mass in English—I thought that Cassidy as Polonius was strange casting. He never perceived himself as a character actor. In his mind he was the leading man, a romantic Romeo, roistering Petruchio, noble Cyrano; yet he had become a Falstaff, brave knight turned fat and ineffectual buffoon, and when he'd come to visit me in Los Angeles I had been his Prince Hal, saying "I know thee not, old man," and turning away from him. He would have bridled at the very suggestion, but in the end Sir John Falstaff for Gavin was pure typecasting.

Ben Nemeroff stepped up to the front of the church, his dark Jewish good looks contrasting with the agonized Aryan-looking Christ that loomed above him. He took a couple of three-by-five cards out of his pocket, shuffled them, looked through them, and then put them back in his jacket and waited for the rustling and coughing in the assemblage to subside. Then he cleared his throat awkwardly and began to speak.

"I'm not an actor like Gavin was; I get scared silly in front of an audience, and I'm scared silly right now," he said. "But somebody has to speak for him, and I guess I'm elected. He wasn't always easy, but he was worth the trouble. He was my best friend for thirty years. And I was his.

"First let me define for you what a friend is. A friend is the one you call when your car breaks down on the Calumet Expressway at three o'clock in the morning and you don't have your checkbook with you and your credit cards are over their limit. A friend accepts you unconditionally, whether or not your politics, your religion, your life-style, or the baseball team you root for happen to be the same as his. A friend gives as much as he takes and then some, loves you for who and what you are and not for how much you have in the bank or what you can do for him. Someone you can laugh with and cry with. Someone you can trust with your life, your kids, your wallet or your secrets. That was me and Cassidy.

"He didn't live the kind of life I'd want," Ben went on, trying to get the shaking in his voice under control, "but that doesn't matter. He lived the life *he* chose, and what's important is that he was a loving, kind, gentle man in a business that was anything but. He gave much and asked . . . very little. Share a jar with him occasionally and not judge him when he had one or two or ten too many. Go with him to the ball game and sit in the bleachers with your shirt off and get rowdy yelling for the Cubs. Listen to his stories about his job and his ladies and the theatrical triumphs that were more in his head than anywhere else. I gave him that—and he gave me so much more in return.

"Is there anyone in this room who can't think of a particular time with him, some incident, some day, and laugh? He lived to laugh, to enjoy, and to make everyone around him laugh and enjoy as well. That's one hell—excuse me," he said quickly, looking upward. "One heck of a legacy. If any one of us can say as much, we'll have really accomplished something."

33

Tessa, next to me, fumbled for tissues, dabbed at her eyes, and blew her nose quietly. Kendra held out her hand and Tessa gave her one from the pack.

"Cassidy had his disappointments and his own private pain," Ben said. "But he had the class to rarely let them show, to not burden his friends with them. He wanted to make people happy, not sad. He wanted to make this city, this world, a little better place than when he found it. In some ways he didn't, but in the ways that are important, he did. For that I thank him. For his love and friendship I thank him. For being a mensch, I thank him."

I held out my own hand and Tessa placed a tissue in it.

"If you knew Gavin well, you know how he loved to quote Shakespeare," Ben continued. "Try this one on for size." He took the index cards from his pocket again, and read, 'His life was gentle, and the elements so mixed in him, that Nature might stand up and say to all the world—this was a man.' " He took his glasses off again and grinned sheepishly. "That was *Julius Caesar.* I read it badly, but I already told you I'm not an actor."

Ben looked up at the choir loft behind us, and lifted an imaginary glass. "So wherever you are, Gavin Cassidy, holding court at a corner table on some quiet little neighborhood Irish cloud where the off-beat angels come to get out of the mainstream—Prosit! Cheers! Chin-chin, *à votre santé,* mud in your eye, here's lookin' up your ancestors, and may the road rise up to meet you." His hand fell limply to his side and his voice, which had grown in strength and timbre during his speech, dropped almost to a whisper. "I'll miss you every day of my life."

The sun was higher and hotter when we finally got outside again. Everyone had filed past the open casket to view the ghastly handiwork of an overambitious mortician and then had gone out past the young priest and Ben and Dolly at the door, and now we were standing around on the walkway and the

34

grass in small clumps, talking quietly among ourselves. I wanted to smoke again, but walking out to the curb didn't seem worth the trouble.

Al Patinkin came up and embraced me. His glasses were streaked and spotted, as usual, but he never seemed to notice. "I wish you'd come home before," he said. "Cassidy would have wanted to see you."

"How've you been, Al?"

He shrugged. "Come see come sah. I survive by not thinking too hard about how I am. Makes it easier. When did you get in town?"

"Yesterday," I said.

"The old town's changed, hasn't it? Everything changes, that's the hell of it. Everything and everybody—except Cassidy. He wouldn't change, wouldn't bend. That's what broke him, finally."

I wanted to ask him what he meant, but we were joined right then by Dolly Nemeroff and the dark-haired woman who'd sat in the front row.

"I wanted to introduce you to Marian Meyers," Dolly said. "She and Gavin were—very close."

I took the dark lady's outstretched hand; it felt cool and dry in mine. She was in her late thirties, maybe older. It was hard to tell. Up close she wasn't beautiful, but there was a serenity about her, and her eyes were large and liquid, set wide apart in her face, complementing her olive skin. She wore lipstick that was a bit too bright for either her coloring or the occasion. "I'm sorry for your troubles," I said.

She smiled. "That's very Irish. Gavin used to say that at funerals too."

"Gavin and I were—"

"I know. I know all about you. From Dolly and from Gavin, too. Of course he talked about you as though you were twenty-one, and that's how I've always thought of you."

"The gray hair surprises me, too," I said.

"The young believe that they are the first discoverers of

35

youth. It's always a shock when they find they don't have the immunity to time they thought they did."

Gary Storm came down the steps from the church and passed by us without speaking or even looking in our direction. Marian Meyers glanced at Al and Dolly, who were deep in conversation, and then turned her back to them and leaned in close so that only I could hear her; her tone was low and very intense. "I have to talk to you," she said. "Can we get together later today?"

"Why don't we ride to the cemetery together and talk on the way?"

She shook her head, almost snorting her impatience. "I'm not going to the cemetery. I can't watch them put him in the ground—I almost didn't make it through this. Are you busy this afternoon?"

"Not that I know of."

She looked both ways, as if to see whether anyone was near enough to overhear, and I wondered if the tragedy that had brought us all together had somehow unhinged her.

"Do you know where the zoo is in Lincoln Park?"

"I was born here, remember?"

"Can you meet me there? The rookery, by the duck pond, at three o'clock. It's very, *very* important."

I said, "Marian, I haven't seen Gavin in years. Are you sure you have the right person?"

She looked at me, her dark eyes sharp, probing. It was a bit unsettling. "No," she said. "I'm not. But I'm asking you anyway."

4

The Lincoln Park Zoo and the rectangular meadow with the fountain and the statue and the flower beds that form a buffer zone between the animals and busy Stockton Drive, stretching northward from Webster Avenue toward the Chicago Conservatory and its thousands of exotic plants and the green smell of moss and damp earth, was more crowded than I remembered, mainly because when I was a kid they didn't take entire classes there on schoolday excursions. Especially not in Catholic schools, where you were excused from attendance for religious or health reasons and not much else. The zoo was a place your mother brought you on the first warm Saturday of spring, and later it was someplace to take an adolescent date. There was always a set routine you followed: turn left past the bears and the wolves and then make a full circle, hoping that one of the big cats would be roaring and pacing in the lion house, to end up at the south end of the zoo where the big Viking ship with a dragon's head on its bow sat under its protective shed, nudging you gently into daydreams of high adventure at sea. Others may have had their own routes of choice, but that one was mine, and I don't think I ever varied it.

I bought some popcorn from one of the rolling stands. I am a sucker for fresh popcorn, and the aroma of it was too much of a temptation for me, overwhelming the acrid smells of the animals and the sweet-sour odor of children, which warred with one another for dominance. I munched on it as I wandered along the zoo's main thoroughfare, the antelope and eland and greater and lesser kudus watching me with wounded resentment at my failure to share my treat. Let them buy their own, I thought.

The rookery is a separate enclave at the north end of the zoo behind the conservatory, its entrance just across the walkway from the elephants. That was another change; the old zoo's single elephant, whose name I recall as Judy, shared the pachyderm house near the Stockton Drive entrance with a lazy and practically immobile hippo. I was surprised to see a large, flap-eared African elephant in the same compound with the smaller, blockier Indian variety. In most zoos they are rightly kept separate, but then that's what Chicago is all about—coexisting and ignoring the rules.

I went in through the rookery gate. Winding slab stone pathways inside skirted an enormous pond, which is home to ducks and geese and swans of all descriptions, and I made my way toward the back of the enclosure, remembering the days when I'd walk the ten miles home from my job in the Loop and cut through the zoo, stopping in the rookery to rest my feet, rest my mind, and, with a foot in either camp, try to sort out the terribly complicated world between adolescence and manhood.

I didn't have much time for reminiscences, as Marian Meyers was prompt. I watched her negotiate the long walkway in her high heels, stepping carefully on the uneven slabs as she came toward me, her mane of black hair glinting red in the afternoon light. I hadn't noticed the red highlights before. She was a fine-looking woman, and I felt glad Gavin had known her toward the end when he'd most needed warmth and sunshine.

"This place brings back memories," I said, going to her, "but then this whole trip has called up lots of them."

"I appreciate your coming to meet me," she said, taking my

38

hand to steady herself. "I know you must have a lot of old friends to see and places to visit. But I needed to talk to someone—someone who cared about Gavin."

"I'm flattered. But it's been years since he and I were even in touch. It was my fault as much as his. He was part of another time for me."

"You're lucky—you weren't around to see what happened to him. You're not judgmental about him, like the rest of them. They all deserted him when he started coming apart. All except Ben." She blinked her eyes rapidly. "Even me. But you're here. You came all the way across the country to say good-bye, and that must mean something. That even though you weren't in touch, you loved him."

"Didn't everybody?"

She sighed. "I did." She waved a hand in front of her face. "For all it mattered. When you love someone like that, you let everything else in life slide, even your work—and I always thought that was the most important thing to me."

"What is your work?"

"I make my living as a freelance copywriter for ad agencies here in town. But my real work is writing novels. I've done three without selling one, but I keep at it."

"That's a tough business."

"Anything worthwhile is tough," she said.

"Shall we walk?"

She shook her head. "I'd rather sit, if it's okay."

We sat down on the cold stone ledge. She'd bought some bird food from the machine by the gate, several slabs of what looked like stale RyKrisp, and she began breaking off little pieces and tossing them into the water, rationing them carefully. The ducks and geese made a frantic rush at the food, converging in a V at the edge of the pond from all points of the rookery as if they hadn't been fed in weeks.

"How did you and Gavin ever get together?"

She said, "We met at a party at Hard Knox College. You remember it?"

39

I laughed. "Remember it? I damn near kept the place in business at one time. You too?"

"No, not like Gavin. But before we were married my husband used to be a regular there."

"Your husband?"

"Ex. Gary Storm."

That little piece of information shut me up. It was hard to imagine this bright, self-assured woman married to an overbearing ass like Gary. She said, "No one told you? Storm was not only my married name, it defined the relationship. Thunder and lightning and gale-force winds. That's why I changed it back after the divorce. Gary and I were coming apart long before I ever started up with Gavin, no matter what he might say."

"You left Gary for Gavin?"

"I left him for me," she said. "Gavin just happened to be there. I'd told Gary I wanted out, and our lawyers were already talking. Getting together with Gavin wasn't in my game plan. I wanted some peace, not another involvement. I don't believe in rebounds; they're unhealthy. But Gavin was everything Gary wasn't—funny, kind, dramatic, going full-bore all the time, as though every minute was too precious to waste on anything more serious than a few drinks and a few laughs. He wasn't the most judicious man in the world, but I don't think he spent a single second being bored. He just wouldn't put up with it." She shook her head. "And God help me, he made me laugh. When you've lived with a man like Gary whose eyes never smile, Cassidy was bound to look good. He was an original, all right. If he hadn't existed he would have invented himself, because he really believed there was a need for people like him in the world."

"There is," I said.

She fiddled with her hair. "We started going together and we fell in love, so hard I couldn't believe it at first. Like a head-on train wreck. I thought I could make something of Gavin and me. I almost succeeded."

40

She was quiet for a while, intent on the ducks and swans, as if their feeding and well-being was her life's passion. I finally said, "What happened, Marian?"

"Beer happened," she said simply. "Gavin loved me too, I'm sure of it—you can't be with someone for five years and not know. He just loved drinking more. I just couldn't compete with three twelve-packs a day. I tried to pretend it wasn't a problem. I cleaned up after him when he vomited all over himself, and I covered him with blankets and let him sleep on the floor where he'd passed out, and I nursed his hangovers and washed his socks, and on those nights when he wasn't too drunk or I could get to him early enough, I'd make love to him. But I finally couldn't handle it anymore. So I gave him an ultimatum, drinking or me, and he called my bluff." She put her head back and sighed. "I hadn't seen him more than twice in six months when he got really sick and went into the hospital. Then I was there three times a day, and all day on weekends." She turned to look at me. "But we both understood that when he came out he was on his own. I didn't stop loving him. I haven't yet. I just had to fix it so he couldn't hurt me anymore."

"I wasn't much of a friend to him lately, either," I said. "I was a Christmas-card friend."

"That's more than the rest of them who showed up today to cluck their tongues and look sad. All except Ben. Ben was the only one who never judged him. Do you have a cigarette?"

I shook one out of my pack for her; it took me two matches to light it in the soft spring breeze. She puffed on it in the manner of someone not used to smoking nor completely comfortable with it, almost like a kid trying to. act grown up.

"Dolly Nemeroff said you're a private detective in California."

"I do investigations for people, yes."

"That's a strange line of work."

"It's an archaic line of work, but it keeps me off the streets."

"Are you good at it?"

41

"If I say yes I'm bragging; if I say no I'm lying."

"Will you do one for me? An investigation?"

"I'm not licensed in Illinois. But I'm sure there are plenty of reputable agencies here in town."

She was chewing off her lipstick, concentrating on getting a hunk of food to a small, dun-colored duck who kept being aced out by his larger and more aggressive neighbors. "Ever investigate a murder?"

"Whoa!" I said. "I don't get involved with homicides. That's the police's job."

Her laugh was a mirthless bark. She aimed a piece of the crispy rye wafer at the small duck, and it plopped directly in front of him in the water. He gobbled up most of it before his companions set upon him, pecking at him and quacking angrily until he surrendered the rest of it. "The little guys don't have much of a chance against the bullies of the world, do they?" she murmured, tossing all the remaining duck food into the pond. We watched the ensuing riot. Ducks are competitive little bastards.

She leaned back on one elbow against the stone, her long trench coat falling open to reveal a black and rust sweater. "How well did you really know Gavin?"

"Twenty years ago we were very close."

"And he was a drunk then, too, wasn't he?" Her smile took the bite out of it. "It's all right, I've heard from the others—from Gavin, too. He was always a heavy drinker, right?"

I nodded.

"Back in the sixties, when dropping acid and popping pills and smoking dope and eating magic mushrooms was de rigueur, did you ever know Gavin to do drugs?"

"No," I admitted. "He was kind of a nut on the subject. He always said that as a cop he saw too many kids get permanently wrecked by putting that shit in their systems. He preferred his highs out of a beer stein."

She was quiet for a moment, perhaps because she was orga-

42

nizing her thought carefully before speaking. Finally she asked, "You know anything about drugs?"

"Just enough not to mess with them."

"According to Gavin's autopsy report, the official cause of death was alcohol mixed with amphetamines. In large amounts, that's a lethal combination."

"I know."

She cast another long look at the ducks and then swung around to face me squarely. "That's my point, Mr. Saxon. He never took drugs in his life. Never. Someone deliberately gave him amphetamines without his knowing it, and it mixed with the alcohol, it killed him." Her brown eyes burned a challenge. "Gavin Cassidy was murdered. Now what are you going to do about it?"

5

I didn't know what I *could* do about it, even if it were true. I had no right poking around in a murder case, and I could easily find myself in pretty torrid water if I got caught trespassing on the turf of the Chicago police. Besides, Marian's accusation rang of overwrought emotion.

If they're any good at all, writers tend to have vivid imaginations, and perhaps Gavin's dying had made Marian lose touch with the real world and manufacture a plot that was better left on the screen of her word processor. It was also possible that she was inadvertently trying to expiate her own guilt at deserting him when he needed her most. Of all the people who turned their backs on Cassidy at the end of his life, she had been the closest to him, and in her mind that may have been the coup de grace. And if that were true, risking my license to check it out would be madness.

It wouldn't have been the first time I've done something illogical or just plain dumb.

But I owed Gavin a little something myself. God knows what might have happened to me twenty years earlier when I didn't know just who I was and what I was going to be, when I felt as isolated and exposed as any postadolescent whose family has just crumbled before his eyes, if Gavin hadn't been there as a friend and mentor to guide me through the treacherous swampland separating youth from manhood. I had learned from Cassidy the things I deem valuable and important—friendship and loyalty and the habit of living life to its fullest even when it means veering dangerously close to the edge—and I'd used them ever since. What he had given me of himself that was destructive—his penchant for tilting at windmills and following the dreams of smoke that led him to the dissolute taverns and flophouses of the Near North Side—I had wisely discarded. And when he came to me for help in California, adrift and purposeless and almost desperate from it, as much as I'd wanted to toss him a lifeline, my own survival rightly took priority over his, and I'd let him use my pullout sofa bed and crunch-style peanut butter and bottled spaghetti sauce without giving him any real support.

So I had a debt to pay, and accepting Marian's challenge, or at least looking into it, seemed to be a small way of discharging it. Too little and too late, but it was the least I could do.

I told Marian Meyers I couldn't accept her money or her assignment, not legally, morally, or ethically. But I did promise I'd make some inquiries on my own.

I didn't know where to start. As far as I could tell, everyone who knew Cassidy had loved him; if not, they simply eliminated him from their life. No one had ever been angry enough with him to do much more than throw a drunken roundhouse outside a bar at three A.M., and by nine it was all slept off and seemingly forgotten. And barflies don't commit murder over an alcohol-induced punch-up.

Cops often make enemies. But Cassidy was no high-level investigator and wore no stripes or gold shield. He worked the streets, writing traffic tickets, rattling the doors of closed shops to make sure they were secure, chasing the kids with the spray cans to keep the neighborhood free of graffiti, checking the IDs of heavily made-up young girls on the prowl on Rush Street. His drinking had prevented him from rising any higher in the department, but it had also kept him away from the big crimes, the murders and drug deals that inspire vengeance. A lot of crazy people out there might fly into a homicidal rage over a parking citation, but they would hardly be liable to slip a beat cop an overdose of amphetamines to go with his twelve-pack. They'd explode on the spot, which is why street cops wear guns and carry batons.

On Stockton Drive I caught a 151 bus, as rattletrap as I remembered, rode back downtown to the Wrigley Building, and descended a flight of steps to the lower level of Hubbard Street where it dead-ends at the river. I had a drink at Riccardo's to kill the stale taste of the zoo popcorn. The sidewalk café was crowded with happy-hour drinkers, all around thirty, dressed for the office, and laughing too loudly.

The bar inside was cool and dark, with its startling *Seven Lively Arts* murals by William S. Schwartz and other Depression-era Chicago artists. You always got an honest drink at Riccardo's, although the intrusion of the TV endlessly playing ESPN behind the bar was an added and unwelcome wrinkle.

I hadn't ever figured to sip Scotch at Riccardo's bar again, but then I'd never imagined returning to confront the scenes of my past again, either. And in my wildest dreams I couldn't have pictured Chicago without Gavin Cassidy. In his own way he was like Hull House and the bandshell in Grant Park and

Wrigley Field and "the Hawk," the killer wind that sweeps off the lake and makes you jam your hands into the pockets of your overcoat and lean into it head down, fighting it at every step. The vacuum his loss created disoriented me here as much as did the unfamiliar new skyscrapers that redefined the skyline.

I finished my drink and walked back up the steps just in time to see the bridge go up. The Chicago River cuts right through the heart of downtown, and when a tall ship wants to navigate its waters going into or out of Lake Michigan, the series of drawbridges that extend some of the city's busiest streets over the river open, stopping traffic for miles in either direction. I stood in front of the Wrigley Building and watched the enormous span of the Michigan Avenue Bridge split in the middle and rise up into the air like a monster from a Japanese movie, accompanied by flashing red lights and the insistent dinging of a bell, as an ore ship sailed by with great dignity, blithely ignoring the inconvenience to the commuters on the streets. Off to the west against the setting sun the bridges of Wabash, State, Clark and LaSalle were rising, too. It wasn't the most efficient system in the world, but Chicago had lived with it for a hundred years now, and nobody saw much reason to change.

When the bridges finally were lowered and the wooden barriers lifted, you could almost hear a collective sigh of relief from the stalled motorists as traffic lumbered forward again. I walked back to my hotel to shower and dress for the evening.

In my room, a little red light on my phone blinked on and off to let me know a message awaited me, and when I contacted the operator I was told a Mrs. Purdell had called. I had to think for a moment before remembering that was Beth Shroats's married name.

"Dolly told me you were here," she said when I returned her call. "I'd love to see you."

"Me too you. Are you going to be at their place tonight? They're having a sort of memorial party."

46

She hesitated for just a heartbeat. "I don't think so. How long are you going to be around?"

"I don't know," I said. "A few more days, anyway. I want to get to know the town again."

"How about dinner tomorrow night at the Como Inn?"

"Are you ready for some heavy-duty nostalgia?"

"Beats hell out of the present," she said.

I took a cab to the Nemeroff place. My driver's name, according to the placard on the dashboard, was Firooz Ghajar, and the manic intensity of his driving, as though India was invading Pakistan, kept me holding on to the back of the front seat. As we barreled north on the Outer Drive, I was reminded of how spectacular the Chicago scenery can be. To my right, Lake Michigan was a blue-gray dropcloth that tiptoed up to the edge of the sky, small waves lapping at the dark blond sand of the beach, which wasn't sand at all but finely ground gravel that was painful to spring-tender bare feet after a winter of enforced absence from the lakefront. In Chicago people use their beaches and parks more than in almost any other city, perhaps because Chicagoans have a zest for their city that never wanes, whether in the numbing blasts of winter or the hellacious midwestern summers.

In Dolly's living room I was delighted to find one of the dearest friends of my youth, Diane Kubo, née Keeshan. A feisty terrier of a lady, Diane had lent a patient ear to our travails and our dreams, always at the cost of a stern lecture, nursed our hangovers and frequently broken hearts, genially disapproved of our carryings-on, and acted as the unofficial mother superior to a crowd of hedonists and revelers at a time in history when the arts took a back seat to political and social conscience.

Her hug was almost fierce, and she pounded me on the back as she kissed me. Her husband, Dave, an industrial contractor and builder, waited on the edges of our reunion. I'm sure he barely remembered me. I hadn't known him very well, since he and Diane only met when I was readying myself for my westward hejira, but he'd always seemed a quiet, pleasant guy who made her happy, and that was the important thing.

Some of the guests I had never seen before, latecomers into the nimbus of light Gavin had cast, but Gary Storm was in attendance, and Kendra and Tessa Niland and Al Patinkin. Bob Eliscu was there, too. I hadn't expected Dolly and Ben to invite him. He had been Gavin's friend but none of ours, a barroom brawler and drink cadger and borrower of money, and it was rumored back then that he was "connected" to some pretty unsavory elements. None of us understood why Gavin put up with Bob, a man of remarkable crudity and charmlessness, but Gavin collected strays like an old lady with a thing for cats, and so the rest of us tolerated Eliscu. It was he with whom I'd squared off in the cramped confines of Figaro's bar so many years before, when Gavin had stepped between us and saved me from the thrashing of my life. Now close to fifty, Eliscu still presented a fearsome visage, a single black eyebrow slashing across his forehead and a mouth downturned with anger at a world that he felt never appreciated him. We shook hands with perfunctory wariness; neither of us is the type to forget old injuries. We had never been friends and saw no necessity to change that situation now.

Dolly had spread a buffet feast for us all: several different kinds of cheese, raw vegetables for the health-conscious, deli roast beef and pressed turkey and kosher salami, rye and shepherd's bread, macaroni salad, green bean salad, rippled potato chips, pound cake and toll house cookies. All I felt like eating were the potato chips, and since I couldn't very well stack a bunch on my plate with nothing else, I elected to skip having anything at all. I poured myself a drink before Diane co-opted me off into a corner, where we hugged again and recited for one another the history of our lives up to the present. I was tiring of talking about myself and wished I had brought a photocopied fact sheet or an audiotape to hand out to everyone with the promise that I'd answer any questions later.

Diane was as animated as ever. I learned that she still dabbled a bit in community theater, albeit now as a producer and director rather than in an onstage capacity, and was on several committees having to do with supporting the Arts in Chicago. She was drinking red wine and it was coloring her lips like a popsicle.

"And just why haven't we heard from you in a hundred years?" she demanded. "No telephone? A chronically broken writing arm? Or couldn't you afford the postage? If we didn't catch you on television once in a while we would have thought you were—" All at once mindful of the occasion, she stopped herself and amended what she'd been about to say to "Among the missing."

"I've already apologized to everyone else," I said, "so let's just say I've been remiss and that I'll go and sin no more."

"You mean you'll even write once in a while?"

"Every Christmas at the very least." I sneaked a potato chip. "I missed you at the church this morning."

"I hate funerals. I mean, what's the point? Gavin and I hadn't been close for years, anyway. I was never as taken with that Irish charm as the rest of you. I got tired of his passing out before eleven o'clock, I hated the way he used Dolly and Ben, and as for Beth! Well, I never made any secret about how I felt. So going to his funeral would've been hypocritical. I came here to see everybody—but mostly to see you." She gave my cheek a grandmotherly, painful pinch between her thumb and forefinger.

"And I'm glad you did," I said, speaking with difficulty until she released my cheek, "because it saved me cab fare all the way out to the bullrushes where you live. I hope we can get together again before I leave."

Dave came up to form the third point of the triangle. "We'll drive in and have dinner one night," he said, "just the three of us, so we can really sit down and talk."

"It's a date," I said. "I don't want to lose you all again."

Diane's eyes turned soft. For all her sometime bluster she was one of the most sensitive people I've ever known, and her question was one I wouldn't have tolerated from anyone else. "Have you seen your father?"

That was Diane all over, forthright to a fault. There are some things you don't talk about to certain people, scabs that never quite heal and are not to be fingered. Knowing it was taboo, she had mentioned the unmentionable: Cyrano's nose, the emperor's clothes, the Pocomoco River from the old Abbott and Costello "Slowly I turned . . ." routine. My father.

I looked away. "No," I said.

She pressed her cheek to mine and walked away with a sad little smile.

Conventional wisdom had it that I'd gotten too high-hat for the Midwest, that I'd left Chicago, friends and loved ones, to go to California and make my fortune in the motion picture industry, that I disdained the community and professional theater groups around town as too small and insignificant to contain my talent, that my overinflated ego had driven me to seek a broader canvas. That wasn't true, or at least it was true in only a small way.

I'd left to get as far away from James Saxon and his prison record as I could.

Now that I was back again, even though I'd spent the last two days trying not to think about him, his presence and proximity hovered over me like a living ghost, as though the moment I crossed the incorporated limits of the city, I was once more fair game.

6

I drank my drink and made another, mainlined a few more
potato chips, and went to talk to Al Patinkin, who was loading
his plate with some of the less healthful comestibles. Al, in the
same frayed blue windbreaker jacket he'd been wearing summer or winter since I'd known him, somehow seemed an oasis
of normalcy. And when Al Patinkin starts appearing normal,
the rest of the world had better get its collective ass to the
nearest therapist's couch for a good talking-to.

"I've never understood it," he said, shaking his bald head.
He'd been bald twenty years ago; he'd probably started losing
his hair in high school. "It's your birthday, you have a party.
You get married, you have a party. Someone dies, you have a
party. It's a barbaric system." He slurped at some bourbon from
a plastic party glass; Al always made noise when he drank.
"You know why we're celebrating?"

I knew, but I figured I was going to hear it anyway.

"Not death. You don't make a party for death." He grabbed
a celery stick stuffed with cream cheese, chomped at it, and
waved what was left like a symphony conductor during a
particularly présto movement. "We're celebrating Life. Our
own. That we're still alive, that it wasn't us they put in the
ground this morning."

"Maybe you're right," I said.

His eyes danced behind his Coke-bottle glasses. He was a garrulous sort, always late with the mail because he'd stop along his route to deliver diatribes on the mayor, the president, the state of live theater in Chicago, the perennial misfortunes of the Cubs, or whatever else happened to be current and controversial, to anyone who would listen. For all anyone ever knew, Al was lonely and asexual, another jolly elf who'd never passed through emotional puberty. He was sometimes a bore, often exasperating, but he had a heart as big as a Chrysler.

"I'm always right," he reminded me. "You know that. It comes from studying human nature on the street every day." He slapped me on the back, jarring my drink. "Miss you, you old son of a bitch." The rest of the celery stick disappeared, and he spoke with his mouth full of it. "Cassidy missed you too, you want to know the truth."

I wasn't sure I did want to know the truth, but I didn't tell Al that.

"If he could have hung out with you in L.A. and made a living doing little acting jobs, it would have turned his life around. That's what he always wanted, a Screen Actors Guild card. So being a cop was just settling; he didn't really know what else to do. Even so, it was a real gut shot when they put him on suspension."

I put my glass down on the buffet table. "I didn't know he'd been suspended."

Al shrugged. "He wouldn't talk about it. Of course, lately I only saw him when he was nine tenths in the bag, so our conversation was pretty much surface. But it wouldn't have made any difference. You know him, he never dumped his troubles on anybody else. It was about a month ago. They kept it hush-hush, but and all of a sudden there was Cassidy out making the rounds day and night, Rush Street, Old Town, Ontario, getting into brawls at Ditka's, going at it like I'd never seen him. And I've seen him go at it pretty bad. It hit him hard, getting kicked out, I know that. He chalked it up as one more

52

failure. For a guy as full of life as Cassidy, he sure as hell never figured out how to use it."

"Or survive it," Gary Storm said. He had come up behind me and caught the last few words of the conversation. "He never learned there are certain rules you follow, laws of cause and effect. You can't just march along doing whatever the hell you want whenever you want to do it."

Ordinarily I was able to ignore Gary; it had been many years since he was even a part of my reality. But bad-mouthing Gavin Cassidy seemed singularly inappropriate tonight, and I decided to call him on it.

"Why not?" I said. "I do."

Gary's mouth twisted into a smile that was more of a sneer. "Then you're an asshole too."

"What do you mean by 'too'?"

He raised an eyebrow, the supercilious bastard, and gave a knowing little shrug. "You've been away too long to get all righteous and smug, so don't talk tough with me, pal. I've been here all along, and I can tell you he wasn't even close to the Cassidy we all knew and loved. Maybe his brain got pickled."

Because I was a guest in Dolly's home, and out of respect for the departed, I didn't answer him, but I had to turn away from him to keep my mouth shut. He bent over the table to construct a roast beef sandwich with cheddar cheese, mustard, and mayonnaise. He never knew how close he came to wearing it home.

Kendra came up beside me and defused the tension, putting one arm around Al Patinkin's shoulders and the other around mine. "How are my two favorite men?" she said. "Are you getting enough to eat?"

"More important is enough to drink," I said.

Al grabbed a couple of carrot sticks and shoved them into his mouth. "Boy, it's great seeing you two together again," he said, and then he winced. "Sorry, that was insensitive. Guess I'm still stuck in the early seventies. But you know something, I think I liked it better then."

I decided to bail him out, as I had so often when he stuck his foot in his mouth. "It's good to have all of us together, Al."

"Listen, let me know if you need a ride for as long as you're in town. I'm at your disposal." He grinned. "I drove you home pie-eyed often enough when you were a kid."

"I don't remember that," I said.

"Oh yeah, you were a real jag-off. But we loved you. Still do." He walked away, chewing happily.

"Al hasn't changed a bit," I said. "He was born fifty."

Kendra nibbled on a chip. "I hate it being awkward like this. With us, I mean."

"Nothing awkward about ancient history."

"If it makes you feel any better, leaving you for Gavin was the biggest mistake of my life."

"It doesn't make me feel any better. Once it would have, but not now," I said. "Any chance we can get together while I'm here, just the two of us?"

She fidgeted. "I'm sort of involved with someone right now. . . ."

"I didn't say sleep together, I said get together."

She laughed in spite of herself.

"Anyone I know?" I asked.

She shook her head, not meeting my eyes. "He's a musician, a bass player. Or he tries to be. The fact is he stinks at it, but he's twenty-three and can fuck all night." She looked up, defiant, angry, lost. "Have I shocked you?"

"No," I said.

"Shit. I tried." She brushed her hair out of her eyes with the back of her hand, a gesture I remembered the way I remembered my whole life. "He doesn't exactly fit in with the group here, which is why I didn't bring him. Sorry about that. I'll bet your curiosity is killing you."

"Come on, Kenni, lighten up."

She arched her long neck. "Is that one of those California expressions?"

I sighed. "We're old friends. No reason why we shouldn't be civil, is there?"

"I wouldn't blame you if you weren't. Some hurts hang on a long time. . . ."

"We were kids. No matter what romantic fantasy we were caught up in, I think we knew we were just way stations for one another. There's no hard feelings anymore. Just good memories."

"It must have been humiliating for you. For what it's worth, I'm sorry."

"I understand it. I think I understood it even then." I took her hand and gave it a squeeze. "We both still had a way to go. We needed to experience a lot more things before we were ready for a picket fence in Glencoe."

"Oh, it was a learning experience, all right. It taught me to beware of alley cats, no matter how prettily they purr." She finished the wine in her glass and poured it full again from a bottle on the sideboard.

I saw Ben approaching; I was never so glad to see anyone in my life, because there was nothing more I could think of to say to Kendra Dane. Ben had a tall, good-looking young man in tow, someone I'd seen at the funeral that morning but hadn't recognized. He had close-cropped blond hair and a semimilitary bearing and wore a sprayed-on gray single-breasted suit; I could have shaved with the crease in his trousers. Ben introduced him as Darren Oraweic, and explained, "He was Gavin's partner. On the force."

"Nice to meet you, Darren," I said. His handshake was firm, and there was warmth and sorrow in his ice blue eyes.

"Same here," he said. "Cassidy talked about you a lot. Every time you were on TV he made all of us watch. He said you were the only celebrity he knew."

"I'm no celebrity. I work in pictures or TV once in a while, that's all."

He gave me a tight smile. "To Cassidy that was pretty hot shit, you." Oraweic, like many Chicagoans of Polish descent, appended the word *you* at the end of sentences. "He would have given anything to be in your shoes. He was a good copper, but he wasn't a happy one."

"Was he, Darren? A good cop?"

"The best," he said almost with reverence. "I lucked out getting partners with him. He was some teacher. I could tell you stories . . ."

"Would you? I'm going to be in town a while, and I'd like to hear them. Can we meet sometime?"

That seemed to startle him. When we use offhand platitudes like "We should get together" or "I could tell you stories" and someone takes us up on it, we get disoriented. He looked around for support, but Ben and Kendra had drifted off to another set of guests. "Sure. I don't know what I can tell you, but, uh, when? I'm off tomorrow."

"Tomorrow's good."

He was a nice kid trapped by his own innate good manners, and I felt crappy about putting him on the spot. He was not yet abraded by the job into thinking that the only class of humanity that exists is crooked and corrupt, not yet stripped of whatever idealism had led him to the police academy in the first place. "I was gonna go to the ball game tomorrow, you."

"I practically grew up at Wrigley Field. Can I join you? The tickets are on me."

We made our arrangements, although he wasn't certain as to what I wanted or why, but a free ball game doesn't come along every day. It was the least I could do for taking up some of his precious off time. I knew some strings to pull for good seats, but they were strings I didn't want to pull, didn't even want to touch. I decided I'd visit the ticket broker across the street from my hotel.

I wanted to find out what Gavin Cassidy had been up to, who he might have run afoul of in the course of his work. He hadn't been the kind of cop to keep things from his partner, I knew that, and if I could get Darren Oraweic to open up, perhaps I could satisfy myself as to what really happened, one way or the other. Intellectually I had to dismiss the wild accusation Marian Meyers had made at the zoo that afternoon, but emotionally it was eating a hole in my gut like a Chinese water torture with battery acid.

"It isn't often we get a movie star in our midst." Bob Eliscu had moved in on me like a December 7th sneak attack. His voice had a rasp I didn't remember, as though someone had kicked him in the throat. Knowing Eliscu, that was entirely possible. And a consummation devoutly to be wished.

"How've you been, Bob?" I said as if I cared.

"Ah, a buck here, a buck there. Rough deal for Cassidy, huh?" He ran a hand through his hair, which I couldn't help noticing he was now dying jet black. "Just about everybody gave up on him toward the end. He was getting to be a pain in the ass."

"Give it a rest," I said. "He's not even cold."

"Hey, you weren't around here, you don't know. He really pushed the old sword-of-justice bit down everyone's throat for a while, and it got tired."

"What do you mean?"

He poked a thick finger into my arm. "Just because you wear a badge doesn't mean you can't cut an old friend some slack. For Cassidy, if you're not part of the solution you're part of the problem. He started taking that uniform a little too serious. I mean, him and me were pals from way back. But all of a sudden he didn't want to know me anymore."

"I wonder why," I said.

"Hey," he said, suddenly on defense, "everybody does things they wouldn't want in Mike Royko's column, you know? But Cassidy, he changed. The older he got, the tighter his ass. And he wound up getting it in a sling."

I felt an adrenaline rush. "Oh? How's that?"

"Ask me no questions," he said, holding up a callused hand.

I shook my head. *"You* sure haven't changed, Bob."

Bob Eliscu ran his tongue around his lips. "Nobody calls me

Bob anymore. Now they call me LSQ. It's what I call my company. Because of my name."

"LSQ sounds like a World War Two landing barge."

His eyes narrowed. "Yeah? Well Saxon sounds like an ex-con."

I felt something very cold and dangerous forming just under my breastbone, an icy and familiar pain, and I clenched my hands so tightly my fingernails bit into my palms. After a quiet deep breath I spoke very carefully. "My father *is* an ex-con, Bob. Is your father a landing barge?"

It can't be said that someone with such ruddy skin can flush, but Eliscu's face darkened several shades, and a muscle at the side of his eye jumped. "I should have torn out your fucking tongue years ago when I had the chance. Damn Cassidy for stopping me."

"If you'd care to try again, let me know. I'm not nineteen anymore."

"None of us are," Tessa Niland said firmly, stepping between us, "and you'd both do well to remember that." I don't know how long she'd been standing there or how much she'd heard, and I didn't care; the rage was upon me and I would have gladly squared off with Bob Eliscu right there in the dining room. "Now you two stop it! This is hardly the time."

"Hey, no problem," Eliscu said. "I wouldn't want to mess up his pretty gray hair."

We watched him move away; he rolled like a gorilla when he walked. I poured myself another Scotch. I was drinking too much, but the good news was I didn't have to drive home. I was badly shaken, and I put my glass down on the table and shoved both hands into my pockets to keep them from trembling.

Tessa said, "You're not going to let a low-grade moron like that upset you."

"He's a real bite in the ass."

She put her arms around me, drawing me close to her, the pillowlike breasts, still firm, pushing against my chest. "Why do you still let it bother you about your father?"

"How could it not bother me? Most people carry their father's picture in their wallets. The only one I have of mine, there's a number across his chest."

"It was a long time ago."

"Tessa," I said wearily, "it seems like everything was a long time ago."

Her eyes, big and brown, suddenly looked like Bambi's after Man shot his mother. She had been one of Gavin's string too, back when we were all young and thirsty for each drop of life we could suck up, and the object of the game was to Experience. We looked at each other and smiled the smile of mutual survivors.

I wandered all over the Nemeroff house, living room, dining room, kitchen, and cozy back yard, where people were telling funny, affectionate anecdotes about Gavin Cassidy with sorrow and loss behind the laughter. Probably no one would have laughed louder than Gavin. Or been sadder, either.

I was standing out back near a redwood picnic table when Kendra found me. "Do you have a ride back?"

"Yellow Cab."

"I'll drive you."

"It's out of your way."

"Nonsense," she said. "I live downtown now. I have an apartment on North State Parkway." She raised her perfect eyebrows. "I spend my whole life without ever leaving my zip code."

Of course it took at least fifteen minutes to say all my good-byes. The people I really cared about I'd see again; those I didn't know or didn't particularly like I felt no pangs about leaving. I was beginning to think coming to Chicago had been a gigantic mistake, caused by a rush of grief and guilt; better I had just sent flowers for the casket.

Kendra drove down Addison Street to Sheridan Road and turned right past the Indian totem pole that has stood sentinel beside the drive for as long as I can remember. I didn't know why it's there or what it signifies, but I'd always been intrigued by it as a child, as were most kids of my era with anything Indian. She turned onto the drive at General Sheridan's huge equestrian statue near Belmont Avenue and headed downtown.

"You never married?" She made it a statement more than a question.

"No. I came close once or twice. I spend an inordinate amount of time walking around with my heart on the mend. I seem to be attracted to women who are bad for me." I bit my lip. "Sorry, I didn't mean that the way it sounded."

"Think nothing of it," Kendra said. "At the time we were really right for each other, but as you say, people grow up."

She exited the drive just before Oak Street, and as we headed south on Michigan Avenue she said, "Damn Cassidy for dying, anyway!"

"It was thoughtless of him, wasn't it?"

"It stirred up a lot of stuff that should have been left buried. Old feelings, old hurts."

We stopped for a light at Pearson Street, and the amber light reflecting off the Water Tower softened the planes of her lovely face. She looked over at me, her eyes dark and serious now, not the pixie I'd fallen in love with so many years before. "Do you want me to come up with you?"

I wasn't expecting that, so I had to think about it for a moment. Almost forgotten hot Chicago nights and the memory of fumbling under skirts, of the wonder of discovery and the acknowledgment of adulthood and potency came flooding back to me. And nights of despair at the betrayal of first love, the empty alcoholic hazes, 4 A.M. walks on wind-tossed Oak Street Beach trying to sober up while I fended off the gay cruisers who staked out that particular patch of sand in the dark. I shook my head. "That might not be such a good idea."

"I will if you want."

"You're involved with someone."

"I'm always involved. It isn't important." She smiled.

"What's the matter? Afraid my body won't be like it was when I was seventeen?"

"I'm not exactly seventeen anymore myself."

"Well then, what the hell? There's no law against it, is there?"

"It's . . . inappropriate."

"Jesus!" she said. "Give me a break. There's been nothing between Cassidy and me for fifteen years."

"It has nothing to do with Cassidy," I said.

"It shouldn't." She gripped the steering wheel of her Taurus station wagon so tight her knuckles whitened. "You know why Gavin and I stopped seeing each other?"

I shook my head. "I'd left for California by then."

"Would you believe a case of the clap?"

I didn't know what to say. Feeling a little sick, I rolled down the car window and breathed in the fresh air.

"I was so stupid and naive, for about three weeks I thought it was a yeast infection." She leaned her head against her hands on the wheel, exhausted from carrying around emotions that she thought had been put aside years ago.

"I'm sorry, Kenni." I squeezed her arm.

"Damn it," she said softly, and raised her head. "Why did you let me get away? Why didn't you fight for me? Fight Gavin? You and I should have loved each other more."

I closed my eyes. Tuxedo-clad drivers waited beside a line of hansom cabs, tourist bait that was another new wrinkle in my native city, strung out alongside the tower. In the air was the sharp smell of horse manure.

7

The next morning brought one of those balmy days when staying indoors was unthinkable. They say that Chicago generally has one day of spring separating winter from summer, and I was lucky enough to have been in town for it. I walked down Ontario Street to a little café called the West Egg and plopped myself down at an outdoor table, where I ordered coffee and a croissant and pored through both Chicago papers. "Kup's Column" was still the mainstay of the *Sun-Times,* as it has been since my earliest memory, and Mike Royko still held forth in the *Tribune.* As I read the local news it amused me to think that even though I had been away so long, now, as before I left, Chicago had a mayor named Daley.

After breakfast I walked around a bit. The neighborhood east of Michigan is now called Storyville. It never had a name before, because there wasn't much there besides warehouses. Now it's one of the city's more prestigious residential and business addresses, due to the regeneration of the area called North Pier and a staggering amount of high-rise construction. A beautiful young woman wearing an olive green suit and brown calf-length boots hurried by, her blond hair in a sexy pigtail down her back. It's a look I find particularly appealing. I glanced at my watch. Ten o'clock; she was obviously late for work, but not too late to give me a quick, noncommittal smile. It was refreshing, almost bracing. In Los Angeles you hardly ever see anyone on foot; we all exist wrapped in the steel cocoons of our automobiles. But Chicago is an eye-contact kind of town.

I went back to the hotel and watched game shows for an hour, then set out again, strolling west. I jumped on a Clark Street bus, and as we clattered northward I marveled at the gentrification of what had once been a pretty disreputable street. There are now a proliferation of eating establishments with purple or green awnings, and several turn-of-the-century stone buildings have been remodeled into sidewalk cafés; apparently a lot of people like to sit outside on a heavily traveled thoroughfare eating arugula and goat cheese salad and designer pizzas while choking on automobile exhaust. On the way, I even counted three Thai restaurants within four blocks of where the Chicago Cubs play their home games. When I was a kid no one knew what a Thai restaurant was.

Unlike the newer suburban or downtown ballparks and stadiums around the country, Wrigley Field is in the middle of a residential neighborhood. You just go north on Clark Street and all of a sudden there it is, rising blue and gray among the six-flat apartment buildings that ring its northern and eastern perimeters, a ballpark that is of the city. Chicagoans bitch about the 1988 addition of lights as a break from tradition, but in my view it beats hell out of having Wrigley bulldozed and replaced by a new stadium out in the soulless suburbs.

The atmosphere is much like a small-town carnival. A Dixieland band performs on the sidewalk near the Sheffield Avenue entrance, and bizarrely dressed street vendors hawk souvenir merchandise of all descriptions: plastic bats, baseball caps, giant beach towels, sun visors, pennants and banners, and a remarkable variety of shirts which bear either the team logo, caricatures of the more popular Cubs, or legends like ST. LOUIS SUCKS, none of which are sanctioned by the team or the league. Chicago makes up for an almost fifty-year championship drought by turning a trip to Wrigley into a raucous, horn-tooting block party, held eighty-one times each summer.

Darren Oraweic was waiting for me at the Addison and Sheffield gate. Today he wore a bright blue Cubs sweatshirt over a pair of neatly-pressed white jeans and blue Reeboks. He was munching from a bag of peanuts purchased from a side-walk vendor who was assuring the faithful that they were much cheaper than those sold in the ball park and tasted even better. Only by his watchful eyes and his stiff back could you have made Darren as a cop.

"It's amazing how thirty thousand people get a Tuesday afternoon off." I said as we shoved our way through the crowd. "Maybe the whole city is out of work."

"In this town, bosses understand about ball games," he replied. "People's grandmothers die eight and ten times a season when the team is winning."

We walked up some concrete steps and out into the stands. I've always considered myself somewhat lacking in the senti-ment department, so the fluttering in my chest and the con-stricting of my throat took me by surprise. Probably no place in Chicago holds the nostalgic kick for me that Wrigley does. I grew up here, learned about life and fair play and strategy and, through the brushback pitch, getting even. When I was a kid, Friday was Ladies' Day, and a woman could get into the grand-stand for the cost of the tax on a ticket. My mother, a loyal fan and a rabid Ernie Banks rooter, brought me here every Friday there was a home game, and what she lacked in hard knowl-edge of the chess like intricacies of the sport she made up for in unquestioning home-team boosterism. We always sat under the huge screen behind home plate because she feared getting hit by a foul ball, and whenever a hitter tipped one back the whole crowd would go "Whoooo-oop!" as the ball rolled down into the waiting hands of the bat boy. The screen is gone now, along with the whoops. I missed them as much as I did the noisy and colorful streetcars that used to clank down Clark Street and Broadway, but being there again reminded me that many of my mother's happiest and most carefree moments had been spent in what everyone used to call Cubs Park.

It's a great place to watch a ball game because of its intimacy. There isn't a bad seat in the house, and the field boxes are close enough to the players that one can practically smell their breath. At Dodger Stadium in Los Angeles it's easy to tell who has a lot of money and who's important in the movie business, because the attendees all wear their status to the game like ermine cloaks, unable to shake off the Hollywood syndrome even for nine innings. At Wrigley the moment you walk through the gate, bullshit is left behind and you're just a fan out for a good time, a bratwurst on a bun, a beer, and a Cub win in the sun. A lot of the men come straight from the office, carrying their briefcases and wearing phone beepers at their belts, their ties loosened and their jackets folded in their laps. But their office personas fall away at the first pitch.

Our seats were just to the third base side of home, in the twelfth row up. A great location, justifying the outrageous price I'd paid for the tickets. We watched batting practice as Andre Dawson, who has the body of a cougar, effortlessly lined pitch after pitch into the left-field bleachers. The crack of wood against horsehide is one of the most satisfying sounds in the world, and I had to be sharp to avoid being too drawn into the excitement to find out some of the things I wanted to know.

I got us a couple of beers—indispensable at a Cubs game—and settled back in my seat. The sun was warming the back of my neck, counteracting the wicked wind that always blows off the lake about a mile away.

"Tell me about Cassidy," I said.

"He was a hell of a guy, that's all I can say. More guts than any ten coppers I know, and more heart, too." Darren Oraweic smiled a little. "Half the time when he made a collar, he'd have the perp talking about his family or baseball or the weather before they got back to the station. The guy would have completely forgotten Cassidy had just arrested him."

"What about the other half?"

65

He took a swallow of beer. "When he had to be, he was one tough mick, you. He was born to the Job. He could always tell when something kinky was going down just by the smell of it. Unbelievable. The street people never fucked with him—they knew better." He turned toward me in his seat, batting practice forgotten in his eagerness to share war stories. "There was this one time, he saw these two guys talking on the street. They were just talking, but Cassidy nudges me and says, 'Drug deal.' There wasn't no question in his mind; he just knew. And if there's one thing Cassidy hated it was drug dealers. Because they sell their shit to little kids, and Cassidy always said he didn't want any scumbag feeding *his* kid poison, you."

I looked at him. "What kid?"

Oraweic stared out at the field. "Just a way of talking," he said. "Anyways, we was right on Rush Street at Cedar. You know where it comes together with State?"

I nodded. "That's where we all used to hang out."

"Well, nobody hangs out there now, you. Bunch of kids from the suburbs drive in on Saturdays to score a little dope, pick up on a little pussy. It's like a goddamn zoo. Anyways, so he follows this one skel to an apartment building on West Elm, just because he didn't like the looks of him. He tells me to cover the rear. I'm like, call for a backup, but Cassidy says he don't need one. So I go into the back yard and he goes upstairs, yells 'Police!' and kicks in the door. Five guys in there, all with guns. One of 'em opens up and Cassidy blows him away, shoots the kneecap off another one, and the other three are face down on the floor with their hands behind their heads before I can get up the stairs. Damn place was like a high school chemical lab—enough schmeck to keep every hype on the Near North Side high for a month." He ran a hand through his close-cropped blond hair. "Cassidy had seen the elephant, all right."

"The elephant?"

He grinned at me. "Copper talk for being in a shoot-out or a life-threatening situation. I guess it's from an old British hunting expression. It wasn't the first time for him, either. He had enough departmental commendations to cover his whole chest, and you know how big that was."

I spoke very carefully. "Darren, wasn't what he did illegal? I mean busting into a private apartment without a warrant?"

"Probable cause," he said.

"But there was no probable cause. Just instinct."

Oraweic looked around us as though there was an Internal Affairs snitch sitting in every other seat. "When it got to court," he said, lowering his voice, "Cassidy said he saw the guy passing dope on the street."

"But that's perjury."

"That's a pussy word, you. Look, if coppers didn't stretch the book a little bit, the only arrests we'd ever make would be for pissing on Michigan Avenue at high noon. Shit, we perjure ourselves almost every time we go to court. Even for a lousy traffic citation." He was warming to his subject now and didn't even notice that batting practice was over and the ground crew was dragging the infield, smoothing it out so a hard grounder wouldn't take a bad hop and violently extract the teeth of a charging shortstop. "You go to traffic court because some slob decides to fight his citation. The judge asks if you recall the incident. How the hell you gonna remember a ticket you wrote forty-five days ago when you've wrote about three hundred since? So you say yes, because if the guy didn't speed or run a red you wouldn't of cited him in the first place, you. And if you tell the truth and say you don't remember, everybody from your sergeant down to some wiseass reporter from the Trib thinks they got to you."

"Got to you?"

"Bought you off. So you say you remember even when you don't. From there it gets pretty easy to kind of falsify a report for probable cause. Or as a favor, say to a guy who owns a bar, and you say the fight you broke up started out on the sidewalk and not inside the bar so the guy won't get his license pulled. Or when you catch a monsignor from a parish on the West Side

67

getting head from a hooker in a parked car off LaSalle Street. You just look the other way, you."

"Kind of a white lie," I suggested.

"Sure—like the drug deal. If Cassidy had gone by the book, those guys'd still be cooking H in their apartment and selling it for school kids to shoot into their arms. Didja know that more than three quarters of the felonies committed in this town are drug-related? That made Cassidy fucking crazy, so he did something about it whenever he could. Now you tell me what's right."

We stood up for the national anthem, and then the Chicago Cubs took the field, their pinstriped whites gleaming in the sun. They were playing their archrivals, the St. Louis Cardinals, and as the Cards' manager brought the lineup card to the plate a chorus of catcalls erupted all over the park.

The Cubs pitcher blew a fastball by the Cardinal's leadoff hitter for a strike, and the boos turned to cheers. Chicago baseball fans have learned to rejoice over the smallest triumphs.

At the end of the third inning the Cubbies were ahead 3–0 by virtue of a double, a walk, a single, and a triple, and I decided it was time to eat. I went beneath the stands and found a concessionaire who sold bratwurst and carried a cardboard tray with four sandwiches, two bags of the expensive in-house peanuts, and two more beers back to our seats. I found that in my absence St. Louis's Pedro Guerrero, for whom I used to cheer in Dodger Stadium, had hit a towering home run with a man aboard and made it 3–2, quieting the crowd considerably.

"Why did Cassidy get suspended, Darren?"

He chewed thoughtfully on his brat. "I don't know for sure."

"He was your partner. How could you not know?"

"Look, they don't tell me everything, all right? I heard rumors, but I don't spread rumors on my partner, you."

"Who'd know for sure?"

"The chief of police."

"Who that would talk to me?"

"Why's it so important?"

"Darren, when I was younger than you are now, Gavin Cassidy was my friend. He's dead now, and I've been hearing a lot of shit about him and I want to find out for myself."

He wiped some mustard off his chin with his napkin and wadded it up and threw it underneath the seat in front of him. "Probably the guy knew him best on the job is Cap'n Mayo. Ray Mayo. They go way back; he was Cassidy's chinaman."

"Chinaman?"

"You know. Somebody higher up who kind of takes care of a guy, watching out for his ass, you."

"In Los Angeles they call them rabbis."

"Yeah," Oraweic said. "But Mayo probably won't tell you, either."

"Why not?"

"The same reason I won't."

"Which is what?"

He looked out at the field as Shawon Dunstan hit a whistling line drive to the opposite field and muscled into second base head first. The crowd began a rhythmic clapping and foot stomping that threatened to bring the old stadium down around our ears. The St. Louis pitching coach trotted out of the first-base dugout, arriving at the mound a few seconds after his belly did, and signaled for some left-handed relief.

"You're not a copper, you," Oraweic said.

I took out my wallet and handed him the photostat of my private investigator's license. "I'm not exactly a civilian, either."

"I thought you was an actor."

"I'm that too."

He handed the stat back. "I still don't see this is any of your business. We keep our shitty laundry inside the department, where it belongs."

"This is more than laundry. You just got through telling me Cassidy hated drugs. Doesn't it strike you funny that's what killed him?"

The skin on his face tightened, emphasizing the sharp Slavic planes of his jaw and cheekbones, and he became all cop, suspicious, on guard.

"What are you saying?"

"That I want to know all I can about Gavin Cassidy's last days, and I'm going to find out, with or without you."

The relief pitcher, a southpaw with dazzling speed, retired the next two men in order, and the Cubs took the field again.

"Pretty good stuff, the lefty," Oraweic said.

"You were Gavin's partner, Darren. I'd think you'd want to help if you could."

I could see he was having trouble adjusting to the concept. It's bad enough for a young cop when his partner and mentor dies; thinking someone might have helped that death along is tough to deal with. He drank his beer thoughtfully.

The Cardinals tiptoed through their half of the seventh inning, and then Harry Caray, the Cubs' radio and TV voice, leaned precariously out of the broadcast booth on the upper level behind the plate and led the entire crowd in the seventh-inning-stretch ritual, the singing of "Take Me Out to the Ball Game." Caray can't carry a tune any better than he can keep a steady beat, but the effect is nonetheless exhilarating, and every eye in the park was on him, joining in, having a blast. Only in Chicago.

"How can I help you?" Darren Oraweic said.

"Start by telling me where I can find Captain Mayo."

His shoulders slumped, and he sat down, finishing off his second bag of peanuts. He brushed the shells from his lap and then dusted off his hands. "You never talked to me, all right? I don't even know you," he said finally.

"Agreed."

"Mayo's about four blocks from here. At the Halsted Street station."

He probably would never have told me if I couldn't have found out anyway.

8

Unlike their counterparts in Los Angeles, the police stations of Chicago do not resemble motels, microchip company head-quarters, or neighborhood recreation centers. They look like what they are, possibly because Chicago maintains and repairs its old buildings, whereas in Los Angeles anything constructed before 1958 is bulldozed and turned into a strip mall. I walked up the stone steps and through the doors, clutching a plastic bag containing a bright blue Cubs T-shirt I had bought to take back to Marvel. I wished he could have been at the ball game with me.

In Chicago the uniformed police wear checkerboard hat-bands, giving them the appearance of taxi drivers. But I wouldn't have mistaken the bespectacled sergeant who sat behind the desk: you don't win stripes on your sleeves by thinking like a cabbie.

"Would it be possible to have a few words with Captain Mayo?" I said.

His jaws worked a wad of chewing gum as if he were being graded on it. "What about?"

I took out my license and showed it to him. "I'm a private investigator from Los Angeles," I said. "Call this a courtesy visit if you want."

The sergeant sighed; he'd been hoping I wasn't some space cadet who'd wandered in from the street to complicate his day. "Cap'n's kind of busy for courtesy calls."

"Tell him I'm an old friend of Gavin Cassidy's."

That brought a flicker of interest behind the wire-rimmed glasses. He nodded at a bench by the wall. "Have a seat, sir," he said, and picked up the phone at his left hand. I sat down on the hard bench next to an elderly black woman who rocked back and forth, moaning quietly, while the sergeant mumbled something into the mouthpiece. He must have been talking to a superior, because he stored his gum in his cheek while he spoke.

After a bit he hung up and called, "Few minutes."

I wanted to have a cigarette but the rocking lady next to me might have been offended. When you live in California, where as a socially loathsome habit, smoking in public is right up there on a par with weeny wagging in playgrounds, you always think twice before lighting up. So I sat and examined the plaques and commendations on the walls along with framed photographs of Mayor Richie Daley, the police commissioner, and the district commander. In Chicago the DC is the top cop in the precinct, usually appointed by the mayor as a favor to the ward boss or alderman; every once in a while the favor system, on which the city is run, works, and a genuinely good cop rises to the top.

Finally I walked back to the desk, where the sergeant was filling out official-looking forms in a childishly cramped hand. "Did you know Cassidy, Sergeant?"

He didn't look up from his paperwork, mainly because he made a concerted effort not to. "Everybody knew Cassidy."

"Were you friends?"

He raised his eyes, two smooth blue-gray stones in his face. "Cap'n Mayo won't be much longer, sir."

I returned to my bench. The woman had stopped rocking and was now mumbling under her breath.

After about fifteen minutes a female officer who looked like

Pat O'Brien appeared at my side and instructed me to follow her. We walked up two flights of stairs and down a corridor musty with fifty years of stale smoke and stale felonies and stopped near the end of the hall by a door inset with a frosted-glass panel.

"In there," she said.

Captain Ray Mayo was in his middle fifties, a rail-thin man with skin the color of the first sunburn of the season. I thought I recognized him from the church the day before. He stood and shook my hand, indicating a hard metal chair on my side of his desk. He looked at the plastic bag under my arm, imprinted with the big red *C* of the Cubs.

"Come from the game?"

"My first time at Wrigley in about seventeen years. I bought my kid a T-shirt."

"How'd we do?"

"We won, four–two."

He nodded, satisfied. "Good. The Pirates lose tonight, we tie for second. You're a private star from L.A., huh? You working on a case here?"

"Not exactly."

"Not exactly," he said, tasting the words. "Got some ID?"

I put the bag down on the edge of his desk and hauled out my ticket again. He scrutinized it. Then he gave it back to me. "This doesn't make you a shamus in shul, Mr. Saxon. What do you want?"

"I'm a friend of Gavin Cassidy's," I said. "I came into town for the funeral."

"So?"

"An old friend, like from twenty years back."

"How do I know that?"

"I'm telling you."

His laugh was like autumn leaves crunching under a foot, with as much good humor. "If I believed everything people say in this office, the jails'd be empty and there'd be blood on the streets. You might be some goddamn reporter."

"I don't know how I can convince you," I said. "I knew him back in the Hard Knox College days—Figaro's, the Cloister Bar. Remember when he took a leave of absence and went out to California for six months or so? I was the one he stayed with out there."

He nodded. "Okay, so what can I do for you?"

"It's been suggested that his death might not have been kosher."

"Who said that?"

"It doesn't matter."

"It does to me. We don't like cop killers."

"Neither do I, especially if the cop was a friend."

He lifted a heavy-grained, curve-stemmed briar pipe out of a wooden rack and began stuffing it with black tobacco from a desk humidor. "The ME says it was a combination of alcohol and amphetamines, and it doesn't surprise me. Cassidy was a drunk. I covered his ass I don't know how many times in the last ten years, including when he fired his weapon while under the influence. Christ, I remember one night, a lotta years back. He'd been working graveyard shift on Rush Street. He got off duty at midnight, went and tied one on someplace. And then he marches down to Michigan Avenue and discharges six rounds up at the Lindbergh Beacon on top of the Palmolive Building." He rubbed his nose hard, as if it itched internally. "The beacon's gone now, and they don't even call it the Palmolive Building anymore. But you can imagine the kind of tap dancing I had to do to keep him from getting booted."

I didn't even try suppressing a smile. The mental picture of a drunken Gavin trying to shoot out the Lindbergh Beacon was delicious. Vintage Cassidy.

"But there's just so much you can do," Mayo said. "A copper operating at half capacity is about as much use as tits on a bull. That's why he was rattling doors and writing traffic citations. He wasn't good for anything else."

I was about to tell him that Darren Oraweic, Gavin's partner, had a different assessment of his abilities, but I remembered just in time that I'd promised not to mention his name. Instead I said, "Why was he suspended?"

He shook his head. "That's department business."

"If his death was kinky, it's my business too."

"How do you figure?"

"Because he was my friend."

"I told you, that doesn't cut any ice in here."

I squared my shoulders and did something that was abhorrent to me, but when in Rome, you do as the Romans do, and in Chicago, you use whatever juice you have. "Does the name James Saxon cut any ice?" I asked, gnawing at a piece of loose, ragged skin alongside my thumbnail.

He frowned, drumming a rhythmic pattern on the desk with his fingertips, which I recognized as Ravel's "Bolero," and sat up a little straighter. "Tailback for the Kansas City Chiefs?"

I laughed, because he was right. "Try *Jimmy* Saxon."

"What's Jimmy Saxon to you?"

"He's my father."

"Ah," Mayo said, looking at my license again, and his face flushed a darker red. "The man is connected."

"I'll be honest with you, I haven't seen him in years. We don't get along. But I'll rattle his cage if I have to."

He tamped the tobacco down tight with his thumb. "That a threat?"

"I don't want to be confrontational, Captain, I'd just like a little help. Now, are we in business?"

"What was your question again?"

"Why was Cassidy on suspension?"

"Go fuck yourself," he said mildly, pointing the stem of his pipe at me, "and your old man, too. This is a police station! I can't release confidential information about my men, no matter who your father is. Coming in here waving your dick around, who the hell you think you are?"

I started to get mad and then I counted to five—that was as far as I had to go before I rethought my position. Not only was I being an asshole, I was alienating a guy that could be either a big help to me or a powerful enemy. I said, "You're right. That's why I don't get along with my father, shit like that. I was out of bounds."

That was as close to an apology as anyone ever gets from me, and it must have been effective, because his face lost some of the angry red flush that had spread across it.

"As long as you know that," he said. "Now what else can I do for you?"

"You were Cassidy's chinaman. You knew him."

"As well as I knew anybody. I loved the son of a bitch, even though half the gray hair in my head is because of him." He lit his pipe with a kitchen match and momentarily disappeared in the resultant haze of thick smoke, like a magician at a Lions Club social. He fanned it away from his face and it lazily swirled out the one-inch opening in his window and out over Halsted Street. "What's your point?"

"You know how he felt about drugs, then. That the chances of him ever taking uppers was slim to none."

"A drunk's liable to do anything."

"Not Cassidy. Not drugs."

He puffed thoughtfully for a while. Fat bursts of smoke drifted ceilingward; half the Apaches in Arizona must have lit signal fires in answer. Finally he said, "It doesn't work that way. Look, what are you coming to me for? We've got enough to do just keeping our citizens from offing each other on the streets without going out to look for more work. I have people to answer to. I can't just go off and investigate what was officially ruled an accidental death."

"No," I said. "But I can."

He dropped his chin so far onto his chest his shoulders were level with his ears. "What do you want from me, Saxon?"

"A free hand to poke around without your guys rousting me out of town," I said. "A sympathetic ear if and when I need it. And a point in the right direction."

He stood up and looked out the window, and I moved across the room to stand behind him, peering over his shoulder at the line of high-rise apartment buildings that rimmed the lake for miles, stretching from downtown north to Evanston. A Halsted Street bus clattered by, belching noxious fumes into the atmosphere. "What a city," he said. "It runs on the system. Always has, for a hundred years or more. You stay inside the system and you survive. Step over the line and you're a joke in every saloon in town. You go along to get along." He stuck his pipe between his teeth and turned to face me. "You remember when Jane Byrne got elected mayor?"

I nodded.

"She won because she promised she'd sweep all the machine politicians right out the door. And she did, too. Then she tried to get things done, and she found out she couldn't, because she'd stepped outside the system. So she had to crawl into bed with the same guys she'd campaigned against in order to get the snowplows out, or else the whole city would have shut down like Back-of-the-Yards on Good Friday. And now you want me to put my ass out on the line. I didn't get captain's bars by putting my ass on the line."

"Not even for a good cop."

"A dead cop. A dead, drunk cop."

"He was your cop," I said, standing up. "And your friend. You go home and try to sleep tonight without thinking that maybe there's somebody out there who made him dead."

I started for the frosted door, hyperventilating in my anger, but his "Saxon!" stopped me. I turned and looked at him.

"Come on back here a minute."

I sat down again, this time on the edge of the seat.

He said, "Were you ever on the Job? Before you went private, I mean."

I shook my head.

"It's a shit way to make a living. A copper's like a garbage collector, tell the truth; they're both there to serve the public. But coppers sometimes forget and get mean to the people they're s'posed to be serving. It happens to everyone. You see an old woman, her nose busted and her teeth knocked out

77

because she wouldn't surrender her purse, or a harmless old wino who's been set on fire for the fun of it, or a six-month-old baby who's been butt-fucked, you get mean, whether you want to be or not.

"Every copper starts out idealistic. He wants to stand up for truth, justice, and the American way, and since he doesn't have a cape to fly around in he does the next best thing and gets himself a badge. But then he learns the expectations. He learns that he's expected to participate, to be a regular guy. Otherwise he finds himself shunned."

"Are you talking about being on the take?" I said.

He was almost chewing on the pipe smoke, tasting it like a fine wine. "It's offered without being asked for. At first he rebels, he gets indignant, he don't take and he kicks ass if anybody offers. But finally it wears him down. It's got to. You don't blame anyone, it's just the Fucking Job."

He leaned back against the window. "Tell you a story. There was this rookie, see, full of piss and vinegar and wanting to do something for his community. They put him on Rush Street—a mistake, because the Outfit still controls Rush Street, but hey, scheduling fucks up, it happens. So this kid—brand new badge, gonna change the world, right?—he's strutting around with a three-foot hard-on, feeling the piece hanging on his hip—*feeling* it, you understand?"

I nodded.

"So he goes into this restaurant and there's two chickies sitting at the bar, obviously out to do a little business, and he checks their ID and finds they're fifteen and sixteen. And the club owner comes over and asks him what's the deal and he tells him. The slimeball says to this kid cop that he doesn't understand the way things work, and the kid says nobody's gonna peddle baby ass while he's on the beat, and he chases the jailbait back home to Rogers Park.

"This is on a Saturday night, now. And Monday the captain calls him in and reams out his ass like it's never been reamed before. Says there's been complaints about the kid shaking

78

down the bar owners on Rush. And the old man says he won't have that kind of shit in his squad, that the kid won't last on the Job very long with complaints like that in his jacket, and he hopes the kid gets the message."

I shook my head. "And you gave him the reaming?"

"No," Mayo said, "I *got* the reaming. Civilians like you are pretty quick to judge coppers as fascists and Nazis, but the truth is, you don't know jackshit about it."

"You're missing the point, Captain."

"You're missing the point," he shot back. "To a copper there's two kinds of people—policemen and assholes. And I don't see your badge."

I said very quietly, "Cassidy was my friend. I loved him. I don't care what he did; if anyone hurt him I want to know it. And I'd think you'd want to know too."

Ray Mayo went back to his desk and puddled down into the chair. He knocked his pipe against the heavy yellow glass ashtray, each knock like a pistol shot in the quiet room, went through the whole ritual of ash removal, broke the pipe apart and blew wetly through the mouthpiece. He didn't look at me for a long while, not until the embers in the ashtray had stopped smoking. Then he did.

"I'll put out the word that we've talked," he said. "Look around for a few days, if that's what you want to do. But no John Wayne shit in my town. You find anything kinky, you come to me with it. I'll nail your nuts to the mast on top of the Sears Tower if you don't. You hear me?"

"Give me some names."

"Did you hear me, I asked you?"

I nodded. "We understand each other, all right. Now where do I go first?"

"Right back to California, if I had my way." He put the pipe back in his breast pocket. "You might want to start by having a heart-to-heart with Martin Givney. He's—"

"I know who he is. Thanks, Captain. I'll stay in touch."

"See that you do, boyo."

I opened the door and was halfway out into the hall when he called my name again. When I looked back he was holding the Cubs bag in his hand. "You forgot your T-shirt."

9

It seems as if the Como Inn has been a fixture on North Milwaukee Avenue since prehistory. It's a sprawling place, with a lobby adjoining its classy, spacious bar. The dining areas are divided into cozy rooms decorated in the classic old-time Italian restaurant style, the way they were before the advent of goat cheese salad and designer pizza, and if you're seated in one of the far reaches of the building, you do well to leave a trail of bread crumbs so you can find your way back to the table from the john. Mobsters used to eat there, and politicians and visiting movie actors and the rich folks from Lake Shore Drive, too. Mike Fritzel's is gone, now, and Henrici's and Gibby's and the Bovary; along with the Berghoff on Adams Street in the Loop, the Como Inn is one of the last restaurant survivors of Chicago's good old days.

I waited for Beth in the bar, drinking a Laphroaig neat, pleasantly surprised that they carried my favorite Scotch; not one bar in a thousand stocks it. Over in the corner a piano player was committing bodily injury to Jerome Kern's "The Folks Who Live on the Hill," and my fingers itched to elbow him off the stool and finish the song myself. Maybe one of these days when the acting jobs dry up and I get too old for the private investigating business, I'll get a gig playing jazz piano in a saloon and show them all how it's done, collecting tips in a big brandy snifter and trying to discourage people from requesting "Feelings" or Barry Manilow songs.

Beth Shroats Purdell appeared in the archway, and I rose to meet her. She was as beautiful as ever, even though there were streaks of silver in her dark chestnut hair, which, as always, she wore short. Sultry in her twenties, she had become patrician in maturity, but as lovely as she was she carried an air of melancholy, a sadness that seemed to press down on her. When her eyes teared up as she caught sight of me, I wasn't sure they were tears of happiness at the reunion. A lot of years of living take the starch out of you if you aren't careful, and the set of her shoulders suggested that Beth hadn't had a particularly easy time of it since she had reigned as one of the Near North crowd's beauties. As we stood in the cocktail lounge at the Como Inn and hugged, I realized that except for a love scene we'd done together on stage in a play called *Tea and Sympathy* when I'd been nineteen and she twenty-five, this was the first time I'd ever held her in my arms. Her hair smelled faintly of gardenia.

"You're gorgeous," I said. "Even more so than twenty years ago."

She smiled up at me with the familiarity of experiences shared. "You grew up into a real charmer, didn't you? I figured you would." She kissed me quickly on the mouth. Pushing forty as I was, it was strange to think of myself as having "grown up" into anything.

The hostess led us through the labyrinth of dining rooms and ensconced us in a cozy high-backed booth with an imitation Tiffany lampshade hanging over the table. The place catered to an older crowd, and the lighting was soft and flattering, to treat kindly those sags and wrinkles that might be more apparent in harsher illumination.

"So tell me all about Beth," I said.

"My life story in twenty-five words or less?" She took a cigarette out of a tortoiseshell case, and I lit it for her. I didn't remember her as a smoker, but I couldn't be sure; time has a way of distorting things. "Let's see," she said. "I was married for a while, to a playwright named Paul Purdell. I don't think you ever met him. It lasted for three years, which was about two years too long. I still had some idealism left then, and I thought being with a playwright was . . . a significant way to live your life. After supporting him for three years, it became less significant by the minute. I have a fourteen-year-old son, Kevin. Right after the divorce I took him to live in Paris for a year—also significant, and oh so intellectual, Hemingway and Gertrude Stein and Henry Miller. Or so it seemed at the time.

"Now I have a place on South State—Printer's Row, they call it, where people never used to live until about five years ago. Kevin goes to junior high. I'm in the claims department at Blue Cross, I wear a suit to work every day, and I still mess with little theater occasionally. Mostly when I get bored. Diane and Dolly and I have breakfast one Saturday a month, and otherwise I'm SuperMom couch potato. Is there a movie in all that, do you think?"

"Probably there would be if you filled in all the blank spaces."

"Everyone has blank spaces they don't want to fill in," she said, using the dry delivery that had enlivened so many drawing room comedies at the NSSTG. "Don't you?"

"A few," I admitted. "One of them was the hopeless crush I had on you when I was a kid."

She flushed prettily. "I never knew that. You never told me."

"I didn't have the nerve. I always figured I was too young for you."

"You were too young for me *then*," she said. "But now you're all grown up. A body could just about take you anywhere." She squeezed my hand to reassure me she was kidding. "So how's Hollywood?"

"Nobody lives in Hollywood unless they're a drug dealer or a hooker or a transvestite. I have my office there, but I live in Venice, just two blocks from the ocean, on a canal with a bunch of very noisy ducks." And then I told her what I'd been doing for the past twenty years, compressed into about four sentences, because I was so tired of hearing it. I guess I didn't fill in many blank spaces either. Her eyebrows went up a notch when I confessed I was more private investigator than actor, and another notch when I told her about Marvel. But Beth was a cool one, always had been. Her perpetual composure was part of her appeal; you never knew exactly what was going on in the depths of those green eyes.

"So we have a lot in common, then," she said. "A shared flaming youth, and we're both single parents of teenage boys. How in the world did we survive either one?"

The waiter arrived with his expectant pen. Beth chose tortellini en brodo. I was glad she hadn't turned into one of those people who have strange and trendy eating habits, such as vegetarianism or only eating grains or insisting there be no ice in the ice water. Nothing can spoil my dinner quicker than having it with someone for whom dinner is not a meal but an agenda.

I ordered veal Marsala.

"Veal?" she said.

"I've always been a veal man. Ten years ago no one ate it because it was bland; now no one eats it because it's politically incorrect. But I was a rebel when you knew me, and if you call veal a rebellion, I guess I still am."

She smiled faintly, remembering. "I was, too. Free love, feminism, artistic integrity, and not following the rest of the lemmings into the lake. It sounds good when you're young and crazy. But I gave up on all that years ago. The price of rebellion is just too high." A look of pain crossed her face like the shadow of a scudding cloud, and then she sat up a bit straighter and put her hands on the table on either side of her plate. "And so the Prodigal returns after all these years. For Gavin's funeral?"

I nodded.

"Why? I know you were close a long time ago, but you hadn't been in touch with him in ages."

"Don't rub it in that I've been a lousy friend. That you don't see someone for a long time doesn't mean you don't care. Gavin is part of me, of why I am who I am."

She took a heavy drag on her cigarette and blew the smoke out into the aisle between the booths. "He's a part of all of us."

"I didn't see you at the funeral," I said. "Or at Ben and Dolly's last night."

"I'd worry if you had. I wasn't there."

"Any particular reason?"

"Of course," she said shortly. "Are you detecting now? Is this an interrogation?"

"I didn't mean it to sound like that."

She sighed. "I'm sorry. I forget that you've been gone so long, that you're several times removed from recent history. You don't know—unless someone else told you."

"Told me what?"

"Ah. Now we get to one of those blank spaces." She ground her cigarette out in the little round glass ashtray imprinted with the restaurant's logo and immediately took out another one. I leaned over to light it for her, and she said, "You're a real dinosaur, aren't you? Nobody lights a lady's cigarette anymore."

"Nobody calls them 'ladies' anymore, either. Look, you don't have to tell me anything you don't want to, Beth."

"Everyone else knows, why not you? After all, you were part of the inner circle. It's no secret: Gavin was Kevin's—my son's—father."

Being at a loss for words has rarely been one of my problems; in fact glibness has landed me in more trouble than reticence ever has. However, I was finding myself struck dumb with monotonous regularity on this trip, and I felt a great urge to return to the hotel, pack, toss the Cub shirt into the wastebasket, board a plane for home, and play some one-on-one with Marvel under the basket I'd affixed to the garage door, forgetting about Chicago and the people in it. I didn't know where to look—certainly not into Beth's face.

"When he came back from California," she went on, answering an unasked question. "It was as much a surprise to me as to anyone else. We'd been friends forever, and you just don't fuck your friends. But he was so . . . sad then. Defeated. We went drinking one night, just the two of us. You were gone, Ben and Dolly were married, so was Diane, Gary had become intolerable, and Eliscu was off somewhere, maybe in jail. And Al Patinkin, he's a love, but not the guy anyone might choose to go tie one on with. Gavin and I were the last of the Mohicans. So we went to Knox College, to the Scotch Mist, to Figaro's— and finally, drunkenly, to bed."

She stopped talking as the salads arrived. When the waiter slipped away she didn't touch her fork but picked up a bread stick and nibbled it thoughtfully. "It went on for six months or so. He was one of the most romantic, intense men I've ever been with. You knew the fun Gavin, the figurehead on the prow of the *Good Ship Lollipop.* With me there were soft times, times when he'd talk about his dreams. They were good ones— just not very realistic. He dreamed big, but in reality he was happier bumming around with people like Bob Eliscu. And that just wasn't my thing. I was ready to call it off, frankly." She toyed with the breadstick. "And then I started throwing up in the mornings."

I was pushing lettuce leaves around in the dressing but I wasn't really interested in eating them.

"Obviously, my pregnancy was an accident—no one in their right mind would ever target Gavin as husband material. When he found out, he got scared. Panic in the streets. He wanted me to get rid of it. I was going to, I even made the appointment, but in the end I chickened out. I'm a prochoicer; everybody should do what's best for them. I just didn't think I could live with it.

Gavin said he wouldn't marry me, that he'd only make me miserable, and I knew he was right. But he offered to support the kid for as long as necessary." She brushed at her cheek. "Gavin didn't have a pot to piss in back then, so I didn't want his money. But I did want a father for my son. That's where the rebellion ended—I wasn't going to raise a child alone. And Paul Purdell had been after me for a long time, since before I started with Gavin. When he still wanted me, even after he found out about the baby, and offered to give it his name and raise it as his own, I couldn't say no."

"What about after Kevin was born? Did Gavin—"

"No. That was part of my deal with Paul, that Gavin stay the hell away from us, and from Kevin. Gavin didn't like it, but he accepted it with as much grace as possible under the circumstances."

"What about after your divorce?"

"Too late. He'd started to drink heavily by that time. And after all those years, it seemed kind of silly for Gavin to suddenly start playing attentive father. Or passionate lover. We left things as they were."

"Maybe if he'd had the responsibility of a child he might have straightened out."

" 'If' is the biggest word in the language," she said. "My concern wasn't straightening out Gavin Cassidy, it was raising my son."

"So he never really knew Kevin?"

She shook her head. "Not in the way you mean. Oh, we'd see each other from time to time. On the street, at a party. Just around. A couple of times I'd be walking on Wells or Rush with Kevin and we'd run into Gavin in uniform. But I don't think Gavin ever spent more than ten minutes at one time with Kevin. He always paid special attention to him and made a fuss over how big he was getting, but Kevin's a beautiful kid and lots of people pay him compliments. He knew Gavin was his father, but 'father' has always been an abstract concept to him."

"That's the saddest thing I ever heard," I said.

"Isn't it?" she said. "But it saved Kevin from grieving when Gavin died, and that, at least, is good." She took a deep breath and let it out slowly. "So now you know why I didn't go to the funeral. Too many conflicting emotions that I chose not to deal with out where everyone could see me."

I squeezed her hand and held it tight until our salad plates were cleared and our entrées were served. There didn't seem to be a whole lot more to say.

Coffee has a way of loosening the tongue, even more than alcohol, and when we were having ours, an espresso for me and decaffeinated for her, Beth said, "It's almost unreal to think of Chicago without Gavin. He done me wrong, as the saying goes, but I loved him for what he was. A lot of people didn't, but I always did."

All at once I was alert. "Which people didn't?"

She waved smoke away from her oval-shaped face. "The old gang didn't exactly stay together over the years. He broke with Gary over Marian. And he and Eliscu had some sort of beef—which is the best thing that could have happened."

"What kind of beef?"

"Who knows? Bob Eliscu has never been exactly kosher, and maybe Gavin finally got fed up with him. I never knew that whole story. And of course Diane . . ."

"Diane and Gavin had a fight?"

She opened her purse and checked her makeup in a compact mirror. "Not a fight, no. I don't think Diane ever had much use for Gavin after Kevin was born. She's my friend, and she thought he was a louse for what he did to me. She was right, of course; but if I forgave him, I couldn't see why she couldn't."

I signaled for the check. "I didn't know they were on the outs."

She snapped the compact closed. "He was just hard to take at the end. Ben still loved him, of course. And Big John."

"Big John Washington? He must be in his eighties."

"And better than ever," she said. "He's playing at a blues

club on Rush Street. The blues are in these days. *Is* in? Anyway, he's quite the cult figure in Chicago now."

I looked at my watch. It was just past nine, and in Chicago that's early. "Let's go see him, Beth. Can we? It's been a long time, and I always loved his music."

She considered it a moment. "I'm not in much of a nightclub mood," she said. "I just wanted to see you, for old times. You go on ahead, I'll just head home." She put out a hand and touched my face. "You look great. We all check the TV listings to see when you're in something. From now on, if you're going to be on, drop a note, okay?"

We walked back through the maze of intimate dining rooms and out to the sidewalk, where the parking valet waited for Beth's claim check.

"Can I drop you somewhere?"

"That's all right," I said, "I feel like walking. I wish you'd change your mind, though."

She shook her head as if a cloud of gnats were swarming around her eyes. "Come back sometime without a reason—or because you want to see us again. Right now I want to get in bed and pull the covers over my head and try to forget how we're all getting old." She put her arms around me and pressed her cheek against mine, and then she kissed me, our first real kiss, one I'd fantasized about many times as I watched her at the NSSTG or at Hard Knox College. Then she pulled away, smiled, and kissed the air next to my ear. "Be well," she said.

Her car pulled up to the curb and she got in and drove away to curl up with her ghosts. I didn't think they'd keep her feet warm.

10

The Blues Box used to be an Armenian restaurant, or what passed for one back in the sixties, four steps down from Rush Street, where they served a reasonably authentic shish kebab and the bartender wasn't all that motivated to check IDs if your money was on the bar. As I walked in I remembered with embarrassment going in there for dinner one night when I was nineteen and ordering a brandy Alexander as an aperitif.

It had changed a lot. Its name was different, for one thing, and the decor was so minimal as to be nonexistent, white-washed brick walls and anonymous linoleum on the floors. It was dark enough to make getting around difficult, except for the spotlighted performing area in the middle of the room. Impossibly small round tables painted flat black were scattered around the stingy floor space, and on a Tuesday evening only half of them were occupied, mostly by young, affluent singles making too much of their own noise to enjoy the music. No one greeted me at the door so I made my way to an empty table near the wall and sat down to wait for the harried waitress to notice I was there.

I didn't care how long I sat unattended; I hadn't come for the booze. An enormous black man sat on a straight chair in a circle of light with an acoustic guitar and a Bob Dylan–type brace around his neck that brought a gleaming silver harmonica to within inches of his lips. Big John Washington's shaved head, sweat-gleaming, nodded in time to the music. His eyes were nearly closed, and the pain of the down-and-outers of whom he sang made me shiver as it always had. "Levee Camp Moan" was the song, sounding like it came from the bottom of a gassy swamp. He was six foot four or so, and six ax handles wide, well over three hundred pounds, and by my reckoning he was close to eighty years old. From when I'd last seen him twenty years earlier, he hadn't changed that much. His eyebrows were whiter and he'd put on thirty pounds, and scoliosis had bent his shoulders. His red and white flannel shirt and denim overalls were not an affectation. They were what he'd worn as a boy in the red-dirt southern hamlets where he'd been raised, and he had never felt the necessity to change his style. A legend to devotees of folk music, he still thought of himself as a po' boy from Mississippi and dressed accordingly.

Big John had been a mainstay on Thursday nights at Hard Knox College back in the sixties, his payment for the gig whatever came back to him in the large peanut butter jar they'd pass around after each set. I have never been a die-hard blues fan—my tastes run more to modernists, postbeboppers like Kenton and Brubeck and Bill Evans—but I was touched by the power and poignancy of his singing, and on Thursdays I was always in the back room of the College and not out at my usual haunt in the bar.

"A Heineken, please," I told the waitress. No unpronounceable single-malt Scotch when you listen to the blues, not to really listen. The correct drink is Sneaky Pete or Annie Green Springs or red rye whiskey that could peel the chrome off a trailer hitch, but there was a limit as to how far I'd go for the sake of authenticity.

The waitress didn't look five minutes out of her teens, but she pointed with authority to the tent card warning atop the table. "There's a two-drink minimum."

"Then bring me two Heinekens," I said. I was easy.

Big John finished the song to a smattering of applause, wiping his head and face with a handkerchief. Then he mumbled his thanks into the microphone and went into "Moon Going Down," and when he sang it you could see it disappearing behind the piney woods.

My beers arrived with no glass and my server exacted instant tribute; I was evidently sitting too close to the exit to be trusted to run a tab.

I sensed someone standing to my right and I looked up. A kid, no older than twenty-two, leaned against the wall, even though there were several empty seats, and I figured he didn't have the price of the two-drink minimum. Handsome and fresh-faced in only the way a kid can be, he held a battered guitar case in his right hand, and with his left he fingered imaginary struts as he leaned forward, mesmerized, his mouth partially open, his foot tapping, watching Big John across the room in the spotlight. His eyes were shining, and adoration turned up the corners of his lips as he listened to the blues, digging it, living it. Almost in pain, I had to look away.

Oh kid, I thought, don't lose it. Hang on to the rapture, the eagerness, the innocence I see in your eyes. Keep the reverence without turning tough and cynical. Don't sell out to the suits, to the M.B.A. degrees, to expectations that belong to somebody else. Don't let them knock the wonder out of you. Don't let the years suck the joy away and leave you dry and brittle and middle-age bitter. Don't turn in your guitar for a briefcase and a car phone, because the music inside you is all you've got to call your own.

Don't grow up, kid. You won't like it here.

When the set was over and canned music began blasting over the sound system, I got up and went over to where the old blues man was putting his guitar into its case. "Hello, Big John," I said.

He looked up at me and frowned, fighting for a name and a place, his eyes squinting in the half light. Then all of a sudden he smiled with his whole face. "Lord God," he said, and threw his arms around me, and I almost disappeared in his bulk. "Lord God Jesus, where you been, son? Where you *been?*"

"I live in California now," I said. "I came in to Knox College to tell you good-bye before I left, remember?"

He laughed ruefully. "Big John don't remember so good no more." He gripped me around the biceps with both hands and held me at arm's length. "You changed some."

"Pushing forty."

"Pssss! Still a baby. You got a long road yet."

"I hope so. Let me buy you a drink."

He shook his massive head. "Don't use it no more. Don't use the drink, the cigarettes, the shit, nothin' a'tall. Not even gage. I smoked me enough gage to last me ten lifetimes, but not no more."

"Sounds like you got religion."

"Never lost it," he said quietly.

We repaired to a small booth near the kitchen, and his eyes danced as I answered his questions about what I'd been doing since he'd seen me last. He nodded when I told him I was a private investigator, beamed when I mentioned my acting career. Big John's beaming could light up a coal mine. "You always done that," he said, "I remember so. You done them shows in the back room at Hard Knox. Now you an actor for real. Awright!" He squeezed my forearm, and it was like a bear bite. He had sausage fingers, thick for a guitarist, but he employed them like a backwater Segovia. "You back to stay now?"

"I can't stay but a few days, Big John. I came for Gavin Cassidy's funeral."

His eyes got sad. "Yeah, I heard about that. That was a sorry thing. Cassidy was righteous good to me."

"He was a righteous good man."

"Cuz of him I don't do junk no more."

"Why's that?"

Big John got misty-eyed remembering. "He bust me six, maybe seven year ago. We's in this pad over to North Clark,

92

gettin' to feeling good, you know, ridin' the white horse. Cassidy an' some other po-lice, they come smashin' through the door, say ever'body on the floor. Then Cassidy, he grab me, hustle me downstairs in the bracelets. He throw me up again' the wall an' say, 'Big John, you gots to choose. You goes to jail or you goes to a hospital and git you clean.' He coulda bust me, y'unnerstan', like he bust everybody else there, but he don't. He knows I got me a record. He say, 'Big John, you my friend, I don' wanna take you downtown—but you gots to choose.' I tell him I don' wanna go back inside, no way! So he drive me to some place over to Halsted Street an' check me in. I stay there six weeks, with doctors an' shit, and I keep axin' who gonna pay for all this, they tell me don't worry, it been took care of. I figger Cassidy care enough about Big John to pay to get him clean, least I kin do is stay that way. So no more drink after that, no more nothin'. And I feels better, too." He rubbed at his eyes. "I just seen him two, three week ago, he come in here. Man was down so far he cudden even see no light, 'cuz they bust him off the po-lice."

"Do you know why, Big John?"

"Aw, you know him, he don't say 'bout his trouble. He just sit here to drink an' dig. Drink real bad, worse'n ever." He knotted a fist the size of a catcher's mitt. "He buck the system, man, he always buck the system. I tole him some day they'll hang your white ass—then they done it." He took out his handkerchief again and wiped both hands on it. "A lots a cats was gunnin' for Cassidy. People he think be his friends, too."

"What friends?"

He shrugged. "Guys like that Storm, an' that LSQ. They rumbles with Cassidy, but it don' come to nothin'."

"Who else?"

He smiled shyly. "You know me, man, I don' mess with politics an' all. Just lee me alone to play my music. I don't know no names."

"Politics. Was Cassidy in trouble with the political boys?"

"What I hear, he cross somebody downtown."

"They say Cassidy died from drugs, Big John. Did you know that?"

"Shit!" His voice had an angry edge for the first time. "I know him with drugs. Ain' no way. No way!"

I sipped on my Heineken, rolling it around on my tongue, but I wasn't thinking about the nutty taste. "You going to play again tonight?"

"Naw, I do the one set is all. They bring in some new groups. I just fills in between."

I dug into my pocket and brought out a twenty-dollar bill. "John, I appreciate the information. Here, in case you bust a string or something."

He pushed it back at me. "I takes tips for the music," he said, low and serious. "Not from friends, hear?"

"This is for the music," I said, and put the twenty in the pocket of his flannel shirt.

The kid from back near the door stood a few feet away, looking hopeful. Big John waved him over.

"How you be, son?" Big John said, shaking hands solemnly. "Siddown here a minute." He looked at the kid affectionately. "I keep tellin' him no white boy kin really sing the blues, but he don' lissen to me."

"I can't sing them like you can," the kid said. The clipped tones of the North Shore were in his speech.

"You been practicin'?"

"Sure, four hours a day."

"You should to be doin' your schoolwork," Big John scolded, pronouncing it "woik," in the Deep South way.

"I practiced what you said the other night," the kid said. "Can I show you?"

"You gonna worry me till you do, ain't you?"

The kid grinned and started to undo the clasps of his guitar case.

I stood up, hating to leave. But the kid needed Big John Washington a lot more than I did. He was like a Pony League pitcher getting pointers from Koufax or Gibson, and I was only

94

in the way. I leaned down and hugged the old bluesman's massive bulk. "Big John, I've missed you."

"Don' stay away so long, then," he said in his gravely whiskey voice. "You come back, hear? Tomorrow night or some time 'fore you goes back to California, you come back early—an' lissen." He broke into a smile again, all shiny teeth and beaming fat cheeks. "Maybe you learn somethin'."

"I wouldn't be a bit surprised," I said.

I walked up the steps and out onto Rush Street. The Hawk was flying high tonight, a cool wind swooping in off the lake a block away, and I hunched my shoulders against its chilly bite.

Around the corner on Oak Street is a little bar called the Acorn on Oak, and I went inside and listened to a fabulous piano man named Buddy Charles who knows every great song ever written and every raunchy one, too. I sat at the bar awash in the nostalgia of the Berlin and Porter songs and in my own remembering, drinking Glenlivet, which was the best they could do for me in the way of single-malt Scotch, more appropriate to the music. I was troubled, and all but convinced that Marian Meyers was right about how Gavin died. Finally, at three o'clock in the morning, I walked down Michigan Avenue, the wind at my back, and back to my hotel, where I fell asleep on the bed with all my clothes on.

11

I rented a car the next morning, a red Pontiac Sunbird. It wasn't the cheapest way to get around Chicago, but it was better than waiting for a bus or trying to flag down a taxi in the rain, which was well-nigh impossible once you left Michigan Avenue. And I had a lot of places to go.

Southport Avenue, for instance. It used to be home to Chicago's German community because of its proximity to the meat-packing and rendering plants of the Northwest Side, where many of its residents worked. When the stockyards closed down, Southport underwent a change, and gentrification set in. Now it's schizo, a neighborhood in search of a character, blocks of red brick warehouses interspersed with two-flat buildings either spruced up or in need of a face-lift, and an occasional upscale restaurant with a seductive neon sign in the window offering nouvelle cuisine or some exotic ethnic specialty.

G. Storm, Inc., occupied one of the warehouses, so begrimed that its original color was lost forever. It had once been called Southport Chemicals, but Gary Storm had inherited the business from his father, and his ego had driven him to immediately put his name all over everything. Gary was the kind of guy who would name his house, probably something like Stormhaven.

He had started out here as a receiving clerk, never letting anyone forget that he was the boss's son. As far as I'd ever been able to figure, he bought scrap chemicals from oil refineries, barreled the stuff up in his warehouse, and sold it somewhere else at a profit. I couldn't imagine who would want to buy the waste products from oil, or why, but apparently someone did. It wasn't the kind of career kids grow up dreaming about, but it had made Gary moderately well-to-do.

I parked across the street from the loading dock and went into the building through an old-fashioned steel door that had rusted and warped over more than fifty winters. A middle-aged woman in the glass-enclosed office told me Gary was "out on the floor" and waved an imprecise hand to show me where. I walked through another door and out into the main room of the warehouse. The smell of oil was sharp, as well as a musty odor that they'd never get out, even if a group of newly rich young entrepreneurs bought and gutted the place and turned it into a Northern Italian trattoria.

All around me workers, mostly black, were trundling great barrels of foul-smelling stuff on dollies, and more than once I had to perform a veronica to keep from being run over. Gary Storm was out in the middle of everything, chewing out one of the warehousemen. In his shirt sleeves, his wide patterned red suspenders were bright against his white shirt, and I noted that the broad shoulders seemed to have vanished with the sports jacket. He was developing a paunch, and his face was mottled with anger as he berated his employee for some breach of procedure. I tried not to listen, so I never found out what the offense was, but I imagine Gary talked to all his employees that way. He'd always possessed a supercilious air, a way of tilting his head back to look down his nose at you that made you want to smack him, and whenever he laughed you could take it to the bank that the joke was on someone else.

"Get your head out of your ass for a change!" was his final

shot to the unlucky employee, who quivered with humiliation as Gary whirled on his heel to walk away. He caught sight of me, and for a split second he registered his shock, then covered it quickly and walked over, tucking a clipboard under his arm.

"Schvartzes!" he said, rolling his eyes. "I guess God missed them when he was passing out the brains because they're so hard to see in the dark."

It was fingernails on a blackboard to me. I said very evenly, "My adopted son is black, Gary."

It only took him aback for a moment, and not enough to apologize or even make a rueful, embarrassed gesture. He just pretended it had never happened. "This is a surprise, a TV star in my humble warehouse. To what do I owe the honor?"

"You said to look you up, so here I am."

"I didn't mean in the middle of a workday."

"I thought I'd buy you lunch."

He looked at his watch. "I can't. Too much work. I'm going to grab a quick sandwich later."

"Do you have five minutes?"

He frowned at the idea that my visit might be other than idly social. "What's up?"

"I just want to talk."

He ran a hand through his white hair and motioned with his head for me to follow him. We went back into the office, and he snapped, "Rose, you're out to lunch!" to the woman at the desk, his manner no less brusque than it had been out on the warehouse floor. He obviously ran his business like a Marine Corps drill instructor.

Rose looked up at the old-fashioned wall clock with the skinny Roman numerals. I remembered a similar clock in Sister Concepta's classroom. It was ten minutes to twelve, early for lunch. She started to protest, then reconsidered and shrugged into her coat, her mouth an angry slash.

Gary waited until she was out of the room before he sat down on the corner of her desk and casually set his leg to swinging. "I hate this goddamn place," he said. "It smells like old people, old times. I've been here too long. I'm building a new ware-house out on the Northwest Side where I can do the processing as well, cut out the middleman. As a matter of fact, I've chatted with Dave Kubo about contracting it for me. Hell, if you can't throw a little business a friend's way . . ." He didn't complete the thought. "What's on your mind?"

"What makes you think anything is?"

"Don't insult my intelligence. I never had anything against you, but your boyish charm always escaped me somehow. You didn't drop by here to have a heart-to-heart with me."

"That's a pretty good assessment."

"Maybe I should have been a detective. So?"

"I want to talk about Gavin."

His leg stopped swinging in mid arc. "I've talked enough about him to last a lifetime."

"I know you didn't get along in recent years."

"That's the understatement of the season."

"Well, that's what I want to talk about."

"How I felt was no secret, and it's no secret why. Him and my ex-wife."

"I heard."

A muscle jumped along his jaw. "I figured you would. Our so-called friends love to gossip about it. That's why I stay the hell away from them for the most part. As for Gavin, he was a prick, and a tiresome alky to boot."

"That's pretty harsh." Keeping my temper in check was like trying to ride a bronco, but I managed. Sometimes I amaze myself.

"Goddamn right," he said. "There's a gentlemen's code. There's a million broads in the world, and you just don't date your friends' ex-wives or girlfriends. It shows a lack of class. He had a definite penchant in that area, and you of all people should know it."

I ignored the dig, but it hurt as badly as he knew it would. "If you felt that way, why go to the funeral?"

His smile was the kind born to be slapped off his face. "I

don't know why. Maybe for the satisfaction of seeing Marian cry. Or maybe to make sure they buried him deep." He sat back, waiting for my reaction. He got it. I felt my teeth clenching hard and my eyes, as Marvel would say, getting all Chinese, narrowing and turning up at the corners as they always did when I was angry.

"I suppose that makes me a shit," he said easily. "It won't be the first time I've been called that."

"Probably not."

"Is that what you came here for? Seems like a waste of an afternoon." He looked at his watch again, as though he wanted me to think every second of his time spent talking to me was a precious jewel squandered. "You can still make the Cubs game. Or are you Hollywood guys more into surfing?"

"Suppose I said that I didn't think Gavin Cassidy died a natural death?"

It rattled his composure, but not much. "I'd say you were blowing smoke. What do you mean, not natural? He died of a million beers too many. He'd been treated for it, hospitalized for it. Christ, they should put his liver in the Museum of Science and Industry." He swung off the corner of the desk and stood nose to nose with me. "Where do you get off showing up after all this time and making a crazy statement like that? Somebody put a burr up your ass or something? Was it my loving ex?"

"Gavin died of an overdose of drugs and alcohol. He never used drugs."

"Who says?"

"Everybody. He was a drunk, but he was no druggie."

He stroked his beard thoughtfully. It was the gesture of a much older man—or maybe he had turned into a much older man inside, plugging away at a business he hated, a busted marriage still rankling, wearing ascots and blazers in a hopeless attempt to deny the clock and the calendar. "Are you saying somebody killed him, deliberately? Well, that's goddamn absurd!" he sputtered. "You're taking this private eye crap too much to heart, you ask me."

"I didn't ask you," I said, "but I do have a few other questions."

"Like did I kill him?"

"That wouldn't have been my first one, but since you bring it up . . ."

"Of course I didn't! I admit I thought about it, when he first took up with Marian. Any husband would. You know the kind of mental pictures you get in your head when it's your wife and your best friend?" He tugged on the end of his nose; Gary seemed inordinately fond of feeling his own face. "If fantasizing murder was a crime, we'd all be in Joliet. But after all this time, after she dumped him because he wouldn't quit drinking, what would be the point?"

"How do you know why she dumped him?"

"You forget what a small town this really is." His mouth twisted. Ugly. "I ought to knock your teeth out."

"You're welcome to try. Look, Gary, there's something about this that just doesn't sit right with me, and I'm going to find out what it is. The only place I can start is with people I know hated Gavin, and that's what brought me to you."

"Well, I'm flattered to be included in that august company, but he wasn't worth hating," he said, standing too close. "Poor sick slob of a drunk, what's to hate? He was his own worst enemy anyway. I didn't like him, I resented the Marian business, but I came to terms with that long ago and simply eliminated him—both of them—from my life."

He backed away and went behind the desk—and not a moment too soon, either. I hate people yelling in my face.

"You want to make a list of the people with a grudge against Cassidy?" he shouted, tossing the clipboard noisily onto the desk, where it bounced once and skittered off onto the floor. "You'll need a whole pad of paper, and you can put your own name on there too, because of Kendra."

"That was twenty years ago, Gary."

"Right. And for twenty years—more than that—Gavin fucked people over, because in his alcohol-pickled brain he thought he was the king of Ireland and could do no wrong. Everyone he came in contact with has the scars. You, me, Marian, Kendra, Beth, Eliscu—the Nemeroffs worst of all because of how he used them. God knows who else!"

"Lower your voice. I can hear you."

He came back around the desk and stood in front of me again, his belligerence bristling around him like the spines of a hedgehog. And he didn't lower his voice. A fine mist of spittle sprayed my face as he hollered into it. "Well, hear this, then. He was an easy guy to hate, and if you'd been around here you'd have realized it, just like the rest of us. Because he was an immoral, using, arrogant, drunken shit-pig Mick!"

I have been accused, on occasion, of being too quick to anger. But I thought about it, about his racist remark earlier and the one about the Irish just now, about what he'd said at the Nemeroffs on Sunday night and what he'd just said about my friend, and how close he was standing to me as he screamed. I calculated all the angles, computed the possible ramifications, and then I backhanded him across the face. He staggered back a few steps, touching his mouth with a kind of wonder. His fair skin clearly showed the reddening mark beside the outline of his white beard.

He was trying to decide if he should do something about it or not, and when he reached the correct conclusion that if he manifested any aggression at all I would beat the piss out of him, his shoulders slumped and he sat down on the edge of the desk again.

"You're no better, Saxon. You never have been. You were always Cassidy's little shadow." He pointed a warning finger at me. "Get out of here before I call a cop and have you booked for assault." He was smart enough to stay far enough away that a roundhouse swing couldn't reach him. "And about Cassidy's death, you breathe the slightest accusation about me to anyone and my lawyers will make you wish you'd never been born."

102

Threats about lawyers usually make me laugh, but I kept my amusement under tight rein. I just walked out of his office and his warehouse, leaving him to rub his reddening face. I probably shouldn't have hit him, but it's rare you get to do something you've wanted to for twenty years, and I'm a great one for taking my opportunities where I find them.

12

The headquarters of Chicago's Fifty-fourth Ward Democratic Organization is on the second floor of a two-story building on the North Side, and to get to it I drove by all the places of my childhood. I passed the Elks Memorial building on Sheridan and Diversey, recalling dimly that my mother used to take me there to climb on the huge bronze elks that flanked the broad white expanse of steps. Across the street in the park were two statues that resonated in memory. One was a shiny gold representation of Alexander Hamilton, facing the lagoon in the shadow of a marble slab. The other was a stylized tribute to Goethe, "the Mastermind of the German People," if the inscription on the base was to be believed. The statue, featuring a fellow resembling Arnold Schwarzenegger surrounded by large hawklike birds, had been erected in 1930 by the Germans of Chicago and was a landmark, but it didn't stop most Chicagoans from resolutely pronouncing the philosopher's name, and the Near North Side street christened in his honor, "GO-thee." I'd pronounced it that way too until I got to the University of Illinois and was laughed at.

On the northwest corner is a building that once was headquarters for the union of meat-cutters and butchers. Now it's a medical center; make of that whatever you wish.

I drove farther north, past the cemeteries on Irving Park Road. In Los Angeles we hide our graveyards behind walls and trees as if we're ashamed of those who had the bad grace to die; we want no reminder of our own fragile mortality. But in Chicago the headstones are easily visible from the street beyond a steel fence topped with a roll of barbed wire; whether that's to keep the rest of us from getting in or the residents from getting out, I didn't know.

The elevated station at Wilson and Broadway probably hasn't been refurbished, or even cleaned, since before World War II. Even in the best parts of Chicago the El goes racketing through the neighborhoods at all hours of the day and night. Along with the lake, it sets the pulse and rhythm of the city. But Uptown, where I'd run, could never have been called one of the best parts. Since I left, it has nearly disintegrated.

The Uptown Theatre, with its beautiful ornate facade towering over Broadway, was boarded up and forlorn. Argyle Street, once a haven where Jewish refugees from the war in Europe met to shop and swap stories, is now completely Vietnamese, as if when Saigon fell everyone there packed up and moved to Argyle. I've never felt more a stranger than here on the streets where I had played cowboys and Indians between the parked cars and slurped cherry Cokes bought from drugstore soda fountains that aren't there anymore.

I felt odd returning to Uptown. The home and playground of my childhood had become a slum in my absence, and I couldn't escape the gnawing feeling that it was somehow my fault, that if I'd stayed around to take care of it, Uptown would somehow have hung on.

At Bryn Mawr, which locals always pronounced BRIN-more, I turned north, noting that the old Bryn Mawr Theatre was shuttered and for sale, too, and I wondered if all the movie palaces of my youth, now closed and deserted, remained standing as a silent rebuke to me for frittering away so many childhood afternoons in their magical dark. After two more blocks I found what I was looking for.

The plasterboard sign stretched across the front of the building was as big and garish as that of a traveling circus, a comparison that carries the ring of truth: 54TH WARD DEMOCRATIC ORGANIZATION it said in red letters on a white background, and beneath that in smaller black letters was the name of the mayor. Smaller still, but in vivid blue type, was the Alderman's name and title. Everyone knew his name, but in the twenty-six years since he'd first been elected to office he was referred to simply as the Alderman, as if there were only one in the world. I found a place to park on the street and went upstairs.

At one of the desks sat a woman in her fifties with sandy reddish hair, which was crimped and permed against the frizzing humidity that plagues the Midwest all year long. The skin of her face, heavily powdered, was the color and consistency of raw cookie dough. For some reason she wore dark wraparound sunglasses, making her look like a fat white Ray Charles in drag.

She picked up a pencil at my approach, holding it vertically in front of her like a cross to ward off vampires, even though she had a real gold one around her neck on a too thin chain. "Help you?" she said.

"Is Mr. Givney in?"

"Did you have an appointment?"

"No, but tell him it's Jimmy Saxon's son."

Her plucked and drawn-on eyebrows did a judgmental samba behind her glasses, and she put down her pencil and went into an inner office, giving me a chance to look around. Old-fashioned venetian blinds filtered bars of sunshine through the unwashed windows, and motes of dust danced in the light. Elderly desks scarred by a thousand cigarettes and twenty thousand heels were spaced unevenly around the

105

room, each with a different kind of rolling chair, some wood with worn seat cushions, some vinyl-covered metal. Large cork panels that smelled like the ruins of an apartment fire had been mounted on the walls next to every desk to accept the thumbtacked busywork of the ward, and in several places I saw duplicates of a flier printed on red paper, inviting the faithful to a fund-raising cocktail party and buffet in honor of the Alderman, which was set for the following evening at a neighborhood restaurant's banquet room. In prominent positions on the wall were carefully posed black-and-white photographs. The one in the middle was, not surprisingly, of the mayor, flanked by smaller pictures of the Alderman and Martin Givney, and there was a blank space where a large frame had once hung; I assumed that it would be occupied again as soon as there was a Democrat back in Springfield. The office's sole nod to modernity was a small desktop computer in a corner, its screen glowing amber. I was willing to bet none of the old-time ward regulars knew how to work it.

The redheaded lady tottered out on heels too high and said, "Right in there, please," pointing to the office from whence she'd come. I went past her, catching a whiff of scented powder that reminded me of an old-time drugstore.

Martin Givney half rose from behind his desk in greeting. He was as barrel-shaped as when I was nine or so and was required to address him as Uncle Martin, but in the intervening years the barrel's capacity had almost doubled. His face was round and wide as a melon, as canny as an old fox's. I recalled that face in my living room, at the ballpark, at my mother's wake, always wreathed in cigar smoke and red from a jar of Irish. But it had changed.

Some Irishmen don't age as gracefully as other ethnic strains. They tend to show their years in a sagging of the muscles around the eyes and mouth and in a tracery of wrinkles out of which wily eyes twinkle. Martin Givney had to be eighty-five if a day and looked every minute of it, his face pouched beneath the eyes and chin, pendulously jowled, and seamed across the forehead and from the corners of his nostrils to his mouth. His poundage and more than half a century of smoking allowed him to breathe only with great effort. Through most of his lifetime he had been district leader of the Fifty-fourth Ward, running it as his own personal fief, dispensing patronage, largesse, and five-dollar bills discreetly palmed in a hearty handshake on election day.

But his sphere of influence didn't end at the boundaries of the Fifty-fourth. Givney was also a committeeman with the Cook County Democratic Organization and a member of the statewide party power structure, and for fifty years he had quietly collected and accrued power the way a miser hoards gold coins, spending it sometimes benevolently but always wisely and with his own good firmly in mind, which is why he had weathered the political changes of half a century with hardly a wave to rock his steady and formidable boat.

"By the sweet saints!" Givney said, pumping my hand. "When Mrs. Meany told me who it was my heart skipped a beat, and at my age that gives a man cause to worry." He patted his chest over his heart the way you'd try to soothe an agitated dog. "So it's home you are after all these years. And a grown man with gray hair, too. I remember you in short pants, with your nose running. How time slips by us, doesn't it?" He had been born Back-of-the-Yards in Chicago and as far as I knew had never been to Ireland, but he spoke as if he'd just stepped out of steerage. "And you're the living image of your dear mother, God rest her. Kathleen was like a daughter to me—I've never quite gotten over her passing. And now you've come home to Chicago at last. Back to stay, are yez?"

I shook my head. "Just passing through."

"Say hello to my grandnephew Owen Maguire," he said, pointing to a compactly built young man in a chair near the wall, one leg cocked insolently up over his other knee. Maguire nodded, taking my measure, and I nodded back. About twenty-seven, he didn't look as if they'd been easy years. There was scar tissue around both his cold blue eyes, and he wore a diamond stud in his left ear. Another sign of the times. When I was a kid men didn't wear earrings on the streets, not if they cared to make it safely to the corner.

"Sit down, sit down," Givney said. "Lord, hasn't it been forever? Where do you live now? Out west, isn't it? I recall your father saying you were out west somewhere." The way he said it made it sound like the OK Corral.

"California."

"Yes, your dad himself said so. So what is it you do out there exactly, out west?"

"I'm a buffalo skinner," I said. "Mr. Givney, I'm in Chicago for the funeral of a friend, and I think you knew him: Gavin Cassidy."

Immediately, smoothly, the features transformed themselves into a mourner's mask, corners of the mouth and eyes down-turned. Martin Givney was a fine actor, better than any of us. "A terrible thing. When an officer goes down isn't it a terrible thing? Never mind it was not in the line of duty, when we lose a policeman we lose something of ourselves, what makes our city clean and decent. I was prostrate. Prostrate, you under-stand. We sent a wreath." He glanced at Maguire for corrobora-tion and got a curt nod. "I don't recall, now, did he leave a family?"

"No."

"Ah. A pity. A family gives a man an anchor. It's a good thing to know there'll be someone left to mourn your passing. Myself, I have five kids, twelve grandchildren, and three great grand-children. And don't they all live right here in the ward, by the by. They never found it necessary to stray far from hearth and home to make their way in life." He said it airily, but I can recognize an implied rebuke from fifty yards upwind.

"Two sons and a granddaughter are attorneys-at-law," Giv-ney went on. "It makes me proud. And proud to know that when I go, there'll be a big crowd of them to send me off. The good Lord notices things like that. 'Look at old Martin Givney,' He'll say, 'and doesn't he have a fine turnout?' " He sighed a musical sigh, descending the scale from high C. "Gavin Cassidy's was a sad passing nonetheless, and I was sorry to see the back of him. Friend of yours, you say?"

"That's right."

"Well, my sympathies to you, then, and I know the Alderman joins me in those sentiments. A fine officer and a fine man he was, Cassidy, a credit to us all."

"He was a fine officer. That's why it's hard to understand why he was suspended from the department."

Owen Maguire uncrossed his legs and then recrossed them, polyester on polyester. Givney fiddled with his tie, a wool one that had been pulled down to below his second shirt button. His smile was all avuncular tolerance. "That's not the essence of the man, son, not important to his loving memory, if yez take my meaning. Why not remember him as the fine friend and kind man you knew him to be?"

"I'm trying to, but people don't seem to want to let me. So I want to find out why he was kicked off the force."

"Now why do you imagine I'd know that?"

I had to laugh at that one. "Mr. Givney, there's not a single thing that happens north of the Chicago River in this town that you don't know about."

He beamed for a moment. "You think I don't know what goes on south of the river, too? You underestimate me."

"Then what happened to Cassidy?"

"And why should that interest you?"

"Because people are whispering about him, and he's dead and can't defend himself."

"Look, son," Givney said, not unkindly, "there are pressures that come upon a man that his friends never know about, and if they don't they have no call to be making snap decisions. You can't judge a man's whole life on a single mistake, not until yez walk a mile in his shoes." Years of campaigning had taught him to speak as if his every word would someday be engraved on the base of a monument.

"What do you mean, mistake?"

"We all make them, y'know. Look at your own dear father. Jimmy made a mistake, he paid the piper, and now he's back at his job with never another word said about it. Poor Gavin Cassidy's with the Lord now. Let it be."

"Do you mean you don't know why he was suspended?"

"My uncle means he doesn't want to talk about it," Owen Maguire said. His voice was high-pitched and nervous, a rubber band stretched too tight. He uncrossed his legs and put both feet on the floor.

I stared him down. "Is that what your uncle means?"

Givney said, "Now, now. Owney knows it does no good to defame the dead."

"Defame? If you tell me why he was suspended you'll be defaming him?"

With a man as beefy as Givney, you never know whether he's shrugging or not, but his shoulders rose a bit and he put his chin down, which spread his jowls wide. "The lad made an error in judgment is all. Forgivable enough in an ordinary man, but for an officer of the law, sworn to uphold—"

"What kind of an error in judgment?"

Givney picked up a half smoked dead cigar from the ashtray in front of him, one end chewed ragged, sloppy with spit. Owney Maguire made as if to get up and light it for him, but Givney waved him back to his seat and lit it himself with a wooden match. "You cut a man no slack, do you?"

"Any reason why I should?"

Givney smacked his lips like a goldfish, and rank gray cigar smoke drifted into the light streaming through the slats of the blinds. "I knew your grandfather Ryan," he mused. "Got him his city job. Structural inspector, it was. I watched your mother grow up. Danced at her wedding, and gave her husband, your father, a job too, right in my own organization. After his troubles the job was still waiting for him. That's the kind of good friend I've always been to the Ryans and Saxons."

"Be a friend to me, then, and tell me why Cassidy was kicked off the police force after twenty years."

"He wasn't kicked off, as you say," Givney said. "He was suspended without pay, pending an internal review."

"Let's not split hairs, Mr. Givney."

"You used to call me Uncle Martin, I believe."

"Old news, Mr. Givney."

He studied the spitty end of his cigar like an entomologist deciding whether a specimen was worthy of mounting. "I tell you this for the love of your mother, though she'd spin in her grave knowing you've come to devil me this way." His eyes almost disappeared behind the protective breastworks of the fleshy pouches that surrounded them. "Your friend Cassidy, God rest his soul, tried to solicit a bribe from a public official."

I clenched both fists on my lap. "Jesus Christ!"

"Blessed be His holy name," Givney interjected.

"I don't believe it."

"Believe it or don't. The charges were leveled and Officer Cassidy never even raised a voice in his own defense."

"You mean he admitted it?"

"No. The man wasn't stupid. But he didn't deny it, either."

"Cassidy was the most honest human being I've ever known."

"Honesty is a relative thing, boyo," Givney said, leaning back in his chair, throwing his arms out wide. "This is the big city here. Nobody gets something for nothing. Or expects it. Chicago operates on the philosophy of the quid pro quo." He chuckled. "You remember your Latin from Catholic school?"

"If you give something to me, I've got to give back something to you. Is that it?"

"Don't moralize to me! This city works, and as long as it does the good people who live here don't look too hard at the how and the why of it. And why should they? They know when they're well off. It's people like me, like your dear father, that keep this city running." He put his meaty elbows on the desk.

"Let me tell you a little story. There's a party one night about two years ago, on Rush Street in one of the restaurants there. Brynie Boyle, the chairman of the Fifty-seventh Ward commit-

111

tee—you know Brynie? no matter—Brynie is holding a little gathering of good friends to discuss the pros and cons of a zoning issue there in his district, and among them is Judge Stanton Stein of the municipal court, who owes his seat on the bench to the self-same Brynie Boyle. Now I'm talking about two men who are in their seventies, comrades and compatriots for more years than you've got on the earth, and they've been in the trenches through more than one war together, fighting off that goddamn woman and our little black brothers from the South Side both, and I'm happy to tell you they've both come through it intact, which is more than I can say for a lot of people who didn't have the grit and the gumption to hang on when the sea got a bit rough. So now, when Brynie rises to introduce Stanton—and Brynie had had a jar or two, I'm not denying that—he says to the assemblage, 'I'd like you to meet one of my oldest and dearest friends, Stanton Stein, the best judge that money can buy.'

"And so the good judge—remember his advanced years, now, we're talking a man with a pacemaker and hearing aid—leans over and cracks Brynie right across the mouth, in front of God and everybody. And while Brynie is standing there, stunned speechless as if the sword of judgment has just fallen on his head, the judge says to him, 'Brynie, don't you ever dare say such a thing like that again—*in public.*' " He laughed uproariously, as though hearing it for the first time, and over in the corner Owney Maguire was yucking it up too.

"I'm not sure I get the point, Mr. Givney."

He stopped laughing and caught his breath. "I hoped you would. The point is that in Chicago the quiet payoff is a way of life, and nobody gives it much attention one way or the other. Everybody has his own agenda, young lad, and no one passes judgment because of it."

"Anyone who claims that Gavin Cassidy was a crooked cop is a lying sack of shit," I said. I was staring at Givney, but I heard Owney Maguire shift in his seat, just in case his services would be needed.

They weren't. Givney returned my stare. He could do the hard look with the best of them—he owned the patent on it. "Shame on you," he finally said. "It's a sad day when a man has no loyalty to his own people."

And then Martin Givney began to chortle. He was so amused that eventually his laughter turned into a massive coughing fit. Maguire leapt to his feet and poured him a cup of water from a thermos pitcher on the windowsill, pounding him gently on the back while he drank it.

Givney wiped his eyes with his fat hand. "I'd love to sit and reminisce with you, lad," he croaked, "but I've work to do here, and you're kind of in the way. Owney, why don't you show young Saxon the way out?"

Maguire came around the side of the desk in front of me, arms hanging at his side, flexing his fingers. I stood up, noting that I had about three inches on him.

"You'll hear from me again, Mr. Givney," I said.

He gulped some more water. "I hope not, frankly. I can't say I care for your attitude. It's disrespectful, and it shames your mother's memory. I don't like that. I held you on my knee, lad."

"I remember," I said. "Your breath stank of cigars and cheap whiskey."

Givney hauled himself to his feet and leaned both hands on the desk, the weight of his shoulders and chest pulling him forward like a lowland gorilla. "You're making a mistake," he said, each word a little chunk of ice.

"How's that?"

"It wasn't cheap whiskey. It was the very best Irish. Always. You'd do well to remember that."

He nodded at Maguire, who gripped my arm hard just above the elbow and began steering me toward the door.

"Have you had your breakfast yet, Owney?" I said.

"Why?"

"Because if you don't take your fucking hand off me I'm going to rip it off and feed it to you."

Owney Maguire looked at Givney, a subtle signal passed between them, and he released my elbow.

"You're a tough bastard," Givney wheezed. "Like your dear father. Dumb like him, too."

"I'll be sure to give him your regards," I said.

13

Marian Meyers lived in a sixty-year-old clapboard house near Belden and Clark, just a few blocks from the zoo. The entire neighborhood is old and well kept, and Marian's house sported a relatively fresh paint job, white with blue and gray trim. In the burnished light of a Chicago spring, it was a pleasant-looking place, the kind of solid midwestern house some people would like to have grown up in.

On the front porch, a two-seater swing stood next to a faded wicker end table, in hopes of summer. The door was of sturdy wood with a thick leaded-glass insert masked by three layers of white net curtains. I rang the bell and the harsh sound echoed inside the house. In a moment Marian Meyers opened the door.

"Well, hello," she said. Her black hair was pulled back into a semiponytail peeking over the left shoulder of a flowered print shirtwaist dress.

"Got a minute?" I said.

"Sure, come on in." She stood aside, and I stepped into the foyer. Directly ahead of me a narrow staircase led to the second floor, and to the left was a set of heavy wooden sliding doors opening into the living room. That's where she led me. It was sparsely appointed, the furniture old but expensive, and the sunlight through the tall window gave the room a feeling of warmth and coziness, even though there was no rug on the well-polished hardwood floor.

"I was writing," she explained, almost apologizing. "My office is upstairs."

"I don't want to interfere with your inspiration."

She made a sour face. "My inspiration is in neutral right now. Can I get you something? Iced tea, or a beer?"

"Nothing, thanks." I sat down in a burgundy easy chair, sinking low into the cushion, and Marian sat opposite me on an uncomfortable-looking sofa.

"I hear you've been a busy boy," she said. "My loving ex called a while ago. I'm flattered—most of the time he cuts me cold. Today I couldn't get him to stop talking. He was raising hell about you."

"I didn't mention what we discussed."

She brushed at a strand of hair at her temple. "He says you slapped him around. Did you?"

"I slapped him," I admitted. "Not around. It's all semantics. Marian, why didn't you tell me Gavin was on suspension when he died?"

She looked blank. "Was I supposed to?"

"I expect a client to give me all the information they can up front. It saves time and energy."

Her big dark eyes narrowed; she was thinking about becoming angry. "I'm not your client—you made that very clear to me. I thought you were doing this for Gavin."

"You're right. But I expect some help. Tell me about the suspension."

She clasped her hands between her knees. "I don't know anything about it. It was one of the times right after he came out of the hospital, and he told me they'd pulled his badge. I assumed it was because of his drinking."

"That had nothing to do with it. I heard Gavin put the bite on some public official and got nailed for it."

"I didn't know that," she said, and her shock seemed genuine. "He never mentioned it."

"Didn't you even ask?"

"I figured if he wanted to tell me, he would." She rose and went over to the window to stand silhouetted against the light, which came through the skirt of her dress. She had strong, solid legs. "I can't believe Gavin would bribe anyone," she said to the street outside.

"Neither can I. That's what's bothering me. Did you know he was involved with the boys in the Fifty-fourth Ward?"

She turned to look at me, her face drawn. "Ben got him into that. I didn't think it amounted to anything."

I struggled up out of the deep cushions of the chair and came toward her. "Ben? What's he got to do with it?"

"I don't know." She hugged herself as if from the cold, even though the temperature was in the seventies. "He's some sort of *macher* with the party over there, or tries to be. I knew Gavin knew those people through Ben, but then he knew everybody in town. That's how he was."

"He never said anything about the suspension?"

She looked up at the curlicued design of plaster leaves and vines on the molding that circled the room just below the ceiling. "He'd rant about it when he was drunk sometimes. If you recall, we weren't . . . together at that point, so I wasn't with him all that much. Once, a few weeks ago, when he was pretty bad—so bad that I was just walking out the door because I couldn't stand to see him like that for another minute—he yelled after me, 'They don't give a shit about you. Even when you fuck your own friends for them, they kick your ass out on the street.' I didn't understand what he meant. I still don't." She chafed her arms. "He was in no condition to tell me that night. But in his ramblings, he mentioned Bob Eliscu. And you."

"Me? I hadn't seen him in years."

116

"I knew that," she said, "and when I asked him about it a few days later, he clammed up. I know he had a great sense of loyalty to the people from the old Hard Knox days, even the ones that didn't like him anymore, like Gary. But I don't know what you, or any of them had to do with his getting suspended."

I put my hands on her shoulders and turned her to face me. "Marian, you're the one who thinks he was murdered. Who do you think killed him?"

Her eyes got very liquid, and she pressed her lips together until they were white. Then she drew a ragged breath and said, "Gavin had been killing himself for years. Whoever slipped him a lethal dose of amphetamines just hastened the process."

All of a sudden she looked very haunted and tired and used up. I put my arms out and she moved into them and put her head against my shoulder, and I felt the sobs she was trying to stifle shake her whole body. Finally they stopped, and we just stood that way for a while, looking out at the sun-dappled grass without really seeing it, hearing the traffic on Clark Street a block away.

Bob Eliscu's office was on Western Avenue near Belmont. When I was growing up that area was known for what was then the world's largest amusement park, Riverview, with wild rides like the Bobs and the Flying Turns, and spooky Aladdin's Castle in which evil spirits in Day-Glo colors jumped out of the darkness at you, and the floor beneath your feet bucked and rattled and contained supercharged jets of air that would blow girls' dresses high above their waists. With the popularity of slacks and pants for women the air-blower declined, and so did Riverview. There is a shopping center where it used to stand, a Dominick's supermarket and a Toys-R-Us. It's quiet and respectable now, and a little more joy has disappeared from city life.

LSQ Associates was a storefront. If Bob hadn't told me about his new nickname, I never would have found him in the phone book. When I walked in, there were no associates in evidence, nor anyone else for that matter. It was a long narrow room that almost disappeared into darkness toward the back. There were four unmatched desks, two against each wall, and each had an old-fashioned black telephone on it. A wall calendar featuring photos of big beautiful women in tiny swimsuits was the only decoration. Miss May was a voluptuous brunette kneeling in the surf with wet sand all over her thighs. It looked uncomfortable.

I heard a toilet flushing in the back, and in a few moments Eliscu came out tucking his shirt into his pants. I was grateful he didn't want to shake hands.

He didn't look glad to see me. His voice was like crumpling cellophane. "I didn't figure you for a visit."

"Neither did I, but life's full of happy accidents." I looked around at the bare walls. "Nice place you have here. What do you do?"

"I'm a factor," he said.

"In what?"

He scowled. "Jesus, you don't know much, do you? Look, I'm busy here. Without the bullshit, whaddaya want?"

"To talk about old times," I said.

"You and me don't have any old times."

"No, but you and Cassidy did."

He stared at me, then went over to the desk nearest the front door and picked up a pack of Camels. "So?" he said, shaking a cigarette out of the pack.

"At the Nemeroffs you said that Cassidy wouldn't cut you any slack even though you were old friends."

He lit his cigarette but didn't say anything. His lumpy jaw jutted out like an underslung bulldog's.

"Do you want to explain that to me?"

"Why should I?" he demanded, coming closer to me than I liked. "It was between him and me."

"Well, now it's between you and me," I said.

"Fuck you, Saxon."

118

"Or it can be between you and Captain Mayo of the Chicago PD. Your choice, Bob."

"It's none of your goddamn business."

"I'm making it my business."

"Why?"

Several replies occurred to me, including the truth. But I didn't feel like sharing that with Bob Eliscu. LSQ. I had disliked the man for so long that I wanted to keep him at more than arm's length, even though his cooperation might give me the answers I was looking for. "Because," I said, like a little kid confronting a classmate in the schoolyard.

"That's no reason," he said.

"Fine." I turned to go. "Mayo will contact you."

"Wait a minute!" LSQ said.

I stopped, looked at him, waited. There was a thin sheen of sweat on his face. Flop sweat, we actors call it, like when you suddenly can't remember your next line.

"I don't want any cops poking around," he grumbled. "No cop ever gave me nothing but grief. They think every fucking day is Christmas."

I waited some more. Finally he said, "Sit down, for chrissake, you're starting to spook me."

That was my intention, but I didn't tell him that. He took a chair from behind one of the other desks and swung it around so I could sit across the desk from him.

"What do you want to know?" he said quietly.

"You and Gavin had a beef. You said he didn't want to know you anymore. Let's hear about that."

"Christ, that was a long time ago."

"How long?"

He thought about it for a few seconds. "Two years—no, more like three."

"Okay."

He took a deep breath to collect himself. "I was trying to move some merchandise for some people—"

"What kind of merchandise?"

119

"What's the difference?" His voice went up half an octave. "A factor moves merchandise for other people."

"Why couldn't they move it themselves?"

As if explaining to a not too bright child, he said, "It wasn't exactly kosher."

I nodded, content with that for the time being.

"So Cassidy finds out about it. Don't ask me how, cops have their snitches all over town. But he finds out. And he comes to my house, and he says I either shut down right now this minute, or he blows the whistle." He stopped and took another breath. Maybe so much smoking was cutting down his wind. He should quit. So should I.

"And?"

"This was not an insignificant deal for me. This was substantial bread. So I says to him that we oughta talk. He says there's nothin' to talk about. I says, not even five percent?" He made a face.

"And what did he say?"

"He beat the crap out of me. In my own fucking house." He shook his head at the injustice of it all.

I said, "And did you cease and desist?"

"I had to," he said. "He woulda had every blue-suit in town crawling up my ass if I hadn't. It cost me about a quarter of a million bucks in commissions, too—*and* got me in a lot of trouble with some people I know."

"What people?"

He shook his head. "Not a chance. Not if you pull out my fucking fingernails."

"Did you tell your friends about Cassidy? Give them his name?"

"I don't give names—not to them, not to Cassidy, and sure as shit not to you. That's how I stay healthy."

"I won't push you on it," I said, figuring it had all happened too long ago to worry about.

"Wouldn't do any good if you did." He crushed his cigarette

120

out and immediately lit another one. "I haven't had a sweet deal like that since. Cassidy really did the job on me."

"Was it drugs, Bob? This merchandise?"

He looked over my shoulder through the plate glass window, studying the traffic whizzing by on Western. "I make a buck where I can. I don't need any so-called pals turning moralistic on me."

"The way I see it," I said, "he did you a favor."

"How you figure?"

"Anybody else he'd have locked up. He gave you a chance to back out. Because you were his friend. You ask me, you don't know the meaning of the word."

Eliscu—or LSQ or whatever the hell he called himself now—hunched his head down and studied the end of his cigarette. Philosophical precepts apparently made him nervous.

"Why was Cassidy suspended just before he died?"

He looked up sharply. "Nothing to do with me."

"I never said it was. I'm asking a question."

"Go ask it somewhere else," he said. "I've had more of you today than I can take."

"You also said the other night that he wound up with his ass in a sling. With the boys in the Fifty-fourth?"

"I'm telling you," he said, and there was a vague undercurrent of warning in his voice that I should have heeded. "You're asking the wrong guy."

"Who's the right guy, then?"

He inhaled a ton of smoke and blew it at me through pursed lips. "Gone by to see your old man lately?" he said, and I could tell he enjoyed saying it.

The six-flat on Kenmore Avenue looked squat and ugly, its buff-colored brick facade now faded to uncertain yellow. The lawn that separated it from the sidewalk was uncared for and bare in spots, and the two huge urns on either side of the steps, once repositories for ivy plants that snaked down the stone and

121

into the front yard, now just held dry gravelly dirt, cigarette butts, and a polystyrene Big Mac container that won't biodegrade for the next five hundred years. On both sides of the building itself were pathetic-looking bushes in need of trimming. A couple of beer cans had been tossed there by someone who'd first squeezed them in the middle.

I sat in the car a long time, my stomach twisted into a granny knot and a tight, tense steel band constricting around my forehead like some medieval torture device. I had a cigarette, ground it out in the ashtray, then lit another one, drumming my fingers on the steering wheel as the smoke swirled around me in the closed car. Finally I got out and went up the walk.

In five of the six front windows there were paper shades pulled down to screen out the light. On the top floor right, there were lace curtains, as there had always been, probably the same ones that had hung there for twenty-five years, now dingy with age and cigarette smoke. "Lace-curtain Irish," they called them, and you could see why. I opened the front door and stepped into the hallway, smelling forty years worth of evening meals, corned beef and cabbage and garlic and onions and beans and *chale* bread and fish and inexpensive cuts of beef. The smell of an old apartment building is a constant, a perennial fragrant monument to generations that have passed through.

I walked up the steps over the familiar pattern of fleurs-de-lis in the threadbare carpet. A high heel would probably catch in one of the rents and the wearer would break her neck, but it was unlikely someone with high heels would visit here anyway. It wasn't a high-heels kind of building. At the second-floor landing a three-foot square of different carpeting had been laid with no attempt made to matching even the color of the original. I continued on up to the top floor, turned to the door on the right, the one with a tarnished brass 6 affixed to it, and raised my fist to knock. I held it there for an uncertain moment, looking at the white knuckles of my hand as if they belonged to someone else. From inside, a radio newscaster droned too low for me to hear what he was saying. I was finding it hard to swallow. At last I did, like gulping an orange whole, and then took a deep breath and knocked. I tried to step back, wanting to run down the stairs, but some sneaky son of a bitch had nailed my feet to the floor when I wasn't looking.

The man who opened the door was old, over seventy, I knew, but somehow I'd expected him to look the way he had the last time I'd seen him, and the fact that he didn't was a severe shock to me. He was shorter than I remembered, about five seven, but perhaps age had shrunk him an inch or two. He had a full head of coarse, iron gray hair that he'd combed with his fingers, and his day-old beard stubble was white, making him look even older. His eyes were yellow-brown and dull; they'd seen too much in too many years. His clothes—a pair of baggy slacks, a maroon cardigan sweater, and a shirt that must have cost at least five dollars new—hung loose on his skinny frame, the way old people's sometimes do. Dangling from the left corner of his mouth was a half smoked cigarette I knew was a Camel; the smoke curled up into his eye as it always had, giving him a squint. The skin on his face was puffy and wrinkled, the color and texture of an old grocery bag. He looked at me and the cigarette wiggled a bit as he attempted the smallest of smiles, his lackluster eyes brightening a bit.

"Hi," I said when I finally found my voice. It was inadequate, ineffectual and banal, I knew, but it was the very best I could come up with under the circumstances.

"Hello, kiddo. I heard you was in town. C'mon in," my father said.

14

James Saxon is a fourth-generation German-American from the West Side, the unpronounceable surname having been Anglicized decades before, but when he married my mother, Kathleen Ryan, he converted to Irish. From their first dance as husband and wife at the wedding reception at the Bismarck Hotel, he became as Gaelic as Paddy's pig.

When I was breech-born two years later, a portent of the stubborn and difficult person I've grown up to be, my mother nearly died, so there were no more little Saxons to come, and my mother's failure in her duty as a good Catholic wife to provide a brood of devout children for the Church was to cause her much personal anguish. I was baptized in her home parish, Saint Aloysius, while my father stood by beaming, predicting to anyone who'd listen that I would grow up and go to Notre Dame to distinguish myself on the gridiron. Stardom with the Fighting Irish was really his second choice, but I guess dedicating my infant soul to the priesthood was laying it on a little thick, even for him. When it came time to begin my education, there was never any question that I would go to parochial school at Saint Al's, there to learn my catechism along with the three Rs. And though James Saxon, now called "Jimmy" by his cronies, was wont to make ugly anti-Catholic jokes at home, such as "The definition of a nun is someone who ain't had nun and don't want nun," which my mother deplored and I puzzled over, his public face was both Irish and devout.

By virtue of his birth in Kilrush, County Clare, my maternal grandfather Ryan was politically connected. On the civic payroll as a structural inspector, which gave him the license to goof off most of the day, it was through his influence, or rather that of *his* chinaman in the Fifty-fourth Ward Democratic Organization, Martin Givney, that the man his daughter married, my father, was able to bail out of his failing small-appliance dealership on Ashland Avenue and go to work for the city as an electrical inspector, something he knew as much about as he did biochemistry or the finely evolved breathing apparatus of sea mammals. Lack of expertise rarely got in his way.

He went through the motions, visiting stores and bars and offices, peering perfunctorily at the wiring before writing violations in an officious and occasionally vindictive manner. But how he really earned his keep—and I knew this about him from the moment I was old enough to sort out the differences between my schoolmates' fathers, who were small businessmen and accountants and merchants, and my own—was as Martin Givney's bagman, the flunky who goes around with a leather satchel delivering and collecting political payoffs, kickbacks, tributes, and bribes. A combination public relations expert and forward observer, he was at the same time the symbol of the higher authority of the political organization for which he worked, as well as a sort of cannon fodder.

Jimmy wasn't a terrible husband; I never heard him say a harsh word to my mother other than an occasional "Don't devil me, Kathleen, I'm not up to it." He delivered his paycheck intact and on time, and there was never a whisper or hint of other women. His drinking was a minor annoyance more than a real problem. He just wasn't a particularly good husband. Today they call men like him workaholics, driven by their jobs to earn and achieve, but it wasn't the work or the profit Jimmy Saxon loved. It was the camaraderie and good offices of capable and powerful men who smoked cigars and drank the best Irish, who made policy and bestowed jobs like blessings on their cronies, who couldn't walk half a block on the streets of the North Side without being greeted by name, and with respect. My father was seduced by the male bonding of the smoke-filled political back room. He ignored my mother and me to spend all of his time with his mistress and true love: the Fifty-fourth Ward Democratic Organization.

As for his parenting skills, I am hard-pressed to remember any. Save for an occasional annoyed swat on the behind that I richly deserved, I was not abused or mistreated in any way. In fact, for a time, until I entered my rebellious period, Jimmy was rather proud of his kid, and I recall a Sunday when I was about seven, being carried on his shoulders into Shanahan's Grill on Devon Avenue—Chicagoans call it "De-VAHN"—the day after I'd gotten a ground-ball hit and turned it into a home run with Jerry Hallen on base in a Park League baseball game. In Shanahan's, where a Jew or an Italian or, God forbid, a Protestant entered at his own risk, I was passed around from hand to hand to be admired like my father's bowling trophy.

In adolescence and beyond, when my interest turned to artistic pursuits like jazz piano and the theater, my father was disdainful and made no effort to hide his disappointment. "You can't make a living acting," he'd warn me, or "You run into a lot of fairies in the acting business." So as soon as I was able, I proved to him and the rest of the world that I could indeed make enough from acting to at least eat, and that my heterosexual drives were in perfect working order. He never came to see me in a play unless he brought some political cronies with him. His interest in my budding career was based solely on how many points it could score with the big boys.

During my sophomore year at the University of Illinois in Champaign-Urbana where I was majoring in theater arts—my choice of a lay school over Notre Dame, or at the very least Marquette, involved a considerable loss of face for my father, who never let me forget it—a political scandal erupted on the

North Side. The powers that be were shocked, *shocked*—to discover that under-the-table payments were being made for political favors in the Fifty-fourth Ward. Mike Royko wrote about it; "Kup's Kolumn" mentioned it twice a week; the local newscasts used it as their lead story on those rare evenings when no sexually motivated murders were reported. City electrical inspector Jimmy Saxon was the name mentioned most often. He was indicted for accepting bribes, and I transferred from downstate to the university's Chicago campus to be with my mother during the ordeal, venting my frustrations on small stages like the North State Street Theatre Guild and in pseudo-intellectual bars like Hard Knox College.

Kathleen Ryan Saxon took the scandal hard. Her hair turned lank and brittle, her skin sallow, she lost weight rapidly and developed an ulcer. Jimmy copped a plea and was sentenced to four years in prison, of which he served twenty-nine months, and though he lost his job with the city, during his incarceration the salary checks from the Fifty-fourth Ward never stopped, because Martin Givney came by the apartment and announced that he took care of his own in adversity as well as in plenty, and that as long as there was breath in his body Jimmy's family would want for nothing. In the meantime, my mother faded; while Jimmy was stamping out license plates she contracted pneumonia, lingered six weeks and died, and was buried next to my grandparents in the Ryan plot in the Saint Aloysius cemetery. The doctors could call it what they would; to my mind it was shame that killed her.

Four months after her death I moved to California to become a professional actor. Hi-diddle-dee-dee. I hadn't seen Jimmy since his trial. I'd never expected to again.

When my draft board summoned me near the end of the Vietnam War, it occurred to me that I might not be coming back, and since I've never been one to leave loose ends dangling, I wrote my father that I'd be going to Fort Dix, New Jersey, for training. He was out of prison by then and back in the apartment on Kenmore Avenue, and he dropped a note wishing me good luck. I guess it worked—I sat out the war in Georgia producing and narrating instructional videotapes for the Signal Corps, while Jerry Hallen, who had preceded me in the Park League batting order and scored on my home run, went to the Mekong Delta and returned in a body bag. When I got back to Los Angeles a civilian, I sent Jimmy my new address, and save for an occasional Christmas card when I was particularly full of seasonal cheer, that was it.

He wrote me a few letters over the years. One I recall, after I'd done a *Movie of the Week* for ABC, scrawled on Democratic party stationery:

March 3, 1978

Hiya, kiddo,

Was watching the TV the other night and surprise! There you were. You took a pretty good part in that. I'm real proud of you. We're getting ready for St. P's day here. It's a lot of hard work but everybody has a good time. Saw you in a picture a few weeks back too. You must be doing pretty good out there and know a lot of stars. Bet you make pretty good money too. Things are okay here but tight. I don't work for the city any more so have to make do on my check from the ward. Hope you like it out in Calif. We always look for you on TV.

Dad

I sent him a money order for four hundred dollars the next day and can't recall any communication between us since.

I went into his living room—my old living room—and the waves of nostalgia made me dizzy. The couch was the same, with the same flowered slipcovers my mother had made for it twenty-five years ago. The cherrywood dining set, bought on time and always too big for its corner, was polished and looked almost new. The old Kimball spinet still stood against the wall, and the sheet music on its stand was a Mozart prelude I had once played. Atop the piano in a silver frame was a black-and-white picture of my mother taken at the peak of her beauty, when she was about thirty-two years old, her soft eyes luminous even though the print had dimmed and browned with the years. Next to it, in a smaller frame, was my high school graduation picture, which surprised and touched me. I even recognized the ashtrays, brimming as they were with Camel butts. I don't think Jimmy had moved a piece of furniture or bought anything new for the place since I'd left it.

"You look good, kiddo," my father said. He touched his own hair. "You got gray."

"How've you been, Jimmy?"

He flapped his arms out from his sides and then let them slap against his flanks. "You know," he said. "I'm here. At my age what more can I ask for? I still miss your mother every day of my life. But I do my best." He threw his shoulders back for a moment. "I'm a precinct captain now. You know, press the flesh, get the vote out." The ash on his Camel was dangerously long, and he flicked it off into an already full ashtray. "You want coffee or something?"

"Don't go to any trouble."

"It's made," he said, walking into the kitchen. "I drink it all day long." I recalled, when he said it. Jimmy carrying a cup of coffee around the house was an enduring image. He came out with a Cubs mug for me; I noticed his hands shook a little. "Black, right? See, I remembered."

I was still standing in the middle of the room as if I were afraid to touch anything, but he motioned me into one of the dining room chairs and took another one himself.

"So. The old hometown pretty much the way you left it? Or lots of changes?"

"Some things have changed, some not," I said. The coffee was strong and bitter from all day on the warmer, and a few grounds floated in it.

"Well, that's the thing, kiddo. Life goes on, you gotta go with it or you wind up eating dust watching the ass-end of the parade. How 'bout you? You a married man now?"

"No. I adopted a son, but I never married."

"I have a grandson!" he said. "You got pictures?"

"Sure," I said. I took Marvel's school picture from my wallet and handed it to him. This was going to be good. I knew he wasn't expecting a black grandson.

He looked at the photo without changing expression and then handed it back to me. "Good-lookin' boy," he said. I was suddenly ashamed of myself. I'd hoped to shock him. Now I was glad I hadn't. "He lives with you?"

I nodded. "We have a little house near the ocean."

"Good," he said. "Good. So you're doing well?"

"I've got my own business. I'm a private investigator."

That raised his eyebrows. "I thought you was an actor. When did all this happen?"

"A long time ago," I said. "I still act."

"Yeah, I saw you in something a few months ago. Can't remember what it was."

"Probably a commercial."

"That was it. Soup. You were eating soup." He ran his hand over his whiskers, and the raspy sound carried clear across the table. He made a noise that might have been clearing a frog from his throat, or something else. "Well," he said, "I don't imagine you came all the way to Chicago just to see me."

"I came for a funeral."

"In that case I'm glad it wasn't to see me." He smiled, but not broadly. After seventy, jokes about dying are pretty dicey. "Anyone I know?"

"I think so. Gavin Cassidy."

He sipped at his coffee, his hands shaking even more, and then he put the mug down carefully and warmed his hands on it. "Ah, shit," he breathed. He pushed himself away from the table and went over to the piano, where he picked up the photo of my mother and stood looking at it, his eyes going soft and damp. He studied it as if to memorize it.

"You and me haven't been what you call close all these years," he said after a time, putting down the picture. "It

130

wouldn't've been my choice, but it's the way you wanted it, and I respected that, because I guess I had it coming. But you're the only family I got. And I'm your father. Like it or not, there's just one to a customer, and I'm yours. I don't want to fight with you now."

"I didn't come here to fight," I said, going over to him. "But I would like to know about Cassidy."

"He was your friend, not mine."

"I know, but I asked someone about him, and they told me to talk to you."

"You wouldn't have come here otherwise, would you?" His naked hurt was like a hot knife in my throat.

"I don't know. Probably not," I admitted.

He shoved his hands deep into the pockets of his baggy pants and hunched his shoulders. "Well, you're forthcoming, anyway. You got that from your mother." His eyes went to the photo again. "She always spoke her mind, never mind who liked it or didn't. It's a good quality. You got most of your good qualities from her. God knows I didn't pass many on to you." He squinted up at me. "You favor her, too. Green eyes and that stubborn jaw. . . ."

He looked for a moment as if he would throw his arms around my neck. The impulse was there, I could see, and for a moment it threw me into a panic, because I had no idea how I'd react if he did. Instead he just hunched over some more, looking even older and smaller. "Where'd we go wrong, kiddo?" he said. "You and me."

"You went to prison and mom died."

He nodded sadly. "You know, I wish you'd waited for me to come back before you left. We could've talked."

"We had nothing to talk about."

"There's always something to talk about."

"I couldn't. I had to get out of here."

"You blame me," he said, not a question. "For her. You're a very judging man of other people. You always were like that, even when you were a kid. Look, I did some wrong things, I

131

admit that. I did wrong things in the eyes of the law and I paid for it. But I always made a living here, to send you downstate to school and to provide for my family."

He looked around, buffeted by his own ghosts. "The place isn't much now, but it wasn't bad growing up here, was it? I did the best I could." He began wandering around the room, touching things with a kind of reverence, as if he were in some sort of ancient shrine, not his own apartment. "When I come back from the joint and your mother was gone, I couldn't leave here. It was like if I stayed, there was always a part of her I could keep with me."

He stopped and looked straight at me. Jimmy Saxon was not an imposing man, had never been the kind of father that could freeze me with a warning look. But there was something about the way he was staring at me now that sent cold crawly things scurrying down my back. "You didn't have those feelings, family feelings. At least not where I was concerned. You left town because you blamed me, because you were ashamed of me. And now you show up out of nowhere and you blame me for your friend Cassidy, too."

"I don't even know what happened with you and Cassidy," I said. "I didn't know you were even aware of his existence until now."

"Oh, I was aware," he said. "I remembered him from your acting days. That's why I hated to do what I did."

"What *did* you do?"

He walked across the room a few times, his hands in his pockets, not really pacing, but as if he had somewhere to go and was barely going to make it on time. Finally he wheeled around to stare at me. "All right," he said, and wagged a cautionary finger at me. "I don't tell you because I owe you anything, but because I want to, you understand? I'm your father, and there's no owing."

I nodded.

"A few months ago. There was a rhubarb going on in City Hall—there always is, isn't there?—about a zoning ordinance.

132

The boys were at work, y'know, the back-room boys, making deals and trading favors. Business as usual; that's how it's done. Well, apparently your friend heard—wrongly, I might add—that some money had changed hands under the table. I don't know where he heard it, but that was his impression. So he come to me. I don't know why, maybe he knew I'd talk to him, on account of you and him being friends, or maybe because he remembered my . . . trouble all those years ago. He said he knew what was going on and that he'd keep quiet if we made it worth his while."

"Cassidy would never do that," I said.

"Ah, you don't know! You haven't been around here for so many years, you don't even know the lake is east anymore. The man was having his own difficulties, you could see it on his face. Hey, it happens to people. With him I suppose it was the drink, with others it's gambling or women or those drugs. Whatever it was, he saw a chance for some easy money and took it. A lots of guys would've. Christ knows I understand that, better than anybody. I know what it's like when you're in a corner."

"And what happened?"

He sat down and took some more coffee. "I learned my lesson a long time ago, kiddo. That's what prison's for, you know, to give a fellow time to reflect on how he can change things for the better. You do a lot of reflecting living in a cage. So when he come and put the arm on me, I did what a good citizen is s'posed to. I went right to Martin Givney and told him about it. I wasn't going to be part of anything like that, you know, not with my record."

I sat opposite him, toying with my coffee mug.

"Now, number one," he said, "you got to bear in mind no one had done anything wrong here, there was no wrongdoing. It was legitimate political business—that's how they run the city—and Cassidy was way out of bounds. And number two, Mr. Givney don't take well to threats. He hasn't run this ward for thirty-five years by turning tail when somebody threatens him. So he got right on the phone to the district commander there. They called Cassidy in on the carpet and yanked his badge."

"That's it? No hearing, no chance to defend himself?"

"They'd scheduled a hearing for next month," he said. "I don't s'pose it matters much now."

"It does to me."

He put his hands flat on the table. I noticed the liver spots on their backs. "Leave it alone," he said. "The man's dead, and so is the issue." His fingers curled into fists. "I haven't seen you since you were a kid, for chrissakes, what do you want to fight with me for? All these years, now you want to get even?"

"It's not getting even."

"That's how it looks from here."

"For what it's worth, whatever I felt about you years ago, it's over with. I'm not here to lay a guilt trip. It has nothing to do with you."

"Then drop it," he said. "For my sake. For your mother's memory."

I pushed the coffee mug away from me. "That's fighting dirty."

His mouth turned down at the corners, and he chewed on the inside of his cheek. "I don't know how to reach you. I never did, did I?"

"You never tried," I said, hating that it came out mean.

He waved a hand in front of his face, erasing the blackboard of his life. "I never figured to see you again, kiddo. I'd written you off. Not in my heart, mind you, because I see you on TV and I bust my buttons with pride. But I never figured you and me would ever . . ." His voice quivered, from age and emotion, and his eyes were red-rimmed as he struggled with his self-control. "Look, let's us have dinner, just the two of us. Maybe take in a ball game or something. It'll be like old times."

"Jimmy," I said sadly, feeling like the lowest worm ever to crawl out from beneath a rock, "when did you and I ever go to a ball game?"

15

Saint Aloysius hadn't changed a bit—the church, that is, not the saint himself. One of those cathedrals built to accommodate the great wave of European immigration in the early part of the century, its huge dark stones had borne the years well. I stood across the street remembering the masses, the liturgies, the candles, and the way the incense made my eyes smart and my nose tickle, and how my mother would reach over and give my thigh a savage pinch to stop my youthful wiggling on the hard pew. This was my home parish, half Italian and half Irish, even though the priests were all sons of the Ould Sod—the dour Father O'Gara, scourge of the confessional, and Father Kaveny of the booming bass voice and the breath reeking of spirits that could knock you over from across the room.

Behind the church was the school where I had quaked in terror of Sister Concepta and Sister Michael, who taught mathematics and science, respectively, though little of their efforts had managed to sink into my thick German-Irish skull, despite their liberal utilization of flexible steel rulers. Sister Bernadette, an apple-cheeked young woman whose family lived in the neighborhood, had been in charge of my literary education, and it was a matter of pride with the parish boys to see which of us could get her to giggle and blush. I wondered if she still might be there, older and wearier but still with the twinkling eyes. The others must be with their Lord, or else they were a hundred years old.

I strolled across the street, my heart a timpani in my chest, and around the side of the sanctuary to the small neighborhood cemetery with its wrought iron fence. I went through the gate, noting that it needed oiling. The Ryan family plot was easy to spot, with its tall stone angel standing sentry over the smaller headstones, and I moved toward it as if in a dream.

Kathleen Ryan Saxon
1921–1973

Being a firm believer that gone is gone and visits to a cemetery are unappreciated by the departed and a waste of time for the living, I hadn't been to the grave since the day of its initial occupation, so this was my first look at the small marble headstone. I remembered the ones next to it, those of John Francis Ryan and Moira Doyle Ryan, my grandparents. Moira died before I was born, and my grandfather was a foggy memory, a crusty pixie with hard and callused hands and a funny little cowlick, who had evicted me from my bedroom and onto the sofa for eight months when I was about five while he took his time dying in stages.

But I remembered my mother with warmth and sorrow, her thick mane tied up in a cloth as she did her daily cleaning, then loosened and brushed before my father came home for dinner. Quick to anger, she was possessed of a stern gentleness, and sometimes the laughter she'd try to hide behind her hand would burst forth as suddenly as a summer rain, a kind of vacuum-cleaner laugh that would shake her frail shoulders and fill her green eyes with happy tears. She had started to gray early, and she used to scold me that she'd earned every gray hair, mostly from trying to keep up with me. Later, when my own hair began silvering at a young age I viewed it as some sort of cosmic payback.

The Ryan plot, like most others in the small graveyard, was well tended, beginning to green for the summer. I leaned over and plucked a stray weed from the mound that sheltered my mother. I rolled it around in my hand, feeling the loss as I hadn't in many years, letting it emerge from where I'd stuffed it, tasting it as bitter as rust. Coming here was a different kind of masochism from visiting Jimmy, but the pain was as keen and deep.

Someone was coming down the path that ran alongside the fence: a priest, in his early fifties, short and swarthy and obviously of Mediterranean extraction, reading from his missal as he walked. He sensed my presence and made eye contact, his smile professionally priestly.

"Hello, Father."

"Afternoon," he answered. "I don't think I've seen you here before."

"I went to school here. I moved away. Haven't been back for a long time."

"Not much has changed," he said. "I'm Father Scalisi."

I told him my name and walked over to shake hands through the vertical bars of the fence. "This was Father Kaveny's parish when I was a kid."

"Father passed on about eleven years ago, and Father O'Gara the year after that. I've been here ever since."

Kaveny's death didn't surprise me, but it hurt me nonetheless. He'd been the only one that made parochial school tolerable, because his theology had a decidedly practical bent. It had been his considered opinion, for instance, that the Cubs suffered a championship drought of such mammoth proportions because they were all a bunch of Protestants. A priest with a mind-set like that could almost make being Catholic fun.

"And what about Sister Bernadette?"

He frowned with the effort of remembering. "I think Sister went to Africa many years ago to aid the hungry and unfortunate. Angola or some such place, as I recall. I can look it up if you wish."

137

That was like Sister Bernadette. Even when she had been Mary Frances Healy, eldest of a tribe of eight who lived in a two-bedroom flat on Winona Avenue, she had manifested the kindness and compassion that had eventually led her to the veil. She had become the bride of Christ, but what a wonderful secular wife and mother she would have made, a lovely and caring human being who made everyone she touched feel good about themselves. I hoped she was well, that death and famine and civil war swirling about her mission hadn't dimmed her laughter, or worse.

"That's all right, Father."

Father Scalisi glanced at the headstones. "Did you know the Ryan family?"

I pointed out the graves. "I *am* the Ryan family, what's left of it."

He clucked his tongue in sympathy. "Mr. Saxon—Jimmy, I believe it is—comes here often to visit his wife. Every two weeks or so. And to pray."

I tried not to show my surprise at that particular new wrinkle. Jimmy Saxon's Irishness had always stopped a good bit short of the church door.

"Is there anything I can do to help you?" he asked.

Once he might have helped me, when I was buying what he was selling, when time and cynicism and a dollop of common sense hadn't knocked the Trinity for a loop in my soul. Now it was too late. I just shook my head.

"Did you want someone to hear your confession?"

I hadn't been to confession since high school, except once in Tijuana when I used a confessional as a hiding place, so it didn't count. Possibly if Father Kaveny were still alive he could have talked me into it—or frightened me into thinking that if I didn't, the Cubs would *never* win again—but not Father Scalisi. I smiled weakly. "I don't think so."

"I understand, my son." He didn't, of course. He was programmed not to understand lapses in faith, but he had to say it anyway. "Well, God is here for you if you want Him. Or even

138

if you don't," he couldn't resist adding. He looked up at the sky, dark with approaching dusk, and waved at the cemetery in general. "It's a fine evening. Spring is finally here, I think. Stay as long as you like."

He resumed his walk, and I turned back to my mother's grave. I needed answers, all sorts of them, and for a moment I'd thought I might find some here. But there was only a neat mound of earth and a small white marble stone.

The sun was almost gone when I drove up to the front of Dave and Diane Kubo's house on the Northwest Side a few blocks from where the North Branch of the Chicago River makes one of its gentle jogs. Their house was an impressive brick three-story with turrets and bays and mullions and a gabled roof, built around 1900 and remodeled several times since, its age making it a landmark and a white elephant simultaneously.

I had called Diane and asked if I could come out for a visit, and though she'd volunteered to cook a dinner, I declined, grabbing a sandwich on my way. Ceremonies and celebrations of the good old days were not what I was after right then. I wanted to be with people I cared about; I needed a friend to drink with. If I went back to my hotel I knew I'd sit alone in the bar downstairs all evening, hunched over a Scotch and a pack of cigarettes, ignoring the blare of the TV and the happy babble of my fellow customers, pointlessly wrestling my own demons and drinking the night.

Dave came to the door, a glass already in his hand. "Come on in," he said, "it's good to see you." He led me through the vestibule, where a sweeping staircase disappeared into the upper reaches of the big house, and into a sitting room that fronted the street. The ceilings were high and beamed, and one entire wall was a built-in bookcase with a stone fireplace in the middle. To the left of the fireplace were what must have been Diane's books—collections of plays, books on the theater and the arts, popular fiction, and matched bound sets of Dostoyevski and Tolstoy. The heavier tomes were on the other side of the hearth, Shirer's books on World War II, real estate manuals, books on architecture, and state and municipal codes, all of which, I'm sure, reflected Dave's reading habits.

In one corner were twenty or so books that looked dog-eared and well thumbed—a one-volume Shakespeare with the Atwater Kent illustrations that made Lear look like those pictures of the North Wind you find in third-grade readers; a paperback *Cyrano de Bergerac* without its front cover and nearly falling apart; a *Best Plays* anthology without a dust jacket. A few Spiral notebooks, a tattered Stanislavski's *An Actor Prepares,* a not quite so battered hardback of Charlton Heston's *An Actor's Life.*

"Those were Gavin's," Diane said when she saw me looking at them. "Hello, love." She was curled up in a big leather chair and lifted her face for me to kiss, putting her hand on the back of my neck as I bent down to her. "Marian gave them to me. It was about all he owned, except his clothes. She thought I could use the books on theater more than she could. It was very sweet of her, wasn't it?"

Dave gestured around the handsome, cozy room, the *seigneur* showing off his holdings. "This is your first visit here, isn't it? Sure, we didn't buy this until long after you'd left. What do you think?"

"Great house," I said sincerely.

He rolled his eyes. "It's a big hole we throw money into. Maybe before we die we'll get it half finished. Do you want the grand tour now, or after you've had a drink?"

"I don't want *anything* until I've had a drink."

He went to an antique sideboard and poured a Glenlivet over ice. "This is right, isn't it?"

I nodded, and took a swallow before I sat down on the enormous velvet sofa. The Scotch hit bottom and spread out, desensitizing naked nerve endings. If I always needed a drink as badly as I needed that one, I'd hurry to the nearest AA meeting.

140

"What have you been doing?" Diane asked. "Seeing all the old sights?"

"Sort of," I said. "I saw my father."

Surprise flickered across her face and then away, like a soft moan in a dark bedroom at four A.M. "I didn't think you would. That must have been tough."

I nodded. The velvet was soft under my outflung arm, textured and gently used, like the house itself. There was no fire on the hearth but it felt as though there were. The dark woods and soft carpets had absorbed the warmth of the afternoon sun and were now giving them back to the room.

"We wanted to take you out to dinner," Dave said. "How long are you going to be in town?"

"I don't know yet. I have a few things to check out. About Gavin."

"Gavin?"

Without mentioning Marian's name, I told them my theory about Gavin's opposition to drugs and how I didn't think it likely he could have died from an overdose.

Diane put her hand to her face, which was white and drawn. "What are you saying?"

"That something is very wrong."

She gave a breathless little laugh that held no amusement. "That's crazy."

Dave said, "That's a pretty serious allegation."

"You're damn right it is."

"Who'd want to do that to Gavin?" Diane said.

"A lot of people, it seems. It's a shock to me, because I've been two thousand miles away, but Gavin wasn't going to win any popularity contests around here. You said yourself that you didn't have much to do with him."

"I resented what he did to Beth," she said. "And to a lot of others. But that was nothing new." She turned her hands palms up in front of her, as though balancing a tray. "People grow away from each other over twenty years. That's just . . . change."

141

"Gavin couldn't have changed that much."

Dave sat down on the other end of the sofa, tinkling his ice. "Don't take this wrong, I'm just asking, but how do you figure it's your business? It's officially been ruled an accident."

I shrugged. "Call it intellectual curiosity."

Diane said, "Well, what if it is true? If someone deliberately tried to . . ." She shook her head, unable to say it. "Aren't you afraid you might get hurt?"

"I'm afraid of that every time I drive the San Diego Freeway," I said. "But I do it anyway. You can't live your life worrying that a piano's going to fall on you."

"You can if you're always standing under pianos."

"That's the trick," I said. "Knowing where to stand. You've obviously never heard the story of the merchant of Bagdad."

Dave frowned. "The what?"

I settled back against the cushions, the alcohol making my head buzz. "A wealthy merchant of Baghdad sent his servant to the marketplace one morning. The servant came back shaken and terrified. 'Master,' said the servant, 'I saw Death in the bazaar and he raised his hand to me. I must run to Samarra and hide from him in the home of my cousin.' "

"Lord!" Diane said, "do we have to listen to this?"

"It's short," I assured her. "So the merchant gave the servant a bag of silver and sent him off to Samarra. And then he went down to the bazaar himself and sought Death face to face. When he found him he said, 'Why did you threaten my servant?' And Death said, 'I raised my hand in surprise at seeing him in Baghdad this morning when I had an appointment with him tonight in Samarra.' "

Dave shivered, taking a long swallow of his drink. Diane said, "Wasn't that the theme of a John O'Hara novel?"

"It was," I said. "The point is, you can't run away from things in fear, because your worst nightmare will find you wherever you go. Gavin told me that once."

"Are you a fatalist?" Dave said.

"No, just the opposite. I think you have to grab hold of your life and take control of it. Otherwise you're at the mercy of others."

"I'm not sure I'm following you," Diane said.

"Gavin chose to perceive himself as a victim. His life didn't work out the way he wanted, so he drank, cursing the gods for his bad fortune. He ran to hide from his problems in Samarra. I won't. I can't."

Diane shook her head. "When you left here, wasn't that running away? Your own chartered flight to Samarra?"

I polished off my drink. "Sure. I was just a kid. Now, Samarra is permanently off my itinerary."

Dave took my glass, and then Diane led me through the beautiful old house. Except for the den, the kitchen, the entryway, and the guest bathroom downstairs and one bedroom and bath upstairs, the place was pretty much unfinished. I understood what Dave meant about throwing money into it. Old houses nourish the soul, but remodeling them can become a lifetime project.

"It'll be done soon," Diane said. "K and K—our company— is into a development that's going to be very profitable as soon as it all comes together. It's been a long haul, but . . ." She lowered her voice, even though Dave was downstairs. "Dave made some bad investments. We hung on by our fingernails for a while. But then he got lucky." She shook her head. "No, not lucky. He got smart, and he got off his behind and took control of his own fate. People do that, you know—that Samarra business is a bunch of baloney."

We made our way down the uncarpeted steps. A white powdery substance from the unfinished drywall rubbed off on my coat sleeve, and I brushed at it ineffectually. "But sometimes other people grab control of your fate and you can't do much about it."

She stopped a few steps below me and turned to look back up at me. "You mean Gavin?"

"Somebody slips you a lethal mickey, it's pretty hard to take control."

We went across the entryway to the den, where Dave was waiting with fresh drinks. "I can't believe anyone wanted to kill Gavin Cassidy," Diane said. "But if they did, why is it your problem?"

"Because he was my friend," I said. "Wouldn't you like to think I'd do the same if it were you?"

16

I'm not completely objective about Lincoln Park West. It's possible that, except for the park itself and the Chicago Academy of Sciences, Lincoln Park West is not what it used to be. Or perhaps it never was; I view it through sweetened memory. One night in particular has resonated over time—a chilly October when two silly postadolescents decided to walk home from a movie, the mist soaking their clothes, stopping to kiss beneath every fog-shrouded streetlamp and finally, swept away by the drumming of their own hormones, moving against the dark outer wall of a public toilet and rearranging whatever clothing impeded their urgent upright act of love.

Today the hotels that line the street are sad, dusty reminders of what once was and should still be a desirable residential address overlooking a park. No longer way stations for the transient, now they are the end of the line, convalescent homes for the lost, where people like Gavin Cassidy huddle to hide from the forces that threaten them, drinking, doing drugs, hooking and hustling, giving up the fight, and watching the world pass languidly by on the street below, to wind up poached in their own urine on the tattered carpeting, OD'd on their poison of choice.

I left my car in a public lot in the park and walked about a block and a half to the hotel in which Cassidy had lived and died. It was named after a local Indian tribe which, thus honored, was then ignored, because there is nothing remotely Native American in the hotel. The vintage art déco metal smoking stands next to the cracked vinyl couches and easy chairs in the lobby, not purchased new from some trendy whatnot shop but survivors from the original decorating scheme, are about as historical as the place gets. A young man at the desk stood sentry in front of a bank of mailboxes without any mail in them; the residents didn't get many letters from home. The clerk was obviously a college student working part time, with a blue corduroy jacket that had fake suede patches on the elbows, a frayed plaid shirt, and a knit tie. His brow was furrowed above his glasses, a philosophy major, possibly, postulating on the meaning of man's existence. I would bet he took himself, and the world, very seriously. It's one of the failings of the young.

I introduced myself and flashed my PI license at him and asked what had been done with Gavin Cassidy's personal effects.

"Nothing yet, sir. The rent was paid up on his apartment until the end of the month, and legally we can't remove his belongings until then."

"You mean they're still up there?"

He nodded in the affirmative. "Except a few books. His . . . friend took some books out. Not many."

Those were the books Marian had given Diane, I was sure. I said, "I wonder if it would be possible for me to go up there and have a quick look around."

"I couldn't let you do that, sir," he said. "It's against the rules."

"I promise I won't steal anything."

"It's out of the question." People with no power in life who are given a tiny taste are the most pompously authoritarian of all.

I took two twenty-dollar bills from my pocket, put them down on the desk in front of him, and smoothed the wrinkles out of Andrew Jackson's face.

"I was a friend of Officer Cassidy's," I said. "It would mean a lot to me."

He looked at them over the rims of his glasses with utter contempt. "You think you can buy everything?"

"I don't mean to insult you," I said.

"Then put your money away." He was unlike any flophouse desk clerk I'd ever met. Where were Percy Helton and Elisha Cook, Jr., when you needed them?

"I really am an old friend. I'd hate to see anything of value get sold off to the junkman or stuffed in a warehouse somewhere. You can understand that. One man's trash is another man's treasure."

He pursed his lips in a thoughtful air kiss. "It'd mean my job."

"I won't tell anybody."

He cogitated some more. Rules clashed with ethics, both clashed with curiosity. Curiosity won, a unanimous decision. "I'll have to go up with you."

"Okay."

He flipped up a piece of the countertop, opened a little gate, and came out from behind the desk, locking the gate with one of about thirty keys on a long chain hooked to his belt loop and ending up in his pocket. That's something else you don't see anymore, key chains. The boy was very young to be a walking anachronism.

We got into a small elevator with a sliding metal safety gate, and up we went with a groaning of gears, the car jerking and shaking as though a herniated Atlas was sitting on the roof raising it hand over hand. At the third floor the young clerk opened the gate and the solid door and led me down a hall

146

redolent with the odors of a residential hotel that's been around too long. They weren't the gagging smells of a slum where food rots in the halls and transients pee in the stairwells; it seemed as if the hotel residents here were just too tired and used up to vacuum or take out the trash or remember to flush the john.

Gavin's digs were at the end of the hall, the windows fronting onto Lincoln Park West. On the worn carpeting in the hallway in front of the door was a white powdery film someone had tracked there days before. The clerk opened up with a passkey. "Mr. Cassidy's apartment," he said, but it was really a single with a small kitchenette built into one wall and a Murphy bed built into the other, and a bathroom no bigger than one you'd find in the sleeping compartment of a cross-country train. There was no extra space for sit-down dinners, for a bunch of guys to have beer and watch a ball game, or a playful shower with a friend.

The desk clerk, who had told me on the trip up in the elevator that his name was Eugene—possibly because he didn't believe the elevator would ever make it to the top and if we were to die together he wanted us to be better acquainted— stood with his back against the door, eyeing me suspiciously as I poked around in the one closet and in the space where the bed was stored upright during the day.

I didn't know what I was looking for, but I grew more glum by the minute. The detritus of other people's lives is always a downer. In the closet were two well-worn but pressed blue uniforms, and two pairs of spit-shined black shoes. On the top shelf were two uniform caps with their checkered bands, bills also shined and gleaming. Gavin's civilian clothes were not so well cared for. He had one suit in a kind of glossy black material, several tweed sports jackets and one worn camel's hair, an overcoat, a raincoat, and a zippered leather bomber jacket, and various sneakers, work boots, and a pair of dress shoes in a jumble on the floor. Toward the back was a pair of black galoshes, covered with a whitish film from the salts the city's snow-clearance crews dump on the streets each winter.

147

On three shelves built into the wide, flat alcove where the bed folded into the wall were stacks of theater programs, some dating back more than twenty-five years. More than a few were from the North State Street Theatre Guild, and some had my name in them as well as Gavin's, and I resisted the temptation to take them all over to the sagging easy chair near the window and read them carefully, playing whatever-happened-to? with all those would-be actors whose names I had forgotten. There were also two scrapbooks full of clippings, reviews, and stagey theatrical photographs. Gavin as Macbeth, as Petruchio, as a paunchy Stanley Kowalski, and some "head shots," not the kind that professionals use but moody, atmospheric poses that made him look by turns satanic, sexy, and mysterious. Not one of them would have gotten him an acting job out in Los Angeles. Probably not anywhere else, either.

Standing against the wall in a corner of the bed alcove was a dueling saber in an old-fashioned leather scabbard. I took it partway out and ran my thumb along the edge of the blade. It was dull, had never been sharp. A stage prop Gavin might have used once. He was a dreadful fencer, I recalled, but had never bothered taking a lesson.

In a dresser between the two windows, next to the steam radiator that must have clanked out symphonies on cold nights, I found Gavin's shirts, mostly blue; socks, all black; and underwear, white Ts and boxers; enough of each for about a week and no longer. A Cubs shirt like the one I'd bought for Marvel, a gray warm-up jacket wadded into an untidy ball, a green Police Athletic League T-shirt with the sizing still in it, making it feel brand new. The clothes were anonymous, might have belonged to any old bachelor with no place to go. Gavin, who had roared through Shakespearean heroes like a road-company Olivier, had led a generic, plain-wrap private life.

"Any treasures?" Eugene said from the door.

"I'm not finished," I said. I went into the bathroom. The medicine cabinet yielded an old-fashioned shaving mug and brush, a jar of shaving soap, and a razor that lifted your whisk-

148

ers with one blade and sliced them off with the other, if the TV commercials were to be believed. Two toothbrushes, both blue, and a can of tooth powder, quaint and touchingly old-fashioned. There was also a plastic bottle of Advil which I opened, spilling the contents out into my palm. The tablets were what they were supposed to be. No amphetamines. No poison. Just Advil.

Beneath the sink was a can of cleanser and a dirty sponge. A bottle of green mouthwash. An aerosol can of bug spray. A dried-up piece of soap. A chamois rag stiff with black shoe polish, the round flat can of polish itself, almost all gone, bespeaking a good cop who always wanted his shoes looking sharp.

I went back into the main room, melancholy sweeping over me like a shadow across the sun. A fifty-year-old man should have more to leave behind, possessions and toys and personal effects to mark his passage through life. Except for the photos and programs, Gavin Cassidy could have been just any sad old derelict who'd checked out leaving no spoor. Eugene hadn't deserted his post by the door, but he was now engrossed in removing part of a split fingernail with his teeth and barely looked up when I came out of the bathroom.

I went to the kitchen area. A two-burner stove with an oven big enough for a Cornish game hen and not much more. Inside the refrigerator were perhaps thirty cans of beer. No surprise there. The overhead cupboards yielded more beer, a few mismatched dishes and glasses, and from Hard Knox College, Gavin's old pewter beer mug, which he'd wave about as he declaimed "Let the games begin!" when an attractive and as yet unknown woman walked through the door. I took the tankard from the shelf, feeling its weight and texture in my hands, and something very like pity pressed down on my chest. It was the only truly personal item in the entire apartment. No clutter, no warmth. Just grime on the windows and more of the whitish dust on the carpet.

On the dresser was a seventeen-inch portable TV set, some

law enforcement pamphlets, the television listings for the previous week from the *Sun-Times,* and a tiny address book, which I opened and thumbed. Gavin had handwriting like a nine-year-old's, tiny and scratchy, going both above and below the lines. The entries were mostly familiar to me: the Nemeroffs, Beth, Kendra, LSQ, Marian, Al Patinkin, even though most of the names weren't spelled correctly, e.g., "Nemarrof." And Ben was his best friend. Gavin was a notoriously bad speller, and often the traffic citations he wrote while on duty had been springboards to merriment around the courthouse. I shuddered at what he might have done with *perpetrator.* I looked on the S page; my name and number weren't there, my own fault more than Cassidy's. I pocketed the address book, glancing up at Eugene in case he had any complaints about it, but he was still gnawing on his finger, now working on some dead skin surrounding the nail, and hadn't noticed.

"You about done?" he said.

"About." I picked up the TV magazine.

"Doesn't it give you a funny feeling, going through a dead man's things?"

The smarmy way he said it annoyed me. "Why do you want to know? You writing a book?"

"As a matter of fact, I am," he said. Just what I needed—someone taking notes.

On the front of the magazine, scribbled over the face of Roseanne Barr, were two phone numbers, one written in ballpoint pen and the other with a red felt-tip. I leafed through the magazine quickly, smiling at Gavin's circling of a late night showing of the José Ferrer version of *Cyrano de Bergerac;* I never knew why he identified with that role so strongly, except perhaps that Cyrano was noble and brave and often misunderstood, and Gavin probably saw himself that way too.

"My novel is going to be about a young man, alienated from the mainstream, who's trying to find some rationale for his existence in an urban environment that is both hostile and materialistic," Eugene said.

150

"Sounds good." I opened the TV listings. In the margin of the program log for Thursday, one week earlier, the day before Gavin's body had been found, he'd written:

STORKO!!!!

He had gone over the letters several times with his ballpoint pen until they stood out bold and dark, and he'd put a box around them, too. I had no idea who Storko was. Maybe a long-legged, pointy-beaked Japanese movie monster. In any event, it seemed pretty important to Gavin.

"It's kind of a twentieth-century *Candide,*" Eugene told me.

"What is?"

"My book."

"Oh." I folded the magazine into my jacket pocket. "How's it going to end?"

Eugene smiled mysteriously. "I don't know yet."

I walked past him and out the door into the hallway, giving the apartment one more quick look. "Make sure you put a lot of sex in it."

He followed me out. "Are you serious?"

"Nobody will read it if there's no sex. Come up with something kinky, like blond identical-twin bisexual Norwegian bondage freaks."

He locked the door and walked with me to the elevator. "That's sick," he said.

When I got back to my hotel I dragged the Chicago telephone directory out of the desk drawer and looked up Storko. I don't know what I was expecting to find—Irving Storko, Louis Storko, Dolores Storko? There was no listing for anyone by that name. I looked further to see if there was a business called Storko, a preschool or a diaper service. But no luck.

I took the TV magazine from my pocket and looked at the two phone numbers. Neither rang a bell with me, but there was no reason why they should. I dialed the one written in red felt pen. After four rings a connection was made, and an answering machine clicked on.

The first thing I heard was a big band, probably Les Elgart or his brother Larry, someone of that ilk, playing the song "Chicago." Then the music faded down to just background, and a woman's voice, rather pleasant and well-modulated but with the flat, nasal *a* of the Midwest, informed me, "You've reached the Mayo residence. Sorry, but Ray and Ginny can't come to the phone right now. You know how it works—wait for the sound of the beep, leave a brief message, and we'll call you back soon as we can. Thanks." The last word was said almost coquettishly and came out sounding like "thinks."

There was about five seconds of audio presence and then a high tone. I hung up, mainly because I had nothing to say to Ray or Ginny. Gavin had evidently called Captain Mayo some time the week before he died. I wondered if he'd reached him or his wife, or, like me, gotten the machine.

The other number, written across Roseanne Barr's forehead, as opposed to Mayo's, which sprawled across her cheek, was in the same color ballpoint as the *Storko* notation on the Thursday program log. I didn't know if that was significant or not, but I decided to find out. I dialed the number and waited.

"D and B Novelties," a young female voice said after the third ring. Well, now I had a name, anyway, but it didn't do me much good. I'd never heard of D&B Novelties, and now that I had them on the phone I didn't know what to do with them. I wrote down *D&B* on the pad on the nightstand.

"Does the name Gavin Cassidy mean anything to you?" I asked.

"Pardon me?" the girl said. "Is *this* Mr. Cassidy?"

"No—"

"You wanted to speak to a Mr. Cassidy?"

"No, I—"

"I'm sorry, there's no one here by that name. What number were you calling?"

I told her.

"There's no Mr. Cassidy here, sir. Are you sure you have the right number?"

"May I—speak to the boss, please?" It was the only thing I could think of that would keep me out of an Abbott and Costello routine.

"The sales manager?"

"Whoever runs the place," I said.

"He's out of the office right now." She sounded as though she might be a college freshman, but not much older. "May I tell him you called?"

"Who *is* the boss?" I said.

"That would be Mr. Nemeroff," the girl said. "Mr. Ben Nemeroff."

17

The evening was a balmy one, presaging a hot Chicago summer that would surprise no one, but the fresh feel of rain was in the air. It was a clean smell, a cool one, the kind that makes you long for the rain to come. I drove north leisurely, since I wasn't really expected anywhere. The orange sun was settling behind the smokestacks of the industrial West Side, and ahead a black Corvette ran interference for me through the last vestiges of rush hour traffic. I could see a head of long blond hair behind the wheel, and every so often the driver would reach out a languid bare arm wearing a thin gold bracelet and dispose of her cigarette ashes. I couldn't even see her face, but her arm was as erotic as hell, as compelling as any Siren song. I wanted to follow her to wherever she was going, even if I ended up foundered on a rock, to forget all about Gavin Cassidy and Jimmy Saxon and Storko. I'd invite her for a drink, maybe for dinner, and flirt and play the elaborate courting rituals of the twentieth-century male. They were tiresome, the games and gambits, but leagues ahead of what lay in store for me that evening—the Fifty-fourth Ward Democratic Organization fund-raiser I'd seen advertised on flyers in Martin Givney's office.

The restaurant they'd chosen for their event was a sprawling one-story on the North Side, near Foster and Clark, the old Swedish neighborhood that was now called Andersonville. I guess nobody told them that was the name of a particularly brutal and notorious Confederate prison.

It was the kind of landmark joint that families patronize decade after decade for Sunday night dinner. It featured dull, basic American food, turkey and chops and meat loaf with mashed potatoes and brown gravy, all right out of the Betty Crocker cookbook, and once a week an exotic special, spaghetti with meatballs and sourdough bread. Only three of the waitresses had been there less than twenty years, and most of the patrons probably knew them by name, knew the ages of their grandchildren, and could remember when their husbands were still alive.

The Fifty-fourth Ward had taken over the banquet room and ballroom at the rear of the restaurant for their fund-raising affair this evening, so as not to interfere with the regular traffic in the dining room. I didn't have a ticket, but the woman at the card table just outside the main ballroom, nearly hidden behind the dozen American flags that perched on the table in gold-painted holders, was only confused for a moment before she accepted my fifty dollars and let me in. Political fund-raising parties don't turn away people with money in their hand. A flustered-looking thirty-year-old, she was probably married to some up-

and-coming precinct captain and had been pressed into service tonight against her will. She was wearing a dark gray dress and had black stockings with a pattern that looked like something unspeakable was crawling up under her skirt.

In the main ballroom a five-piece band was playing, loudly and gamely, if not well. Their repertoire probably stopped somewhere between Dick Haymes and Rosemary Clooney; the youngest sideman was in his fifties. Since the ward is divided almost equally between the Irish, the Italians, and the Jews, the musicians alternated between "Galway Bay," "Funiculi, Funicula," and "Hava Nagila," and in true egalitarian fashion mangled all of them.

The guests grouped themselves by ethnic origin. They stood around in little clumps, florid big Irishmen with pale eyes, olive-skinned Italians in shiny suits, distinguished-looking gray-haired and gray-skinned Jews, each group casting side-long glances at the other two and politely forcing smiles when they made eye contact. Chicago has many constants, and one of them is the wariness that one ethnic group feels for another. Irishmen, for instance, think Italians are gangsters; Italians think the Irish are drunken brawlers. Neither trust the Jews, who consider the Irish and the Italians pushy immigrants. Pigeonholing people into insulting stereotypes is a way of life in Chicago, where the coexistence between ethnic groups and descendants of various European nationalities has always been one of wary tolerance rather than true melting-pot brother-hood. But in the last twenty-five years there have only been two colors to the city's politics, black and white, and no matter how the first- and second-generation residents might distrust each other, they all band together as a voting bloc against the blacks, the largest single political entity in Chicago. It's a lot easier for the Irish to work with the Poles, and the Germans with the Italians, than for any of them to get into political bed with the blacks. Chicago is one northern city that never quite got the message about the civil rights reforms of the late sixties.

Tonight the Italian husbands were relishing the occasion,

155

pressing the flesh and laughing too loudly as they exchanged cigars and showed off their clear-skinned young wives. The Irish clinked glasses, muffled their cigarette coughs, and spoke of problems in the parish, the shameful lack of attendance at early mass, and Gowan Corman's good day at Arlington Race Track the day before, hitting an exacta and a trifecta. The Jewish precinct captains stayed off in one corner and talked to each other about their businesses, their homes, and their children at the University of Chicago. All the wives seemed long-suffering in their shiny dresses and just-done-this-afternoon hairstyles, not wanting to be there and making very few bones about it. Among the younger women the blondes were a trifle too blond, too brassy, too busty, and their young husbands kept a hand on them, holding their wrists or the backs of their necks or slipping an arm around their waists, as if they didn't maintain physical contact the young wives would run away with someone from another ethnic group or, God forbid, a Republican. Everyone seemed to be the slightest bit overweight.

It's often been observed that the only difference between Democratic fund-raisers and Republican ones is that the Democrats feature a little more polyester and a little less food. The cuisine on this particular Thursday was spread out over two long sets of picnic tables, one at each end of the room and both laid out with identical items in metal warmers. Everything in the containers was some shade of brown. There were deep-fried cheese balls, deep-fried zucchini and potato puffs, paler egg rolls, darker meat balls, crumb-covered fish cakes. The only things that splashed color on the spread were the miniature hot dogs, of course red but floating in a viscous brown sauce, and the same flags and holders that had greeted me at the hospitality table in the foyer.

I joined the line at the service bar in the corner. Having scanned the crowd for a familiar face and not finding one, I decided I needed some fortification for whatever lay ahead. I reached the line at the same time as a pleasant-looking gray-haired woman in a shiny white dress with an orchid pinned at the shoulder.

"Go on," she said, stepping back to allow me to get ahead of her in line. "You don't have one yet; I'm on my second."

"No, no, ladies first." Maybe Beth was right and I am a dinosaur.

She smiled tolerantly. "It's okay. I'm the Alderman's wife." She gave me a motherly push ahead of her. I hadn't the heart to tell her she was sacrificing her place to someone who didn't even vote in her husband's district.

I surprised myself by ordering a bourbon and soda, but I tend to try and blend in with the natives when I'm away from home, and Chicago is still a bourbon place, especially away from downtown. And the annual political shindig is the kind of party where you either leave at seven thirty, having made the obligatory appearance and shaken hands with people you can't stand, or you hang around until the bitter end and make a complete fool of yourself.

As I moved from the bar the music stopped and the Alderman, a sixtyish man dressed in plaid golf slacks, a tan sports jacket, and a tie better suited to the boardroom at IBM, stepped up on the stage with a three-by-five card in his hand. He put on his glasses and read with difficulty. "We want to welcome Father John Keogh from Immaculate Heart," he said, his mouth too close to the microphone, distorting his words as if he were talking through a tissue-paper-covered pocket comb. "Where are you, John?" He put his hand across his brow in B-movie Indian fashion and looked out across the crowd. "There you are! Father Keogh, everyone!" Two people applauded without much enthusiasm; everyone else totally ignored him. A priest is a big deal on Sunday, or when the monsignor comes to visit. At a cocktail party he's just a guy in a funny collar.

Aldermen are elected officials, members of the city council, and dispensers of favors on the grass-roots level. They can provide the cushy patronage jobs to their people only as long as they are able to get out the vote for the mayor. In Chicago the mayor holds the ultimate power, controlling approximately ten thousand jobs. At one time, the figure was ten times that, until the federal government stepped in to ensure that garbage collectors, road crews, and maintenance workers wouldn't lose their jobs just because they belong to an out-of-power party or an out-of-favor faction.

The Alderman had been around so long, weathering the changing winds of local politics, because no matter who sat in the big office in City Hall, he was able to coerce, cajole, and convince the faithful to go to the polls to cast their ballots the "right way," even some voters who had been dead five or ten years. It was generally supposed that the Alderman knew the location of all the buried bodies on the North Side, when in fact he knew none of them. He left that kind of low-level espionage to his district leader, Martin Givney, whose creature he was.

After the band played another number, "Dear Old Donegal," with the bass player, drummer, and piano player joining in on the "Lanagan, Flanagan, Milligan, Gilligan" chorus, the Alderman once more mounted the stage to welcome Sam Matzkin, the vice president of the Edgewater chapter of the B'Nai B'Rith, and his lovely wife Esther. Once more no one paid the slightest attention, and the Alderman didn't seem to notice.

So far my fifty bucks had bought me a drink, the privilege of listening to two badly-mangled ethnic songs, and the chance to look at some inedible food. I began looking around, hoping to cut my losses.

The first familiar face I saw was my father's.

He was dressed in what was obviously his good suit, a blue shirt, and a metallic blue tie, and he had shaved since I'd seen him last. He looked more surprised to see me at the political party after twenty-four hours than he had been when I showed up on his threshold after seventeen years.

"You're just about the last fella I'd expect to see here," he said. "Didja get anything to eat?"

"No. Everything looks so good I can't decide."

"Come on," he said, "I want to introduce you to some people." He grabbed the arm of a passerby, a little fireplug of a man with a jaw like a speed bump in a parking lot. "Ed! I want you to meet my son. He's a Hollywood actor—you probably see him on TV sometimes."

"Oh, yeah," Ed said, not having the foggiest idea who I was. "Sure. Nice to see you." He pumped my hand uncertainly and left as soon as he could.

We did the whole my-son-the-actor bit for about five minutes until I lost patience. Nobody recognized me from my film work, and it was terrible to watch my father degrade himself fawning on them. I took him over to the food table. He seemed pleased that I was joining in the party, and since it cost me nothing to make him happy I filled my plate with little brown things while we talked.

"Jimmy, what do you know about Storko?"

"Who?" He looked genuinely puzzled.

"Who is Storko?"

"I don't have a clue what you're talking about," he said. "Sounds Wop to me, but I'm not familiar with him." He pointed over to the third of the room where the Italian contingent had gathered. The cigar smoke was thickest there, hanging over the groups of sharply dressed people like a gray predawn fog. "You oughta ask one of those fellas over there. They might know this Storko." He popped a greasy egg roll into his mouth and tried not to grimace while he chewed it. "The name don't even ring a bell with me."

The grease from the deep-fried food was soaking through the bottom of my paper plate. "It might have been someone Gavin Cassidy knew."

Jimmy shied away from me as if I had a disease that could be passed on by proximity. "Gah-damn it! I thought we got through all that crap yesterday." He gripped my arm, hard, something that always triggers my temper. If he hadn't been my father I would have thrown him across the room. But you don't hit your dad—that's the rule.

"Will you find a new song to sing?" he said into my ear.

"Will you just quit it? Jesus God, you get something between your teeth and you shake it to death." He lowered his voice to a hiss. "You're not making any friends around here, kiddo, I can tell you that. I don't like getting phone calls about your behavior. I didn't like it when you were twelve and I don't like it any better now." He combed his hair with his fingers and lit a cigarette, and I hated the way his hand shook when he did it. "The other thing is, you're not doing me a whole hell of a lot of good, either. How does it look when Mr. Givney has to call me up to complain about you? Now let it loose!"

His head suddenly dropped nearly onto his chest, as if someone had removed all the bones in his neck, and he looked like a tired, defeated old man. "For the love of Jesus, let it loose!" he said again.

I put the plate of brown food down on the serving table before it fell apart all over me, and touched him on the back. "Don't worry, Jimmy. You're off the hook."

I looked over my father's head and saw someone else I knew: Ben Nemeroff was talking earnestly to a knot of middle-aged men and women on the other side of the ballroom. One of the men wore a blue blazer, a red paisley tie, and a colorful knitted yarmulke that was fastened to his hair by two large bobby pins. There was a spot of blood the size of a dime on the pristine white collar of his shirt that corresponded with a nasty-looking shaving cut on his neck. The woman with him was in ice blue satin, against which her ample body strained; the red plastic frames of her glasses swooped diagonally up toward her temples and made her look like a cartoon pussycat. Ben didn't see me until I was practically on top of them.

"My God!" he said, "what are you doing here?" He was momentarily flustered but composed himself quickly, smiling his usual happy smile, and introduced me to the two couples with him. I didn't catch their names.

"Can we talk for a few minutes, Ben?"

He smiled again, excused himself from the others, and piloted me away with an arm casually thrown around my shoulders. "This isn't a terrific time for me," he said.

"I didn't know you were into politics," I said, and I'm afraid I made it sound like a dirty word.

He shrugged his shoulders. "What politics? As far as I'm concerned, they're all full of crap. Look, it's business. You see the little flags and flag holders on the tables, out in the lobby? They get them from me. Come election time, they want to send out letter openers or bookmarks or pot holders with the candidate's name on, they get them from me. They want to run a promotion, I get the prizes for them. At cost." He looked around as if he was afraid someone might hear him. "In the meantime, they see to it some nice orders come my way. Nothing huge; city offices, things like that. But it keeps my doors open."

I sighed. "Oh, Ben . . ."

He shook his finger at me. "Listen, boychik, I know what you're thinking, and you're way out of line. I'm my own man and always have been, but I'm running a business. I belong to the Chamber of Commerce, the North Side Merchants Association, and I'm recording secretary of the men's club at the temple. So I suck around a little! What's so terrible about that?" He gave me a pitying look. "You actors, you don't even know the way the rest of the world lives. We don't live in little boxes all by ourselves. We have to get out and spread the word."

"What word?"

"The word that we're here, that we're part of the community!"

The Alderman took the microphone again when the band finished "Chen a Luna" to welcome Mr. and Mrs. Anthony Scarantino from Tony's Plumbing Supply.

"Did you know your neighbors here in the community were the ones that got Gavin suspended?" I said.

All the color went out of Ben's face and he looked around again, this time in near panic, and both hands fluttered in front of his face as if they had independent lives and were mating

161

just under his chin. "What are you saying? I don't believe you're saying this to me—not here. What the hell's the matter with you? Are you crazy?

"Something was going down around here and Gavin got wind of it, and they had him bounced to shut him up. And they might have gone further than that, Ben."

A mustache of sweat beads broke out on Ben's upper lip. "You don't even live here! What do you know about it? About anything? You don't know what you're talking about."

"Who's Storko?" I said.

"Who?"

"The week Gavin died, maybe even the day he died, he called you at the office, and I think it had something to do with someone named Storko."

Ben looked intently at the carpet as though he were making an estimate, and the voice I heard behind me told me why. "Young Saxon," Martin Givney said. He had sneaked up on me, remarkably light-footed for such a heavy man. Owney Maguire, his little shadow who goes in and out with him, was at his elbow. Givney nodded rather severely at Ben. "Good evening to you, too, Mr. Nemeroff."

Ben burbled something and started to ease away. I looked at him and he froze in place. Whatever was going to happen, I wanted him to see it and hear it.

"Isn't it a marvelous affair?" Givney said, breathing heavily from his walk across the room. "It's a wonderful thing when the people in the ward can forget their differences and come together in common cause, to raise a toast to their neighbors in the true spirit of the party that's nurtured them."

"A wonderful thing," I said.

"Which makes *me* wonder just what brings you here?"

"I had a sudden yen for fried cheese balls."

"Did you? And have you had some?"

"They were yummy," I said.

"Then perhaps it'd be a good idea if you were to be on your way."

162

"And miss the rest of the party? You haven't seen my clog dance yet, Mr. Givney, to say nothing of my tarantella."

He looked at Owen Maguire. "It's a pleasure I'll have to postpone till a more propitious time."

Ben was sidestepping away, a cute little crab shuffle that was fooling nobody. He was white around the mouth and looked ready to cry.

Martin Givney's eyes bored into me from beneath his heavy brows, and they weren't twinkling or smiling anymore, and all at once I realized how he managed to so thoroughly intimidate everyone that got in his way. The avuncular cloak of affability had fallen from his shoulders to reveal the bunchback toad beneath.

"What would possess you, f'r heaven's sake, to come to a political event like this? This isn't some game, Saxon," he said, each word spit out with the precision of small-arms fire. "These people are all here having a good time, but the reason behind it is as solemn as a heart attack, and there isn't a soul here who doesn't know that. I don't care how they do out west, but we take our local politics pretty seriously. We're here to do serious work for this city and for the people of this ward and this organization, and I'll not have things disrupted by some out-of-town malcontent going around asking silly questions and bringing disrespect down upon the memory of his dear mother."

"Mr. Givney," I said, "you mention my mother one more time and I'm going to forget you're a hundred and ten years old and punch your lights out."

This exchange had all been accomplished rather quietly, heard by only a few over the strains of the band's rendition of the theme from *Exodus,* but now a small group began congregating around us as the Alderman, up in front of the band, searched the crowd in vain to introduce the missing Dockerty brothers from Wilson Avenue Auto Parts.

"You're gonna be policin' up your teeth in a minute," Owney Maguire croaked at me, and I replied, "The cheaper the crook,

163

the gaudier the patter," because I'd read it in Dashiell Hammett years ago and had always wanted to say it sometime; I'd never get a better chance.

"You're awfully far from home to be talking tough," Givney observed.

"I was born here," I said. "This is home."

"Not anymore it isn't. You don't even live in Chicago. You're a silly, moralizing man who has the collosal effrontery . . ." He paused, loving his own rhetoric, rolling it around on his tongue like a fruity cabernet—"the effrontery to think you know what's good and what isn't for everybody else in the world, and you come in here passing judgment on people who have given the better part of their lives to seeing to it that this community, this city, fulfills the needs and the hopes and the dreams of those who live here. Go away, young Saxon. Go back to your world, and leave us to ours. There's nothing for you here anymore."

I wondered if he knew when he said it how much it would hurt. The truth often does.

18

Leaving the city of your birth is akin to renouncing your citizenship in a country. You can't go back again and expect open arms and warm acceptance. A perception of betrayal exists, of defection, and I guess the hometown crowd never quite trusts you again, because you left them for what you considered greener pastures and they stayed to tough it out.

Or maybe it was just me. Maybe it was because I'd made such a holy mess of everything I touched since I'd arrived back in town that people were treating me like a cockroach and closing ranks against me.

I slunk out of the ballroom with nearly all present looking at me except the Alderman. He was busily working the room like a celebrity chef at the opening of a new Hollywood pizza emporium, patting backs, recalling names, and mumbling non sequiturs, serenely unaware that anything in his well-ordered world might be amiss. Near the door I caught my father's eye; he looked away, probably wishing with all his heart that I was someone else's kid and therefore someone else's embarrassment, that he could turn to his cronies and say, "Isn't it a dirty shame, a nice-looking boy like that?" without being tarred by the same brush. Ben Nemeroff just looked woeful and pitying, shaking his head at my rash stupidity, but there was more than a little worry in that crease between his eyebrows. I felt like the duke of Buckingham being banished from Richard's court.

There were still a few stragglers coming into the restaurant as I was leaving it, more of the polyester-and-white-sock crowd, hurrying to get to the tables before all the cheese balls were gone and before all the important people had left, to make sure they were seen and their participation and ongoing loyalty duly recorded somewhere, so when the favors came due for distribution and the list of good guys and not-so-good was updated, they'd be in the right column. I was thankful that the latecomers, at least, had not witnessed my public humiliation, although I was sure they'd hear a much enhanced version before they even got to the potato puffs. It would be the story of the year, even better than the one about Brynie Doyle and the judge, and the resultant conclusion would be that Martin Givney had vanquished a dragon and made the world safe for the Fifty-fourth Ward Democratic Organization again. Chicago political machines are a hundred years ahead of the rest of the

165

world; they have always operated on the principle that the most valuable player is the one who can make chicken salad out of chickenshit.

I just ducked like a mob kingpin running the gauntlet of reporters outside the grand jury room and aimed myself in the general direction of my car. A dull red pain pulsated on the crown of my head like the bubble light atop a police car, working its way down behind my eyes, the logical result of stress. The rain, a promise earlier in the evening, had arrived in the form of a fine, stinging mist.

I heard someone running behind me. "Saxon, wait up!"

I stopped and turned around. Owen Maguire was coming toward me, his short legs pumping. Why was I not surprised? Martin Givney never did his own muscle work. Besides, at a dead run it would have taken him four days to get this far, even when he was younger. I bent my knees just slightly and leaned forward on the balls of my feet, ready for just about anything.

"Taking a walk in the rain, Owney?"

He came up to me and stood squarely in front of me, his hands on his hips, a banty rooster about to crow. There was more than a little of the young Jimmy Cagney in him, that cocky, brash self-assurance, the slight side-to-side wigwag of the head. In Cagney it had been charming; in Owney it became a character flaw.

"We gotta talk."

"So talk," I said.

He blinked his eyes rapidly against the falling mist, looking up at me. "Okay, so you don't like me—"

"I don't even know you," I said. "But if I did, I probably wouldn't like you."

His lips were thin, white surgical scars in his face. "You're jaggin' off, Saxon, and you're gonna wind up gettin' hurt."

"Nice of you to worry about me."

"My uncle is ticked off at you already. He wants you to go back where you came from and get out of his hair."

"And he sent *you* to tell me?"

166

Flushing, he moved his shoulders around, possibly honing his Cagney imitation or maybe because the rain was getting down his collar. I know it was getting down mine. "This has nothin' to do with my uncle. This is me to you. Look, whattaya givin' us shit for? We never did anythin' to you. Your father, he works for my uncle. He don't need problems either."

"Are you threatening my father?"

"Don't be a dipstick, okay? Nobody's threatenin' anybody." Maguire held his hands out from his sides as if to show me he wasn't carrying a spear or a club. "I just wanna make you understand where we're comin' from."

Inside I could hear the band going into a spirited version of "The Irish Washerwoman," and I imagined all the Micks in the place putting down their drinks and cheering and clapping their hands in time to the music, their green polyester ties swaying with the rhythm. No one would turn loose his dignity and common sense to dance the jig, of course, because you don't want to call undue attention to yourself in front of the big boys and have them think of you as shanty. No matter how much they might laugh, after the dirty glasses are washed and the ashtrays are emptied, nobody really likes a life of the party. You just keep a low profile, do what you're asked when they ask you, and there'll always be a job for you, or a chunk of city business that somehow hasn't gone through the normal bid process, or the big boys will drink in your bar or eat in your restaurant or drop the gentle hint that you're the best dry cleaner or plumber or bookmaker in the whole ward, and your business stays open and prospers—just as long as you put the right candidates' posters in the window and show up at the right block parties and contribute to the right charities. And this above all, to thine own party be true on election day.

I reached my hand up and rubbed the back of my neck where the pain had dripped its way down like spilled battery acid. "Owney," I said, "I've known where you people were coming from since I was eight years old."

"Come on, for Christ's sake! My Uncle Marty don't want

167

trouble with you. He's got a soft spot for your whole family, y'know? He really loved your mother."

The frustrations of the week and of the evening had been piling up inside me like a shaky pyramid of canned vegetables in a supermarket, needing but one too many to topple the whole thing. Owney Maguire's invoking my mother to get me to back off was the last can. It wasn't as though I hadn't warned them inside—I'd warned his uncle, anyway, and Owney had heard me. The band of dull pain that had been tightening around my head snapped, my common sense and self-control went with it, and I swung a wild overhand right at him. I don't usually lead with my right, but anger had clouded my judgment as much as my headache had. Normally I think it out better before I slug somebody—that way I keep from getting hurt—but this was pure reflex, and not a very good one.

Owney pulled his head back out of the way about two inches, seemingly without effort, so that my knuckles barely grazed his cheek. He hadn't even moved his feet, just kind of tucked in his chin and let the blow sail by him. It was impressive ducking, but he was feeling so proud of himself about it that he wasn't expecting the follow-up left uppercut to the stomach, and it caught him solidly, surprising him.

He grunted and staggered back a few steps, but though his black eyes burned dark and hot and the veins in his neck and forehead were standing out like highways on a three-dimensional road map, he made no effort to retaliate. His normally ruddy Irish complexion turned flaming crimson, and his fists were balled so tightly at his sides that his knuckles resembled white macadamia nuts on the backs of his hands.

It was the knuckles that tipped me off—flattened and misshapen and too large, in uneven rows. I was watching his hands to see where his first punch would be coming from, and that's when I realized why he hadn't even tried to hit me back.

I dropped my hands and just looked at him. "You're a pro boxer, aren't you?"

He nodded.

168

"And if you hit me, it's assault with a deadly weapon."

"Somethin' like that."

I felt like shit. Again. It was becoming a way of life for me. It seemed like forever since I'd felt good about myself. But putting the slug on Owney Maguire was like hitting a guy whose hands were tied. Guilt stampeded me. "Why didn't you tell me? I wouldn't have swung."

He ran a hand over his stomach, wincing a little. "You hurt me, you bastard."

"I'm sorry. Really." I had an impulse to extend my hand to him, but I didn't think he'd accept it. I lit up a cigarette instead, and noticed my hand was shaking almost as badly as my father's did. Owney got his own cigarettes out, reached out, steadied my hand, and lit one from my quivering match. He didn't exactly blow the smoke in my face, but close enough to deliver his message.

"How many fights did you have, Owney?"

"Thirty-one," he said. "I was twenty-eight, two, and one draw before I quit." He pointed to a shiny pink scar over his left eye. "This was from the last one, and I figured that was enough. Where's your car?"

I looked over at it several rows away in the restaurant parking lot. The carbon lights shining through the falling mist turned everything the same ghostly color. Even us. Pale, with washed-out features and eyes of dull obsidian, spooky dumb-show mimes struggling mightily to walk into the teeth of a strong wind.

"Come on." He motioned with his head for me to follow him, and we started toward my car, two buddies out for a stroll and a smoke in the rain. "I been around a few places, and I know what's what. I don't like to see a guy be stupid for no good reason. You're rammin' a wall, goin' against my uncle in Chicago. This is pretty much his town."

"He can help me, and he won't."

He spit on the pavement. "He don't do nothin' for no one unless there's somethin' in it for him."

169

I looked over at him. "Coming out here to talk to me—what's in it for you?"

He smiled a little, like it hurt him to do it. "I'm not my uncle." He Bogarted his cigarette, all the classic movie toughies wrapped up in one small package. Next I expected him to do Edward G. Robinson. "It took some guts to get in my face yesterday," he said. "And besides, you look to me like a guy who's hurtin' bad. It didn't cost me nothin'."

"Owney, did you know Gavin Cassidy?"

He shook his head. "I think I met him once, but I didn't really know him. He hung out on the Near North and River North and Wrigleyville. I mostly run north of Wilson Avenue. I don't know what really went down, him gettin' crunched with this bribe thing. But I can tell you this much right now: whatever my Uncle Marty says he did, that's the story. That's how it'll go down on the books, and nobody'll tell you nothin' different in this town, not if they got a brain in their head." He looked at me, and a half smile twisted one corner of his mouth, as if smiling hurt. "You know how it works as good as me. You're from here."

That was good to hear, at least, and from a surprising source. Maguire was the first one to even acknowledge I might belong here.

"Look," he said, "I don't have any schooling, I just made it outta high school by a cunt hair, you know? I'm just a tough Mick. Everybody else in my family got the brains, I got good hands. So nobody paid much attention to me when I was growin' up, and my Uncle Marty, he just let me hang around to run errands for him, light his fuckin' cigars, and laugh at me when I did dumb things. I fought middleweight; welterweight at first, and then I put on a couple a pounds and moved up in weight class. I was pretty good—well, the truth of it is I was just okay—but I figured out real quick I didn't like gettin' hit, so I hung the gloves up while I could still breathe through my nose. And there I was, the family clown, workin' for my uncle again, still doing dumb things. Your father, he was the only one ever

170

treated me like I was human. When I was in high school and flunkin' out, I'd bring my homework into the office, and Jimmy, he'd drop damn near whatever he was doin' and help me with it. Not just tellin' me the answers, but explainin' to me, so I'd understand it for myself. Later on, when I started fightin', he was always there at ringside, you know. My uncle never was, but old Jimmy, he never missed one of my fights. So I figure I owe him. I can't give nothin' back to him, but you being his son, maybe I can keep you from gettin' into a lot of trouble here you won't be able to handle."

I couldn't believe what I was hearing. This was some other Jimmy Saxon he was describing, some sternly gentle, Ward-Cleaverly parent who wore a suit and tie to read the evening paper; not the guy who walked around the house in the tops of his long underwear and baggy pants with the suspenders down around his hips. Maybe, like Owney Maguire, I should have brought my homework to the Fifty-fourth Ward Democratic Organization offices, because God knows my father was never *ever* home when *I* needed him. I wasn't yet out of short pants when I learned to live without him. I leaned against the side of my car, stunned, and so jealous of Owney I could barely see straight. Pretty ridiculous, at my age.

Wasn't it?

"That's real nice of you, Owney," I said, squeezing it out of the clenched fist in my throat.

"Just tryin' to help."

"You really want to help me?"

He shrugged. "If I can without gettin' my own ass in a sling. You go back to California and forget about it. It doesn't cost you nothin'. Me, I gotta live here."

"Just some information." I took a deep breath. "Who's Storko?"

"Storko? Never heard of him."

"Think," I said. "You never heard of a guy named Storko? Never heard the name? Your uncle ever talk about him? Or did my father? Anyone?"

171

"No," he said slowly, really thinking about it. "That's a pretty funny name. I'd've remembered it."

"It couldn't be a nickname? Like a tall skinny guy who looks like a stork?"

He laughed.

I scribbled my phone number at the hotel on the inside of a book of matches and handed it to him. I hadn't written my number on a matchbook since my singles-bar days, and back then I hadn't handed it out to pugnacious little Irishmen. "If you *do* hear the name, call me, okay? I'll be here a few more days. Just call me."

He looked at the matchbook, then put it in his pocket. "Look, go home to Hollywood," he said softly. "Forget Cassidy, forget this Storko guy, forget about all this shit. You can't do nothin' about it anyway, and I don't want to see you get hurt, or your old man, either. I—I really care about him, y'know? I mean, he treated me like I was his own kid."

I unlocked my car, my headache now full-fledged and punishing my eyeballs like the relentless pounding of the surf.

"No, he didn't," I said.

19

Friday had that fresh grassy smell of a morning after the rain, even though there isn't much grass around Storyville. I got up early, showered, and dressed casually. For breakfast I walked over to a place near the river called Chris—A Café, I suppose to distinguish it from Chris—A Drugstore and Chris—A Hardware Store.

After my omelette and coffee I ransomed my car from the pricey garage where I'd left it and drove over to Wells Street in Old Town. It isn't the Old Town I knew. Its heyday was in the late fifties and early sixties, Chicago's answer to Greenwich Village when the artsy young Rush/Clark/State Street crowd had moved farther north and west, turning carriage houses and storage units into restaurants where customers were urged to eat the free peanuts on the tables and toss the shells into the sawdust on the floor. Old Town is *really* old, now, sad and tattered beyond the banners that stretch across the streets to announce houseware sales, and the astringent elegance of the fern bars.

I fed the parking meter, lucky to find a spot at all at eleven o'clock on a Friday morning, and trotted up the steps of a faded town house. Some of the buildings on the street had been spruced up, restored or remodeled, with bright primary colors trimmed with white wainscoting and newly painted wrought iron grillwork, but this one was dusty and bowed with time, its paint blistered and flaking, showing its age. Weren't we all?

The apartment was the first-floor rear, and when I knocked the door was opened almost immediately by a kind-looking woman in her sixties whose big brown eyes were a lot younger than that. The entrance to the apartment was in the kitchen, and behind her I could see a kettle steaming on the range top.

"Yes?" she said.

I told her my name and that I was an old friend of Stretch Knox whom he hadn't seen in a long time, and before either of us could say anything more a familiar voice roared from the next room, "Well, ask the man in, for God's sake, don't both of you stand out there jawin' in the hall."

The lady and I exchanged smiles. "I'm Alice Orr," she said, looking over her shoulder. "I guess he wants to see you."

I followed her into the parlor, which was lined on three walls with bookshelves stuffed with old magazines and newspapers, as well as worn volumes of sociological and political theory. Stretch Knox was sitting in an easy chair by a bay window that overlooked a lush green garden growing in a patch of back yard surrounded by buildings on all sides. I wasn't surprised to find him in cotton twill pants, heavy round-toed shoes, and a blue cotton work shirt: summer or winter, I'd never seen him wear anything else. The plaid shawl over his knees was a new wrinkle, though, as was the palsy in his hands and the constant bobbing of his head. He was, by my reckoning, eighty-two years old, and I guess he'd earned the right to wear a shawl on his knees.

"How ya doin'?" he said gruffly. He didn't make any effort to get up or shake hands; he might have seen me last Tuesday instead of seventeen years ago. Nothing ever surprised Stretch; he'd complain and bellow no matter what crossed his path. He took whatever change might come along as a personal affront but accepted it as the normal way of things, whether it be baseball on artificial turf, the upsurge of Republicanism, or

174

women who objected to being called "gals." He always growled and snarled as if he was madder than hell at everyone, and indeed he was angry about a lot of things. He would intimidate you for the first five minutes with his cranky-old-bastard routine, or longer if he thought he could get away with it, until you saw the pussycat underneath.

He was a chimney sweep by trade, believe it or not—Stretch was a walking anachronism and always had been—but he'd spent more than one night as a guest of the city or county for his rabble-rousing speeches in the pocket park once known as Bughouse Square, and he was convinced that he was on every list of subversives in the files of the FBI. He probably was. When he'd first opened the bar he called Hard Knox College, it was less a means to make a living than it was a political forum for himself, his friends, and occasionally his enemies, a freewheeling watering hole where anyone with a cause could rail against the injustices and inequities of the world without fear of a nightstick across the face and a ride downtown in a Black Maria.

All this was pretty much before my era at Knox College, of course. By the time I discovered it, when political dissent had become the preserve of the long-haired young who took it to the streets with protest songs and marijuana, it was the creative types that gravitated to Knox College, folk singers like Big John Washington, artists like Kendra Dane, and actors like me. Stretch must have thought we were pretty fluffy, with our artistic and intellectual pretensions, but he put up with us anyway, grumping and grousing all through our one-act play festivals, our jazz jam sessions, our poetry readings, our love affairs, and our occasional fights, as on the fateful and much-talked-about night when Cassidy and I got into a shoving match over Kendra at the bar.

It was the only time we'd ever exchanged harsh words—no, that isn't right, because we didn't exchange any words at all. It was quick and explosive, and unless you were looking right at us you would have missed it. It was the only time when, for

175

scant seconds, our friendship threatened to unravel. The strained feelings, the hurt and resentment, had been between Kendra and myself, almost as though Gavin had no part in it, or maybe neither of us was willing to point a blaming finger at him. He and I never spoke of it, except that the first time I saw him after Kendra informed me that she'd slept with him and would continue to do so, he'd thrown his arm around my neck in greeting and given me a bear hug that almost snapped my head off, whispering, "Courage, my friend. Life is in the striving. There will be other days." Looking back on it now, it was pretty puerile, but at the time it seemed as profound as the sea.

On the occasion of our one hostility, a Thursday night in winter when the slush and wind was keeping all but the regulars from attending the festivities at Knox College, Gavin and I were on adjoining stools at the bar rather than at his usual table, and he had been drinking heavily all evening long. He was feeling morose about something; it was one of his usual modes. Gavin was always either morose, seductive, or bombastic while urging his troops into the breach of Agincourt. Someone stopped by to chat for a moment—people always did that to Gavin, even those who didn't know him—and idly asked how Kendra was.

Deliberately misunderstanding the question's syntax, Gavin had waxed eloquent on the subject of how Kendra was. "She's absolutely astounding. Young, vital—a perfect, passionate sexual animal. Inventive, creative, and constantly surprising." And he'd turned and beamed at me. "You trained her well, my young friend, and for that I'm ever in your gratitude."

The cruelty, or rather the thoughtlessness of it had hit me like a bucket of ice water, hurt like a sword thrust, stunned like a sledgehammer blow, and I'd swung on Gavin without thinking about it, before I realized that I didn't really want to hit him because *(a)* he was my friend and *(b)* he was too drunk to defend himself. So at the last possible moment I changed my mind and pulled my punch, opening my knotted fist so that I wound up shoving him in the middle of the chest. Surprised and off balance, he slipped backward off the stool with a silly, stunned look and sat down hard on the floor, his tailbone thudding against the planks and his legs splayed out in front of him, still holding his pewter tankard in his hand, having spilled not a drop. He had no idea, then or later, why I had hit him.

Stretch knew why. And behind the bar, he was yelling, "Now, quit it, God damn it! Quit it!" He rather enjoyed fights involving outsiders, strangers to Hard Knox College with whom he had no emotional involvement, but he couldn't stand it when two of his own were in intramural conflict.

Now I smiled down at the old man in the chair. His leonine gray hair was sticking up in all directions as it always had—Stretch didn't believe in combs any more than he did capitalism—and I marveled that even at his advanced age he hadn't seemed to lose any of it. I tried to ignore the involuntary bobbing of his head, as if he were constantly agreeing with me.

"You look great, Stretch," I told him.

"Well, you don't," he snapped. He examined me with a critical eye. "Look at your goddamn white hair. You turned into an old man." He turned his attention to the woman. "Alice, get this old guy a beer or something."

"Stretch, it's ten o'clock in the morning!"

He hitched the blanket up around his waist. "Ah, Jesus, I lose track of the time sitting here. Whattaya want, then?"

Alice said, "I have water on for tea."

"That'll be fine, thanks." She smiled and went into the kitchen. I said to Stretch, "You always did like younger women."

"Don't remind me." He frowned in concentration. I realized he was trying to speak and having a little trouble doing it. "So! You're a movie star. Every time you're on the idiot box, Diane Keenan calls me up and tells me. I never watch, though." Suddenly enraged, he shouted, "You think I have nothing better to do than watch you in some silly damn show? You know how many books in the world I haven't read yet?" He

177

rubbed violently at his nose with a callused hand, his head nodding like that of a toy dog in the back window of a low-rider's automobile. "And time's running out," he finally managed to stammer.

"You'll outlive us all, you old fart."

He burrowed into the chair like a nesting animal. "I outlived Cassidy, didn't I? Never thought I would, by God, but here I am looking out the window at this pocket jungle back here, and him six feet under. I guess that's why you're in town. You shoulda come back while he was still alive to appreciate it." He wiped a hand over his face. "At least you came to see me before *I* check out."

"Did Cassidy come to see you?"

"Oh, yeah," Stretch said, "just about every week, when he wasn't in the hospital himself. He'd come in the mornings like this, sit and shoot the shit, drink four beers while I was having tea, tell me all the silly gossip I didn't care about. Sometimes he'd read to me, and I never had the heart to tell him he stank at it. God, he was a lousy actor!" He looked away, out into the shrubbery in the back yard, his mouth working. "I think he knew that deep down, and it ate him up. Cassidy was unhappy all the years I knew him, but especially at the end there."

"Why so much at the end?"

"You know how I feel about cops," he said, his bristly eyebrows lifting.

"Cossacks, you used to call them."

His head nodded spasmodically. "Cassidy once told me, a long time ago, that he didn't want to be a cop at all—which wasn't exactly big news—but that as long as he wore the badge he'd be the best goddamn cop that ever was. I liked that, even though he was too dumb to know he was a capitalist tool." He frowned, shifting in the chair in an effort to get comfortable, and was silent for a while. I thought he was considering what to say next, but then it hit me that he was trying to get the sentence out of his mouth. Something was happening inside

178

his head that didn't correspond to how he wanted his muscles to respond.

Finally he found his voice. "When he had to do bad shit on his friends it really hurt him. Stuck between loyalty and how he saw his duty was a hard place for him to be."

As long as it had taken to say, it had been worth waiting for. I sat forward, the skin on the back of my hands prickling. "What friends? What shit?"

Alice Orr came in with a tray of tea and fixings, a classic of rotten timing. I poured myself a cup, refusing lemon, milk or sugar, and Alice fixed one for Stretch with all three. She must have sensed she was interrupting, because she smiled a sheepish apology at me and tiptoed back into the kitchen.

"What shit did Cassidy have on his friends at the end, Stretch?"

He peered over his glasses at me, his mouth working. "Most people have things to hide."

"From a cop?"

"Sure! Bunch of storm troopers. But it's not just them now, it's everybody minding everybody else's business, and it's a pain in the ass! Smoking, drinking, abortion, eating meat, wearing furs, using condoms, gay or straight, black or white, male or female. You can't piss in a bucket without ten different people getting offended!"

"Stretch, who?"

"You're starting to sound like a cop yourself," he said. "What's the damn difference? You show up after half a lifetime, trailing stardust behind you, and all of a sudden you care!"

That one closed up my throat. I said, "That's a little rough, isn't it?"

"Shit!" he said, dripping disdain. "You can take it. You're supposed to be a big tough private eye."

"Private investigator," I corrected him—being called a private eye is one of my pet peeves. "How did you know that?"

"I know a hell of a lot about you. I make it my business to. You were like the baby of the family—even though you took off

179

and we never heard a word from you." He tried to sip at his tea, but his hands were shaking too badly and he couldn't get the cup to his mouth. Instead he blew on it to make me think it was too hot and put it on the table next to his chair. The cup rattled noisily, and without meeting my eyes he hid his trembling hands beneath the shawl on his lap.

We talked for another hour or so, about people long gone and the Chicago we'd known, history as ancient as the fall of Carthage. Every so often he'd hesitate before he spoke, frowning with the effort, but he didn't stammer once he got started, and when he was on a roll, bemoaning the general state of things and how all of his "kids," those of us who had matriculated from Hard Knox College, never came around anymore, his hands didn't quiver as much at all. The palsy in his head never quite stopped, though at times it was less noticeable than others.

When it became obvious he was tiring, I took my leave of him. I wanted to hug him, but Stretch Knox came from an era where heterosexual men did not hug each other, or show much emotion at all. Six four in his prime, lean and hickory-hard, he was the quintessential proletarian radical, and whatever might be plaguing his last years he was not going to go gentle.

"Don't stay away so long," he grated at me as I was leaving. "Come back the next time you're in town."

"It's a date," I said.

It was one of those obvious lies we sometimes tell to make human existence endurable. Both Stretch and I knew we'd never see each other again.

As I made my way through the cozy kitchen, Alice Orr emerged from the bedroom.

"I'll see you out," she said.

We went out onto the stoop of the building into sharp, high-definition sunlight. The Wells Street traffic belched its fumes into what a few hours earlier had been a fresh, clean morning.

180

"I'm glad you came," she said. "Stretch is, too. Don't feel bad, he's always that gruff—but then, you know that."

I took her hand. "Is there anything I can do?"

"There's nothing any of us can do." She looked toward the towers of downtown, squinting her eyes against the light.

"Parkinson's?" I said.

She nodded. "You know your diseases, Mr. Saxon."

"Jesus, I'm sorry. I'm glad he has someone like you who cares about him."

"We've been together for about twelve years now. He was old even then, but he was healthy. Now . . ." She stuffed her hands in the pockets of her smocklike apron. "The best thing I do for him is pretend I don't notice the shaking hands and the halting speech, even though he knows I do. It's our little game."

I squeezed her hand, let it go, and started down the steps. She said, "It's a small apartment, and I can't help overhearing whenever Stretch has a visitor. I heard you talking. I heard Gavin Cassidy, too."

I stopped, one hand on the wrought iron railing.

"I don't know exactly what it was all about," Alice Orr said, "but it was last week sometime, a few days before he died, and from what I was able to glean, Gavin wanted Stretch's advice because he was going through some sort of moral crisis."

"What about?"

"About Marian Meyers. Not wanting to hurt her." She raised her eyebrows and shrugged. "That's all I heard, really, and Stretch didn't talk about it afterward. But I remember Gavin saying, 'I don't want to hurt Marian, but I'm a cop.' If that's any help to you . . . ?"

"More than you'll ever know," I said.

20

It wasn't that far from Stretch Knox's place to Marian's, about a five-minute drive, but there was no answer when I rang the doorbell. She must have gone somewhere to shake off her writer's block, because apparently she wasn't upstairs in her office. I really wanted to talk to her, but I didn't know where she hung out when she wasn't at home, so I had to give it up. I went to a liquor store on Clark Street, bought a six-pack of Heineken dark, and went back to the hotel and watched the ball game on TV. I suppose I could have gone to Wrigley and taken my chances on getting a decent seat, but I wasn't really in the mood to sit in the sunshine and cheer. The ballpark is a happy place, and I didn't feel happy.

I went through four bottles of beer while the Cubs lost that afternoon, and afterward I called Marvel. We chatted for about ten minutes; he was anxious to tell me about his week, about how he went two-for-four in his ball game the day before, and I told him about Wrigley Field. I really wanted to share the Cubs with him, but I was glad I hadn't brought him on this trip, to drop him into a nest of middle-aged people he didn't know and bore him with nostalgia. My taking on a case wouldn't have helped either.

Sometimes Marvel's sense of humor overtook his common

sense and he could be acerbic and cutting, but at least he was ever accepting of me, on my side no matter what, and an ally with a sympathetic ear whenever I needed him. There didn't seem to be anyone in Chicago of whom I could say the same at the moment.

I hung up, leaned back on the bed, and gave myself over to missing him. Eventually I snoozed. I woke up at eight o'clock and called Marian again, but there was still no answer. I changed clothes and strolled over to the Loop, past the Chicago Theatre, now dark but designated a historical monument, and remembered the great movies and stage shows I'd seen there. On the next block was Marshall Field's department store, the original one with the big clock on the ornate facade. Many a Chicago rendezvous has begun with "Meet me under the clock." Field's archrival, Carson Pirie Scott & Co., was only a block farther away. I remembered my mother dragging me shopping through both of them.

On Adams Street, just off State, the old German restaurant called the Berghoff was still there, and I went in to eat, more interested in the architecture and design than the food. We don't have places this big and sprawling in Los Angeles, with Old World murals and real wood paneling. Some of the waiters were Puerto Rican now instead of German, but the Berghoff hadn't changed much anyway, and I was glad I'd taken the trouble to come downtown.

I was going to go back to the Acorn on Oak later, but unlike Los Angeles, Chicago doesn't get started until late in the evening, so I strolled up Michigan to the river, walking off the sauerbraten I had consumed. I watched the floodlights dancing off the brilliant white of the Wrigley Building for a while until the wind off the lake got to me. Then I crossed the bridge and went back to my hotel.

Two men in light-colored, inexpensive suits were sitting in the tastefully appointed lobby, as out of place as two altar boys in a high-security federal pen. One look told me they were not guys you fooled with, maybe because they had eyes like hard little marbles. One of them, the blond with the disappearing hairline, looked like an ex–collegiate outside linebacker now run to fat and selling insurance in a small town in Iowa, and the other one was short, ferret-faced, and dark, with a habit of licking his lips all the time, so that they were chapped red.

"Mr. Saxon?" the linebacker said. He got up from the sofa where they'd obviously been waiting for me, his pendulous Saint Bernard jowls swaying as he came across the lobby.

I looked at him and nodded. He had me cold.

He didn't shake hands. He didn't say his name. He didn't introduce Ferret Face. "I'm from Major Ackerman's office."

My mouth dropped open. "Morris Ackerman?"

Ferret Face joined us. *"Major* Ackerman," he corrected me. He sounded as if someone were pinching his nose.

Major it was, then, although nobody had ever ascertained in what army Morris Ackerman was an officer. Perhaps they were afraid to ask. Ackerman was the statewide political kingmaker, the guy who allowed people like Martin Givney to function. Givney and the Alderman, for all their power and clout, were simply local pols, first lieutenants to Ackerman's field-grade commander. On Capitol Hill there wasn't a senator or congressman of either party who would dare refuse the major's phone calls, and it was tacitly understood that if you wanted to discuss presidential politics, Morris Ackerman was one of those you sought out to talk about it—if you knew what was good for you. The governorship of Illinois was solidly in Ackerman's pocket, of course, as was every elective position in the state, and he divided his time between his office in Springfield and his real headquarters, Chicago, where he owned a mansion on the Outer Drive near the Museum of Science and Industry— and nearly as big—and a condo overlooking Oak Street Beach.

The linebacker went on, "The major would like a few minutes of your time."

"Are you sure you have the right person?" It was hard to believe Morris Ackerman was even aware of my existence, unless he watched soup commercials in his spare time.

"Your name Saxon?" Ferret Face said.

I allowed as how it was. "What does Ack—the major want?"

"You'll have to ask him," Linebacker said.

I glanced at my watch. It was after nine. "Are we talking about now?"

"You have someplace better to go?" Ferret Face licked his lips, and it was an aggressive, hard-ass kind of lick, a wolf coming upon a moose herd after the first thaw. He was somewhat confrontational; I guess he thought he could afford to be, with the Linebacker at his side and the major behind him.

"Let's do it," I said, resigned. Ackerman wasn't one to make requests; he gave orders. There was little doubt in my mind that a no wouldn't have been accepted with good grace, so as long as I had to pay my respects one way or another, I might as well do it standing up.

Their car, parked right in front of the hotel, was a long gray Oldsmobile with tinted glass windows that would have made more sense somewhere like California or Arizona where the sun shines all the time. Here the advantage was that no one could see in from outside. The car was just beneath a street sign warning NO STOPPING AT ANY TIME. No cop in the city—or in his right mind—would write out a citation for Morris Ackerman's car. I wondered if one of Gavin's last official acts might have been to tag the major with a parking violation.

Ferret Face was the designated driver. I sat up front next to him with Linebacker in the back, hanging over the seat, his pork ribs dinner, probably from Randall's, still on his breath. A spot of red-brown sauce had found its way onto his white shirt where his stomach slopped over his Sansabelt waist.

"Where are we going?"

"To see the major," Linebacker answered. Not exactly a news flash, but I'd get no further amplification, so I shut up and enjoyed the short ride.

The building they brought me to on Lake Shore Drive was just south of where the massive Potter Palmer mansion had dominated the lakefront for so many years until it was torn down to make way for an apartment house. This was an older building, built of huge dark brown stones, which had once stood proud and alone overlooking the lake. Recent construction had squeezed it between two larger and newer high rises, so that from the outside it seemed dwarfed and cramped. The doorman was in his fifties and so at ease greeting the visitors to the building that he must have spent his entire adult life in livery. He spirited the Oldsmobile through a stone archway, and Ferret Face, Linebacker, and I got into an elevator at the rear of the lobby. Ferret Face pushed the twelfth-floor button with a finger whose nail sported a half moon of black dirt.

We stood in the attitude of elevator passengers all over the world, staring at the overhead floor indicator, not touching or even acknowledging our fellow riders, even though we were acutely aware of one another. There was no music in the elevator, for which I was grateful. Bad enough being taken someplace I didn't want to go without being subjected to "You've Lost That Loving Feeling" with strings and a celesta.

The car stopped and the door opened directly into an apartment that took up the entire twelfth floor. Ferret Face stood aside so Linebacker and I could step out onto a highly polished hardwood floor. The bigger man nudged me in the back and we turned right, toward what was the living room.

The windows stretched forty feet across the room, taking various bends and dips with the contour of the building. They all faced eastward to the lake across the drive, and a window seat covered with white cushions ran along beneath them. It must have been a spectacular place to watch the sunrise. Diffused lighting in several different areas made it look even bigger than it was. The furniture was modern, expensive, mostly done in whites and blues, and the fine rug on the floor was a pale champagne color. Sitting on the window seat in one of the bays was an elderly, bespectacled little man in a white shirt and tie and a gray wool cardigan. He looked like a retired accountant, or a tie salesman, or somebody's uncle. Major Morris Ackerman. Givney, Big John Washington, Stretch Knox,

Jimmy Saxon, Ackerman: the world seemed full of flinty old men who smelled of milk that wasn't quite fresh.

"Mr. Saxon, sir," Linebacker said.

"Come on over here, Mr. Saxon," the little man called, waving for me to join him. As I crossed the room I heard my escort heading the other way, toward the far recesses of the apartment.

"I'm Morris Ackerman," he said. He had an enormous balloon of cognac in his hand and swirled it around to warm the amber liquid. He didn't offer me a handshake, either. These guys could use a few lessons in basic etiquette.

"I know," I said.

His eyes danced behind his thick lenses. "Know me, eh?"

"I was born in Chicago."

"Sure you were, that's right." He swished the brandy at me. "You want something to drink?"

"No, thanks."

"Some cheese and crackers? Chips? I've got the nacho-cheese-flavored kind, I've got sour-cream-and-garlic—"

"This isn't exactly a social call, is it, Major?"

He looked over his glasses, his feelings hurt. "It's what you want it to be," he said. "We need to talk. You can't talk and drink at the same time? Or have a cracker?"

I shook my head, and he shrugged his shoulders as if I were hopeless, indicating I should sit on the window seat with him. I sat, my back to the window, with the uneasy realization that the only thing between me and a twelve-story drop to Lake Shore Drive was a quarter of an inch of glass. I tried to ignore the vertigo that made me momentarily giddy.

"What brings you back home?" Major Ackerman said. He took a cigar from his shirt pocket and rolled it around in his fingers but didn't light it. He passed it under his nose several times, seeming to take sensual pleasure from the feel of it. "You just come back to see your dad? Spark some old girlfriend? Catch the Cubs while they're hot? What?"

"Personal business," I said.

"Business." He shook his head sadly. "It gets in the way, doesn't it? In the end, business equals dollars. It's always dollars that separate people, don't you think? Black or white, Jew or gentile, everybody wants dollars. You can promote yourself some pussy, you can get your entertainment off TV, but dollars is what it all boils down to." He smelled the cigar once more and then put it back in his pocket. "I asked my associates to bring you here because I want to talk to you about business, Mr. Saxon. Dollars."

"I'm always willing to talk about dollars."

"I'm glad to hear that," Morris Ackerman said. "I'm very glad to hear you say that, because as long as a man can talk about dollars there's always the hope of an agreement, a rapprochement between gentlemen. That's how it's done. Dollars is the grease that keeps the wheels turning. Not just in government, but all over. It's the essence."

He inhaled his cognac, eyelashes fluttering from the fumes. He had the act down perfectly, and I didn't want to ruin the moment by saying anything.

"This is an election year," he said, "as I'm sure you know. Elections are *my* business. I watch them, I play with them the way some people play with toy trains. I try to put spin on them so they come out my way. It's an ancient and honorable profession, and you can check the election results the last thirty years in Chicago and agree that I'm damn good at my job. Well, I hear you're damn good at your job, too."

"Where'd you hear that?"

"I find out what I need to know. It's never a good idea operating out of ignorance."

"Okay, I'm good at my job. Now what?"

He sipped at the cognac and smacked his chops. "There's a congressional district out in California that I'm particularly interested in this year. It's the Mimosa Beach area down south of L.A. That's not too far from you, is it?"

"Hop, skip, and a jump," I said.

"Right. Now, there's a Republican gaining strength in that

area, name of Birkenshaw, Thomas Birkenshaw. He's a local guy, was on the Mimosa Beach City Council; now he's a state representative. Made his bones by demolishing the incumbent there. He's been growing in popularity for the last two years. If he gets the nomination for Congress, he's going to give our boy a pretty rough time of it in November."

"What's this got to do with me?"

"I'd like Birkenshaw looked into. Investigated. I want to know what he has for breakfast, I want to know how regular he is, I want to know if he has a tootsie or two on the side, or a gambling habit, or drinks a bit too much. I want his blood pressure and his cholesterol level and whether or not he trims his nose hair. I need ammunition to fight him, and I need someone smart and thorough to find it for me. You being a private investigator out in California, I thought you might be just the man for the job." He smiled, swirling his brandy, holding it up to the light and looking through it. Whatever he saw pleased him.

I said, "That's very flattering, Major. But what would you have done if I hadn't been in Chicago right about now?"

"Hired someone out in California. We have people." He smiled expansively, whitely. His dentures were very good, but you could still tell they were dentures. "Since your father is such an old friend of mine, and since you are here, I thought I'd ask you first, let you take a crack at it."

I didn't say anything. He wasn't through talking, and we both knew it.

"Now, we mentioned dollars," Major Ackerman said. "The job pays pretty well. Fifteen hundred a week, plus your expenses, of course. And that's for . . ." He stopped, pretending to calculate. "Ten weeks."

"That's very generous," I said.

"We realize you have other clients, so we wouldn't expect you to be exclusive. But do the best you can, and ten weeks ought to wrap it up just fine."

"Of course you need me to get to work on this right away," I said.

He sat back, his shoulder against the window, and folded his hands over his small paunch, very pleased that I was getting the idea. Twelve stories below us the traffic on Lake Shore Drive made moving ribbons of light that bent along the shoreline. "Right away, yes." He smiled, seemingly delighted with my perspicacity. "Tomorrow. You could catch a flight out of O'Hare first thing in the morning."

"Do you mind if I smoke?" I said, and he granted permission with a wave of his brandy balloon. I took out a cigarette and lit it, then looked around for an ashtray to put the match in.

"Over there someplace," he said, pointing to what they used to call a "conversation grouping" of furniture in the middle of the room. I took a heavy crystal ashtray off the coffee table and brought it back over to the window with me. The smoke stung my throat and lungs. I was going to have to quit smoking. Again.

"I have a little problem, Major," I said.

"Is that so? Something I can help you with?"

"Probably. A friend of mine was murdered in Chicago, and I hate like hell to go home until I find out who did it."

He looked genuinely shocked. "Murdered? Whoa! That's not so good, murder. Who got murdered?"

"A policeman name of Gavin Cassidy."

He looked at me over the tops of his glasses. I had an English lit professor at Illinois who used to do the same thing. "You aren't putzing around; that's serious stuff." He looked out the window at the moonlight shimmering on the lake.

"Too serious for me to drop what I'm doing."

He twisted up his mouth. "That's disturbing. That's very disturbing for me to hear at this point."

"You checked me out, but not thoroughly enough. You want me to stop asking questions and bothering your people and go back to California because you've offered me some sort of bullshit job. I don't operate that way. You don't give any more

190

of a damn about Mr. Birkenshaw's having a girlfriend on the side than I do—if there is a Mr. Birkenshaw."

"There is," he said, "and we would like to get enough dope to shoot the son of a bitch down in flames. But you're right. And I won't insult your intelligence: I do want you to stop asking questions and go home. I'm sorry about your friend, I'm sorry you think someone deliberately took his life, and I can only assure you with all my sincerity that we're not in the murder business." He gave me a particularly smarmy smile. "We don't have to kill people. We've got too much power. I can make one phone call"—he raised the brandy balloon and pointed one finger of the hand that held it toward the telephone—"one phone call, and there's hardly anyone in Chicago whose job wouldn't be on the line. I know about everyone in this town what I'd like to know about Tom Birkenshaw. I don't have to kill anyone. Don't be a goddamn fool."

He got up and wandered the room, one hand in the pocket of his full-cut trousers. "Now here's as honest as I know how to be. Yes, I want you out of our hair, out of town. The Birkenshaw job is just a little added incentive, but it don't sit right with you, I'll give you the fifteen thousand anyway, you don't even have to get off your ass. I won't jerk you around. You're in the way of things you don't understand here, and the real purpose of our talk is to get you out."

"I don't want to get in anybody's way, Major. But I'll find out what happened to Cassidy whether it gets in your way or not."

His lips pursed up as though he'd just tasted a rotten oyster. "You're a tough nut to crack, Saxon. Your father is easier to deal with."

I crushed my cigarette out in the pristine bottom of the ashtray and cleared the smoke out of my lungs. The sauerbraten burned in my stomach like a hot stone. I wished I had a Tums.

"Jimmy is wiser in the ways of the world," Ackerman said. "Maybe that comes with age and experience. You're a young guy, gray hair or no; you haven't learned that yet."

"Thanks for the good advice, Major. It's my burning ambition to be just like my father."

He suddenly roared, "Your father does what he's told, because he knows what's good for him! He does just what I tell him to do, no more and no less, and if you had a fucking lick of sense you'd do the same." The color rose in his face along with his voice, and some of the brandy sloshed out over the edges of the balloon.

I didn't answer him. I couldn't.

Finally he said, "All right, so you can't be bought. Bully for you. I s'pose you're pretty proud of that?"

"I'm a credit to my species," I said.

"Well, there's more than one way to skin a cat. Can you be reasoned with? Can I ask you to drop this inquiry as a personal favor to me?"

"I know about Chicago favors. Tit for tat. Let's trade favors, maybe. Do you know anyone by the name of Storko?"

The Major's face grew dangerously red as I watched; someone inside his head was turning up the thermostat. Then all of a sudden his shoulders slumped and he seemed to relax. A smile cracked his face. "I tell you I want you to stop asking questions, and what do you do? You ask me a question. You're truly a putz, do you know that? A textbook case of a stupid putz. There's always two ways to do things, the hard way and the easy way. Only a putz chooses the hard way."

He shuffled across the room toward the foyer, where the elevator shaft divided the enormous apartment in two. He looked older standing up than he did sitting down. "Rogatz!" he called, and in a moment Ferret Face appeared, his jacket unbuttoned.

"Take Mr. Saxon away, will you?"

Ferret Face—I guess his name was Rogatz—came over to where I was sitting and motioned with his head for me to get up. Linebacker came out of the back of the apartment and stood there with his finger on the elevator button.

"I can find my own way back," I said.

Ackerman leveled me with a dead stare. "I wouldn't think of it."

I stood up and went over to the elevator, conscious of Rogatz behind me and Linebacker waiting for me, his jowly face set in a scowl. I said, "You can't buy me and you can't reason with me, Major, and you're unable or unwilling to trade favors with me. What now? Have your goon squad lean on me?"

Morris Ackerman looked at me with what might have been disgust or pity, it was hard to tell which, and then nodded at Rogatz and Linebacker. "I don't know what else to do," he said.

Beneath the tracks of the El, the elevated train system that ties the city's disparate neighborhoods together, is a dark nether-world most Chicagoans rarely see, lonely as a crypt after the sun goes down. Crumpled newspapers ride the wind through shadowy corridors of stout, aging wood and skeletal steel never touched by direct sunlight. Derelicts wrapped in filthy rags huddle against steel and concrete pillars and poke through trash bins behind six-flat buildings with gray-painted wooden back stairs. Terrier-size rats roam at will, kings of the jungle, because no stray cat in its right mind would venture down under the El. Discarded fast-food containers, beer cans, used condoms, and other urban flotsam cover the street floor like wall-to-wall carpeting, and the atmosphere is poisoned by smells of rotting garbage, urine, and dying hope.

The Oldsmobile pulled to a stop beside a huge concrete pillar about a block from Belmont Avenue. This time we'd all sat in the front seat, me in the middle, Rogatz driving, and Linebacker between me and the door, his spicy breath making me gag.

"Get out," Rogatz said. He'd left the motor running. Line-backer opened the door and levered his ponderous bulk out onto the street, grunting at the effort, and waited for me to follow. I slid across the fake leather seat and got out, waiting, hoping for the cavalry to come bugling over the hill, or at the very least for a parade to pass by. I stood with Linebacker until

Rogatz came around the car to us, and I saw he held a leather sap.

"You look like a smart guy," Rogatz said, his ferrety nose seeming to twitch. "But I guess you're not. You're not smart enough to know you don't go up against the major. That's not good sense." He had the sap in his right hand and he ran it almost tenderly through his left, feeling its weight and thickness and leathery texture. It was obviously a sensual experience for him, and almost embarrassing for me to watch.

Linebacker said, "He's not a smart guy. He gets offered an easy out and good bucks besides, and he turns it down."

I hate it when people talk about me as if I'm not there.

Rogatz said, "Whyn't you take it, you dumb schmuck?"

" 'Cause he's stupid," Linebacker said. He shook his head, frowning, saddened I'm sure at the tragic flaw of hubris that was bringing me down like a hero in a Greek tragedy. Or maybe it was the barbecue sauce repeating on him.

I didn't say anything. My supply of witty repartee had dried up like a runny nose after an antihistamine shot.

"You're a lucky guy, Saxon," Rogatz went on. "I've taken out most of a guy's teeth with one swipe of this. I could break your back without any trouble, or smash your jawbone." He waved the sap at me. "But Major Ackerman said he don't want you marked up, so this won't be too bad. Just enough to convince you to mind your own business." He looked around to make sure we had a relative amount of privacy. About fifty yards away, against the back fence of an apartment building that had once been an enclave of lace-curtain Irish and now housed twenty Puerto Rican families, a filth-encrusted wino huddled under an anorak, hood up around his ears, knees against his chest like a fetus, watching us with booze-dimmed but comprehending eyes. His bottom teeth showed, like a death's-head's. He looked straight at me, and a moment of understanding passed between us: he couldn't help me and I shouldn't expect it. His presence certainly didn't cause Rogatz concern; winos were nonpersons, and if he didn't like it he could just go huddle someplace else.

Rogatz surveyed the area like a guy trying to decide where to spread out his beach towel. Finally he said, "Stand up against that pillar, there."

Linebacker took hold of the back of my neck with one slab-like hand and shoved me face first against a steel stanchion studded with rivets, which held up the huge wooden beams forming the superstructure of the El tracks. I hit it with my palms and pushed myself backward and to the side, propelled by my momentum, and drove my elbow into the big man's face. His nose gave under the impact, making a crunchy noise. A scream leaked out of his throat, and he staggered away, hands to his face and blood spurting from between his fingers.

I whirled around to face Rogatz, who was caught surprised, and I braced my back against the pillar and kicked out at him. He moved backward, too quick for me, and my heel caught him on the thigh. It hurt, I'm sure, but that wasn't where I'd aimed, and it didn't even slow him down. He moved in again, and my next kick went into the pit of his stomach. Again my aim was off, a little too high, but this one doubled him up. He clutched his gut and thought it over, trying to catch his breath.

"Hold it!" Linebacker rasped, and I looked over at him to see that he'd found a little snub-nosed .32 somewhere and was pointing it at the widest part of my body. Blood poured out of his nose, and he'd thrown his head back to try to slow the bleeding. He looked like a fat, unrepentant aristocrat on his way to the guillotine in a tumbril.

"Put that away before I shove it in your ear," I said. "If you kill me Ackerman'll have your ass, and you know it."

His eyes flickered to Rogatz for a moment, and I knew I'd spoken the truth. He wasn't going to shoot me, and that at least made me feel better. He started moving toward me from my left side, slow as a creature in a nightmare, spitting out the blood that was running from his nose into his mouth. Rogatz was on my right, also advancing, holding the sap out in front of him like an elephant's trunk. I couldn't bolt straight forward because I'd have to run around the Oldsmobile, and the steel pillar was at my back. I'd have to stand and fight.

It wasn't much of a battle. Linebacker made a quick rush and when I turned to meet it Rogatz brought the sap down across my shoulder. It was like a tree falling on me. The pain made me dizzy and set my ears to ringing. My entire left side went numb, which was almost a blessing, and I sagged to one knee. And then Linebacker was all over me, his bulk smothering me, blood from his battered nose running onto my face, and I was down and under him, on my stomach, my arms pinned to the cobbled surface of the street. At those close quarters I realized he needed Arrid as much as he did Listerine.

"I told you you weren't very smart," Rogatz said through his teeth, and I could hear the sap whistling through the heavy air. "Now it's gonna be worse."

21

State Street abruptly stops its northbound meander at Division Street, at which point it affects calling itself North State Parkway, taking every precaution against being confused with its better-known source street. The Ambassador East Hotel, with its fabled Pump Room, still caters to new and old money, the gray suits and designer labels, and many of the gracious brownstones are still one-family homes. No one ever "gentrified" the

Parkway because it never fell into the kind of shoddy disrepute that many formerly elegant city neighborhoods did. It was and is one of the most desirable residential areas in Chicago.

My taxi was a deadly guided missile driven by one Azim Mahboubian-Fard, and it deposited me in front of one of the brownstones that had been cut up into fashionable, roomy apartments. I had been half lying on the plastic-covered back seat, and I'm sure a groan or two escaped me during the bumpy trip. I was sweat-soaked and feverish, going in and out of delirium, and Mahboubian-Fard had cast more than one wary over-the-shoulder glance to make sure his passenger hadn't expired on him, which would cause him to spend time doing paperwork and explaining to the authorities and would surely cost him the rest of his night's profits. He was glad to see me go.

I'm not certain how I got from the curb to the steps of the brownstone, but I remember what it was like going up. It was one of the many variations of Hell. White flames licked at the backs of my legs and around my lower back, and I pulled myself up, foot by foot, pausing after every step or two to catch my breath. My kidneys ached, and I was afraid I would pee blood for a month. The chilly wind whipping in off the lake two blocks to the east was no help at all in stanching the flow of perspiration that poured off me with every effort, but it turned it unpleasantly cold and clammy. When I finally got to the vertical row of doorbells inside the vestibule, I felt as if I'd climbed Annapurna.

I leaned on the bell until I heard the answering buzzer. Almost falling through the inner door, I lurched down the hallway to the apartment I was looking for.

Kendra Dane opened the door wearing a long white jersey nightgown with a pink rose at the modest neckline. Her small nipples poked at the fabric. For some reason the rose made her look unbearably young and vulnerable, almost the way she'd looked the first night I'd kissed her, when she was sixteen years old. The slack-jawed surprise on her face at seeing me there gave way to concern, as she took a better look and saw that if I hadn't been holding on to the wall I would have surely fallen on my face.

"Jesus, you're white as a ghost," she said.

"Had some trouble." I spoke carefully through my teeth. Longer sentences were a problem. Battered ribs do that to you.

She stood aside and opened the door wide, and I went past her into her apartment. It was one large, high-ceilinged room in the front, one of those all-purpose efficient rooms with a kitchen against one wall and a dining room set directly under a hanging lamp, smart and modern-looking against the highly polished hardwood floor. A young man sat on the white sail-cloth sofa near the windows, and I use the word *young* advisedly. He had on a pair of stone-washed jeans and nothing else. His bare feet looked white sticking out of his frayed cuffs.

"Mark, you have to go," Kendra said.

"Who the fuck is he?" Mark said. Arrogant little prick.

"I'll explain later."

"You'll damn well explain now," he said, standing up. He was tall and skinny, and had very little hair on his chest. Kendra must have waylaid him in mid paper route.

"I'll damn well not explain *ever,* if you're going to be an asshole." She snatched up a plaid shirt from the back of a chair and hurled it at him. "Now get out."

The toughest thing in the world is to maintain your dignity when you're putting your clothes on. If I hadn't been in such pain I would have felt sorry for him. He struggled into the shirt without buttoning it, then picked his dirty sneakers and tube socks up off the floor and stalked barefoot through the door. "Hey, fuck you, bitch!" was his parting shot.

Kendra shook her head. "The young are so articulate." She noticed I was leaning against the wall for support again. "Come over here," she said, and helped me from the wall to the sofa, where I collapsed. Mark's ass had made the cushion warm.

"What happened to you?"

"A difference of opinion," I said tightly. "Mostly they worked on my legs, but the back and kidneys, too."

"Who did?"

I shook my head, and the movement sent messages of agony all through my body. A moan bubbled up from depths I didn't know I had.

She ran to the kitchen cupboard and took down a bottle of brandy and a glass. It wasn't a snifter or anything fancy, just a glass like the ones you used to get when you finished eating all the jelly. The brandy was a supermarket house brand and didn't deserve a better glass. She poured generously and handed it to me, and I shook so badly I could barely get it to my lips. It was like drinking fire.

"I don't remember them stopping, or leaving," I said finally, when the burning in my throat and stomach made me forget just the tiniest bit the way the rest of my body felt. "I must've passed out."

"How'd you get here?"

"Cab."

"Why here?"

"Nowhere else to go. It was that or lie there until the birds came and covered me with leaves."

She took the glass from me. "Take your shirt off."

I fell back onto the cushions. "I'm not sure I can."

She hovered over me like a harried mother, as I struggled to sit up enough so she could help me out of my jacket and unbutton my shirt. I heard her suck in her breath when she saw my back.

"Bad?" I said.

"A day at the beach. Pants." It was an order.

I got unbuckled and unzipped, but the effort just about knocked me unconscious, and she tugged off my shoes and gently pulled my gray slacks down over my feet.

She nudged me over onto my side. "My god," she said.

She poured me another brandy and went into the bathroom. I heard the water drumming into the tub, loud and metallic. I looked over my shoulder at the backs of my thighs, remembering Lenny Bruce's definition of a Spanish dancer as a guy trying to catch a glimpse of his own ass. A ladder pattern of angry red welts crisscrossed my legs. Rogatz was very good with the sap, inflicting maximum pain with minimum permanent damage. It's the kind of skill that only comes with experience. There were probably a lot of people that Morris Ackerman wanted hurt but not marked; at least, not where it showed.

I sucked greedily at the brandy but stopped at the second swallow. Eventually it would make me sick, and there was no way I could move quickly to someplace I wouldn't do any damage. I put the glass on the floor, feeling silly lying there in my shorts.

Kendra came back in. "Can you get up?"

"With a little help."

She held out both hands and I grabbed them and pulled myself up, muscles giving silent screams of outrage. I limped into the bathroom, leaning much of my weight on her, but she bore me up without a murmur. She was a strong lady, always had been.

Steam from the tub had fogged the mirror and left a film of moisture on the walls. "Sit in that for a while," she said. "I put some epsom salts in; that should draw some of the pain away."

"Some isn't enough."

"One step at a time," she said.

Kendra had one of those over-the-edge whirlpool attachments, and she bent down and turned it on, setting the water to swirling gently. She pulled down my shorts and I stepped into the tub, holding onto the wall for support. The temperature was just this side of scalding—as if I needed more pain—and it took me a long time to get in. But after the initial shock when I sank down into it, it was soothing and healing, the wet heat digging into the cramped, bruised muscles. I put my head back against the edge of the tub and closed my eyes, feeling the water's weight lulling me into semiconsciousness again.

It must have been about half an hour later—you lose track of time when all you know is pain and all you want is the cessation of it—when she came in and turned off the whirlpool attachment, hauled me out of the tub, and dried me off. Then she led me into her bedroom, fed me some more brandy so that I was punchy and floating above myself, and laid me flat on my face on a big fluffy bath sheet. She smeared some sort of salve on me, which smelled of menthol and felt incredibly cold on my hot, almost parboiled skin, and expertly manipulated my legs and thighs with her fingers. Each feather touch was enough to send me through the roof, but I knew whatever she was doing would eventually ease the hurt, and I gave myself to it, sinking deep into the feeling.

I don't know how long she kneaded me; I spaced out into another time and place. But I was aware of her covering me up with a blanket, and then later, easing in next to me, her body against me, and as I slipped into the deepest stages of sleep I was aware of her crying softly against my shoulder.

"You're good," I said. "I'm really impressed."

Kendra held her hands up in front of her and wiggled her fingers. "Magic," she said.

We were at the little breakfast nook between the kitchen and the living room. One small window looked out on the side yard and the brick facade of a new apartment building next door. I had coffee in front of me and a half finished glass of fresh orange juice at my elbow; I had used the first half to wash down a couple of codeine capsules Kendra had provided. She drank black coffee too and nibbled on dry whole wheat toast. We were both wearing white terry-cloth robes that she used in her therapy sessions. It was a cute little domestic scene, as in a commercial. Any moment I would tell her how good the coffee was, and she would astound me with the news that it was new instant crystals.

"All the aches and pains gone?"

I shifted uneasily on the pillow she'd given me to sit on. I was sore from mid-back down to my ankles, but the fire had gone out of it, and the bruises had turned from bright red to dull purple. And apparently the damage to my kidneys was minor, because I was functioning normally in that area. "It doesn't feel like they'll ever be gone, but they're calmed down some. Thanks."

She arched her long neck. "Are you going to tell me about it? You owe me that much, I think."

I toyed with the handle of my coffee cup. "Gavin got on the wrong side of some powerful people before he died," I said. "People who don't like questions. I guess I asked one too many."

She brushed toast crumbs off her lips. "Who are we talking about here?"

"Morris Ackerman."

"You must be nuts. Get on a plane and go back to your beach bunnies and palm trees."

"I can't do that," I said.

"How did it become your problem?"

"You've known me too long to ask that, Kenni."

She stood up, undoing the sash on her bathrobe and then retying it tighter. "Sense of obligation to your dead friend?" she said. "Don't be a chump. He had none to you."

"What do you mean?"

"You think I just woke up one morning out of a clear blue sky and decided I'd rather be with Gavin than you?" She put her hands in her pockets. "He was after me from the beginning. He thought you were too immature to handle me, and he never missed a chance to tell me so." She barked a little laugh. "Finally he talked me into it."

"A stiff prick has no conscience," I said.

"So how come yours is bothering you?" She suppressed a smile. "Your conscience, I mean."

"Because I think Gavin was killed. Deliberately."

The color drained from her face. "Go to the police," she said.

"Officially, they aren't interested."

"Then drop it. They know more than you do. If they say it's closed, it's closed."

"This is more than Gavin with me now." I ran my fingers lightly over the back of my leg; it hurt, and the skin felt raw. "This is personal." I took a slug of orange juice, which was a lot more rejuvenating than the coffee. "Kenni, have you ever heard of anyone named Storko?"

She shook her head. "Who is he?"

"I went through Gavin's apartment. Storko's name was written in the margin of the TV listings on the day Gavin died."

She looked at me as if I'd suddenly begun speaking in tongues. "In the margin of . . . ? You *are* nuts. Maybe it's from what happened to you, and it'll go away when the bruises do."

"He wrote two phone numbers there as well. One was his captain's and the other Ben Nemeroff's. I think he called them and tried to tell them both about Storko."

"And?"

"As far as I know, he never reached them."

"And you think you can find out?"

I finished the orange juice and got up carefully, flexing first one leg and then the other, stretching my aching lower back. I was in pain, but I was functional. Eventually I was going to be all right. "I'm planning to."

"In your condition?"

I shrugged, and it hurt when I did it. "It's the condition I'm in," I said.

She was past forty and starting to put on some weight, not a lot, just enough to make her cuddly. She had reddish-brown hair, kindly brown eyes, and the kind of skin that would sunburn easily, and she was wearing a pair of red shorts with a white sleeveless blouse and holding a tall plastic glass of iced tea with a lemon wedge floating around on top of it. She looked like a nice woman, which was the way she sounded on the answering machine. She probably called herself Ginny so as not to be confused with the movie star of the forties, Virginia Mayo.

"Mrs. Mayo?"

"Yes?" she said pleasantly.

"Would the captain be in, by any chance?"

She frowned. "It's Saturday, Mr. . . . ?"

"Saxon," I said. "I'm sorry. I wouldn't bother him if it wasn't important."

"Of course," she said. "Won't you come in?"

It was the kind of nice, middle-class home you'd expect a medium-rank Irish cop to live in, near O'Hare. I followed her through a spic-and-span living room, noticing the color photos of two good-looking boys and a pretty girl at various ages scattered all over the end tables and knickknack shelves. Down two steps I could see an airy den with a pool table.

"Ray's in the back yard," she explained, and took me through the wood-paneled kitchen to the back door.

Ray Mayo was in a lawn chair reading the morning paper, the sports section. He wore dark blue shorts, and his yellow polo shirt didn't have a little animal sewn on the pocket. I mentally gave him five points for that. As Ginny and I came out the back door he glowered at me so fiercely I immediately took three points away.

"Christ, it's my day off!" he said.

"Some iced tea, Mr. Saxon?" asked Ginny.

"I'd like that, Mrs. Mayo, if it's not too much trouble." I knew it wouldn't be; there was a big jar of it sweating happily on a redwood table.

"It's sun tea," she explained, pouring me a glass. "A slice of lemon?"

"No, that's all right."

She looked at her husband uncertainly, then at me, and then she excused herself and went back into the house.

"You've got brass balls, hunting me down at home on a Saturday," Mayo said.

"I apologize, and I'll only stay long enough to finish my tea," I said, going over to him.

"Why are you walking like Grampa McCoy?"

"Actually it's more like Gabby Hayes," I said. "You know a guy named Rogatz?"

He sat up a little straighter, squinting at me. "That explains the walk," he said. "A meaner dog I've never met. He hangs out at Pachinko's on Rush Street and runs errands for the big boys. He hurt you bad?"

"You know anyone that hurts you good?"

He put the frosty glass against his face. "Sit down, why don't you?"

"I'm more comfortable standing."

"Then I'll stand, too. I don't like people looming over me when they talk." He got up. I'd never seen a guy his age so lean and hard, but it wasn't a health-club kind of hardness. Part of it was metabolism, and the other part probably from eating bad guys raw. "Rogatz works for Morris Ackerman."

"Is that late-breaking news? Film at eleven."

His eyebrows arched. "Are you pressing charges? Is that why you're here?"

"I'm not much for lost causes. There's as much chance of nailing Ackerman and his people in this town as there is of Mike Ditka winning the Nobel Peace Prize."

"What'd you do to piss them off?"

"That's what I'm trying to find out. Captain Mayo, Cassidy pulled his suspension for supposedly soliciting a bribe."

"I know that. I couldn't believe it. I still don't. Cassidy was a drunk and a fuck-up, but he was clean as a whistle all his life, and I'd go to the communion rail with that one."

"It was my father that filed the complaint."

He sagged a little and leaned his behind against the table, rattling ice cubes in his glass. "Your father, huh? Jesus, Mary, and Joseph!" He stared out across the back yard toward the detached garage near the alley, not looking at anything in particular. A purple grackle screamed abuse at us from the

205

branches of an elm tree. "You're saying Cassidy found out something he shouldn't've and Ackerman and Givney used your old man for a frame to shut him up."

"That's my reading. Did he call you the night he died?"

"I don't know. We weren't home."

"How can you remember that right off the bat?"

"Christ, it was only last week. I can tell you where we were: the Cubs were playing Montreal and the DC—the district commander—got tickets and invited Ginny—Mrs. Mayo—and me." He showed all his teeth when he smiled. "They don't play so many night games that I wouldn't remember."

"Cassidy didn't leave a message on your machine?"

He shook his head. "He didn't like talking to machines. I tried telling him a phone was a machine in the first place, but he wouldn't listen."

"If he hung up without leaving a message, wouldn't you be able to tell?"

"Not if he hung up before the outgoing message finished. It'd just reset automatically."

I swatted at some winged thing that was buzzing around my nostrils. The iced tea was good in the warm sunlight of mid-morning. "Does the name Storko mean anything to you?"

"Should it?"

I told him.

"It's nobody local," Mayo said. "You never know when the scumbags will import out-of-town talent, but it's nobody I ever heard of."

"How about the fat guy hangs out with Rogatz?"

"Big blond guy with a beer gut? Nah, that's some Polack name, Wizdnitski or something. You saw him; would *you* call him Storko?" He coughed out a dry laugh. "Porko, maybe."

"Cassidy found out something about somebody named Storko the day he died. He was trying to tell you, and I'd be willing to bet that's why he's dead."

"Slipping a guy a lethal dose of amphetamines doesn't sound like a wise guy's MO."

"It's a new world."

"You want me to put a man on it?"

"I can't tell you how to run your squad. If it was me I'd try to get a line on Storko."

He wiped a mustache of sweat from his upper lip. "You think this Storko killed him?"

I shrugged.

"Just because he wrote 'Storko' in his TV magazine?"

"In the margin of the listings for the day he died. I don't believe in coincidences. And most cops don't, either."

Mayo took a long swallow of the iced tea. "Pretty long reach, isn't it, Saxon?"

"It's all I've got," I said.

"I've got something," he said. "It probably doesn't mean anything. I was processing Cassidy's papers. Strictly routine. His pension, his life insurance."

I stood up a little straighter, ignoring the pain that rippled up and down the backs of my leg's like a lover's tease. "Life insurance?"

He nodded. "Cut-rate through the department. I think it may surprise you."

22

I took a cab to the South Loop, this one piloted by one Sid
Treffman, who was even crazier than Azim Mahboubian-Fard.
He not only drove as though the hounds of hell were on his
heels, but he complained all the way that Chicago was unliva-
ble because people let their dogs shit in the street. The backs
of my legs hurt so badly each time he hit a bump or a pothole,
right then I wouldn't have cared if Chicagoans curbed their
elephants in the gutter.

It annoyed me that my rental car, which cost me twenty-nine
bucks a day, was parked in a garage a half block from my hotel,
at eight bucks a day, and I was cabbing all over the city and
paying the freight. But I was too stiff and sore to drive a car and
resolved to turn it back in as soon as I had a moment.

The South Loop used to be one of those places nobody in
their right minds ever visited. Minsky's Burlesque Theatre and
the Star and Garter used to be over there, less than a mile from
the glitter of Marshall Field's, along with a large cadre of what
we once called bums and winos. Several major printing compa-
nies had their headquarters in the squat buildings of heavy red
and brown brick, and chances are if you were alive in the
forties and fifties and had a telephone directory in your home,
it was printed on South State Street. Then the grind joints

closed, the printers relocated, and some enterprising young developer got the bright idea of converting the print shops into condominiums and apartments. Thus was Printer's Row born.

I found the building I wanted and took a creaky old elevator that had gone through a purely cosmetic face-lift up to the third floor.

When the door to Beth's apartment opened I had to catch my breath. The adolescent who stood there wearing a puzzled expression might have been a Gavin Cassidy clone. The same blue eyes, the same sandy hair, the wide shoulders and deep chest, the same Grade AAA Irish stamp on his face. Whether or not Cassidy had ever chosen to acknowledge the boy as his son, the visual evidence was there, obvious to anyone with half a brain.

"Hi. You must be Kevin," I said. "I'm a friend of your mom's."

He shook my hand listlessly and glanced over his shoulder at the TV. The Cubs game was on. Beth came in from one of the other rooms, wearing a white sleeveless blouse, lime green shorts, and sandals. Her body looked every bit as good as it had twenty years before. "Who is it, Kev— Oh."

"Sorry to bust in on you on a Saturday without calling," I said. "I can come back some other time, if you'd rather."

"No, that's okay," she said. "We weren't really doing much."

The boy stepped aside, and I walked into the living room. The furniture was inexpensive, more suited to a suburban patio or a sunroom than to a living room in the heart of downtown Chicago, but it was light and pleasant, rattan with tropical floral prints, in contrast to the heaviness of the walls and ceilings and the massive dark brick front of the building across the street. The air conditioner was blowing hard, making it almost uncomfortably cool in the apartment. I didn't sit down.

"Kevin," Beth said, "why don't you go into your room and watch the rest of the game?"

Kevin stumbled over to the TV, switched it off, and headed for the rear of the apartment, emitting the same kind of put-upon sigh I was used to hearing from Marvel when I made a similar request. It made me feel at home. "Great-looking kid," I said. "I don't need to tell you who he takes after."

"No," she said. "You don't. Every time I look at him I see Gavin."

"Is that a problem?"

She smiled a bit too brightly. "Certainly not. I adore Kevin. He can't help it who he looks like. And as you said, he is a great-looking kid. He's a good kid, too. I apologize for his manners."

"Don't," I said. "I have a teenager of my own, and I'm used to it."

"Well, this is a pleasant surprise," she said, but there was a troubled line between her brows that told me it wasn't as pleasant as all that. "Can I get you something cold to drink?"

I shook my head. "We have to talk, Beth."

She sank down onto the rattan sofa. "If it's about Gavin, I really have nothing more to say."

"Then just listen," I said. "You'll be hearing this anyway, but I wanted it to come from me."

She just looked at me, waiting for the shoe to drop.

"Gavin had a life insurance policy," I told her. "Plus some accrued pension benefits." I took a slip of paper from my pocket. At Ray Mayo's place I had jotted down the figures. "The total is in the vicinity of two hundred twenty-some thousand dollars. And change." I looked at her, hard, and she didn't meet my gaze. "Kevin is his only beneficiary."

Her olive skin turned pale underneath, and she put a hand to her throat. Her nails, I noticed, were cut businesslike short and sported clear polish. "My God," she said.

She stood up suddenly, wringing her hands in front of her; her breathing had grown quicker and deeper.

"Did you know about this, Beth?"

She darted a glance at me, then away, but she really had no place else to look. Finally she met my eyes and said, "I knew there was a policy for Kevin, but . . . My God, that's—"

"A lot of money. Put that in a CD and let it sit awhile, we're talking about a lot more. Your son is, not exactly a rich man, but with proper management he'll be pretty comfortable."

She covered her face with her hands.

"I didn't see the policy or the pension, so I'm just guessing here. But I imagine the money is given over to you in trust until he's twenty-one."

She didn't move, just stood in the middle of the shag rug, swaying, her face covered. I went to her and put my arms around her; that seemed to be my job these days, comforting people. It wasn't a role I was completely suited for. Finally I took her wrists and gently brought her hands down. Her face was ravaged, despairing.

"All those years," she said, "I didn't think he gave a damn about Kevin—about us. It hurt Kevin, too, although he'd never admit it. Every boy needs a father to look up to."

I fought down the sour feeling in my stomach. "Yeah."

She gave me a quick hug and went into the kitchen. I heard the refrigerator open and close, and in a moment she was back with two sweating cans of beer. I took them from her and popped them open, then returned one.

She took a long swallow, wiping her mouth with the back of her hand, and sat down on the rattan sofa again.

"Beth," I said, "you're close to Dolly, aren't you?"

She nodded, staring off into space.

"How tight is Ben with the politicians up north there?"

She looked up at me. "What do you mean?"

"I don't know what I mean," I said. "I don't know if I mean anything. Gavin ran afoul of those guys, and Ben is in bed with them somehow. It might not mean a damn thing, but the more I hear, the more I want to know."

She put the beer can against her forehead, then took another long slug. "Ben is a precinct captain. That's all I know about it." The vertical line between her brows deepened. "Why?"

I said, "I didn't see Gavin's policy. But it had a double-indemnity clause. If it can be proved that Gavin's death was in the line of duty, an accident, or due to 'misadventure,' the policy pays double."

"Misadventure?"

"Come on, Beth, you handle insurance claims, you know very well what that means. If it's determined that Gavin was killed, the total jumps to about three hundred twenty thousand."

Outrage replaced shock in her green eyes. "Surely you're not suggesting . . ."

"I'm suggesting that the circumstances of his death are a bit peculiar, and the police are beginning to think so, too. If it's true, it'd behoove you to help me as much as you can."

She slumped back against the floral cushions, her legs splayed out at an unattractive angle. "I thought you were asking a few too many questions at dinner the other night. What have you got to do with all this?"

"Officially, nothing," I said. "Personally, everything. I've already taken a beating for asking too many questions, in case you were wondering why I'm standing up. That makes it personal. And an extra hundred and fifty grand should make it personal for you, too. Now, will you help me?"

All the air seemed to go out of her, like from a sat-upon whoopee cushion. "If I can, of course."

"Do you know of a friend or acquaintance of Gavin's named Storko?"

"I told you, I hardly saw Gavin in the last few years."

"What about Ben? Or Dolly? They ever mention that name to you?"

"What is it, Storko? No, I'd remember. Why?"

"Because," I said, "Gavin found something out about Storko, and I think he was killed to keep him from telling anyone about it."

She fingered her lower lip, twisting it enough that it looked painful. I could barely understand her when she said, "What are you going to do?"

"Find Storko," I said.

* * *

Ben answered the door. I could hear an opera playing on the stereo inside. I'd never seen him in blue jeans before. He wasn't the type. They made him seem neither trendy nor like a cowboy. They didn't seem to help his disposition, either; he didn't even ask me in before he went after me angrily.

"Do you know," he said, "that you have the whole damn city mad at you?"

"That's why I want to get in off the street," I said.

Reluctantly he stood aside and let me past him into the house. The music was Verdi, I would have guessed, but then my exposure to opera ended when Ed Sullivan's show went off the air and I didn't get to see Roberta Peters every week. He snapped the stereo off.

"What did you hope to accomplish by coming to that party Thursday night and making a scene?" he said, following me in. "It made me look bad, it made your father look bad, and it made you look like a complete schmuck!"

"I don't give shit for your image, Ben. Or my father's, either. And I'll worry about my own, thanks."

"I don't understand you." He stood in the archway between the living room and the vestibule with his hands on his hips, watching me, and then he said, "What's wrong?"

"What?"

"How come you're walking funny?"

"I can't tell you. It'd make you look bad." There was an upright piano against the wall, and I went and leaned on it to take some weight off my legs. "Dolly home?"

"She's at temple," he said. "What do you want?"

"That's a little abrupt, isn't it? Come on, Ben!"

"No, *you* come on!" He advanced like the legions of Rome, jaw thrust forward in unaccustomed pugnaciousness. "We don't hear from you for years and years, and all of a sudden you walk in here like you belong and expect the rest of us to roll over with our legs in the air. You practically accuse about four

213

different people of a murder that isn't even a murder, and you tell *me* to come on? Screw you, pal."

"Nobody's accusing you of anything," I said. "Except maybe a bad back."

"Huh?"

"A chronic weakness of the spinal column."

He looked away. "You've got no right saying that to me."

"I might as well," I said. "You accept whatever you're told because it's expedient for you to. You're so dog-whipped by the back-room guys with the diamond pinkie rings, you're willing to swallow anything." He started to speak but I raised my hand to silence him. "You've got your priorities screwed up, Ben, and your loyalties, too. Gavin was your friend."

"You're damn right he was. Because nobody else would put up with him. You think it's easy nursemaiding a bottle baby? If I had a nickel for every night I went out looking for him or had to take him back to his place because otherwise he would have just lay down in the street and died, I could retire to Florida."

He paced the room, angry, aroused, the bitterness suddenly let loose and torrenting over the dam. "I have a life, buddy. A wife that I should have spent time with, instead of running around taking care of a grown man whose whole reason for living was to self-destruct in flames."

"That was your choice," I said.

"It was my only choice! Who else gave a shit about him? You? You left to do your own thing, and when he followed you out to L.A., you slammed the door on his nose."

"You know damn well why I left."

"Sure—a terminal attack of no guts. So your old man got into some shit, so what? Mine gambled away all the money he ever made, which wasn't much, and my mother had to darn socks and buy day-old bread to make ends meet. Kenni's father couldn't even take a crap by himself. Everybody's got father problems! But Saxon the Sensitive couldn't face up to it, so you ran! And when Gavin needed a lifeline, you were too busy

214

trying to be a star! So he came back here, and I took care of him for the rest of his life—and a good hunk of mine. You call that fair?"

It stung, worse than the pain in my legs and back. "Where is it in your contract that it has to be fair?" I said.

His dark eyes snapped. "Opening up a smart mouth always did come easy for you. No, it doesn't have to be fair. But you've got try to even it up a little. I have a business to run, and being associated with the guys in the ward organization helps me out. Sure I kiss around Givney, like everybody else on the North Side. So what? I couldn't survive if I didn't. Survival is just about the best all of us can do. Me, Kenni, Beth, even Gary Storm, jerk that he is. God damn you for showing up here like some recording angel and judging us for it!"

He hurled himself into the overstuffed chair in front of the TV, where I'm sure he sat every evening and no one else ever did. It was that kind of easy chair. "Everybody's got their own ax to grind, pal. Christ, even Marian, and she loved him."

"What do you mean?"

He looked up at me, wounded. "Marian asked Gavin to stop drinking and he wouldn't, so she left him. But what nobody seems to talk about is the other half of the deal: Gavin agreed to go to AA if Marian would marry him."

"Gavin?" I said.

"Sure, Gavin! Hey, the guy was no kid anymore, and he knew it. He figured at long last, after a lifetime of screwing around, that it was time to settle down with someone he loved. But Marian wouldn't do it."

"Why not?"

"Because, dickhead, Gary pays her a bundle in alimony, about four times what Cassidy made in a year. If she got married the money machine would shut down, and she'd have to give up writing her precious shitty novel! So she said she wouldn't marry Gavin, and he said he wouldn't quit drinking unless she did. That's how it ended."

I limped over in front of him, noting that he wouldn't raise his eyes to meet mine. He kept his hand over them as if he had a headache. Ben Nemeroff didn't yet know what a headache was.

"Ben, you must have heard something. From Givney or his people about what their problem with Gavin was."

"You hear lots of things."

"Tell me one."

"I can't."

"You won't."

"I can't!" he said, finally glaring up at me. "Givney called me a few months ago and said he was having trouble with Cassidy. I told him I didn't know anything and couldn't help him, and I never heard about it again."

"And did you tell Gavin?"

He looked down again, and spoke so softly into his chest that I barely heard him. "It wasn't my business."

Neither of us said anything. The only sound in the room was the ticking of the antique ormolu clock Ben had inherited from his mother. It sat atop the piano in quiet judgment.

Finally I said, "You just let them come get him without even warning him it was going to happen?"

He gripped the arms of his chair. "I don't know anything about that," he said through teeth clenched tight enough to hurt. "I know *chotchkes*. I don't know politics and police crap!"

All of a sudden he wilted completely, his head falling forward. "Do me a favor? Go back to California. Just . . . go back."

"Sure, Ben. If you'll do me a favor in return."

He looked up.

"Stop breaking your arm patting yourself on the back for being such a good friend."

I went toward the door. I felt the way Hans Christian Andersen's mermaid had—every step was like knives. As I was letting myself out I caught a glimpse of him. He somehow had gotten smaller, and the overstuffed chair was practically engulfing him.

23

There was still some residual light in the western sky, but for all intents and purposes the day was gone as I climbed the steps to Marian Meyers' house, holding on to the railing. My back and legs were starting to stiffen up again, and it was becoming difficult even to move. I could understand why some old people simply give up. Combine the aches and pains and the diminished capacities with the disillusionment that comes to everyone if they live long enough, and all the uses of this world begin to seem as weary, stale, flat, and unprofitable as they did to Hamlet. And right now I was as achy and disillusioned as any cranky octogenarian watching TV game shows all day long and making his grown children miserable because the soup isn't hot enough or the mail didn't come until two P.M.

Marian looked startled when she answered my knock and saw me standing on her porch. She also looked beautiful. Her makeup was subtly more dramatic than I'd seen it before, and she was wearing a peach-colored silk blouse and form-hugging linen slacks—not the kind of outfit one associates with a quiet evening at home. Behind her and to my left the lights in the living room were romantically low, and mellow music played on the stereo. She seemed to be handling her grief like a champ.

"I hope I'm not disturbing you."

She consulted the slim watch on her wrist. "Uh . . ."

"We need to talk," I said. "Just a few minutes."

She pursed her lips the way people do when they bite into a tart cherry pie. "All right," she said, and turned back into the house. I followed her, leaving the door open. When I got inside I was able to identify the music as Johnny Mathis. People of our generation always put Mathis on when they want to get laid.

"What's the matter?" she said as I hobbled into the living room. "You're limping."

"That'll teach me not to argue politics." I managed to get to the mantel, where I could lean. "Are you expecting someone?"

She looked away. "What if I am?" she said. "Life goes on."

"It has nothing to do with me. And I guess there's nothing in your divorce settlement that prohibits dating."

The shock hit her hard. "What?" she snapped.

"I'm sure you heard me, Marian."

"Who have you been talking to?"

"Everyone. And they all have different stories. I'm getting pretty sick of it, too."

"I don't know what you mean."

"I thought I made it pretty plain," I said. "But then you're the novelist—you could probably put it better."

"I can't say I care for your attitude."

"Join the club. I'm about as popular in this town as the Black Plague. But you got me involved in this, Marian, and we *are* going to talk. Now, or we can wait till your friend gets here." I crooked an arm on the mantel, hating the theatricality of the pose, but it was the only way I could stand comfortably. "Your call," I said.

"Just what is it you think you've discovered, that you come in here and make demands?" she asked, approaching me angrily.

"I'm not demanding anything," I said. "I'm just here to talk to my client."

She shook her head. "It was a mistake ever confiding in you. I'm sorry I did. Why don't we just forget it?"

"Did Gavin Cassidy propose marriage to you?"

Something went flat behind her eyes. "That's not your concern."

"That's what you think, lady. You turned him down so you wouldn't have to give up your spousal support."

She gnawed off most of the lipstick she had so carefully applied. "What if I did?"

"You had your chance to throw him a life preserver when he was alive, but your bank balance was more important. Now that he's dead it seems awfully important for you to find out how he died. Why the belated concern?"

"You insensitive son of a bitch!" she spat, and her open hand cracked across my mouth. I don't cotton to being hit, but under the circumstances there didn't seem to be much I could do about it. My face was the only part of my body that hadn't been in pain, and now she'd fixed that, too.

"Did that make you feel better?" I said, rubbing my lower lip to take the sting away. "Well, I'm tired of everybody else's feelings. Everybody pouts and gets wounded when I ask questions, and they trot out all their excuses and bitch about their own little troubles. And for all the weeping and rending of garments and the fancy eulogies, no one really gives a shit what happened to Gavin Cassidy."

She raised her hand to hit me again, and I grabbed her wrist hard, twisting just a little, and the corners of her mouth went white with pain and shock. "I don't think so," I said quietly. "Not twice." I don't manhandle women, but not twice. Not today.

We stood that way, nose to nose, for about ten seconds, and her eyes were as full of hate as any I'd ever seen. On the stereo, Johnny Mathis was entreating us to "Walk my way." Finally Marian relaxed and I relinquished my grip. She moved over and snapped off the music, and the house was suddenly too silent, with nothing to mask the sound of promises broken and trust betrayed.

"So I'm a lousy human being," Marian said. "Take me to court."

"I never said that."

"You think I'm proud of myself? I'm a single woman and I'm not so young anymore, and I haven't yet figured out a way to support myself and keep this house and do the work that I love. So yes, I take Gary's money, and yes I turned Gavin's proposal down so I could keep it. You think I haven't cried myself to sleep every night since?"

"Sure," I said, "you're just a sensitive soul."

"I don't know about that. But I do know about guilt." Her dark eyes flashed again. "All of us loved Gavin, sure. But we all let him down one way or another." She shook her head. "We couldn't help it: he asked too much."

"What's too much for a friend?"

"Vampires suck blood," she said. "But Gavin sucked away your essence. That's what he did to the people who loved him, because he was like a child, he couldn't take care of himself. And now, because you abandoned that child and it died, your conscience is eating a hole in your gut, just like the rest of us. My guilt made me ask you to investigate his death, and your guilt made you say yes." She brushed a strand of black hair out of her eyes, and perhaps the beginning of a tear as well. "So save us the moralizing, okay?"

There was a thin mustache of sweat across my upper lip, and I wiped it away with a knuckle. I think the last time I'd felt really good about myself was when I cooked those steaks for Marvel eight days before. For a guy whose ego feeds on his own self-image, that was a starvation diet. But I had to give her game, set, and match. She'd nailed me pretty good. "I think I might have liked it better if you'd slapped me again."

"That can be arranged," she said.

"How about a drink instead?"

She looked at her watch again. "I'm expecting someone."

"If he's the jealous type, tell him I'm your cousin from California. He'll be all right about it."

She shrugged. "In the kitchen. The cupboard over the range." If she couldn't get rid of me, she was damned if she'd be hospitable either.

I laboriously crossed the throw rug and the hardwood floor into the kitchen, and found a bottle of Cutty Sark where she said it would be. I splashed some into a glass and tossed it down neat, enjoying the burning in my throat and stomach. Then I refilled it and carried it back into the living room. Marian was standing behind a chair, her hands clutching the back of it, as if to keep something solid between us.

"For what it's worth, I'm sorry," I said. "I came on pretty strong. But I've had a pretty lousy week, and it got to me."

"Poor baby," she said in a voice like old newspaper crinkling. "It's been one big long carnival for the rest of us."

"Marian, there's a piece missing here. If I can find it I can probably put some answers together. I've asked everyone else and run into a stone wall; either they don't know or they won't tell me. You're just about my last hope."

Her eyes rolled toward the rounded-off ceiling. "Christ, that's the story of my life."

"Storko," I said.

She looked at me. "What?"

"Did you ever hear Gavin mention a man named Storko?"

"Who's Storko?"

"I don't know. That's why I'm asking you."

She shook her head. "I never heard of anyone . . ." All of a sudden she closed her mouth tight and her eyes moved all over the room. "Storko?" she said.

And then she started to laugh. From the gut and through a tight throat, the way you laugh when nothing is really funny, just before hysteria sets in.

She was still laughing when her date walked in the unlocked front door.

"Tell me the joke so I can laugh too," he said. He was a wimpy-looking guy, a little bit shorter than Marian, with owlish glasses and a hairline that had migrated north with the

Canada goose. He was wearing an expensive blue suit, a white silk shirt, and a conservative yellow necktie, all dressed up for a big Saturday night date. The only thing lacking was a clear, square plastic box with an orchid corsage inside.

The sight of him turned the crank up on Marian's laughter, and the dumb, hurt look on his face almost made me laugh too. She held up a hand, trying to will herself to stop, and finally looked away from both of us, gulping great chunks of air. When the spasms subsided, she fumbled in the pocket of her slacks for a tissue and dabbed at her eyes. "Oh, dear," she said. "Howard Gartner, this is—this is my cousin from California." That sent her off on another round of giggling.

Howard Gartner was confused, and I couldn't much blame him. I told him my name and we shook hands. He had the grip of a deboned halibut, but the cologne he wore didn't come from Walgreen Drugs, and he held himself in the way of a man who wasn't worried about meeting the mortgage on the first of the month. Having done the loving and lusting with Cassidy, this time Marian was going for the money.

"California?" he said, clapping me manfully on the back so that my aching, tortured muscles screamed silently. "Whereabouts in California?"

I told him.

"Just passing through?"

"Yeah."

"Business or pleasure?"

"If those are the choices, it must be business."

"What business are you in?"

"I'm a shepherd," I told him.

He didn't quite know how to take me. It's a character flaw of mine. "Ready to go, Marian?" he said uncertainly. "Our reservations are for eight thirty."

She caught her breath again. "Yes, Howard. I'm ready. Just one second." Her tone was that of a mother whose six-year-old was yammering, "Can-we-go-now-Mom?" She found a lipstick in her purse and put some on, and I have no doubt poor

Howard was wondering where the first application had gone. Marian turned to me. "Where'd you ever come up with Storko?"

"Gavin wrote it in the margin of a magazine the night he died.

"S-t-o-r-k-o?"

I nodded. It set her off laughing again, and Howard began examining his fingernails like an archeologist who'd just discovered the thighbone of a triceratops. I could see they had been professionally buffed.

Finally Marian wiped her eyes and said, "Gavin never could spell worth a shit. It's not Storko—it's *Stor Co.* Capital S, t-o-r, capital-C, o. It's the new company Gary is forming when he moves out to the Northwest Side. Storm Company. Stor-Co. He's been talking about it for years."

She picked up her purse and slipped her hand through the crook of Gartner's elbow. "Let yourself out, Cousin," she said.

I sat alone in Marian's living room for a long time, complete with mood lighting, romantic music, and Scotch I didn't particularly care for. There was no compelling reason for me to feel like an idiot, but I did anyway. I should have remembered Gavin Cassidy's total inability to spell even the simplest words. I should have recognized Gary Storm's penchant for putting some version of his name all over everything he touched. And when I thought of how many people I'd asked if they knew "someone named Storko" I wanted to disappear into a hole deep enough to land me in downtown Shanghai at rush hour.

Discovering the secret of StorCo, I realized, didn't qualify me for the grand prize. There was a certain satisfaction in realizing that Gary Storm was somehow involved, but I couldn't cast him in the role of a murderer, no matter how hard I tried. He was too snide, too full of himself, and beneath it all too self-pitying to ever put his ass on the line enough to kill someone. Gary was not the man Cassidy had been; if he ever had to see the elephant face to face, he'd run like a first-grader's nose in January.

Still, he had to be talked to.

I got up from the sofa where I'd been sitting and brooding for the past hour. It wasn't easy. Everything in my body had tightened up and grown stiff and sore again, and going up the stairs to the second floor cost me more effort than I would have believed possible. Rogatz was even better with that sap than I'd realized.

There were three doors opening onto the second-floor hallway. The first was Marian's bedroom, where I had no reason to go. I did notice as I passed by that it was extremely feminine, ruffles and big throw pillows, and on the bed atop the pink comforter, a stuffed unicorn with a sappy expression. Unicorns and Gavin Cassidy; Marian was obviously into myth and fantasy. I skipped the bathroom, too, and went to the third door, which proved to be her office.

Her Rolodex file was what I was after, and I found it on the shelf near the dictionary and thumbed through it. She had all the S's together, but not in any particular order, so it took me a minute to find Gary Storm's home number. His address was in there, too, in the suburb of Schaumburg. It's a fairly new suburb, and probably named after the developer. I wondered whatever happened to the fine old custom of naming towns things like Willow Glen and Cherry Creek and Rolling Hills. I picked up the pastel pink telephone and tapped out the digits. It was a toll call.

I heard five rings before someone picked up. "Storm residence," said a professional voice.

"Is this the answering service?"

"May I help you, sir?"

"Is Mr. Storm in?"

"No he isn't, sir. May I take a message?"

The last time I'd seen Gary I'd slapped him in the mouth, so I doubted he'd return my call, and I told the woman no thank you and hung up. Then I hobbled back downstairs, finished my drink, and left the dirty glass in the kitchen sink.

Somewhere after nine on a Saturday evening, with home two

thousand miles away and a killer running around loose somewhere, and I could barely walk. I could think of but three
options. The first was to go back to my hotel room and sleep,
in which case I'd wake up in the morning too sore to get out
of bed. The second was to head for the Acorn on Oak, listen to
Buddy Charles, drink myself silly, and wind up with the same
result plus a hangover.

I chose the third and called Information for the number of a
taxi company.

"Have you eaten anything today?" Kendra said. She was wearing the terry robe she'd had on that morning, looking fresh and
young. I, on the other hand, was wearing the clothes I'd put on
two days ago, and I'd been through a lot.

"I haven't even thought about it."

She shook her head in dismay. "You have to eat; food is fuel.
You want me to fix you something? All I have is bacon and
eggs. Or I could send out for Chinese."

I sank onto the sofa and put my feet up. It made me feel like
a rubber band being stretched to the limit. "I need another one
of your expert massages," I said. "I hurt all over."

"Why don't you go home?" she said. "It couldn't be worth
all this pain."

"I can't," I said. "I'm too close now. Gary is mixed up with
what happened to Gavin."

"Gary Storm? I can't believe that."

"I'm almost sure of it. Gavin knew something about Gary's
new company, and somebody killed him to shut him up."

She went into the bathroom and began filling the tub. Then
she came back out and said, "Are you going to the police?"

"I'm going to Gary first."

"You expect him to confess to murder?"

"No. I don't think he's guilty of murder. But he's involved,
and he's going to tell me how."

She pulled me up off the couch and helped me off with my
shirt. I grunted with the effort.

225

"What are you going to do?" she asked. "Beat it out of him? You're in no shape."

"That's where you come in," I said, stumbling toward the waiting balm of hot water.

This time I didn't doze. I actively felt the soothing heat, almost sucking it inside me through my pores, letting my muscles fight against the whirlpool effect and gingerly rubbing all the painful places I was able to reach. As much as I hurt, I couldn't concentrate on my physical condition. I was too busy thinking about StorCo, thinking what a damn fool I'd been asking questions about a guy named Storko who didn't even exist. Thinking about Gary Storm. What would a guy who dealt in oil waste have to hide that would be compelling enough to get someone killed, especially someone who was once a friend? That was one of the things I'd ask him.

Kendra came into the bathroom and looked down at me. I was scrunched into the tub up to my neck. Only the necessity of breathing had kept me from submerging my head, too.

"You've cooked enough," she said. "Out."

"Let me stay here a while," I said. "It feels so good."

"Too much isn't good for you. You want to have a heart attack?"

"I've got the heart of a lion."

"Are you kidding, with all the red meat you eat? I bet if the Cubs' team batting average equaled your cholesterol level, we'd have a World Series flag flying over Wrigley. Come on, upsy-daisy."

I wrapped myself in a fluffy, light-blue bath sheet and followed her into the bedroom, looking forward to the ministrations of her strong hands with a mixture of anticipation and dread. It was going to hurt like hell, but in the end I'd feel better.

She bent over me, fingers probing, pushing, kneading, and I groaned, my face buried in a pillow that smelled of her perfume. "Why did you have to come back?" she said, and the pressure of her fingers increased. "Why didn't you just stay home?"

"For a while," I said between grunts, "I kind of thought this was home."

"You can't just drop out for years and years and then come back and upset everyone's lives. Damn you for trying!"

I raised my head, but she pushed it back into the pillow. "Hold still! I'm not finished." Her strong hands worked up my back. "You'll either get what you want or get yourself killed. But you'll keep on trying anyway, won't you? Will that make you proud?"

"It won't make me very proud if I don't keep trying," I said.

"Is that so important?"

"It is to me. It's the way I am."

She didn't answer me but kept on working. After about fifteen minutes it hardly hurt anymore. The memory of the pain was still there, but I felt as if I could function again, for the first time in twenty-four hours.

I rolled over onto my back. "You ought to bottle that."

"Made you feel good, did it?"

"Amazing."

Her mouth twisted into a crooked smile. She undid her robe and let it fall around her ankles. In the dim light coming through the half opened bathroom door, her body looked just the way it had when she was seventeen. "Now it's my turn," she said.

24

Kendra was at the kitchen sink, washing the coffeepot and the mugs and spoons from breakfast, the morning sun streaming through the tiny window. I was at the table, idly pushing a blue packet of Equal around on the Formica surface, feeling better than I had in a long time. The law of compensation had made me forget about most of my aches. Mozart was playing softly on the stereo, and outside in the trees of North State Parkway the birds heralded the borning spring.

"It didn't mean anything," she said. "Last night, I mean. Men always put a lot more store into a night in bed than women do, despite what most people think."

I said, "I hate statements that begin, 'Men always.' "

"I just wanted you to understand, so there won't be any problems or recriminations later."

"Things a little different in the harsh light of day?"

"Not really." She stared straight ahead at the lone catalpa tree in her small back yard. "Too much has happened the last few days, and I was feeling . . . adrift. Insecure. You caught me at a weak moment when I just needed arms around me."

"Glad to be of service," I said. "It was the least I could do in exchange for the therapy." I tried unsuccessfully to keep the edge out of my voice.

She cocked an eyebrow at me. "Your white charger is crapping all over my carpet, so climb down. Don't tell me you never slept with a woman just for the company—or because you were plain old horny."

"Sure I have. I just never found the necessity to announce it to her in the morning. Especially with a history that goes back twenty years."

"I'm just trying to be honest."

"No," I said. "You're just trying to cover your ass in case it didn't mean anything to me either."

"You can't go back," she wailed. "Not to an old town or an old love. There's a statute of limitations." She turned the water off and began drying a mug with a flowered dish towel. "It was very nice. You've gotten better in bed with the years." She looked over at me, but it had been a backhanded compliment, and I was damned if I'd acknowledge it. "But you have to realize it didn't mean anything."

"Methinks the lady doth protest too much."

"God damn it, don't quote Shakespeare!" she said, all but hurling the mug into the dish drainer. "Gavin used to do that all the time. He had a fucking quote for every occasion."

"I'm not Gavin."

"I don't see a significant difference. You're both dead to me. He's in a grave and you're two thousand miles away."

"I'm right here in your kitchen."

She turned and leaned against the sink. "You think you're the first man to sit at that table drinking coffee the morning after? Or the fiftieth?" She drew the back of her wrist across her forehead to wipe away the perspiration. "There's too much water under the bridge," she said. "All the bridges you're looking under. Fly away home, little bird, and root for the Dodgers. This ain't your territory."

I stood up. "You're probably right. You've changed too much, and so have I. We've grown old and cynical and a little bit mean, I'm afraid. Mean-spirited. When we were young, youth was enough excuse to hurt each other out of stupidity and thoughtlessness. Now it's for recreational purposes."

"Isn't that why you're going to go on with this silly murder theory? Because you get your kicks that way?"

"No. Because I have to." I picked up my jacket from the sofa and put it on. "I sort of had the idea that was what last night was all about."

"You're still such a child," she said. "Last night was because I thought if I took you inside me and held you, then you wouldn't be able to get away, to go off and do something stupid."

"Why do you care?"

She fumbled in the pocket of her robe for a cigarette, found one and lit it with a cheap drugstore lighter. "I've buried one ex-lover this week. I can't take burying another one."

In the cab going back to the hotel, I thought about it. To say it hadn't meant anything to me would be to trivialize it; there's something about a first real love that never goes away. It hangs on, to color the rest of your life in ways you'd never have thought possible. It's probably not the best love you'll ever have, but it's the sweetest and the most innocent, and that's worth a lot after you've lived nearly forty years and discovered that life is largely neither innocent nor sweet.

But making love to Kendra was not going to change anything. I wasn't about to turn my entire existence inside out because of it. Kendra was right—you can't go back. Revisiting an old love is a lot like a college football star returning to the empty stadium, a roll of fat around his middle and glasses augmenting the vision that once let him spot a receiver downfield at forty yards. It's a nice feeling, certainly, but not the same. It can never be the same.

I never thought I'd be glad to see a hotel, but when my cab pulled up in front of mine it seemed almost like home. I hadn't been back since Friday evening, my clothes were reprehensible after my little dustup under the El tracks with Rogatz and his fat friend, and I badly needed a shave, so I tried to ignore the disdainful stare of the young woman at the desk when I asked for my messages. She handed me a plain white envelope, sealed with transparent tape.

There was no stamp or postmark, only my name, writ large with a felt-tipped pen. I tore it open and extracted the familiar red, white, and blue ticket folder of United Air Lines. Inside was a one-way ticket to Los Angeles on the three o'clock flight that afternoon, in my name.

"When was this delivered?" I asked the clerk.

She screwed up her nose in a fashion designed to be either thoughtful or cute. It was neither. "I think yesterday sometime. In the afternoon."

"Were you here?"

"I think so."

"Can you remember who brought it?"

"I'm sorry." Her tone turned cool and condescending. "I didn't know I was supposed to notice. If you'd let me know ahead of time . . ."

"Thank you," I said. The snobbery of desk clerks in nice hotels can reach emergency levels. I took the elevator upstairs and put that funny little plastic card that serves as a key into the slot in my door. The air conditioner had been turned to high, probably by the housekeeping staff, and entering was like stepping into a blizzard. I turned it off and fell flat on my back on the bed, just enjoying being there and resting my weary body, checking out the grainy texture of the sprayed-on ceiling.

Fifteen minutes of inactivity was about all I could handle. I sat up, took the ticket out again, and looked at it. Subtlety was not Morris Ackerman's long suit. Well, I thought grimly, it isn't mine either. I had plans of my own, and they didn't include going back to Los Angeles—not that afternoon, and not until I was damn good and ready.

First things first, though, and my priority right now was to get out of my sour-smelling, rumpled clothes. I left them in a pile on the floor and on the pad next to the phone I jotted a reminder to call the hotel valet in the morning. I hadn't expected to stay in Chicago so long; I was running out of wardrobe.

I stood under a hot shower for a long time. Whatever pain I'd experienced had faded under Kendra's tender care to a dull ache, but the water felt good nevertheless. I washed the grit out of my hair, shaved, and used every towel in the place to dry off, a luxury I always indulge in when staying in a hotel. Then I called Jo Zeidler's house in L.A.

"I thought for sure you'd be back by now," Jo said. "Is everything all right?"

"Just great. Anything happening at the office?"

"I don't have the list of messages in front of me, but you did get a couple of calls from your agent, and from a Beverly Hills attorney who I think wants to hire you."

"Can you hold him off a few more days?"

"What's going on there? The funeral was a week ago."

"Complications."

She was silent for a moment. Jo knows me better than almost anyone. "Can I do anything?" she said softly.

"Hold down the fort and think good thoughts," I said.

"Be careful, okay."

"I'm always careful."

"Sure," she said. "You want to talk to Marvel?"

"If he's available."

She put the phone down and I waited for what seemed like a long time. Then I heard someone snatch the receiver up from where it had been lying. Marvel sounded grumpy; it was not yet nine o'clock on the West Coast, and I'd awakened him.

"What's going on?" I said.

"Oh, not much," he replied with forced airiness. "I was jus' layin' here sleeping."

"How's school?"

"Oh, man, it's great. I kin hardly wait to go every morning, an' shit."

"Are you eating okay?"

He gave an exasperated sigh. Kids never understand why adults treat them like kids.

"All right, all right," I said.

He obviously had to weigh his next question to decide whether or not it sounded dependent and childlike. "When you comin' home?"

Home. I liked the sound of the word, the way he dragged out the vowel sound. It made me think of ducks swimming on the canal, of skinny girls in bikinis on the beach a few blocks from the house, of the familiar sights and sounds and smells of my own house. "In a few days. Miss me?"

"Shee-it!" Marvel said. Ask a silly question.

Reassured that all was well in Los Angeles, I put on clean clothes and went across the street to the parking garage, where I ransomed my rented car and headed for the Kennedy Expressway and the drive out to Schaumburg.

There was a newness to the streets, the trees, the grass and the houses that made the suburb seem like a movie set that had been built to last no more than a few weeks. Is American society in the nineties as temporary as it seems? Twenty years from now would any of these people still be living here in these cookie-cutter houses, working at the same jobs and driving a newer model of the same make of car they now owned, or would they move on to bigger and better homes, leaving these to be occupied by strangers who wouldn't care for them?

After stopping for directions at a self-service gas station—minimart, I found the address I was looking for without too much trouble. Gary Storm's house teetered on the edge of ostentation. A sweeping lawn rolled up to the large Tudor, looming on its small hilltop like the Château d'If. I parked at the curb and started up the driveway toward the front door. At the foot of the driveway were two stone pillars matching the facing of the house. There was no iron gate, but I was sure one of these days Gary would decide he needed one and have it installed. I noticed two copies of the *Chicago Tribune* carelessly tossed onto the grass by a passing delivery agent; a closer examination revealed they were yesterday's and today's. Perhaps Gary didn't care what was going on in the world.

The damaged muscles in the back of my legs protested the walk up the inclined drive to the front door, heavy burled oak with a leaded-glass insert of many colors. I rang the bell, which chimed inside like a medieval clock, and waited. After repeating the ring a few times, I wandered around the side of the house to the garage. It was closed, of course, but there was an eye-level window in the door, and enough light inside to let me know there was no car in residence. Gary had probably gone somewhere for the weekend.

Across the street in a smaller and less impressive house I saw a middle-aged man peering out the window at me, making no effort to hide himself, his look hostile and suspicious. This was not the sort of neighborhood where strangers prowling around the garages of absent residents were welcome. I got back into my car and drove off in a hurry.

Back at the hotel I bided my time, laying plans. I had to think it out carefully or risk getting hurt and/or arrested. What I had in mind was stupid, but there are things in life which are not to be tolerated, not if you wish to see your own reflection in the mirror. I'm a firm believer in the payback. Some things just require closure.

When I had it all down pat in my head I spent the rest of the day napping, grabbed a light dinner in the hotel restaurant, and then walked off the meal and the stiffness. I strolled across the bridge into the Loop, but it was virtually closed down, with only a Walgreen's and a souvenir shop open. I went into the drugstore and purchased a large padded mailing envelope. I asked the clerk for two rolls of quarters, which he sold me only grudgingly, and with one of them I bought postage stamps from the machine near the checkout counter. Then I went back to the hotel to wait.

At ten o'clock I made a phone call. When I found out what I wanted to know, I hung up, got ready, and made the fifteen-minute walk over to Rush Street. There was an outdoor café there, and I sat down at a dusty table and ordered a cup of coffee and a piece of pie, neither of which I consumed, while keeping my eye on the entrance to the bar across the street.

Pachinko's, it was called.

The tired waitress kept coming by and glaring at me, and finally I ordered another piece of pie.

"You didn't finish the first one," she accused.

"That's why I want another one. This one got lonesome."

It had been a long evening for her, I was sure, and she didn't need my crap. I resolved to leave an especially big tip.

Finally, at about eleven forty-five, I saw what I'd come for. I slipped ten dollars under one of the plates and went out onto the sidewalk.

Rogatz had come out of Pachinko's and was walking south on Rush, hands in his pockets, wearing an Italian-cut sports jacket that was too silvery and shiny to take seriously. Across the street, I paralleled him. He headed for a multilevel parking structure about a block away. When he turned into it I jay-walked, deftly dodging an oncoming Yellow Cab. I got to the entrance in time to see him walking up the ramp, waited until he'd turned a corner out of sight, and then followed him. The cashier was sitting in his little booth, his head back against the glass, dozing.

The structure was dim, puddles of yellow light fading into dingy grayness, and quiet, the only sound being the traffic humming outside on Rush. I ducked down behind a minivan and watched as Rogatz reached a big gold-colored Cadillac. Why wasn't I surprised? As he fumbled with his keys, his back to me, I walked up behind him, stopping about six feet away.

"Hold it!" I barked. "Drop the keys, hands on top of your head."

He straightened up, his right hand making a move toward his left armpit. "Don't try," I said.

The keys hit the floor with a clank. Slowly he put his hands atop his greasy hair.

"Lace those fingers together. Now!"

He hesitated. "What is this?"

"Shut up and do it!"

He tried to sneak a look over his shoulder at me, but couldn't quite pull it off. "How do I know you're carrying?"

"You want to know bad enough to risk a kneecap?"

It didn't take him long to think it over. He intertwined his fingers and waited while I moved up, reached around him and removed the gun from his holster. It was a .22, a lady's gun much favored by the boys with the bent noses for close-up wet work, ugly metallic blue. I switched it to my right hand and with my left went under his jacket and removed the sap from his hip pocket, transferring it to my own. Then I patted him down to make sure he wasn't carrying any other goodies. He wasn't. I kicked the keys hard and heard them skitter on the concrete. I didn't see where they went, and neither did he. Then I stepped back. "Turn around," I said.

He did, keeping his hands where they were. His mouth was chapped and red from his habit of licking his lips. His eyes widened when he saw me. "Jesus," he said, "I'm surprised you're walkin' around."

"I'm a fast healer," I said.

"Was that you called Pachinko's asking for me before?"

I nodded.

"Whaddaya want?"

"You," I said. "I want a piece of you."

His bravado smile didn't work. "You don't have the guts to shoot."

"Or the inclination." I was enjoying watching him sweat. I waited. He fidgeted and looked around for a rescuer.

"So whaddaya gonna do?" he said. The suspense was killing him. I liked that.

"I'm going to find out how tough you are without a sap in your hand and your fat friend to hold me down." I put the gun in my pants pocket, feeling the weight of it, the cold metal through the thin fabric of the pocket lining. Then I took out the remaining roll of quarters and wrapped my fist around it.

He couldn't believe it at first, or else he would have put his hands down. But he kept them on top of his head for a moment, just as Simon Said.

"You are a dumb fuck," he said.

"Come on, Rogatz," I urged, motioning him toward me.

He took his hands down from his head and let them hang at his sides, his tongue darting out to wet his raw lips, his eyes never still. "Hey, listen, the other night, I was just doing my job." His voice was getting higher, more shrill. Pretty soon it would be up in that acoustic range where only dogs could hear it.

"You ought to find another line of work."

"It was nothing personal, you know."

"It is now," I said. We were between two cars, both parked too close to the wall for him to try an end run. I took a step forward.

"Hey, what about Ski? He was there too. You broke his nose, man."

"I know. That's why I'm not going after him now."

"Listen," he said. "This isn't fair—you're bigger than me." He put out a quivering hand to stop me.

"Everybody's bigger than you, you little prick." I grabbed two fingers of the outstretched hand and bent them back as far as they'd go. Then a bit further. The two little pops, like dud firecrackers, were almost drowned out by his screams. A pretty sickening sound.

He pulled his fingers back, clutching them against his chest, and I stepped forward, putting all my weight into the blow I aimed at the side of his jaw with the fistful of quarters. It caught him hard, spun him around and into the concrete wall, which he slid down slowly. The quarters made a tinkly sound as they hit the floor. My hand immediately went numb and I knew it would ache in the morning, but it was worth it. I took a step forward, ready to kick an extra point with his head, but his chin hit his chest and he fell over sideways. I checked to see if he was faking, but he was sleeping like a baby. The only thing spoiling the illusion of childhood innocence was his jaw, hanging at an unnatural angle, the chapped lips slack and drooling.

I waited a few seconds to make sure I hadn't killed him. Then I went down a flight of stairs, which put me out on the sidewalk on one of the side streets running between Rush and Michigan, and strolled back to the hotel.

Up in my room I ran cold water on my sore hand for a while, and when it felt better I checked the little .22. The serial numbers had been filed off, which didn't surprise me at all. Then I took Rogatz's sap from my pocket, wrapped the airplane ticket around it, and put it into the padded envelope, which I addressed to Major Morris Ackerman on Lake Shore Drive. I didn't think I needed a return address. I put five dollars worth of stamps on it to make sure it arrived.

I went downstairs in the elevator, and as I crossed the lobby the young desk clerk did her best to pretend I wasn't there. There was a mailbox at the corner of Michigan and Ontario into which I deposited my parcel. Then I strolled a few blocks south past the Tribune Tower to the Chicago River and tossed Rogatz's gun into the water off the Michigan Avenue Bridge.

25

Maybe it's the eight hours of cooling off that lets your emotions take a back seat to your common sense, where they belong, or perhaps the mind is rested and fresh, but things always look different after a good night's sleep, and in the morning I decided it was fortuitous that Gary Storm hadn't been home for the weekend. I couldn't very well go crashing in there, no matter what I might suspect. He'd already threatened to sic his lawyers on me, and that was just for a slap in the mouth. What he'd do about a murder accusation I couldn't even imagine. Perhaps call out the Illinois National Guard. I needed more ammunition before I confronted him or called Ray Mayo to spill the beans. And I'd figured out where I could get it.

I called the hotel valet and left my dirty clothes in a bag hanging on the doorknob and then went out for breakfast. When I travel I like to visit as many different eateries as I can, but I was in no mood for experimentation, so the West Egg seemed serviceable enough. It's hard to louse up bacon and eggs anyway. I read the morning *Tribune,* at least the sports and entertainment pages. I didn't think I was up to the bad news of the day on the front page. I had enough of my own, thank you.

The official business of the city of Chicago is handled downtown, in the middle of the Loop. City, state, and federal offices vie for space with the stockbrokers and lawyers of Clark and LaSalle streets, and the profusion of dark suits and eelskin briefcases coexists more or less peacefully with the cottons and polyesters of the civil servants. The government buildings all feature controversial sculptures in their courtyards.

It took me about an hour wandering the corridors of Daley Center, the county building named for the current mayor's late father, to find the department I was looking for. It was a different venue than I was used to, but it was familiar territory nonetheless. Much of a private investigator's work is done in the stacks of records that proliferate in the large cities of America. Millions of acres of forest have fallen to create the paper documents stored in government archives all over the country, documents that turn musty and yellow with the years because no one ever looks at them. Except people like me.

The records for StorCo, Inc., were easy to find. The attractive black woman in charge of such things wore a name badge identifying her as Beatrice Meacham, and she was ten times as pleasant as most people in her job tend to be. I mentioned I was from Los Angeles and she told me her daughter was a junior at UCLA. It was a friendly, Chicago kind of conversation, and she was glad to point me in the direction of the business records. I wished I could put her in my hip pocket and take her back to California with me as a good example to the sullen and often antagonistic civil servants in our hall of records.

According to the application forms, StorCo, Inc., was a four-pronged company that would collect waste oil products, then process, repackage, and sell them. It was a quantum leap for Gary, the next logical step past the firm he now owned and operated, G. Storm, Inc. I knew nothing about the business. I'd learned more than I'd ever wanted to know about oil drilling the year before in Los Angeles on a case that had turned particularly messy, but Gary's operation was about twenty steps further down the line from that, closer to what the M.B.A.s persist in calling "the user end."

240

I'm no lawyer, either, but from what I could tell the articles of incorporation had been properly filed, listing Gary Storm as the principal stockholder and CEO. Other shareholders were Esther Storm, Gary's eighty-something-year-old mother, who owned a ten-percent block, and someone named Winfield Katz, Esq., with an address on North LaSalle Street. The "Esq." and the LaSalle Street office led to me to the inescapable conclusion that Winfield was Gary's lawyer, and a trip to the yellow pages at an old-fashioned phone booth in the corridor confirmed it for me.

In another room, almost identical to the first one—apple green walls the color of a headache, overhead fluorescent light fixtures every ten feet that hummed about a flatted fifth apart, cardboard boxes bulging with file folders stored on endless rows of metallic shelves—I also found that a parcel of land on the Northwest Side, at the bend of the North Branch of the Chicago River, had been bought by StorCo three months before. The price at which it had been purchased seemed ridiculously low to me, but when you're accustomed to the grotesquely inflated real estate price tags in Southern California, everywhere else in the country seems like a bargain. From the preliminary blueprints it seemed that Gary Storm was thinking big.

Reading blueprints is not my strong suit—I can hardly read the directions for assembling a set of bookshelves—but you didn't need a degree in architecture or engineering to know that StorCo's new headquarters were going to be impressive indeed, with three buildings and a parking lot for more than a hundred cars sprawling over fifteen riverfront acres.

Acres that were located in Martin Givney's Fifty-Fourth Ward.

In a bureaucracy, it's damn near impossible to do anything without getting official permission. Every city is a bureaucracy, and Chicago the granddaddy of them all, so there were several permits on file for StorCo, including a business license. In the same file were copies of construction permits, sewage and water lines and such, issued in the name of K&K Contractors, Dave and Diane Kubo's Company.

Stuffed in the back of the folder, dated three weeks earlier, was another permit, signed with several names that were as familiar to me as my own: people my father had known in the old days of the Fifty-fourth, who had now risen to enough prominence in the city and county that they were able to affix their names to important documents. But this one just about blew me out of my chair.

The pieces all fell into place, and I knew why Gavin Cassidy had died on Lincoln Park West.

I got to Gary's office just after four thirty, just late enough in the day for things to be winding down. Many of the workers had gone home, or were elsewhere; the floor of the warehouse seemed almost deserted except for a two-man cleanup crew who flourished their mops and brooms with authority and conviction.

Gary was at his desk in the glassed-in office, today's suspenders bright blue against the white of his shirt. His face turned red again when he saw me. It was a patriotic color scheme, but I feared for his blood pressure. "Just turn your happy ass around and walk out of my life," he said, getting to his feet and pointing his finger at me like a pistol. "If you think you can come in here and manhandle me some more, you're out of your goddamn mind!"

"What will you do, Gary? Call your lawyer?"

"You're damn right!"

"Does he handle criminal cases, too?"

Uncertainty warred with anger behind his eyes even as his skin color went from red to mottled. He glanced over at his secretary, who stopped shuffling, stapling, and spindling, jumped to her feet, and tiptoed from the room.

"I don't have to discuss anything with you," he said when she'd gone. "I don't even have to talk to you. And I won't."

"Call the cops, then."

242

He hesitated, and I took up the receiver from the phone set on his desk. It was one of those multibutton jobs that require a six-month course at the Famous Acme Electronics School before you can make an outside call. I held the handset out to him, and he cringed in his chair as if afraid I might hit him with it. "Go on, Gary. Call."

He snatched it away from me and slammed it down into its cradle. "All right, what's your problem?"

I took out my notebook and flipped it open to the last entry. "My problem is city permit number 51467771."

He looked down at the desk. One of those big calendar blotters covered more than half the surface, and he seemed to be studying the notations he'd made on it to make sure he hadn't forgotten an appointment. "I don't know what that is."

"That surprises me, knowing how you keep on top of things in your own business. Let me help you out, then. That permit will allow StorCo, Incorporated, to construct and utilize at its new plant site an underground disposal system for chemical waste products."

"So?"

"You just pump it into these large cast iron disposal tanks a hundred or so feet under the surface, right?"

"It's a standard permit, as far as I know. What do you expect me to do with the waste—eat it?"

"You're going to let everyone else eat it instead."

"Obviously it isn't as bad as you think, or they never would have issued the permit."

"They? You mean Harry Gogarty from public works and Frank Skelley from the Chicago Sanitation District?"

"Who?"

"Those are the signatures on the permit—and they're both Martin Givney's boys."

He was grinding his teeth together, hard. "This is a waste of time," he said. "We're not dumping it in the river. The permit is for underground disposal."

"Sure it is, Gary; that's how you hid it. Except the plant is right on the riverbank, out on the Northwest Side where the river bends, and the disposal site is less than five hundred feet from the water. That chemical waste, which as far as I can see is toxic, will leach right into the river to the tune of two thousand gallons a day!"

His nostrils were taking on a pinched, white appearance, as though he'd smelled something bad—like chemical waste.

"Nobody in their right mind would issue a permit like that," I said. "But there are lots of ways to get one in Chicago, and we both know what they are."

He slammed his open palm down on the blotter with such force that it made even him start. "What the hell business is it of yours, anyway? You some kind of religious fanatic? So I'm polluting the river, so what? Everybody pollutes. Christ, it's almost a national pastime. I'm as concerned about the environment as the next guy, but I'm not going to be the only one going broke over it while everyone else cuts corners. Even you. You don't use plastic? You don't add to the crap in the air out in California with your car, your cigarettes, your barbecue grill? Give me a fucking break!"

"I'm trying to," I said softly, "that's why I'm here."

"What are you, the Caped Crusader, going from place to place pointing fingers at polluters?"

"I don't care if you piss in the drinking water at City Hall," I said. "But you paid somebody off for that permit. You'd have had to, and it was more than fifty bucks, or a couple of good seats to a Cubs game. I think Gavin found out about it, and somebody killed him to keep him quiet."

Someone sucked all the red out of his face with a soda straw, leaving him ashen. The idea seemed to truly shock him. He put his hand to his mouth as though he wasn't quite sure where it was and meant to search around with his fingers until he found it. "Gavin? Uh, I don't—what makes you think that?"

"Let's say I have some evidence that points that way."

"What evidence?"

I shook my head. "Talk to me."

244

He took his hand from his mouth and knotted it into a fist on the desktop. "I told you the truth," he stammered. "I don't know anything about that permit. I mean, I know my business, but I don't bother with all that—political shit." He tried a chuckle; it came out a sickly hiccup. Funny how tough he could talk until his back was against the wall. "I leave details like that to—other people."

"I thought you were a one-man gang, Gary. What other people?"

His lips were slack, wobbling the way lips do when they're shot full of Novocain for a root canal, and his face was now slick from the sweat that darkened his beard.

"My contractor. He took care of the building and use permits. It's part of his job. I pay him a flat fee up front, and he takes care of all that stuff so I don't have to worry about it."

Something inside me lurched and went off its axis. I didn't want to hear the answer, but I had to ask anyway. "Are you talking about K&K? Dave Kubo?"

He nodded, his face crumbling along with his empire. He swallowed a few times and then leaned forward with his elbows on the desk, taking his head between his two hands. He was the monkey who heard no evil.

By the time I left G. Storm, Inc., the evening rush hour was in full cry. In another, less complicated time, heading downtown at six o'clock would have been against the traffic, but now with so many people living in or near the Loop, there was gridlock in both directions. Feeling irritated and stressed, I drove directly to the car rental office a few blocks from my hotel and turned the car in. I had managed to live the first twenty years of my life without a car in Chicago, and I guessed I could muddle through another day or two. Cabs are always easy to find near the lakefront, and if you don't mind the maniacal driving, it's an easier way to travel.

Nothing, however, seemed easy to me at the moment. I was sick at heart and sorely troubled by what Gary Storm had told me, and I had to decide what was the best way to handle it. There's no "right" way, of course, not when it involves someone you love. Diane had been my friend forever. It was she who had carefully explained to me that a brandy Alexander was not the correct drink to order before dinner, who had held my hand when Kendra left me for Gavin, and she'd always been there to let some of the air out when my young head swelled too big. It wouldn't do to inform the police about what her husband had done—and what he might have done—without talking to her first. There might be an explanation, or mitigating circumstances. At least I hoped so. It was the least I could do for her. Another debt to pay.

I guess when you're raised in the kind of political environment that pervaded Jimmy Saxon's home like stale cigarette smoke, some of it rubs off. Debts are incurred and they are invariably called in; a gentleman pays his debts.

When I stopped by the front desk of my hotel for my mail and messages, the young woman clerk was gone; in her place was a studious-looking young black man whose clipped speech had originated in the British West Indies. Another student, I figured. Isn't there any such thing as a professional hotel clerk anymore?

"Just one message, sah," he said, handing me the slip. It was from Diane.

In need of bolstering, I went into the bar and had two quick Scotches that didn't make me feel better. They stocked Talisker, a single-malt I don't like as well as Laphroaig but can make do with. Then I went up to my room. The valet had returned my clothes squeaky clean and hanging in the closet, along with a bill that would feed a family of boat people for a year. I kicked off my shoes, shrugged out of my jacket, and punched out Diane's number.

"Gary must have called you," I said.

"He did. God, this is awful. We have to talk."

"I'd say so."

"Can you meet me?"

"You want me to come out to your place?" I asked.

"No, no," she said quickly. "Let's meet somewhere."

"Shouldn't Dave be there, too?"

"Let's you and I talk alone first. I'll come downtown."

"Now?"

"No, about eleven o'clock. Do you know the Wild Cherry on Wabash, right near Wacker Drive?"

"I'll find it. Isn't that kind of late?"

"I have to make Dave's dinner. He goes to bed early, and I can get out."

"Diane—"

"Don't tell anyone, all right? Not until we've talked. Please?"

I'm a sucker for a please. I agreed.

I stripped my clothes off and showered. There wasn't enough hot water in Chicago to rid me of the slightly dirty feeling I had, but afterward I shaved and put on some of the duds the valet had so carefully cleaned for me—dark gray slacks, a white shirt, and a lightweight black linen jacket. If I was going to scuttle a friendship of twenty years' duration, I might as well look sharp while I did it.

I walked over to Pizzeria Uno. In more than a week in Chicago I hadn't been able to indulge my pizza passion, and I didn't know when I'd next get the chance. I put my order in when I first arrived—cheese, sausage and mushroom—then got a Watneys from the bar and went to sit outside and wait for a table. That's the way Uno does it.

It wasn't the same anymore. The pizza was as good as it had ever been, but something had changed. Perhaps I had. Or maybe nothing would have tasted good that evening.

26

Rain hung in the air again, heavy and fragrant beneath the ominous clouds, one of those good midwestern smells that cut right through the traffic exhaust and the diesel fuel and the industrial pollution of the city. It was too early to go and meet Diane, so after dinner I walked around the neighborhood where I'd cut my grown-up teeth, had my first fist fight, lost my virginity, gotten drunk for the first time, and learned how to be an adult. The old North State Street Theatre Guild had been razed years before to make way for an enormous parking lot that was crowded during the day but now, at night, served the overflow crowd from a dance club that had sprung up on a side street. The site of my theatrical debut, I thought, and now someone's parked their Volvo there to commemorate the spot.

As struggling young actors, few of us had owned an automobile except Gavin, but now the cars cruised Rush Street, radios blaring. The once familiar places, those that hadn't been torn down anyway, all had new names and new looks. Figaro's was gone. So was the Scotch Mist. The gay all-night coffee shop on Division Street was no more, replaced by a loud, open bar catering to young kids who drank too much beer, shouted at each other to be heard over the blast of canned music, and threw up in the gutter. No more Cloister Bar, that intimate boite where Lurlene Sanders had once redefined the art of café singing.

No more Cassidy.

Changes. The world rolls on, people grow up, grow old, and die, and things change, as they're toughened by the cold of winter and burnished by the summer sun. It's the natural order, I suppose, but knowing that did nothing to mitigate the sense of loss that engulfed me and left me empty. Almost everything I once knew was gone or transmogrified, and now I was on my way to shoot down the last remaining touchstone I had in Chicago.

Just after ten, when I'd had enough nostalgia to last me a lifetime, I headed for the Wild Cherry. It was only about fifteen minutes away, but I'd have to live with being early. We Californians, products of a car culture that keeps us distant from our fellow man and all wrapped up in a metal womb with an imitation leather dashboard and fuzzy dice hanging from the mirror, aren't used to a lot of walking—after all, we drive to the mailbox—and my feet were starting to hurt. So was my heart. Dave Kubo was the last guy I'd expect to kill anyone, but people do strange things when they're in a corner.

The Wild Cherry was on the wrong side of the river to be fashionable. Wabash Avenue slices through the Loop, and the bar was situated near South Water, just before the rickety El tracks turn westward at Lake Street. Unlike the wood-paneled fern bars of River North, the Cherry was dark and dreary inside. Odors of urine, stale beer, and Lysol assaulted the senses like a physical slap in the face. Occupied mostly by blacks, some elderly white men with gnarled, hard hands and wilted work shirts, and a redheaded hooker who probably couldn't even remember her fortieth birthday, it was not the place I would have picked to while away a few idle hours. I wondered why Diane had chosen it.

Everyone stared at me as I hoisted myself up onto a barstool. I didn't blame them. I looked as if I'd wandered in from the wrong movie. The hooker gave me a brave come-on smile, but her heart wasn't in it. Mine certainly wasn't. The bar top had been wiped but probably hadn't really been scrubbed in twenty years. I ordered a Bud, figuring I'd be safe if I drank it out of the bottle. Had I asked for Laphroaig or even for a Watneys, they probably would have fallen on me and torn me to pieces.

An old movie, *Seven Men From Now,* droned on the TV set amidst the backbar bottles. No ESPN cable channels for the Wild Cherry. Randolph Scott was hunting down the seven men who held up a stagecoach station and killed his wife. A young Lee Marvin was in evidence, too. I'm sure I was the only guy in the place who knew the name of the movie, or cared. I even knew who the director was. I didn't share my knowledge with my fellow drinkers. My guess was there were few movie-trivia buffs at the bar.

I'd gone through three beers—or rather, three beers had gone through me—and Scott had only two men to go when Diane walked in wearing a lightweight black raincoat over a burgundy pants suit and a white silk blouse buttoned to the neck. At the hem of her coat was a dusty white smudge, as if she'd gotten ready in too much of a hurry to check herself in the mirror. Not that Diane had ever given much thought to appearances; she believed other things were more important. The patrons gave her the same sort of peculiar look with which they'd greeted me.

"Nice place you picked out," I told her as she took the stool next to me.

"I thought we should talk someplace where we weren't likely to run into anyone we know."

"Good choice."

The bartender came over and parked in front of us, silently waiting for Diane's order. Dragon tattoos on both folded arms disappeared up the short sleeves of his shirt. He looked like he might have fought bantamweight under the name "Sailor Al" Somebody back in the fifties.

"I don't really want anything," Diane said.

Sailor Al immediately lost interest and went away.

"Let's take a walk," she said.

We went out into the rapidly cooling night, and I tried not to think of what they were saying about us inside. At the corner an elevated train roared around the bend, showering sparks as it headed west. There was a fine mist in the air, sparkling in the arc lights like microscopic diamonds. We turned right, heading for the river. To have gone in any other direction at that time of night would have been courting disaster.

"Gary said you found out about the permit," she said.

"Yep."

She hunched her shoulders under the raincoat. "Dave could be in a lot of trouble. Are you going to tell anyone?"

"I don't know. I wanted to talk to you first."

The sardonic smile I knew so well turned up one corner of her mouth. "Demanding an explanation?"

We reached Wacker Drive, Chicago's famous two-level street, that hugs the south bank of the river. We stood for a bit at the balustrade, looking across to the towers of the Wrigley Building, Riverfront Plaza, and the squat brick and glass headquarters of the *Chicago Sun-Times.*

"I'm not demanding anything, Diane. I'm as sick about this as you are. Just tell me about it, and then we can decide where to go from there."

"We? You mean I have a choice?"

"There are always choices, Diane. We talked about that before."

"Sure—you can choose to live, or not," she said. She raised her head and sniffed the moist air like a golden retriever. "I told you the other night that Dave and I have had some bad luck financially. Contracts that were broken, promises that were never honored. It's nobody's fault, really." Her breath caught in her throat. "Well, maybe Dave's, a little. He's very good at what he does, but he's just too naive, too trusting. So we weren't in good shape at all. We were overextended, with the house and all, and it needs so much work, and—"

"What has this got to do with StorCo?"

She struggled to keep her voice even. "While our fortunes were hitting bottom, Gary has prospered. He's made a lot of money in the last ten years, and you know what an egomaniac he is. He wanted to expand, become one of the wheeler-dealers around here. He decided to form StorCo and build a big new plant to house it. A showplace, he said." She looked at me. "You can't blame him for that, can you?"

I shook my head.

"So I went to Gary and begged," she went on. "He's such a snake I figured he'd get off on throwing K and K a bone. Make him feel like Lord Bountiful. And I was right. He offered about fifteen percent less than he would have to any other contractor, but he knew we were hungry. Dave got the contract."

"And?"

"And life got better all of a sudden. Dave was even walking different, with his head up."

"What about the permit?"

"Part of the contractor's job is to secure the various permits they need to go ahead and build the plant out by the river. It was all included in the fee Gary was paying him."

"And what was that fee going to be?"

Her eyes were expressionless marbles. "It would have amounted to about a seven-hundred-thousand-dollar profit."

"Fat City," I said.

"For the first time in Dave's life." She sighed deeply. "Look, he didn't know anything about oil, about petrochemicals. He just accepted what Gary told him. And when he applied for the dumping permit, he was turned down. He even slipped a few bucks to someone under the table, but he was still turned down." I could hear her teeth grinding. "It almost killed him. He started sitting in the front window, you know? Just staring out at the street. One more time, Dave Kubo snatches defeat from the jaws of victory."

"Why did he think they'd let him dump toxic waste into the river in the first place?"

"You know how this city works!" she snapped. "A few

252

bucks in the right place, a campaign contribution that's tax deductible. It's done every day."

"What happened, then?"

She shrugged. "When you're talking about pollution, it gets a lot tougher than it was twenty years ago. People are more aware of the environment. Now it's a political issue."

A headache was taking root behind my eyes, and I turned my face up to the mist. "Political," I said.

"So it took more than a few dollars."

"How much more?"

"Forty thousand more."

The number impressed me.

"Forty thousand dollars, paid in cash, in small bills, to a representative of one Morris Ackerman. I imagine that some of the money trickled down to the boys in the Fifty-fourth Ward, too." She clucked her tongue. "So there it is. The whole story."

"I don't think it's quite the whole story, Diane. What did this have to do with Gavin Cassidy?"

She looked at me, hard, a thin white line around her compressed lips. Then she turned and started walking slowly west. I took a few quick steps to catch up with her.

"Gavin found out about the permit, didn't he? About the bribe?"

"I don't know how. I suppose policemen have eyes and ears everywhere. But he found out."

"They call them snitches."

She looked over at the hulking mass of the Merchandise Mart. "That must be it, then."

"And?"

"Gavin and I knew each other for longer than you and I. Just like you, he didn't want to tell anyone until we had a chance to talk."

"Did you? Talk?"

"Oh, yes. For hours, one night." She pulled the collar of her coat up around her chin. "In the Wild Cherry, actually."

"What happened?"

"He got drunk, of course. And he gave me—gave Dave, actually—forty-eight hours to withdraw the permit application."

"Or he'd spill the beans?"

She nodded.

"The permit is on file, so obviously you didn't withdraw it. What happened?"

"I went to Martin Givney for help."

I stopped in my tracks. "And Givney got Cassidy suspended by accusing him of soliciting a bribe."

She didn't say anything, didn't look at me.

"And he got my father to make the accusation, knowing Gavin wouldn't call Jimmy a liar because of our friendship."

"I don't know what his thinking was," she said, her face muffled in the folds of her collar. She began walking more quickly. I had to do a couple of skip-steps to catch up with her.

"You're not going to just leave it like that?"

"I don't know what else you want from me," she whined.

"Gavin never denied the charges. He just took it. Why?"

"Because of you," she said. "Because of your father." She looked up into the night sky, searching for a star. She never found one. "And they threatened to go public with the bribe thing and embarrass Gavin's son." She ran her fingers through her dark hair. "A little late for him to start thinking about Kevin, but that was part of it."

I touched her arm, but she pulled away. "I didn't have anything to do with—"

"Quit it, Diane. We've known each other too long. So Gavin kept his mouth shut for as long as he could, and then his sense of moral outrage kicked in and he was going to blow the whistle anyway—a week ago Thursday. And somebody stopped him."

We reached Clark Street, just as the mist began to turn to a light rain, and Diane headed north across the bridge, walking with her head down, scuffing each foot on the cement walkway. There were restaurants across the river, someplace to duck into and stay dry. On the south bank there wasn't much of anything. "Lots of people had reasons to kill Gavin," I said, catching up with her again. "I didn't know that until I started asking questions. Kendra, for one—Gavin left her with a broken heart and a case of the clap. And Beth, who's had a hell of a struggle raising Gavin's son all these years. And Bob Eliscu: Gavin short-circuited his trip to the top of organized crime. Gary, because of Marian, among other reasons. But I don't buy any of that—the timing was wrong. It had to be connected with this StorCo business."

"You have quite an imagination," Diane said.

"I have more than that, Diane. I have proof," I said, thinking of the TV magazine with Gavin's sad notations in the margin.

"What proof?"

"It's not important right now. All that matters to me is who killed him."

A gust of wind came whistling up the river from Lake Michigan, through the man-made canyon of skyscrapers pushing some wetness in front of it. I wasn't wearing a raincoat—I hadn't brought one—and my shirt was getting soaked and sticking to my chest. It was very quiet out there on the bridge. Not many people were going to or from the Loop at that time of night, and those who were would probably use Michigan Avenue.

I said, "Gavin tried to reach Ben the day he died to tell him, so Ben could cover his own ass, that he was going to pull the plug on Ben's political friends and expose the StorCo bribe. But he never made contact. He also tried to call his captain, but Ray Mayo was at the ball game that night."

"What are you getting at?"

"Just before Morris Ackerman had me worked over—"

"He did?" she said. She sounded really concerned.

"Oh, yes, by experts. He told me that they weren't in the murder business—they were too powerful to get into anything that messy. He was telling the truth. An allegation of a bribe wouldn't hurt him, or Givney's people either. It'd cause him a bit of trouble, of course, and probably the forty grand, but for

people like Ackerman that's chump change. Hell, he was willing to pay me fifteen thousand just to go home."

"So?"

"So who would really suffer if that permit was rescinded?"

"Gary Storm," Diane said.

"Gary, yes. But Gary's a businessman. He understands the
ups and downs. If he couldn't build his new plant and dump
waste into the river, he'd figure out some other way to dump
it, if not now, then five years from now. He wants to expand,
but he's doing just fine the way he is. Besides, with his ego at
stake, he'd be much more likely to kill Gavin because of
Marian, and he didn't do that."

She stopped, putting a hand on the iron railing that keeps
people from falling off the bridge, and turned to face me.

"But Dave," I said, feeling lousier about this every second,
"is a different story. First of all, he was the one who offered the
bribe, not Gary. He'd be the one to take the legal heat for it. And
if the bribe story comes to light, StorCo would never get built.
Dave was the one who was counting on the contracting fee to
dig you both out of the hole you're in. And the police labs can
probably identify the odd white dust I found on Gavin's carpet
as coming from the drywall in your house. Look, it's turning to
mud all over your coat right now."

"I can't believe you're saying this."

"I can't either," I said. "But I need you to tell me I'm wrong."

The wind ruffled her hair, the reflected lights dancing on the
moisture clinging to her bangs. "What if I can't?"

I took a breath, and it hurt my chest. "Then I'll have to talk
to someone."

"Dave is my husband. I love him."

"I know." I held out open palms. "Help me, Diane."

The two of us stood face to face in the middle of the bridge,
the rain pittering down, and I thought that if the bridge were
to open now, the two halves suddenly lifting skyward to the
accompaniment of flashing red lights and clanging bells, and
we were caught on opposite halves, we couldn't be further

apart than we were at this moment. A lone taxi rumbled by on its way north, shaking the steel beneath our feet.

She thought for a long time about what she was going to say, deciding whether or not she should, chewing on it to soften it up. "You're wrong," she finally said. "Dave didn't kill Gavin."

I started to sigh with relief when she finished: "I did."

"Diane, don't protect him."

"I'm not," she said fiercely. "I did it, and Dave doesn't know anything about it. Gavin called Dave that day, the day he died, and said he was going to tell his captain about the permit anyway, and I went over to his place to talk him out of it." She snorted an ugly, sardonic laugh. "For old times' sake, I thought. I told him I could fix it so he got reinstated before his departmental hearing. I begged. But he wouldn't listen, oh no. He was so full of himself, full of crap about doing the right thing." Her eyes flashed and her voice, usually well modulated from her years of stage experience, became higher and more shrill. "Gavin Cassidy never did the right thing in his *whole life.* He was a drunk, which is bad enough, but he was a user, too."

She whirled to start walking away, then turned back to me quickly. "Gavin didn't have friends," she went on, the words tumbling out, "he had people he used. I was all right to buy him drinks and let him crash on my sofa, to listen to his drunken slobbering when he was feeling sorry for himself. But when it came to love, to caring, I was just good old Diane the Doormat! Everybody else!" she wailed. "He sniffed around everybody else like an alley cat. Kendra, Tessa, Beth—the list goes on and on. He never once *looked* at me! I was always there for him, but he never knew I was alive."

I squinted at her through the rain, my head spinning. More changes.

"I never knew," I said. "You loved him, didn't you? All these years, you—"

"Yes, I loved him! But I hated him more. And if you think I was going to stand by and let him ruin Dave, let him ruin *us,* you're crazy, that's all. You're just crazy!"

257

She took her hand from the railing and put it into her coat pocket again. "I had the capsules in my purse because I was taking them myself, for depression. Gavin was three quarters drunk anyway, and when I went to get him another beer I just split open a whole bunch of capsules and put the powder in the can when he wasn't looking. Of course he drank it, and another one after that." She smiled, but there was no humor in it. "When I left he was asleep in his chair. I guess he never woke up." Her laugh was more like a terrier's bark. "Poor Dave—he never knew anything about it. He just counted himself lucky that Gavin had died conveniently. That's been Dave's trouble all his life: he sits around doing nothing and waits for outside forces to solve his problems."

I stared down into the water. They'd done a good job of cleaning the river up in the past few years, but not enough yet for kids to swim in it on those hot midwestern afternoons. If Gary Storm built his plant the way he wanted to, the river would be ruined for generations.

"Now you hate me, too," Diane said.

I shook my head. The lump in my throat made it hard to talk. "I don't hate you. I'm just . . ."

"Shocked? Surprised? Meek little Diane, everybody's mother, right?"

I didn't say anything. I couldn't.

She said, "What are you going to do about it?"

I knew what I had to do. There wasn't any question about it. But acid, bitter and strong, was eating a big hole inside me, one that wasn't going to go away. Ever.

She made a little mewling sound in her throat. "I beg you not to," she said. "I've begged Gary, I've begged Gavin, I'm not too proud to beg you too."

"Diane . . ."

"When Kendra dumped you and you turned into a twenty-one-year-old drunk, who listened to you cry? When your father went to jail, who held your hand and made you realize it wasn't your fault? I was like a mother to you. God, I've been your

258

friend forever! Can't you do one thing for me?" She gestured wildly at the shiny ribbon of water that ran beneath us. "Is the goddamn river so important to you?"

"It's not the river! Jesus Christ, it's not the river!"

"Listen," she said, her voice high and tight in her throat, "Gavin was dead anyway. The way he was drinking he couldn't have lasted the year. And what if he had? What kind of a life would he have had?"

"It was *his* life," I said. "It wasn't much of one, but it was his. You had no right to—"

"Right?" she said. "I have the right to protect *me*. You told me yourself that you have to take control of your own destiny. No more trips to Samarra."

"Diane," I said sadly, "if you don't understand, there isn't any point in explaining it to you."

We stood with our elbows on the rail, arms touching, watching the flow of the river, the rain making bright beads on our shoulders. She didn't look at me, and I couldn't look at her. "Are you going to turn me in?"

It's amazing how hard it can be to get one simple word out of your mouth. "Yes."

"Oh, shit," she said. She moved back away from the rail, and when I turned to face her there was a little silver-plated gun in her hand, the kind that fits in the pocket of a raincoat.

"You're not going to use that, Diane."

"You don't think so? Get your hands away from your pockets."

"I wouldn't shoot you even if could. But I'm not carrying a gun. I came here for a funeral."

"For yours, too." She looked around quickly. The Clark Street Bridge was deserted, quiet. There were lights on in the massive cylinders of the Marina City Towers, but even if someone had been looking out a window, there wasn't much they could do.

"Climb over the rail," she ordered.

Little jolts of adrenaline ran through me, making my knees

259

weak, as my acrophobia kicked in. The thought of standing on that narrow ledge with no protective rail between me and an eighty-foot drop into the river froze me to the spot.

"Do it!" she screamed. "Or I swear to God I'll shoot you in the stomach before you go over."

I grabbed the rail with palms drenched with sweat and rain. It was hard to get a good grip. I looked over at her again, but there was no softening in her eyes, and she gestured impatiently with the little gun.

I swung a leg over, the railing digging into my crotch. The backs of my legs didn't hurt nearly as much as they had before Kendra's massage therapy, but they were still sore, and the effort sent painful messages up into my back.

"Go on," she said.

Back near the turn of the century, engineers had dredged the Chicago River so that it flowed backward—away from Lake Michigan rather than into it—in an effort to keep the lake from pollution. I knew that if I went in I'd float upriver, west and then north, and probably wash up someplace near where Gary planned to build StorCo, an irony I didn't find amusing. There was no question of my jumping in and swimming ashore. The impact from this height would knock me unconscious—if it didn't kill me.

My fingers felt welded to the rail. I shifted my feet no more than an inch and tried desperately not to look down, my head spinning and terror clutching my throat. My legs were suddenly made of overcooked linguini. Fear of heights can do that to you.

"Now jump," she said. "I seem to remember you don't swim very well. Unless you've been taking lessons."

I kept my death grip on the handrail. "You don't want to do this, Diane."

"No, I don't. But I have to."

"Where is it going to stop? First Gavin, now me. How many other people are you prepared to kill?"

Her voice quivered as if she were about to cry, and the gun

wobbled in her hand. Dizzy and precariously perched as I was, I couldn't do anything about it. "As many as it takes," she said.

"And you can live with it?"

"I've lived the last twenty years with being the only woman Gavin Cassidy ever rejected; I guess I can handle this. Go on, jump. Don't make this any harder than it is."

"I wouldn't want to do that," I said with more bravado than I was feeling. "But I don't think I'm going to jump. It's easy for you to think Gavin was dying anyway, and if I go into the river you'll rationalize it into a suicide in your own mind. But you want me dead, you're going to have to make me that way. Yourself. With your own hand. So go ahead and shoot."

She looked around again, and I went on, "In the middle of the night someone's bound to hear the shot and look out their window up there in Marina City. You might not get away with it."

"You're just talking," she said. "You were always good at talking." A fleck of white spittle appeared at the corner of her mouth, and under her raincoat her chest was heaving.

"For Gavin you could plead temporary insanity. But kill me, and the jury's going to notice a pattern." I shook my head sadly. "Let it go, Diane." I released one hand from the rail, which made my knees actually knock together. "Give it to me," I said, and reached for the gun.

"Don't!" she said. "Don't touch me!" And then she rushed at me, trying to push me off the tiny ledge, which was hardly wide enough for my feet. The impact knocked me sideways, and my body swung crazily out over the black river, anchored only by my left foot on the platform and my left hand clutching the rail. She hammered at my fingers with the gun, while I tried desperately to get my other foot back on the ledge. Then she started hitting me around the face, but I was so afraid of falling I barely felt it. The muzzle of the gun opened up a cut high on my cheek under my eye, and I tasted my own blood. And my own fear.

She put one foot up on one of the metal crosspieces and

lifted herself up so she could push harder, and I guess the dampness caused her foot to slip, because she tumbled over the railing to my side and slipped past me, her gun flying off into space and making a soft splash several seconds later when it hit the water. I reached out for her as she fell by me, and her fingers wrapped around my wrist. Her weight—she wasn't as sylph-like as she'd been twenty years ago—almost jerked my arm out of my socket, and almost pulled my other hand off the railing. That hand was all that was keeping her weight and mine from dragging us both off the ledge and into the river, and I grunted with the effort, my aching muscles screaming.

"Hang on!" I shouted. "Hang on!" I strained to pull her weight up as she dangled at the end of my arm, and I felt my own fingers slipping. "Try to get your feet up on the ledge!" I yelled, but she just hung there in shock and panic, swaying in the wind, her face upturned to me, blinking against the rain. "Hold on, Diane!" I said.

Something came into her eyes then when they locked on to mine, almost like a sorry smile, replacing the panic. I felt her body suddenly relax and become dead weight. Then her grip on my wrist relaxed, too.

It seemed like a long time before I heard the splash.

27

It was on the books. Bribery indictments were being prepared against David Kubo, Martin Givney, and Morris Ackerman, everybody in fact except Gary Storm, who must have had a good lawyer; the official ruling was that K&K had offered the bribe, not StorCo. Poor Dave Kubo, who hadn't done anything that ten thousand other guys in his position had done and will continue to do as long as there's a greedy bureaucrat or politician who lines his own pocket at the expense of the good of the public, was going to take the fall for everyone. He'd not only lost his wife, the person who kept him going, but he was going to lose everything else as well. He was no killer—he wasn't even a crook. He was just a poor bastard trying to get along in the time-honored way, the way that had kept Chicago moving for a hundred years. I felt sorry for Dave Kubo.

When I laid the whole story out for Ray Mayo it was a simple matter for the forensics lab to match up the powdery drywall from the Kubo house to that found on Gavin's carpet, and to trace the amphetamines in his system to Diane's own prescription. And so the books now read that Gavin was murdered, the insurance company grudgingly paid off the double-indemnity clause, and Kevin Cassidy was a fairly wealthy young man.

The police and the DA did their jobs, and everyone felt

noble. The charges on Givney and Ackerman would never stick, and I knew it: they'd simply pay off somebody else, someone in the prosecutor's office or some judge, the indictments would be quashed, and in another month everyone would forget about them, because Martin Givney took care of the people in his ward and Morris Ackerman took care of Givney, and that's the important thing. It's how the city works. Hell, Mussolini kept the trains running on time.

Marian Meyers wanted to pay me, but I said no. I'd starve on the street before I'd touch a nickel for what I'd done. She invited me to dinner, too, but I turned her down again. I just wanted to get away. Call me Doctor No.

I called to tell Kendra good-bye, and we said little more than that. Take care, keep in touch, let me know if you ever come to town again: banalities to cosmetically touch up a sad conversation between two sad people who'd loved each other once, and *once* was the operative word. I supposed she'd patch things up with her young musician, or more likely find another one.

I called Tessa and promised we'd get together next time, but she didn't sound too enthusiastic about it. When she had told me she'd dropped out of the old crowd from the Near North and become a suburban housewife, she wasn't kidding, and Gavin's death, and Diane's, hadn't made her any more anxious to strengthen old ties. I couldn't blame her.

When I called the Nemeroffs, Dolly hung up on me. I thought about trying to reach Ben at his office, but I had every reason to believe he wouldn't talk to me either. Another friendship down in flames. That night I had more than a couple of drinks with Al Patinkin at the Blues Box so I could hear Big John play one more time, that wail from the pit about being lonely and alone and down to your last dime. The young white kid with the guitar was there again to worship at the shrine, to learn and to listen, so I bought him a few beers too. Maybe I bought everyone in the place a few drinks; you can't tell it by me.

The next day, with one of the top ten hangovers of my life,

I was invited to lunch by Ray Mayo and Darren Oraweic at a little Argentinian restaurant on an industrial stretch of Fullerton Avenue. The help, always happy to see the police when they're smiling, fell all over themselves bringing us *matambres* and *empañadas* with *humitas en chala,* pureed vegetables and spices wrapped in corn husks, and plenty of Argentinian beer. The peppery food did nothing for my condition.

Darren wasn't used to dining with his captain and clearly wasn't completely comfortable with it. He sat ramrod straight in his blue uniform and spoke only when spoken to.

"We owe you, Saxon," Ray Mayo said.

"You don't owe me, Captain."

"Oh, yeah. A biggie. More than a lunch. Right, Oraweic?"

"Yes, sir."

"If it wasn't for you we would have shined the whole thing. And that would have been lousy. When a copper goes down, we like to know why. I'm sorry it had to be your friend who—"

"Right," I said. I didn't want to talk about it.

"You know," Mayo said, "when a man dies, we look at the body, we see someone diminished, someone without life, almost like a puppet after the show when it's laying in a corner and no one is pulling the strings, and then it's sometimes hard to think of the human being that was. Cassidy had his problems, especially at the end, the drinking and everything, but you have to remember him the way he used to be."

"I know," I said. I told myself I was drinking so much beer to put out the spicy fire in my gut, but deep down I knew that spices had nothing to do with it.

"And a good copper. Right to the end, a good copper. Wasn't he, Oraweic?"

Darren Oraweic sat up a little straighter. "Yes, sir!" he snapped out smartly. Then his shoulders relaxed a little and he took a big slug of beer and patted his mouth with his napkin. "He'd seen the elephant, all right."

"We all see the elephant, Darren," I said. "It isn't always big and gray, but sooner or later everyone sees the elephant."

That kept everybody quiet for a while. I was developing my conversation-ending skill into a real avocation.

Toward the end of the meal, when we were having ice cream to cool off our blistered palates, Mayo said, "There's only one thing I wish about this whole business."

"What's that, sir?" Darren was getting gutsy.

Mayo carefully didn't look at me. "There never was any hearing on that charge against Cassidy, the bribe thing. I hate like hell to close the book with that hanging over his record." He slurped his coffee. "Of course, he isn't here to defend himself now, so I guess we'll never know." He set down his cup and stretched, his elbows back behind his shoulders. "Damn shame."

"Are you sure, Captain, that you just don't want it on *your* record?" I asked. "As his chinaman, I mean?"

Ray Mayo's eyes turned to slits in his red face. "Don't presume that everybody has an angle, Mr. Saxon. It's cynical. That's an unattractive quality in someone I was just beginning to like."

I sighed. "Sorry. I was out of line again."

"Don't let it become a habit," Mayo said, and leaned back in his chair. He took out his pipe and a leather tobacco pouch. The Midwest is one of the few places left where you can smoke in a public place and not be treated like a typhoid carrier.

As we got up to leave, Mayo threw a ten-dollar bill on the table for the servers, and I realized that the waiter hadn't brought a check for the meal. Not for a captain of police. Good old Chicago.

"Going back to the Coast now, are you?" Mayo said when we got outside.

"Tomorrow. I have a few things to do before I go."

His eyes sparkled. "Do you? Well, I hope you get them done. I hate loose ends myself."

I turned to Officer Oraweic and shook his hand. "It was good meeting you, Darren. Maybe next time I come to town we can take in another game."

"I'd like that, you." Oraweic almost saluted, then changed his mind.

Mayo and I shook hands, too, and he thanked me again for helping to solve Gavin's murder. "Can I drop you anywhere?"

"No thanks. Like I told you, I have some things to take care of."

His smile was kindly, or as close to kindly as a hard-assed Irish copper like Ray Mayo can get. "Look out for the elephant," he said.

My father was wearing a different shirt and the same baggy pants; he was smoking his eternal Camel, still needed a shave, and looked pretty much the way he always had. He wasn't particularly glad to find me on his doorstep, and that was business as usual, too.

"Hiya," was all he said, and then he turned his back and went back into the apartment, leaving me to follow along after him. I'd come down a few steps since the last time—I didn't even get a "kiddo."

"I'm leaving tomorrow morning," I said, closing the apartment door behind me.

"Going back, eh?"

"Yeah."

"Well, I guess that's home now, that's where you belong."

"So . . . I came to say good-bye."

He puffed on the cigarette, coughing as his lungs filled up, which may or may not be the reason he didn't say anything.

I sat down on the sofa.

"Well," he said, "I was glad to see you when you first got here, but this wasn't exactly a happy visit."

"No," I said.

He wandered around the room, the way he usually did, and it occurred to me that I'd rarely seen Jimmy Saxon sit. Even when he was younger, when my mother was still alive, I never remember him sitting and reading the newspaper or watching the TV, although it was always on at low volume to some mindless sitcom. He had his favorite chair, but he never spent more than two minutes at a time sitting in it. He was a perpetual-motion machine, pacing the perimeter of the living room the way a captive big cat endlessly paces off the limits of his cage. Looking at him now, I saw a man who seemed infused with a kind of manic energy; maybe he prowled all the time in search of a new angle. As old as he was, it worried me that he'd drop from exhaustion.

"We never did get to the ball game, did we?" he said. "Now it's too late—Cubs are on the road. I don't go out to the Sox games, y'know."

"I know." North Siders never go south to see the White Sox play; South Siders rarely venture across the river to watch the Cubs. That's the way of things in Chicago.

"Say hello to your boy for me. What's his name?"

"Marvel."

"Yeah, Marvel. Well, you tell him hello from his grandfather." He smiled, showing his stained lower teeth. "I imagine there's a story behind that someplace. You'll have to tell it to me sometime."

"Uh-huh," I said.

"Well, you're looking well. You grew up pretty good. A good-looking man. And I guess you're happy out there, so that's the main thing."

"Look, Jimmy . . . I'm sorry things had to turn out the way they did. And I hope I didn't—cause you any trouble with your job." It sounded so lame, even I was embarrassed.

He shrugged and puffed, then waved the smoke away from his face with an impatient gesture. "You did what you had to do, I guess." He allowed himself a tiny smile. "We all do what we have to." He wandered over to the dining room set with his small, old-man steps. "It doesn't matter much about me. I'm old. Too old for the rough-and-tumble anymore. Politics in this town isn't fun the way it used to be when the mayor was around. Daley. Richard J., I mean. Now it's a game for younger fellas, skinny guys in dark suits with the telephones in their cars. I don't even *have* a car." He rubbed his hand over his stubbled face. "So I'm prob'ly gonna retire pretty soon anyway. I got some money put by, and a little pension. I'll be okay."

"You sure?" I said. "I'm not rich, but if you run short . . ."

He looked around the living room with its faded forties furniture. "Nah, I'll be fine. Like you can see, I don't have many needs." He chuckled, and it made him hack again. "Whaddaya think, I'm gonna spend my money on loose women?"

I didn't say anything, and all of a sudden he looked anxious.

"Hey, that was a joke, all right? I never ran with women, you know that. I never cheated on your mother, God rest her soul, not one time. Even after she was gone . . ." Sorrow brimmed out of his eyes, wrenching my gut. "I never put a hand on another woman from the day I first set eyes on your mother until this one. You have to believe that."

"I do," I said, sad because of it.

"Some men, they spend their life chasing the ladies. I wasn't like that. I guess my interests were politics and the way the city runs. That's what kept me going." He looked intently at me. "You're a ladies' man, aren't you? You always were when you were a kid, and you still are. I can tell by the way you walk, the way you carry yourself." He looked up at the crack in the ceiling, remembering. "What was the name of that little gal you were so stuck on? Kinzie, was it?"

"Kendra."

"Yeah. Pretty girl—those long legs, I remember. You get to see her while you was here?"

"I saw her a few times."

"Well, that's good." A deep breath heaved his skinny chest, and he started moving around again. "I wish we could've spent some time while you was in town, y'know, but I guess under the circumstances . . ."

"Jimmy—"

"Ah, go on!" he said, waving his hand at me as though he were swatting a mosquito. "I know what you think of me. Always have. We never talked the same language to each other—never knew how. Life don't always lay out like you want it to, so I accepted it. I know I'm a pretty poor excuse for a father, but you're not exactly a model son, either, so the two cancel each other out. Well, that's spilt milk, kiddo. You do the best you can—I did. The best I could. Some of us are made one way, and some another, and me, I'm this way. What is it Popeye says? 'I yam what I yam.' " One thing, though—I never lied to you."

"Not to me, no."

Suspicion clouded his face, and he puffed furiously on his Camel.

"You lied a lot, Jimmy. Not to me, but to others, when it was important not to."

He turned away, paced away, as though distancing himself from me would make what I said disappear. "I don't know what you're talkin' about."

"When you went to prison. You didn't take that bribe, did you? You had nothing to do with it. It was Givney, and you took the rap for him, because you were so fucking desperate for him to like you."

"Don't use that language in your mother's house!"

"Let's not get fatherly now, Jimmy. All your life you've been lying for Martin Givney. And you never stopped to think who else it would hurt. Me, Ma . . . You had your priorities all screwed up. Martin Givney and a bunch of cigar smokers over at the ward were the most important things in the world to you."

He didn't meet my eyes. "Listen, there are things that you just do," he said. "For your friends. For people who are good to you. Maybe they aren't the right things to do, but it seems like it at the time, so you do them. You were too young to understand, kiddo."

I got up off the sofa and went over to him. "Am I too young now? I'm nearly forty years old, Jimmy. What about now? What about Gavin Cassidy?"

All the air seemed to go out of him, and he sank down into

one of the dining room chairs, one elbow crooked over its back. He ground his cigarette out in the ashtray and immediately lit another one. His hand was shaking so badly he could barely put the flame on the tobacco.

"You lied about that too, didn't you? Givney got you to lie because he knew Cassidy wouldn't call my father a liar in public."

He looked up at me, anguish in his eyes. "There are things that you do," he muttered again.

If he hadn't been my father I would have slapped him, old as he was. Instead I shoved my clenched fists into my pockets and walked away from him to look out the window. The rain of two nights before hadn't done much to help the burned grass in the front of the building. Across Kenmore Avenue three little boys played catch on the sloping lawns of two buildings similar to the one where I'd grown up. One of them, a little black kid about nine years old, reminded me of Marvel—the same athletic grace, the same confident cant to his head. I missed Marvel.

"What do you want from me?" my father cried.

It was a question worth pondering. What did I want from a man whose entire value system was so different from mine? What could I expect from someone who had fashioned his whole life after a political system that was serviceable but corrupt? There would be no sudden glory-hallelujah conversation here, no seeing the light, and I'd been stupid to think there might've been the slightest chance. People don't change.

And yet, they do. Everyone I'd known in Chicago in my youth had changed, grown older, grown bitter, grown fat. The city itself had become a different place, at least to look at. And me, I had changed the most of all. Change is, in its own way, a synonym for life. If you don't keep changing, keep growing, you die.

I took the chance. "I want you to go to the district attorney and tell them you lied, Jimmy." I was still staring at the game of catch across the street, but I sensed him stiffen in shock behind me. "I want you to clear Gavin Cassidy's record, and his name."

I heard him take a drag on his cigarette, the sucking, the deep inhale, the quick expelling of the noxious smoke.

"You want me to put my neck on the block, eh?"

"You won't get into any trouble. You didn't swear to it. There's no penalty for lying unless you're under oath."

"What about people that've been my friends for forty years?" he said. "I owe them."

I turned away from the window to face him. "Those people aren't your friends, Jimmy. They're nobody's friends but their own. They let you go to prison for them, for Christ's sake! You don't owe them shit. You've paid them back a hundred times over."

He stood up and started traveling again, from the dining room to the front door, then to the sofa, then across the living room, giving me a wide berth. "What's the point?" he said. "The man's dead. Cassidy's dead."

"He's dead with a dirty record he never deserved."

"He don't give a shit for his record now, for God's sake. I don't see the point."

"I'll tell you the point. Over on Printer's Row—you know where that is? I know it isn't in your ward."

"Don't be funny," he said.

"All right. Over on Printer's Row there's a kid, a young kid. Fourteen or so. Good-looking boy. He never got to know his old man—it's nobody's fault, but that's the way it was, which is a damn shame because now the father's dead and it's too late. So we can't give him his father back. But he thinks that father was a crook, Jimmy. A dirty cop who was on the pad. And that's something that kid's going to live with for the rest of his life. Unless you make a phone call."

"I don't know that kid," Jimmy said. "I don't owe him nothing."

"No," I said. "But you owe me."

"How you figure?" he said, not looking at me.

"I've got a son now, Jimmy, and I know how it's supposed to go. You take care of that kid, you nurture him, you spend time with him, you knock into his head the kind of man he's supposed to grow up to be. I never had that from you—you were too busy with your cronies. And that's okay. I'm not blaming you, it's the way it was, and just like you said, I grew up okay. I never asked you for anything, I never expected anything." I filled my lungs, then let the air out slowly. "I'm asking you now."

He sat down in his favorite chair and put his head down, studying the worn carpet between his feet.

"You're big on paying your debts, Jimmy; you've spent your whole life paying debts. If you taught me one thing, it's that gentlemen pay their debts. That's not a bad legacy to leave a kid. But now I'm calling your marker."

I went over to him, took Ray Mayo's card out of my pocket, and put it in his hand. He didn't look at it for a long while, and when he finally did, he was thorough, turning it over in his tobacco-stained fingers, examining it from every angle. When he got up from the soft embrace of the chair, he was ten years older. It took him quite a while to get over to the kitchen, where the telephone hung on the wall.

He talked to Ray Mayo for a few minutes, and although he spoke too low for me to hear the words I could sense the strain in his voice. I guess Ray told him he'd make an appointment with the DA's office and the police department's Internal Affairs people, because Jimmy nodded, mumbled thanks, and hung up.

"Well, that's that," he said softly to the wall. He came back out into the living room and started walking the perimeter again, slowly, puffing on his cigarette, watching his carpet slippers. I stepped into his path and he stopped, still not looking at me.

"Thanks," I said. "That makes us square."

He raised his head, his bloodshot eyes filled, and I gave him my crooked grin, the one that was the mirror image of his own. "It took a lot of years, Pa," I said. "But we're finally square."

I held out my arms and his frail, bird-like body flew into them.

28

I was *in* my seat, my seat belt *was* fastened, and I was doodling *in* my notebook as the 727 headed west. Outside the plane's window it was dusk, the sun turning the wheat fields of Kansas a vivid orange.

The notes I'd taken on the Cassidy case were still there, and I ripped them out, tore them up, and placed the scraps in the seat pocket in front of me. I wouldn't give them to Jo to type up for me. It wasn't a real case, after all; I'd been on vacation.

At the top of a fresh page I wrote:

THINGS TO DO:

That wasn't like me, but I'd left my paperback in the hotel room by mistake, hadn't found another I liked in the racks at the airport newsstand, and had finished reading the airline's magazine, with its report on all the delightful things to do in San Antonio. The flight attendants weren't worthy of my fantasies, especially since two of the four of them were male, and I didn't have anything better to do than make lists.

Ball game—Marvel, I scribbled. That was a must, a right-away must. I'd take Marvel to a Dodger game, or if they weren't in town I'd call my pal Ken Brett, the ex-southpaw who now works the TV booth for the California Angels, and cadge some tickets for a game in Anaheim. I'd missed Marvel at Wrigley Field, but it was more than that—it's important for fathers and sons to go to baseball games. It's the American way of male bonding. I knew he'd rather hang out at the mall and talk to girls than go to a game with me—that's the way teenage boys are—but when he was my age and I was Jimmy's, I wanted him to remember games we'd gone to together. I didn't want any debts between us.

Bill Laven—lunch, I wrote. Bill was a good friend, a transplanted Chicagoan that I'd met for the first time in Los Angeles. We had lunch every two weeks or so anyway, but I wanted to be sure I called him. I'd lost a lot of friends in the past two weeks one way or another; Bill was one I wanted to hang on to. I wrote down *Zeidlers for dinner,* under that, for the same reason. Jo Zeidler and I saw each other almost every day at the office, but every once in a while I'd remember how much I cared for her, her and her husband Marsh, even though he rooted for the Knicks and the Mets. They'd always been there for me, and for Marvel. I wondered if I told them enough how much they meant to me. I underlined the notation so I'd remember.

Something was bothering me, though. There was a loose end somewhere, and I couldn't figure it out. Maybe it was because I'd just spent some time enmeshed in the political roughhousing of Chicago, but I kept thinking of the dreaded Payback, and I felt incomplete.

I was in no position to pay anyone back for anything. It's hard to get even from two thousand miles away. I drummed my fingers on the notebook until one of the male flight attendants—see, that was how my luck was running—stopped by and asked if he could serve me a beverage.

Jo and Marvel picked me up at the airport and drove me

home. They were both glad to see me, and that felt good. It seemed like it had been a while since anyone was glad to see me—anywhere. It was almost midnight by the time we got back to my house, but I insisted on everyone having ice cream. Before Jo left I asked if she and Marsh would come for dinner Sunday.

Considering it was the first night in my own bed in quite a while, I should have slept better. But I tossed fretfully. Until about five in the morning, when I sat up in bed, smiling.

The next morning I asked Marvel if he wanted to go to the beach.

"The beach?" he said, looking at me strangely. "You hate the beach."

"That's not true. I like to walk on it and look at the ocean. I just don't like baking in the hot sun and getting all oily and sandy."

"What about school?"

"I already graduated."

"I didn't."

I smiled at him. "I'll write a note saying you were sick, all right?"

"Wha's the deal, man?"

"Humor me, okay?"

I called Bill Laven and set up lunch for Monday, then called Ken and arranged to go to the Angels game the next night. As luck would have it, the Chicago White Sox were in town, playing surprisingly well. Then I put on a pair of shorts and a pink polo shirt and packed a cooler with sodas and chicken sandwiches Marvel had gotten from the deli on Windward Avenue.

He was surprised when I headed for the car.

"I thought we was goin' to the beach," he said. He had a surfboard under one arm.

"We are."

"We gonna drive? It's only two blocks away."

"Different beach today."

"Man," he whined, his voice rising the way it does when he's exasperated.

"Different beach, different girls," I reminded him, and he seemed to feel a little better about it.

In the car I said, "We're going to have a houseguest in August."

"Who?"

"A young fellow named Kevin Purdell—Kevin Cassidy. His father is the one whose funeral I went to. I invited him out for a week or two. I don't know if he'll come, but I hope so."

"How old is he?"

"Fourteen," I said.

"Aw, man . . ." Marvel slumped angrily in his seat. "Jus' a little kid! I gonna have to baby-sit him?"

"I'd like it if you'd show him around a little. Take him surfing, things like that."

He gave one of his put-upon sighs, and I said, "He's had a real rough time, Marvel."

His expression softened. Marvel knew all about kids having rough times—he could write the book on it. He said, "Well, I guess it'd be okay."

I relaxed a little. I truly didn't know if Kevin would accept my invitation, but I hoped so. It would be nice having Gavin's son around for a while. To make up for losing Gavin.

I had lost some illusions about Gavin, too. In a way, he'd been diminished in my eyes by the things I'd found out about him; in another, he'd become even more heroic a figure. I suppose the truth lay somewhere in between, as it does with all of us.

We drove down to Mimosa, about half an hour in the weekend traffic, and ensconced ourselves on a blanket about twenty feet from the surf line. Nearby a bunch of guys played volleyball noisily and with gusto. I slopped tanning oil with number-ten sunscreen on my nose and cheeks and watched Marvel hit the water with his board, skimming across the tops of the waves. I could see his grin until he was about fifty feet out.

I snapped on the portable radio to KLON, an underpowered jazz station you can only pick up in the South Bay, knowing that as soon as Marvel returned he'd change it to something I'd hate. I popped a soda and ate one of the sandwiches and then lay face down on the blanket, listening to an Oscar Peterson cut, feeling the sun burn into the sore places on my legs and back. I figured I had about half an hour before I began turning lobster red.

That's how long it took Marvel to finish his first round of surfing. "I'm gonna go git in that volleyball game," he said when he'd come back and dried off.

I grinned at him. Marvel was a killer athlete; those guys didn't know what they were in for.

"Go ahead," I told him. "I've got an errand to run."

As I passed the volleyball net, Marvel spiked a shot that sent one of the guys on the other side of the net slithering into the sand nose first. Business as usual. I walked a block up to Mimosa Beach Avenue and found the address I was looking for. It was an office on the second floor of a building that housed shops selling surfboards and beachwear and health foods. I didn't worry about the way I was dressed. In California beach communities, everyone wears shorts and has sand sticking to them someplace.

The young woman at the desk was pretty, with that California blond, blue-eyed, WASP-y Republican look, and she smiled at me when I walked in the door. She was very young; she should have been playing volleyball herself instead of sitting in a stuffy little office. She had a nice smile. It was nice to have people smiling at me again.

I smiled back. I smiled because I was home, because a pretty girl was smiling at me, and because I was about to exercise the ancient and honored art of the Payback.

"Hi," she said, fluffing her fingers through her hair on either side of her head. "Can I help you?"

"My name is Saxon," I said. "I'd like to see Representative Birkenshaw. I've got some information I think will interest him."